# Love, on the Rocks

Elsie McArthur

# AUTHOR'S NOTE

I started writing *Love on the Rocks* a number of years ago, and completed it during the Covid-19 lockdown of 2020. It was, in part, inspired by my own childhood holidays on some of the many beautiful and diverse islands along Scotland's West Coast.

Inniscreag - where this story is set - is a fictional island, but I have tried as best as I can to reflect the sense of friendship and community that I have experienced myself during visits to this area, especially the isles of Islay, Mull and Skye itself, which features in the novel.

During the Covid-19 outbreak, this small island community was deeply affected by a number of illnesses and deaths, particularly within care home settings. Coincidentally, there is a care home on Skye featured in the opening chapters of this novel. I would like to clarify here that this care home, its physical location and staff are entirely a work of fiction. I myself have no connections with any care home on Skye, and created the building and its location purely to fit the requirements of the plot of the story.

Apart from the island itself, the secondary setting of this story is the distillery where Rachel works. I'd like to thank my husband for his help with the technical aspects of whisky making, although as always, any errors or inconsistencies are entirely my own.

Lastly, thanks to you, the reader, for giving me an audience with which to share my work. I hope escaping to the wild, free, windswept shores of Inniscreag brings you a little joy, makes you smile, and maybe even shed a wee tear.

Right - let's get on with the story now, shall we?

# CHAPTER 1

Not many people had heard of Inniscreag, and that suited Rachel McIntyre just fine, thank you very much. The aptly named "Island of Rocks", along with its hundred or so inhabitants, lay almost exactly halfway between the islands of Skye and North Uist off the North West coast of Scotland; a small, craggy lump of granite jutting out of the sea, home mainly to hardy seabirds and even hardier people. The select few who had heard of it would have fallen into the middle of a very specific Venn diagram, at the intersection of "whisky drinker", "bird watcher" and "rich".

Rachel had not been one of those people. Prior to her arrival on the island, she mainly drank cheap, sweet white wine drowned in lemonade, and her only experience of birds had been the mangy, one-legged pigeons which frequented the windowsill of her grandmother's high rise flat in Glasgow. The expensive single malt that was the island's main export would have been vastly outwith her budget, not to mention tastes, and she would never in a million years have believed that one day she'd find herself running this small, isolated distillery.

Pulling back the curtains across the dormer window of her bedroom, Rachel looked out over the neglected back garden to see grey waves and creamy coloured foam tumbling wildly beyond the sheer drop of the cliff face. The morning sky was hard as steel above the swirling water, the sun glaring behind the clouds but unable to break through.

Inniscreag was certainly less romantic than Rachel had imagined when she decided to up sticks and move here on a broken-hearted whim; a million miles away from the almost Caribbean turquoise waters and white sand beaches she'd remembered from her childhood holidays on nearby Harris. But over the six months she had spent here, Rachel had grown to love the island's barren, desolate landscape. Sometimes, standing alone on the cliff top at the edge of her garden, it felt like she could be the very last person left on earth.

Shrugging on her dressing gown, Rachel shivered as she watched a couple of brave cormorants swoop into the tumultuous, peaking waves in search of fish, before padding downstairs to make her own breakfast.

She was met, as usual, by a plaintive mewing from the back door. Technically Doug, the distillery mouser, was semi-feral and strictly an employee - certainly not a pet. In return for food and shelter in one of the many warehouses, he was meant to keep the site free of rodents and other vermin. But he'd proven to prefer cuddles to mousing, and Rachel enjoyed the feel of his warm, heavy body on her knee while she had her morning coffee. He purred loudly as she opened the door, scurrying in out of the wind and rubbing his damp, ginger body affectionately against Rachel's legs.

"Morning, Douglas," she whispered, bending down to tickle his chin, her voice reverberating around the roomy farmhouse kitchen.

The detached villa she'd been given, rent free, when she accepted the job was really far too spacious for one person. But the smaller, terraced cottages that had once housed the many distillery workers, along with their families, had been left to fall into disrepair in the years since the distillery's heyday. As a result, this was the only property left that was still habitable. Apart from Edith's house, of course, which was even grander, both in scale and decor.

Apart from Rachel, no one else lived on the site now. Just a few weeks after her arrival, the eccentric, elderly owner had finally given in to her declining physical health and admitted herself into a nursing home on Skye. Edith McLeod's mind was still sharp, but her body was failing her.

Rachel missed her. She had taken to the older woman instantly, despite their fifty year age gap. Edith still rang to speak to her every day; sometimes on the pretence of checking in on the running of the site, but more often than not, just for a chat. She had no family of her own, and Rachel got the impression she'd been lonely for some time. Maybe that was why they had bonded so quickly; they were both alone in the world.

The distillery had been in Edith's family ever since its inception, two hundred years ago. Over that time, Inniscreag had gone from being a tiny, illicit still on an unknown island, to one of the most prestigious, high-end brands of whisky in the world. The only down side to this luxurious reputation, however, was that they had become something of a niche product. As a result, sales had fallen in recent years, taking the profits along with them.

Rachel filled her espresso pot and set it on the old range

cooker to bubble, whilst she poured some kibble into a stoneware bowl for Doug and popped bread into the toaster for herself. It was just after seven o'clock, and she wanted to be in the office for the shift changeover in an hour.

As an almost entirely self-sufficient industry, Inniscreag had steadfastly resisted the wave of automation that had swept across most other distilleries in Scotland. Pairs of operators still took shifts day and night, working largely by hand, using age-old techniques to gradually transform water and barley into prize single malt. It was a process that took time, and patience, and skill; an almost magical alchemy, and it all happened with absolutely no input from Rachel whatsoever. Sometimes, she wondered why Edith had even bothered to hire her in the first place.

Glancing at the kitchen clock, Rachel poured her bubbling coffee into a travel mug, topped it up with milk and sugar, and carried it back upstairs to dress.

She enjoyed the casual attire she was allowed to wear in this job; jeans and a polo shirt made for a refreshing change from her past life in pencil skirts and high heels, when she had been the manager of a department store coffee shop back home in Glasgow. However, as she squeezed the top button of her jeans shut and felt her belly strain against it, Rachel cursed herself for giving into Jenny's fruit cake once again. She swore that if there was more in the office today, she would resist. Or try to, at least.

Quickly running a brush through her thick, chestnut brown bob, Rachel grabbed her coffee mug and trundled back down the stairs, pouring a reluctant Doug back out into the windy morning and wrapping her fleece around herself as she followed him into the moist island air.

The grey sky and biting wind belied the fact that it was early March, and supposedly spring. Taking a sip from her coffee, Rachel strode across the courtyard that separated her house from the tiny, timber-clad office - a recent addition - attached to one side of the much larger, and older, stone built still house.

The distillery was a jumble of little, low-roofed, white-washed buildings, with the exception of the maltings and its tall pagoda chimney which rose into the grey sky. As visitors approached along the single road that ran the length of the island, this chimney was the only visible clue as to the nature of the business that occupied the

4

long, narrow outcrop of rock on its westerly tip. From the sea, however, the tall, black letters identifying the name of the distillery could be seen sitting atop the cliffs, stark against the white wall of the storehouse.

"Morning, lass."

The voice that greeted her belonged to Cameron, their master blender. He was a tall man in his early fifties, with a shock of salt and pepper hair, a bushy moustache and warm hazel eyes. A native Gaelic speaker, like most of the islanders, his gravelly voice bore the distinctive lilt that Rachel was gradually becoming accustomed to. He was seated by his desk in the corner of the office they shared, surrounded by shelves containing tiny labelled bottles of golden liquid and various strange looking, copper tools.

Three nosing glasses sat on the table in front of him, each with the merest splash in the bottom, varying in tone from light gold to a deep, rich amber. Cameron raised them to his nose one at a time, taking it in turns to swill the liquid around the glass before sniffing it carefully.

His was a job that Rachel would never be able to fully comprehend - with just the use of his olfactory receptors, he could tell when each individual cask had reached its optimum condition for taste and appearance, and could then mix them together to ensure that every bottle of Inniscreag single malt was absolutely consistent. Although she could never have admitted it to her colleagues, to Rachel, pretty much all whisky still smelled - and tasted - like paint stripper.

"Morning," she replied, flicking on her computer. "What are you doing in so early?"

"Iain's coming off the nightshift; his mother asked me to pick him up." Iain was one of the operators, and Cameron's son. His wife, Jenny, was the serial fruit cake baker, and at least partly responsible for Rachel's ever expanding waistline.

"I'll drop him home when he's done and be back in a while - I just couldn't resist a wee snifter while I waited." Cameron smiled at her, a twinkle in his eyes as he nosed the various casks appreciatively.

Rachel opened her emails and began to sift through the plans for the day. With the production side of things pretty much taking care of itself, Rachel had spent the last six months familiarising herself with the process and absorbing as much of the operator's expertise as she could. Now however, as they approached the busier summer months, she was getting ready to start pursuing her own agenda.

The distillery already had a small visitor centre - more of a waiting area, really, containing nothing more than a few tatty posters and lacklustre information displays. This was where tourists would gather to shelter from the inevitable rain before being led on their tour, and then enjoy a quick sample at the end. Once they were done, however, there was little reason to hang about. Rachel wanted to change that.

With demand for expensive single malt dwindling, one of the distillery's original two maltings had been moth-balled a few years back. The long, barn-like structure now lay empty and unloved, and was steadily falling into disrepair. Rachel, however, saw potential in it. She wanted to convert it into a coffee shop. Hospitality was her background, and she knew from experience how much money could be made simply by selling teas, coffees and a few cakes.

The only stumbling block was getting Edith on board. As far as she was concerned, Rachel might as well have suggested turning her family heirloom into the whisky world's equivalent of Disneyland. After much discussion and persuasion, however, Edith had eventually agreed to let her trial it over the coming tourist season, as long as she kept a tight lid on the budget.

Rachel clicked on an email address she recognised - it was from the contractors over on Skye, who were due to start the renovation work. She fired off a quick reply, confirming that she would meet them off the morning boat the following day. The school Easter holidays were fast approaching, and Rachel was keen to get them in and have the work underway as soon as possible. She didn't want to miss out on the first influx of holidaymakers.

"That's me awa' then," Cameron said, heading for the door. "I'll run Jamie home as well. I'll no' be long."

"No worries," Rachel replied, waving him off as the phone rang. She could see the dayshift operators, Ben and Hamish, pulling into the little car park.

Rachel grabbed the handset, expecting to hear Edith's distinctive rasping voice, roughened by the thousands of cigarettes she must have smoked over her long life. Instead, she was greeted by an unfamiliar English accent.

"Rachel McIntyre?" the voice asked.

"Yes?" Rachel replied, her heart suddenly picking up its pace within her chest.

"I'm phoning from Bayview Nursing Home on behalf of Edith McLeod. She has you listed as her emergency contact? I'm afraid we need you to get here as quickly as you can."

# CHAPTER 2

It was over two hours until the first of the two daily scheduled ferries to Uig on the Isle of Skye was due to depart, but when word got around that Edith McLeod was in need, the islanders soon banded together to help. Hamish, a broad, strapping lad in his mid-twenties, with a thatch of violently ginger hair and a matching beard, found Rachel, flustered, at her desk, just as she ended the call.

"Everything a'right?" he asked, his equally ginger eyebrows furrowed together as he looked at her. When she explained, Hamish wasted no time in ringing his dad - a skipper on one of the local fishing boats - and arranging for her departure from the island as soon as possible.

The main settlement on Inniscreag was called Craigport, although the locals never called it by name and always somewhat ambiguously referred to it as just 'the village' or 'the port'. It was made up of a handful of streets, and contained the island's only hotel - more a pub with rooms, really – a harbour, a small two-room school, the local tearoom-come-shop and a church. Despite being at opposite ends of the island, Inniscreag was so small that the distillery was still only a ten minute drive away. But today, with the nurse's words echoing in Rachel's ears, it felt interminable.

*"We need you to come right away."*

Rachel hadn't given the woman much chance to elaborate, but if haste were such an important factor, and Edith wasn't able to speak to her herself, she could only assume it wasn't good news. As an only child, and having never married or had children, Edith was the last McLeod still living on Inniscreag. Rachel didn't want to think about what her passing might mean for the future of the distillery, not to mention how much she would miss the old woman herself.

Blinking back tears, Rachel was momentarily distracted by the sight of a car pulled into one of the passing places on the single track road. It was bright red, sleek and sporty, with a low chassis and a smooth, contoured silhouette - not the sort of vehicle ordinarily seen on Inniscreag. The bonnet was raised and pointing in Rachel's direction, a figure bent over the engine within.

She drove past at first, intent on getting to Edith as quickly as she possibly could, but then gradually started to brake. He was obviously a visitor, and he looked to be having trouble. Rachel wasn't exactly much of a mechanic, but she could at least give him the number of someone who might be able to help. Reluctantly glancing in her rear view mirror, she put the car into reverse and negotiated her way backwards round the bend, pulling in behind the stricken vehicle.

She climbed out and pulled on her waterproof coat, her boots squelching in the muddy verge as she approached.

"Hello?"

The man jumped at the sound of her voice, jerking abruptly upright and sending his head thumping into the underside of the bonnet.

"Oh my God, I'm so sorry," she cried, rushing to his side.

He stood up straight, facing her with a confused grimace and one hand rubbing the back of his head.

Rachel knew instantly that her assumption had been correct - he definitely wasn't an islander. He was wearing a three piece suit for starters, something she was pretty sure no man on Inniscreag had ever owned. His smart shoes were edged in mud and he had oil on his fingertips. He was tall, with an athletic build, thick dark hair, sharp features and green eyes. Rachel's voice caught in her throat when she tried to speak.

"Are you OK?" she asked feebly.

He flashed her an easy smile - effortlessly warm and friendly, and both playful and charming in equal measures. "Me or the car?" he asked jokingly, gesturing to his head.

"Both, I suppose." Rachel smiled back, feeling an unfamiliar flutter in her chest that she hadn't experienced in quite some time.

"My head will survive," he replied with another friendly smile, turning his attention back to the interior of his car. He had a well-spoken, but still unmistakeably Scottish accent. Maybe Edinburgh or the Borders, Rachel thought. "But I can't for the life of me figure out what's wrong with this car. Don't suppose you're any good with them?" He raised his eyebrows hopefully.

Rachel gave a snort of derision. "Far from it, I'm afraid," she said. "But I could give you the number of one of the local farmers - he'd probably be able to get you moving again."

"Oh, it still goes," the man said. "It's just ever since I got to Skye, every car I've passed has waved at me. I figured there must be something up, so I pulled in to check. But to be honest, I don't really know what I'm looking for." He gave a self-deprecating shrug.

Suddenly understanding the problem, Rachel tried her best to suppress a smile. This was something that had thrown her when she'd first arrived, too.

"First time visiting the Western Isles?" she asked.

"First time on any island," he confessed, casting a sideways glance at the scrawny, bleating sheep who were considering them from the unfenced hillside at the side of the road. "I'm something of a city boy, if I'm honest."

Rachel smiled again. She noticed that his hair was dappled with a sprinkling of silver at the sideburns. He looked to be about her age, maybe a little older. Before she could stop herself, she'd already taken a surreptitious glance at his ring finger and found it bare.

"There's nothing wrong with your car."

"How do you know?" he asked, grinning and raising an eyebrow at her.

"It's an island thing," Rachel explained. "Everyone waves. Doesn't matter if they know you or not; it's just what they do. You'll get used to it."

The man smiled his charming smile again, and ran a hand through his hair. "God, what an idiot!" He laughed, relieved, and lowered the bonnet back down onto his car.

"It threw me the first time, too."

"You're not from around here either?" He was leaning casually against the car now, his long legs crossed at the ankle. Rachel saw him glance at her own vehicle, a rusty old Land Rover with a slightly faded Inniscreag logo on its side.

"Moved here for work," she explained, gesturing to the car. "What brings you to the island? You don't look like our typical tourist; they tend to be a bit more hand-knitted. And waterproof." She smiled again, trying to sound more confident than she felt.

The stranger smiled slowly back at her, making his green eyes crinkle at the edges. "Just a spot of business," he said. "I'll admit 1 am woefully ill-prepared for the surroundings, though." He glanced down at his mud covered shoes. "I'll be heading back to civilisation on the evening ferry."

Rachel tried not to look too disappointed, reminding herself that part of the reason she'd come here in the first place was to get

10

away from all that nonsense.

"Thanks for stopping," the man was saying. "Very kind of you...?" He left a pause, clearly waiting for her to fill it with her name.

"Rachel," she stammered.

"Duncan," the man replied. He extended a hand, still smiling at her warmly, and she shook it.

"It's obviously true what they say about island hospitality," he continued. "I don't think anyone would have stopped for a stranger like that on the mainland; especially not a woman on her own. What if I'd been an axe murderer?" His eyes danced as he looked at her, a playful smirk tweaking at the edge of his lips.

"Oh, I don't need to worry about that," Rachel replied with a shrug. "We all carry shotguns around here. I could take you."

Her answer took him by surprise and he paused for a moment, before breaking into a wide grin and laughing. "I bet you could," he said quietly, giving her a lingering stare that made her excruciatingly conscious of her dowdy raincoat and walking boots. Why couldn't she be wearing a full face of makeup, control underwear and a push up bra when she unexpectedly bumped into flirtatious, handsome strangers?

"It was very nice to meet you, Rachel," Duncan said. "Maybe I'll see you again, if my business ever brings me back to Inniscreag."

"Maybe," Rachel replied, giving him her best attempt at an enigmatic smile, before saying goodbye, and trudging back to her car.

Just over half an hour later Rachel found herself, in an even less attractive luminous orange life-jacket, clinging desperately to the grab rails in the tiny cabin of a rusty old fishing boat. She focused, unblinking, on the undulating horizon and desperately tried to ignore the rising queasiness in her belly. Beside her, Hamish's father, Tormod, stood at the wheel, balancing effortlessly as if his feet were nailed to the floor whilst he navigated them across a grey, heaving ocean.

It was only when they finally berthed at Skye, just under an hour later, and Rachel clambered gratefully back onto solid ground, that she noticed her fists were stiff and sore from the ferocity of her grip on the rail. Flexing them and rubbing at the tender knuckles, she glanced around the little car park and debated what to do next.

Having left the distillery car at the port back on Inniscreag, her main obstacle now was how she'd get from here - Uig, on the West of the island - to the main settlement at Portree, in the East, where Edith's nursing home was located. There was always the possibility of hitching a lift, but right now the car park was conspicuously empty.

"Dinna fash," Tormod assured her, helping her out of her life jacket. "My brother's takin' ye the rest o' the way."

Right on cue, another old, battered Land Rover could be heard, sputtering and lurching along the road as it swung unsteadily into view. An older man with rust coloured hair smiled at her from within. Clearly, the inter-island network had been buzzing well ahead of her arrival.

Rachel climbed in, tossing her bag in the seat behind her, and waved farewell to Tormod as his brother executed a very bumpy U-turn and headed for Portree.

# CHAPTER 3

The nursing home sat on its own at the southern edges of the town, looking out over green hills and the shores of Loch Portree. Or it would have, if the weather hadn't closed in around the island in a cloud of grey haar and drizzling rain. Calum, Tormod's brother, was not a chatty fellow, and they trundled down the A87 in silence, the only sound the endless swishing of his wiper blades as they battled to keep the windscreen clear.

Bypassing Portree's famous multi-coloured houses along the harbour, they circled the outskirts of the town and pulled into a large grey car park next to a low roofed, timber clad building. It was a modern structure, with a glass conservatory at the front where residents could, in finer weather, look out across the road to the water beyond. Calum brought the engine to a shuddering halt, and the sound of the rain drumming on the metal roof was suddenly deafening.

Having been running on a mixture of nerves and adrenalin so far, Rachel found that, now they were actually here, she didn't want to go in. The thought of what might lie beyond those doors scared her.

"I'll bide here for ye, lass," Calum said, the first words he'd spoken all journey. When she looked at him, he attempted a smile. "Ye'll be fine - Edith's a tough old bird. And you are too, fae whit I've heard."

Rachel forced a grim smile, assuming that this had been meant as a compliment.

"I hope you're right," she said, opening the door and rushing across the rain soaked car park to the automated entrance.

A dour faced nurse met her at the reception desk. Her hair was scraped back in a severe bun and the scrubs she was wearing struggled to contain her ample, broad backed frame. Unbidden, the image of Miss Trunchbull from Matilda popped into Rachel's head.

With as few words as possible - most of the islanders she had met so far shared the same efficient conversational style, Rachel reflected - the nurse led her to Edith's room.

She had imagined finding the elderly lady in bed, probably sleeping or unconscious, with feeding tubes or oxygen masks attached to her face. So, Rachel was pleasantly surprised to see her, instead, sitting up in a floral armchair looking out of the window. Her thinning grey hair was neatly combed, and she was wearing a zip up polka dot housecoat with matching fluffy slippers. Edith turned as Rachel entered, smiling and reaching out to her with a bony, liver-spotted hand.

Rachel breathed a sigh of relief, crossing the room to her and taking the proffered hand gratefully.

"Oh, thank goodness you're ok," she said, sitting in the armchair opposite. "You gave me the fright of my life, Edith!"

Her boss - although Rachel sometimes found it difficult to think of her like that - had a pair of tortoiseshell reading spectacles balanced on her nose, the chain snaking around her neck. She shook her head sharply in response.

"Sorry, lass," she said, still gripping Rachel's hand earnestly. Her blue eyes were as sharp and clear as ever, although now she was closer, Rachel noticed that her breathing was slightly laboured.

Edith squeezed her fingers. "I'll nae mince my words, Rachel - I've called for you to bring me home."

"Home?" Rachel echoed. Edith nodded.

"Aye. Now dinna you ignore me like these useless bloody nurses…" Rachel glanced nervously towards the door, where Miss Trunchbull was still hovering, the perpetual scowl on her face. "I'm nae daft, and I can tell." The old lady took a deep, shuddering breath. "I've nae much time left, and if I'm tae leave this world I'd like to do it in the same place I entered it, thank ye very much."

Rachel paused, confused. "What's happened?" she asked. "Why do you think you're going to..." her voice trailed off. She couldn't bring herself to say the word.

"Call it a hunch," Edith replied, her eyes sparkling despite the macabre topic. "Ye get tae my age and there's nae much that'll surprise ye; I can feel it in my bones, lass. Dinna fash," she said, patting Rachel's arm and giving her a reassuring smile. "I'm no' feart. I just want things to be in order, when the time comes."

Rachel felt unexpectedly tearful. She'd only known Edith a matter of months, although it felt like longer.

"I've had a good life," Edith was saying, her eyes still bright. "A long life; one many others would have been grateful for. And I'm ready for it to be over."

Edith had been born during the Second World War, the result of one of her father's brief periods of leave, during which he and her mother had been hurriedly married. Like most islands, Inniscreag had suffered more than its fair share of losses during the conflict; an entire generation of men was virtually wiped out, Edith's father among them. Rachel had seen his name carved into the lonely cenotaph at Craigport, standing stark against the grey waters of the Hebridean Sea.

The distillery had belonged to Edith's mother's people, and when her husband did not return from the war, Mairead McLeod reverted to her maiden name, went home, and never remarried. Edith was raised an only child, and when her mother passed away from typhus, she became the first in line to inherit the distillery from her childless uncle. It had been the only home she'd ever known.

Rachel couldn't help but feel a sense of kinship when she'd first heard the story of the older woman's life. Whilst she had grown up in a run down, working class area of Glasgow - about as far removed from Inniscreag as you could get - Rachel was also an only child, and hadn't been much older than Edith when she too lost her mother. But unlike Edith, who'd never taken a husband - despite many offers, or so she'd told Rachel - Rachel had combatted her own loneliness and desperate longing for a proper family by marrying the first man that came along. Not the best of decisions, in hindsight.

Edith was watching her carefully, and when she spoke again her voice was low and earnest.

"Ye ken why I hired ye now, lass?" she asked, shooting a sidelong glance at Miss Trunchbull. The nurse was still hovering by the door, a fact that was clearly unnerving Edith.

Rachel attempted a smile. "Because of my impeccable references and strong work ethic?"

Edith frowned. "No - because we're the same, you and me. We're made of the same stuff. It's in our bones."

Now it was Rachel's turn to frown. "What do you mean?"

Edith beckoned her closer. "You're one of us now," she explained. "And yer strong, and brave, and honest. So, I ken ye'll do the right thing, when I'm no longer here."

"Edith, I don't understand…"

"The vultures are circling, lass, make no mistake about it. Promise me I can trust you?"

"Of course you can…"

"*Dinna let them have it,*" Edith muttered insistently, pulling her closer. There were specks of spittle on her lips, and Rachel began to suspect that the old lady wasn't anywhere near as lucid as she'd first assumed. "It's ours, d'ye hear me? It belongs to us, and to the island, and I can't go to God thinking they might take it from us."

Scared now as well as confused, Rachel nodded. She'd read something once about the importance of not trying to rationalise with people who were suffering from dementia - the article had suggested that it would cause them less stress just to go along with whatever delirium they were experiencing. So that's what she did.

"I promise," she said, as firmly as she could. "I won't let them take it."

The old woman sighed, a peaceful smile spreading across her wrinkled face.

"There's a good lass," she whispered, patting Rachel's hand gently. "I've made many mistakes in my life, may God forgive me, but you're not one of them. Yer just like I imagined ye'd be…" Her voice drifted off as her eyes closed, and before either of them could say anything else, Edith McLeod was fast asleep.

# CHAPTER 4

Unsurprisingly, the care home was not particularly keen on the idea of allowing an elderly and frail patient to attempt a voyage at sea - albeit a short one - at such short notice. After much discussion, however, and even more scowling from Miss Trunchbull, Rachel managed to negotiate a plan to get Edith home. She was to be allowed to stay overnight in one of the home's spare rooms, and Edith and herself were booked on the evening ferry the following day, giving the care home sufficient time to ensure she had enough medication to keep her comfortable for a couple of weeks. After that, Rachel would have to arrange for repeat prescriptions to be collected from the pharmacy on Skye.

After sending Calum on his way, and belatedly realising that she hadn't thought to bring spare clothes or toiletries, Rachel popped back in to see Edith. The old lady was still dozing in her armchair, mouth open, her bony chest rising and falling. In a surge of unexpected tenderness, Rachel leaned over and kissed her on her forehead, fervently hoping that her macabre premonition would turn out to be wrong.

Before popping to the shops to pick up some deodorant and a toothbrush, Rachel rang the distillery and gave Cameron a quick update, arranging for him to meet the contractors off the boat the following morning instead.

"Just you wait and see - Edith'll outlive us all," he'd said, when Rachel divulged their employer's strange demands. She wasn't sure, however, that he sounded entirely convinced.

As it turned out, after a restless few hours of tossing and turning beneath beige polyester sheets, Rachel was awoken by an insistent rapping on her door at half past two in the morning. Even before she'd crossed the room to answer it, she knew who must be knocking, and why.

"Has it happened?" she asked sadly, leaning her head wearily against the doorframe.

It was a nurse she hadn't met yet, with pink cheeks and curly brown hair. The girl was only young, and looked shaken. She nodded, thin lips pressed together. Rachel briefly wondered if it was the first time she'd seen a dead body.

"A few moments ago," the girl sniffled. Her accent was local. "The alarm went off, but she'd signed a DNR..."

Rachel sighed. "Is there anything you need me to do?"

"Not just now, but they said I should let you know..."

"Thank you," Rachel shut the door, crossing the darkened room and slipping back into the uncomfortable bed. The single room was depressingly bare, devoid of even a radio she could switch on to distract herself. Sleep, she knew, would be a long time coming.

Rachel let a few tears slide down her cheeks. She knew she shouldn't be too sad. Edith had said it herself; she'd lived a long and eventful life, for which many others would be grateful. The thing that upset Rachel most was the fact that she'd ended it in a soulless place like this, rather than at home on the island that had borne her.

Wiping her face, Rachel rolled on to her side and shut her eyes, but it was useless. Every time she did, her mother's image floated before her in the dark.

Rachel had been nineteen the first time she saw a dead body; probably not much younger than the nurse she'd just seen at her door. After years of struggling, one day her mum finally had enough, and succeeded in doing what she had tried to do a number of times throughout Rachel's childhood. When that knock on the door eventually came, while Rachel was off at university and considered herself to be an adult, she'd almost been relieved. They'd barely spoken in years anyway - what was there to be sad about?

She'd identified the body, as requested, and that was that. She was back at her lectures the very next day, and no one would have suspected that anything had happened. Rachel hadn't attended the funeral, and couldn't remember shedding even a single tear over it; all of which made her feel more than a little guilty at the fact she was so saddened by Edith's passing.

The remainder of her student years had passed in the usual bubble of parties, last minute revision, exams and ill-advised one-night stands that were typical of many people's university experiences. But when graduation came and went, and her mid-level English literature degree didn't open very many doors, career-wise, Rachel found herself at an impasse. Eventually, with no job and no uni digs to return to, she ended up living back at her grandmother's flat, and sleeping in the same single bed where she'd spent so many of her childhood nights, when her mother had been unable to look after her.

Granny Peggy had actually been her father's mother. Rachel's mum had been raised predominantly in children's homes and never knew her birth mother. But even after Dad upped and left them when Rachel was just a baby, never to be seen again, Granny Peggy had remained. She had been the only person Rachel could ever really rely on. And then, predictably, Granny Peggy had also died, just weeks before Graham walked into her life.

Rachel sighed, shifting around on the lumpy mattress and trying to get comfy. She'd spent over six months trying to forget about Graham; she didn't need to be thinking about him now.

He'd appeared out of the blue one night, looking to use the toilets in an old-man boozer where Rachel was working behind the bar. He was muscled and tattooed, with floppy jet-black hair that fell into his eyes, and when he smiled at her she saw the flash of a silver stud through his tongue. From that moment, Rachel was infatuated with him.

It was such a stereotypical rebellion; falling for a bad boy. But Graham was charming, and funny, and Rachel found it completely intoxicating to be in his company. Not to mention the fact that following him around to watch his band play in various dodgy nightclubs across the Central Belt gave her an excuse not to think about what she was going to do with her own life.

Five years later, however, when they were newlyweds still living in her Granny's flat, and with Rachel putting in a forty hour working week at the local supermarket while he waited for his 'big break', the shine had well and truly worn off.

She'd toughed it out for another decade though, a fact which she now not only regretted but felt deeply humiliated by. Had she so little self respect? But she'd longed for the family she'd never had growing up, and every time she threatened to leave he promised that he would find a proper job, they'd buy a nice little semi in the suburbs, raise a couple of kids somewhere green and pretty, and Rachel had been stupid enough to believe him.

She laughed at her own naivety - for a while, she had genuinely believed that becoming a dad would force Graham to grow up. After the fourth miscarriage, however, when she'd returned from flushing another baby down the toilet, and he'd barely looked up from his phone for long enough to pat her on the belly and mutter something along the lines of "it wasn't meant to be," she finally realised that she'd had enough. Deciding that she'd rather be alone and childless than trapped in a lonely marriage, she threw him out, started divorce proceedings and signed up to LinkedIn in search of a new job. The distillery had approached her within a week, a telephone interview with Edith soon followed and she'd been offered the job within a fortnight.

And now here she was, alone again in a single bed, wishing that for once, just one person in her life would hang around when she needed them.

Obviously accustomed to their residents passing away in the middle of the night, the care home already had Edith's affairs well in order before Rachel had even made it to the nurse's station the following morning. Her solicitor had been notified, and was on his way there with a copy of the will as they spoke. A doctor had signed the death certificate, and all Rachel would have to do was take it to the Registrar's Office in Portree before she returned to Inniscreag.

Neither Miss Trunchbull nor the young nurse from the previous night were on duty, but the male nurse who explained all of this to her very kindly offered Rachel a much-needed coffee. Accepting it gratefully, she took a plastic chair in the waiting area. With any luck the solicitor would be there soon, and she could start making arrangements to get Edith home like she'd promised.

He arrived not long after ten, a harassed looking man in his mid-fifties, with a paunch hanging over the belt of his trousers.

"Ruaridh Davidson," he said, extending his hand to Rachel as she rose numbly from her seat. She'd been zoned out in front of a subtitled repeat of *Homes Under the Hammer* on the muted waiting room telly.

"Shall we go somewhere more private?" he suggested, ushering them into a vacant office.

Ruaridh closed the door behind him as Rachel sat, unsure of the protocol for a situation such as this.

"Okay, so, I won't keep you any longer than I have to," Ruaridh was pulling papers from his briefcase before he even sat down. "As she had no next of kin, Edith named you as executor."

Clearly, the surprise was evident on Rachel's face.

"You didn't know?" Ruaridh asked.

"No."

"She appointed you six months ago - shortly after you began working for her, I believe?" Rachel nodded mutely in response. "You'll need to register the death, obviously - we have the paperwork for that - and you are also the main beneficiary."

Rachel's head was spinning, and suddenly her throat felt very dry. "I'm sorry... what?"

Ruaridh looked at her, barely concealed exasperation in his eyes. For someone who must deal with things like this on an almost daily basis, he didn't seem to have much patience for the recently bereaved. He sighed loudly. "It's really very simple - Edith had a large estate, but she made very few bequests. I'll handle it all - we'll apply for confirmation and should be able to settle everything in six months or so. You won't have to do much, other than accept what she's left you. Or decline it, should you choose to do so."

"What has she left me?" Rachel asked. She could hear her own heartbeat in her ears.

"The distillery," Ruaridh said. "It's yours."

# CHAPTER 5

Everything beyond that had been a bit of a blur. The whooshing in Rachel's ears intensified, until she had to ask Ruaridh to fetch her a glass of water.

"Are you okay?" he asked, hurrying back in from the water cooler in the hallway. "Shall I call for a nurse?"

"No, it's alright. I'll be fine." Rachel sipped the water slowly, and tried to still the trembling in her hands. "She's left me the distillery? As in, I own it? All of it?"

"Well, you will do, as soon as it's all gone through the courts. It's a bit unconventional, bequeathing an historic family asset to an employee, but there's no other relatives around to contest it, so I can't imagine we'll have any issues on that front."

Still keeping a wary eye on Rachel, Ruaridh sat back down in his chair on the opposite side of the desk. "She's left you the business and all of its capital assets; her personal wealth has been bequeathed to a donkey sanctuary."

Rachel laughed. That seemed more like the Edith she had known. It was certainly less of a shock than finding out that she'd left her family's two hundred year old business to an incomer she'd only known for six months.

"You should know," Ruaridh continued, "that we've had interest in the distillery already."

"What do you mean?" Rachel asked, taking another sip from her water. Her palms were still sweaty, but the rest of her bodily functions were beginning to return to normal.

"Ever heard of Kindred Spirits Ltd?"

Rachel shook her head.

"I thought not - they try to keep the name of the umbrella company out of the public eye. You'll have heard of what they own, though. They're a multi-national drinks firm, and control some of the biggest proprietary brands in the world."

He slid a sheet of paper towards her across the table. It was a letter, topped with a company logo and list of international offices. Rachel scanned her eyes over it as he spoke.

"They had a rep over here yesterday to speak with Edith - word must have got out, somehow, that her health was failing. She's been refusing to sell to them for years, but they keep on trying. Bonus was they didn't realise she'd gone into a home, so they went looking for her back on Inniscreag. I have his name here somewhere…" Ruaridh rifled through his endless sheaves of paper, but Rachel wasn't listening. She'd just reached the end of the letter.

"Duncan Fraser," she whispered. His image flashed through her mind; the sharp suit, green eyes and easy smile. So that explained what the city boy was doing so far from home. And suddenly Edith's last words to her made sense, and she knew what it was the old lady had wanted her to do. *Don't let them have it.*

Ruaridh was watching her. "Do you know him?" he asked.

"Not yet," Rachel replied, with a wry smile. "But I will."

They arrived home the following day. Edith had arranged everything for her funeral, so after the undertakers took over it wasn't long until she was in her coffin and ready for the journey across the water. She'd even arranged for a private charter to transport them back to Inniscreag, in the event that she died at the nursing home.

When they first set out, Rachel felt distinctly uncomfortable – alone, in the little cabin, with nothing but Edith's body for company. She was unable to relax, and paced the floor warily, thankful that the sea was, at least, more peaceful than it had been on her outward journey. But as the craggy shoreline of Inniscreag came into view through the low sea mist, she felt an unexpected surge of pride. It may not have been Rachel's home for long, but she had been entrusted with accompanying one of its most admired residents on her final journey. Laying a hand against the warm oak of Edith's casket, Rachel set her jaw firm and resolved not to cry.

The islanders met them at the jetty; a small crowd, adults and children alike, dressed in sombre colours and huddled together against the rain. Four men - the young operators from the distillery - stepped forward to carry Edith down from the boat. She would be taken home to be laid out before the funeral, so that anyone who wished to could come and pay their last respects.

There was something beautiful about the way they welcomed home one of their own, Rachel thought. The mood was quietly respectful, but there was a matter-of-fact air about it all. There were no euphemisms, no platitudes; people chatted quietly as they exchanged hugs and greetings. It all felt strangely *normal*.

With no hearse on the island, Edith's casket was lifted onto a bier - a raised stand on wheels - and the small procession followed her along the path to her home.

Rachel walked with them, her head down and her hands deep in the pockets of her coat. She wasn't sure how the news of Edith's final wishes would be received. Would these people, who had lived and worked alongside her their entire lives, resent the fact that an incomer they barely knew was inheriting a part of their shared heritage? Rachel wouldn't have blamed them if they had. In fact, she'd have happily given it all up, if it weren't for the promise she'd made to Edith. She'd entrusted her with her legacy; Rachel couldn't risk letting her down.

Even on foot, it didn't take long to arrive at the wrought iron gates of the distillery. Rachel held back for a moment, watching the procession continue up the small hill to Edith's house, before slipping quietly down the path that led to her own home. After the events of the last twenty four hours, she needed some time to be alone.

She found Doug, damp and dishevelled, crouched by her back door. Scampering over as soon as he saw her, he weaved in and out of her legs while she stumbled over him to unlock the door. Doug bolted in before her, a ginger ball of fuzz, making a beeline for the nearest radiator.

Rachel trudged in behind him, kicking off her boots and discarding her jacket as she went. It was only lunchtime, but she was sure no one would mind if she took the rest of the day off. Exhausted, physically and emotionally, she trudged up the stairs to bed.

# CHAPTER 6

"You *own* the distillery?"

Sorcha was looking at her incredulously, one eyebrow raised as her coffee cup came to an abrupt stop halfway to her mouth.

Rachel nodded. "Apparently. Or I will, at least, once all the legal stuff's sorted."

They were in the little tea room at the front in Craigport, the tiny square window behind Sorcha giving a view out over the harbour. It felt more like sitting in someone's living room than a proper cafe, and that's because that's exactly what it was. There were four square tables, covered in hand stitched tartan tablecloths, and a counter at the back complete with a kettle, coffee machine and covered trays of home baking. A set of racks on one wall held a selection of newspapers and magazines, and the lean-to conservatory on the gable end of the building housed a mini corner shop, with milk, bread, tinned goods, and a selection of snacks.

Sorcha's mother, Ishbel, was the owner, but the fact that she left the front door permanently unlocked, combined with the honesty box on the worktop, meant that you never had to worry about whether she was actually in or not. There was even a small dishwasher under the counter - a recent addition plumbed in by Sorcha's husband, Andrew - so that patrons could stack their dirty dishes away before they left.

It was just after four o'clock on a Wednesday afternoon, the day after Edith's casket had returned from Skye, and Rachel and Sorcha's table was the only one occupied. Una was due to join them, but as she was routinely late they hadn't bothered waiting for her, and had already helped themselves to hot drinks and cakes.

"Bloody hell," Sorcha breathed, spreading a thick layer of butter on one of her mother's homemade scones. Sorcha was the headteacher - in fact, the only teacher - of the island's small two-room school. The full roll amounted to a grand total of twelve pupils, three of which were Sorcha's own children.

"What are you going to do?" she asked, her blue eyes wide. Sorcha had the white blonde hair and creamy complexion that instantly marked her as a native islander; unmistakable Nordic blood, which she had passed on to her three flaxen-haired children.

One of them ran in the door just as Rachel was about to speak. They'd been dispatched to play at the pebbly beach down by the shore, but despite the fact it was early spring, an unforgiving wind whipped in from the sea. Maisie's normally pale face was flushed pink with the chill, her long, fine hair tangling around her neck as a fierce breeze rushed in the door alongside her.

"Mum!" she cried. She was ten, but mature for her age, due to being the eldest child not just in her family, but on the entire island. "Fergus keeps hitting Struan," she said plaintively.

"Why?" Sorcha asked, turning to her daughter with an exhausted smile. They had the same heart-shaped faces, only Maisie's was in miniature.

"Struan's winding him up," Maisie admitted, with a weary grin beyond her years. Struan was eight and Fergus six. Rachel smiled; she'd often wished for siblings when she was younger, but seeing how Struan picked on his little brother so relentlessly actually made her grateful that she'd missed out on that particular pleasure.

Sorcha smiled. "Take them both a biscuit," she said, nodding to a tray of chocolate chip shortbread their grandmother had made. "And a piece for yourself," Sorcha added.

Maisie took the treats and scampered back out into the wind without a jacket. Not for the first time, Rachel marvelled at the resilience of the native islanders; even indoors, she still had her fleece on.

"I don't know," Rachel admitted, returning to their conversation and taking a sip from her tea. "I'm touched, but I've barely learned the ropes myself yet. And I think there was another reason Edith wanted me to have it…"

Rachel was just about to explain her boss' mysterious dying request when the bell above the door tinkled again, and Una strode in from the cold.

To look at her, no one would have guessed what Una did for a living. Rachel had been astonished herself when they'd first met, over drinks and a quiz in the local pub just a couple of days after she'd arrived on the island.

Una was beautiful. Objectively, undeniably beautiful. She was dark and tall, with long glossy hair and an elegant, willowy figure. An incomer, like Rachel, she was originally from Inverness, but had inherited her Mediterranean complexion from her Spanish father. She was also the local minister, and, much to the chagrin of the local bachelors, gay.

"Sorry I'm late," she said, pulling off her scarf to reveal the dog collar beneath. She dragged over an extra chair to join them, while Sorcha rose to re-boil the kettle.

"Tea or coffee?" she asked.

"Tea, please," Una replied, folding Rachel into a hug.

"I'm so sorry," she said, squeezing her hand. "How are you?"

"I'm OK. Just a bit shocked, to be honest."

As Sorcha poured Una's tea and brought over a slice of caramel shortcake, Rachel gave them both a quick summary of the conversation she'd had with Edith in the care home.

"She knew she was going to die?" Sorcha said, her eyebrows raised in two blonde, disbelieving arches. "I guess at her age you're kind of just playing the odds, saying things like that."

"It's more common than you might think," Una replied. Given her profession, talk of death or premonitions didn't faze her. "Especially with older people; I think sometimes they hold on until they know everything's in order."

"Well I wish she'd held on until I got her back to Inniscreag," Rachel admitted. She still couldn't escape the feeling that somehow, she'd let Edith down.

"So why do you think she left it to you?" Sorcha asked.

"To protect it, she said. According to the lawyer there's a big multinational drinks firm that want to buy it. Why she thought I'd be up to seeing them off I've no idea."

Rachel shuddered. Over the last twenty four hours, the reality of what she was actually up against had sunk in. A quick Google had shown just how wealthy, and powerful, Kindred Spirits Ltd were. They owned major international drinks brands, not to mention swathes of land and even a few five star hotels. How was she supposed to withstand the kind of pressure they'd be able to apply?

And then there was Duncan. Another quick Google search had taken her to his LinkedIn profile, and proven her initial impression of him as a smooth talking, corporate type to be correct. Probably pretty ruthless to boot. How on earth would Rachel - a department store coffee shop manager who'd been in the industry less than five minutes - stand up against him in a negotiation?

"You're not alone," Sorcha said. "That distillery is part of our bones on Inniscreag." Her face was serious, and her jaw set in a way that made it very easy for Rachel to see her Viking heritage. "No one here will want to see it in the hands of an outsider any more than Edith did. Oh, I didn't mean you," she added in a rush, seeing Rachel's crestfallen expression. "You're one of us now."

Rachel smiled. She hoped Sorcha was right; she had a feeling she was going to need all the help she could get.

After going through the details for Edith's funeral, which Una would lead in a couple of days' time, the three women dropped their money in the honesty box and went their separate ways; Sorcha calling her children in for tea with their granny, Una walking back to the manse just a couple of streets away, up the gentle hill from the seafront, and Rachel making the short drive back along the coastal road to the distillery.

The sky was just beginning to glow orange as she pulled out of her parking space, signalling twilight was on its way. Before long, summer would arrive and the daylight hours would stretch long into the night. Rachel was looking forward to that.

The road as she approached the westerly tip of the island rose steadily, curving along the tops of the rocky cliffs until it reached the stone-walled gates of the distillery itself. Rachel tried not to notice the layby where she'd pulled in to help Duncan just a couple of days before. He made her nervous, and flustered; two responses that would not be helpful during high stakes business negotiations.

Although maybe, she wondered, it might be good that she'd met him before all that began? At least this way, she could be prepared. When he turned on the charm, and those intoxicating green eyes, she would have her defences primed and ready. Hopefully, Rachel thought, being suitably forewarned would help protect more than just the distillery.

# CHAPTER 7

Rachel gave her reflection one last critical glance. With no clothes shops on the island, and her corporate wardrobe abandoned back in her old Glasgow flat, she'd had to make the best of what was available to her.

The black skinny jeans had to be folded up to prevent them from scrunching around her ankles. Not for the first time, she wished for long, slim legs like Sorcha's or Una's, instead of her own dumpy wee cocktail sausages. Pulling on her black Chelsea boots, Rachel hoped that it looked like a deliberate style choice, rather than simply necessary because she was a short-arse.

Paired with her plain white blouse, however, the trousers made her look like a waiter, so she opted for a bottle-green, fine knit cowl neck jumper instead. It was modest enough not to reveal too much cleavage - an ongoing battle which Rachel faced in many tops, thanks to her ample chest - and skimmed her tummy forgivingly without drowning her short frame. Hardly formal enough for a funeral, really, but Rachel consoled herself with the knowledge that it was unlikely anyone else would be overly dressed up, anyway.

Island funerals were very much community events, Una had said. Sorcha would be bringing along the schoolchildren, and the service was being timed so that the operators from the distillery could briefly abandon their posts. Rachel had wanted to close down production completely for the day, but Cameron had, quite rightly, pointed out that this would have been the last thing Edith wanted. The distillery had barely shut a day in its two hundred year history, and the old woman would have been appalled if one of those days of lost production were on account of her, dead or otherwise.

There were still twentieth century health and safety requirements to consider, however, and with the copper stills reaching a heat of two hundred degrees Celsius, they couldn't very well just walk away and leave them unattended. Cameron offered to come to the house in the morning to pay his last respects there, before relieving the operators so they could attend the church service.

Slipping a packet of hankies into her pocket, and quickly running a brush through her hair, Rachel grabbed her handbag, threw on her only vaguely smart coat, and headed downstairs.

The procession began at Edith's house, where Una was waiting alongside the coffin and the distillery workers. The same four operators who had carried her off the boat stood at either corner of the bier on which Edith's coffin had been laid. They would push her the mile or so into Craigport, a reverse of the journey they'd completed just a couple of days before, with everyone else following behind.

Cameron's wife, Jenny, greeted Rachel with a hug. "Dinna fash," she said, tucking Rachel's hand firmly into the crook of her arm without asking. "I'll keep ye right."

They left just after ten o'clock, a straggling line of just a dozen to begin with, but steadily growing in number. A scattering of houses dotted the fields along the roadside, and at each one the inhabitants would step outside and join onto the end of the procession. By the time they reached Craigport almost half an hour later, Rachel guessed the original group had more than doubled; by the time they reached the church itself, almost everyone on the island was following Edith's casket.

Rachel saw Sorcha leading the schoolchildren down the hill from the little schoolhouse, and her husband Andrew walking up to meet them from the harbour. He ran sea life and birdwatching tours on his boat in the summer months, as well as being a part time plumber and odd-job man. A lot of people on the island needed more than one job to make ends meet.

As they reached the gates of the church and Una led them inside, Rachel noticed a cluster of unfamiliar cars parked at the end of the road. With the tourist season not quite upon them, it was unlikely that they belonged to bird watchers or rock climbers; besides, she thought, they looked far too swish and clean to be the vehicles of choice for the island's usual, outdoorsy visitors. And then Rachel realised that one vehicle wasn't quite as unfamiliar as the rest. It was low, and sleek, and sporty, and a rather vibrant shade of red.

Feeling Jenny tug at her arm, Rachel was pulled inside just as she caught sight of his dark head ducking out of the car, followed by long limbs unfolding themselves from the vehicle in a strangely elegant manner. The green eyes were concealed by a pair of sunglasses, and he was accompanied by two women who had simultaneously disembarked from the other cars.

Unable to do anything else but follow Jenny into a pew, Rachel sat down quietly and fidgeted with the edge of her scarf. How dare they gate crash her funeral?

The congregation stood when Edith was wheeled to the altar. Rachel tried to push all thoughts of Duncan and his associates from her mind, watching Una take her place at the pulpit and welcome the mourners, but it was useless; she was preoccupied with rage. She wanted to turn around to check if they had actually had the gall to enter the church itself, but couldn't risk giving Duncan the satisfaction of seeing that he had riled her.

Instead, Rachel focused on the gentle, velvety timbre of Una's voice as she continued to speak. She was good at this, Rachel realised, feeling the indignant fire in her belly gradually recede. There was something soothing and reassuring about the certainty in Una's voice, as she spoke of resurrection and everlasting life. For a second, Rachel almost wished that she shared her faith.

Una's sermon was brief, but heartfelt. There was no eulogy, and only one hymn - *Abide with Me*. As it finished, the mourners trailed out of the church and into the spring sunshine, where Rachel spotted Duncan and the two unnamed women hovering by the gates of the churchyard. They hadn't actually come inside, at least. Maybe they weren't entirely heartless after all?

At this point, Rachel had been warned, it was tradition for the men to accompany the body to the graveside for burial, whilst the women headed back to prepare the wake. However, as Edith's only heir, and in the absence of any direct family members, Rachel had been bestowed the unique honour of going to the grave with the men.

She saw Hamish approaching, his impressive bulk clad in a dark, knitted fisherman's jumper. Gallantly, he took her hand from where it had remained throughout the service, nestled in the crook of Jenny's elbow.

He smiled down at her. "My turn to look after ye' now."

Taking his place at one corner of the bier, Hamish pushed with one hand and held on to Rachel with the other, as the men guided Edith the short distance up the hill to the cemetery. It looked down over the little village and out to sea, the sky clear and the water still, reflecting it like a sheet of glass. There was barely even a breeze, and the calls of the oyster catchers that swooped across the bay carried clear and sharp through the air. It was a beautiful spot, and Rachel knew Edith would have liked it.

Without any further preamble, the coffin was lowered solemnly into the grave and Rachel was invited to scatter some earth on top of it. Then, much to her astonishment, the four young men who had pushed the bier took up shovels and began to fill in the grave themselves. The rest of the men remained standing, watching in silence.

Suddenly lacking the comforting presence of Hamish beside her, Rachel felt alone and uncomfortable, as if she were intruding on something she had no business witnessing. Seeing the cold ground sealed back up over the top of Edith was much harder than she'd imagined, and she felt herself swaying gently. Breathing in deeply, Rachel shut her eyes, praying that she wasn't going to faint.

Once the soil had been packed in firmly, the men retrieved the roll of turf that had been cut away the day before and placed it carefully over the top of the burial site. The finality of it struck her, and suddenly Rachel felt tears brimming her eyes. She was relieved to feel a strong hand grasp her forearm, and looked up to see Hamish back beside her.

"It's done," he said simply, although his eyes were gentle.

Rachel sniffed, nodding her head. The rest of the men were departing now, winding their way back down the hill to where sausage rolls and sandwiches would be waiting in the local pub.

"Sorry," Rachel said, wiping her eyes.

Although she'd experienced death before, she'd never seen it handled with this degree of frankness. Compared to traditions on the mainland, she reflected, actually rolling your sleeves up and filling in the grave yourself seemed like a decidedly purposeful way to deal with the passing of a loved one.

Hamish wrapped a brotherly arm around her shoulder.

"A strong cup of tea and a biscuit, that's what you need," he said, leading her back down the hillside and into the village.

When they reached the pub, Rachel was not surprised to find it full to bursting. The wood panelled room was packed with jostling, chattering bodies, and the mood was unlike any wake she'd attended before. The mourners were talking animatedly, drinking heavily - despite the fact it was not quite noon - and a fiddle player had even started up in the corner.

Rachel and Hamish entered together, each finding a whisky immediately pressed into their hands.

It was one of their own, of course. A twenty five year old single malt, distilled and aged on the island itself; a fitting tribute to their leader. Rachel knew that the bottle would easily have fetched upwards of two hundred pounds on the open market - even more if the pub had been selling it by the quarter gill. Shelagh, the landlady, obviously wanted to mark the occasion properly. The room fell into a gradual hush, as simultaneously everyone raised their glasses.

Rachel suddenly realised they were all looking at her. Panicking, she racked her brains for something appropriate to say, finally alighting on the dimly remembered blessing she'd read at her granny's funeral. She raised her glass, stumbling over the words.

"May the road rise to meet you;

May the wind be always at your back;

May the sun shine warm upon your face;

May the rains fall softly upon your fields.

And until we meet again,

May God hold you in the hollow of His hand."

She felt her voice break on the final line, and was grateful when Hamish's deep bass led an enthusiastic chorus of "*Slàinte Mhath,*" which echoed around the room.

Rachel downed the whisky in one deep gulp, despite her distaste for the stuff. Her empty stomach burned as the fiery liquid hit it. Suddenly deciding that she wasn't hungry after all, she headed outside for some fresh air instead.

She stumbled out into the bright sunshine, squinting after the relative darkness of the cramped little pub. Crossing the road without looking - there were no cars around anyway - she flopped down on the bench next to the cenotaph, looking out over the harbour. Her head in her hands, Rachel took in large, grateful gulps of the salty ocean air and waited for the feeling to pass.

"Hi there."

The voice spoke from behind her. It took Rachel a moment to realise she was holding her breath, before she finally looked up, and turned around to face him.

He was every bit as handsome as she remembered. Taking off his sunglasses with one hand, he reached out and offered her the other, his arm outstretched so that she could see the smattering of dark hair around his wrist where the suit jacket rode up.

"My condolences," he said.

Rachel took the hand reluctantly and gave it a brief shake.

Duncan considered her for a moment, before coming round and sitting beside her on the bench, staring out to sea. "I'm guessing from the look on your face that you've figured out what my 'business' on the island was?"

"Yes, I have," Rachel replied, her voice tight. "Beginning to regret not leaving you stranded at the side of that road."

He laughed, turning and half-smiling at her. "If it wasn't me it'd be someone else," he said. "This isn't personal; I'm only following orders."

"Well that's a convenient excuse for being utterly heartless, isn't it?" Rachel shot back, standing abruptly as she felt her temper flare. "What do you think you're playing at, coming to her *funeral*?"

"Look, I can see you're cross, and that's understandable… we just came to pay our respects."

At the mention of "we" Rachel looked over his head, spotting the two women she'd seen with him earlier, standing awkwardly across the street and watching their exchange. They were also conspicuously formal in their attire, making Rachel feel even more bedraggled in her old jeans and jumper.

Una wasn't far behind them, peering out of the open door of the pub, having clearly come out to look for Rachel after her hurried exit. A concerned frown hung on her friend's face, and though she hovered by the door, she didn't come any closer.

"If you had an ounce of respect you wouldn't be here at all," Rachel muttered between gritted teeth, turning her attention back to Duncan and making a conscious effort to keep her voice low. "Can't you let us mourn in peace?"

Duncan sighed, looking down at his feet. For a second the professional facade fell, and when he looked back up at her, Rachel thought she saw genuine remorse in his eyes. "Please, believe me, I'm sorry about the timing. But we've been sent to do a job."

"You mean buying the distillery?"

"Yes. And we'd like to make the whole process as quick and painless as possible for everyone involved. We understand Edith had no heirs, and that you were her manager for a short period before her death. I think you'll find our offer extremely generous, given the circumstances…"

"She did have an heir," Rachel interrupted. "It's me. The distillery is mine." Duncan frowned at her, his mouth hanging half-open but no words coming out.

"I'm the manager *and* the owner now," Rachel continued, "And I'll be fucked if I'm going to sell it to a smarmy, money-grabbing, disrespectful bastard like you."

Her heart thumping in her chest, Rachel stalked across the road, grabbing a startled Una by the arm and dragging her back into the sanctuary of the pub.

# CHAPTER 8

"Who was that?" Una asked, her expression simultaneously intrigued and concerned. Rachel bustled her over to a table in the corner and waited for her heart rate to return to normal. After the initial toast and a quick round of the buffet, the crowd had started to thin; she was glad for the slightly less claustrophobic atmosphere.

"A problem," Rachel answered with a sigh. "He works for that company I was telling you about; the one that wants to buy the still."

"Oh," Una sat back, eyeing her friend carefully. "Quite good looking, though," she said casually. "If you're into that kind of thing."

Rachel scoffed. "Well, I thought so too, the first time I met him." She briefly recounted the story of their roadside meeting. "Just a pity he's actually a soulless, corporate robot."

They could still see him, through the tiny square windows that looked out onto the seafront. He was pacing up and down the short promenade, talking animatedly to the two women who had rushed over to him as soon as Rachel stormed away.

Shocked, Rachel saw him suddenly take a decisive turn towards the pub and cross the road, before striding confidently through the doors.

The crowd hushed as he entered, immediately sensing a stranger in their midst. Curious eyes turned on Rachel as they watched him advance towards her, Hamish placing his pint glass firmly down on the bar and observing the proceedings with a protective glint in his eyes.

Duncan paused uncertainly in front of her table, clearly not expecting everyone in the bar to be party to their conversation. He opened his mouth once or twice, seemingly searching for the right words before he spoke.

"Listen, we're going to be here for the next week, and you can ignore us if you like, but it won't make us go away. We know your financial situation," he said, pausing for effect, "and we can help with that. This isn't some 'David and Goliath' scenario; we're here to help make this community better. We can invest, and bring more money into your economy."

Rachel just glared at him. She could see Hamish looming

behind him - slightly shorter than Duncan, admittedly, but at least twice as wide - and whilst he didn't turn around, she could tell that Duncan sensed the other man's presence.

He lowered his voice. "Just hear us out," he said, placing a business card on her table. "My number's on there."

Duncan spun on his heels to leave, pausing when he found Hamish's expansive chest in his way. He tried to step around him, but the larger man stepped that way too, and again when he attempted the same manoeuvre on the other side. Every eye in the pub was on them. The islanders may not have known the ins and outs of exactly who Duncan was and why he was there, but they could certainly sense a threat. For a moment, Rachel felt sorry for him.

He paused, taking a deep breath and looking Hamish in the eye. "Would you mind?" he asked, his polite tone betrayed by the slight tremor in his voice. Hamish said nothing; just stared back wordlessly.

"It's fine, Hamish," Rachel said eventually. He stepped aside then, albeit hesitantly, and Duncan hurried outside without looking back.

As soon as he'd left, the normal chatter of the bar resumed as if it had never been interrupted. Rachel turned to Una, seeing her dark eyebrows raised.

"Yep," her friend said, taking a sip from her dram. "That is indeed a problem."

Three days later, it was a problem Rachel was no closer to solving. Duncan's card sat on her desk, taunting her, and while she didn't want to ring the number on it, she couldn't quite bring herself to throw it away, either.

It was Monday morning, and Rachel was going through the distillery accounts. They used a book-keeping firm on Skye to take care of everything, and before now she'd only really concerned herself with day-to-day cash flow or budgets for particular projects and improvements, such as her coffee shop plan. Edith had still been in control of the bigger picture stuff.

But now, Rachel was starting to see what Duncan had been getting at. Whilst cash flow and covering production costs wasn't a concern - for now - if things continued at their current projection, it wouldn't be long until the distillery was operating at a loss. And they didn't have a big enough buffer to be able to absorb that loss for long. They had to come up with a way to increase profits, and fast.

Picking up Duncan's card, Rachel flicked it over absent-mindedly between her fingers. She'd always worked for a bigger company; always had a boss or hierarchy of some kind to guide her. It would actually make life easier for her, in a way, if Kindred Spirits did take over. Assuming they didn't just fire her, that is. It certainly would be an awful lot less stressful than it was right now, and she wasn't even technically the owner yet. It would be months until the probate was concluded, and after just a few days of being in charge, Rachel was already buckling under the pressure.

But Edith's final words to her rang in her ears. *"Don't let them have it."* Which scenario would be worse, she wondered - to ignore the old woman's final wishes, or to be responsible if the whole bloody thing went under with her at the helm? That would destroy not just Edith's legacy, but the livelihood of so many people on this island whom Rachel had come to love.

With a deep breath, she reached for the phone and dialled Duncan's number before she could lose her nerve. It rang half a dozen times, and she began to hope she'd be able to hang up without leaving a message, when suddenly his voice was in her ear. He sounded distracted.

"Duncan Fraser?"

"Uhm, hi… this is Rachel. From the distillery."

She could almost hear him smiling. "Rachel! Good to hear from you. I hoped you'd be calling."

"This doesn't mean anything," she said in a hurry, not liking the smug tone in his voice one bit. "I just thought I should hear you out. Properly. And then I can be fully informed when I tell you…"

"To stuff my offer up my smarmy, money-grabbing, disrespectful arse?"

Rachel felt her cheeks flush. "Something like that," she said, through gritted teeth.

To her surprise, Duncan seemed to be laughing. "I look forward to it immensely," he said. "How does ten o'clock tomorrow morning suit you? We'll come to you? I'm assuming there's not much in the way of corporate meeting venues around here?"

"That'll be fine," Rachel said, ignoring the jibe and jotting the appointment in her open diary, although she knew she wasn't likely to forget it. She could almost feel Edith's spirit watching her, and judging her.

Duncan's voice was in her ear once more; an unnerving, but not unpleasant, gentle rumble. "See you then, Rachel. And promise me one thing?"

"What's that?"

"Leave your shotgun at home."

# CHAPTER 9

Later that night, as she stepped out of the shower and tiptoed on damp bare feet back along the hall, Rachel was glad for the distraction of her weekly Monday evening ritual. Things on Inniscreag ran to a comfortably predictable schedule, and Mondays meant pub quiz.

It was over the quiz that she, Sorcha and Una had first bonded. Just a couple of days after Rachel's arrival on the island, Cameron and Jenny coaxed her into going for a drink in the pub, where they wasted no time in foisting her upon what was, at the time, Sorcha and Una's cosy little team of two.

She'd always suspected that maybe they'd been trying to set her up with Una - her androgynous style sometimes drew assumptions, Rachel knew, and the excited gleam in their eyes when they'd introduced the two women was not exactly subtle. But regardless of their motivations, the three of them had clicked, and had been firm friends ever since. Besides, even if she had been a lesbian, Rachel was pretty sure she'd have been punching well above her weight if she managed to get off with someone as beautiful as Una.

Rachel opened her wardrobe and surveyed the meagre contents for what felt like the millionth time. With most of her belongings hastily abandoned within her granny's flat, Rachel's outfit choices the past few months had been depressingly sparse.

This hadn't bothered her, to start with; in fact, she'd found it quite liberating. Everything here on Inniscreag was decidedly casual, and the small selection of jeans, tops, cardigans and jumpers that she'd brought with her had so far seemed more than adequate. Now, however, that Duncan and his companions had brought a touch of big city corporate style to the small island, she felt more than a little scruffy by comparison.

She sighed, running a hand through her damp hair, before selecting a well-worn pair of stonewashed skinny jeans with a hole in the left knee, a striped boat neck tee-shirt and her cosy knock-off Uggs. She'd put a little make up on and blow dry her hair at least, she told herself. Not that she cared what he thought of her; but it wouldn't hurt to feel as confident as possible if they ran into each other. Which, given how small Inniscreag was, was highly likely.

Having grabbed a quick dinner of toast and tinned soup, Rachel poured Doug another bowl of kibble and left it on the back step for him before she left. The weather had remained fine - still cool, but clear and dry - and there would be a full moon later to light her way home, so she decided to walk into town. A drink or two would be in order tonight, and although there was no police officer on the island to catch her if she did, Rachel would never drink and drive.

She strolled through the distillery gates and made her way down the winding road, not a car in sight. To her right was a barren field, scattered with rocks and bedraggled sheep - which could quite easily be mistaken for rocks themselves, until they moved. To her left, the edge of the island tumbled away in a steep, jagged cliff, down to the deep grey waters below.

A gentle breeze tugged at her hair as she walked, and Rachel knew that her careful blow-dry would be thoroughly undone by the time she made it into Craigport. She didn't mind though; it was worth it for the salty, refreshing taste of the wind on her face.

Rachel had always thought herself a city girl, and she was amazed at how quickly she had settled into life in this tiny community. She loved being out here, alone in the encroaching twilight, listening to the crash of the waves hundreds of feet beneath her while the setting sun sent streaks of pink and orange across the sky. She closed her eyes and breathed in deeply, her hands cosy in her jacket pockets as her feet led her unconsciously along the path. For the first time in her life, she realised, Rachel was beginning to feel at peace; as if she really belonged somewhere.

She opened her eyes as a deep, throaty rumble pierced through the tranquil evening air. It was an engine, no doubt about that; but it definitely didn't belong to a tractor or the decrepit 4x4s that most of the islanders drove.

The road she was following had been sloping gradually downwards, so that Rachel was now walking beside a rocky shoreline rather than along the tops of the cliffs. There was a sharp bend up ahead, where the road swung around to the right. She paused, knowing the vehicle would be approaching on the same side of the road she was on, and stepped cautiously into the verge so as to be well clear before it came hurtling around the corner.

Predictably enough, the car which came too fast around the bend, almost drifting, was bright red, sporty and low to the ground. Rachel stepped as far into the muddy verge as she could, half hidden by the bare, overhanging branches of one of the few gnarled little trees that were scattered across the island, hoping he wouldn't see her. But even before the car had fully straightened up and passed her by, she could already hear the brakes being applied.

Duncan swiftly put the car into reverse and coasted back until he was alongside her, one arm slung over the back of the passenger seat as he looked out of the rear window. His own window was down before he'd come to a standstill.

"Hi there," he said, flashing Rachel that smooth smile. His green eyes were concealed once more behind the designer sunglasses, but he'd changed from his three piece suit into a casual tee-shirt, zippy top and jeans.

Rachel grimaced back, folding her arms across her chest.

"Hello," she said. "Enjoying yourself?" She nodded down at the car. "You know there are other people on these roads, occasionally. And speed limits. It's just as well I heard you coming."

"Maybe you should walk on the right side of the road, then?" he shot back, although the smile remained.

"This is the right side of the road, City Boy. You walk *towards* oncoming cars on a single track."

Duncan ignored her, changing the subject instead. "You look nice," he said, the compliment catching her off guard. "Hot date?"

Rachel rolled her eyes. Obviously, he was being sarcastic. "Pub quiz."

"Oh, I saw the sign!" Duncan said, taking off his sunglasses and propping one elbow on the ledge of the open window. "We thought we might give it a try ourselves, actually. Two nights of sitting in a hotel room - a very small hotel room that I can't even stand up straight in - is giving me cabin fever."

"We?" Rachel asked, hoping that the little edge of jealousy she felt wasn't betrayed in her voice.

"Louise and Fiona," he explained, "the rest of the investments team. You'll meet them properly tomorrow. I'm legal, Louise is finance, Fiona's marketing."

Rachel nodded, not wanting to think about the power-suited, corporate women or what the meeting tomorrow might bring.

"Where are you heading, anyway?" she asked.

Duncan shrugged. "Just fancied a bit of exploring. Like I said, I've got cabin fever."

"Well if you want to explore round here, I wouldn't advise doing it in that," Rachel replied, jutting her chin at his ridiculously impractical car. "Better with a set of walking boots and a compass."

Duncan ran a hand through his hair, his piercing eyes still on her. "Like I said before, I'm not so keen on the great outdoors. I'd rather explore from the comfort of a fine piece of Italian craftsmanship like this."

He put his hand out of the window and patted the door of the car, a gesture which Rachel found so ludicrously wanky that she was actually grateful he'd done it. Much easier not to fancy him when he was acting like a total tosser.

"Like it or not, the great outdoors is all you've got here. This is the only road. You'll get to the distillery and just have to turn back again."

Duncan's impeccable smile faltered for a second, and he gave her a confused frown. "The *only* road?" he echoed.

Rachel nodded. "Yup. I'm afraid you've already experienced all the motoring adventure Inniscreag has to offer. Might have to get your fine Italian shoes dirty if you want to see anything more exciting."

Feeling quite pleased with herself, Rachel turned and continued along the road towards the scattered lights of Craigport, leaving Duncan and his idling Italian engine at her back.

It wasn't long until the low rumbling of his car was behind her once more, just as she reached the outskirts of the village. Rachel turned and smiled at him as the low red roof approached, her arms folded across her chest and her eyebrows raised. He didn't stop this time, but coasted past her and slid into a parking space just up ahead, alongside the harbour wall.

"Told you so," she said, crossing the empty road to gloat.

He was stepping out of the car as she approached, and she found herself looking up at him, a self-deprecating smile on his face. At just over five feet, Rachel looked up at pretty much everyone; but she had to admit, tosser or not, she really quite enjoyed looking up at Duncan Fraser. The wind was ruffling his hair in a way that made

43

him look almost boyish, and nowhere near as slick or intimidating as he had when they first met.

"What can I say?" he said, his arms wide in a doleful shrug. "You were right. No more roads."

"Told you so," she repeated, glancing down at the trendy canvas trainers he was wearing. "You'll need to invest in some sturdier footwear if you're going to be hanging around."

"Well that all depends on the outcome of our meeting tomorrow," Duncan replied, rubbing his hands together briskly. The breeze was cool, but Rachel felt perfectly comfortable in her light puffer jacket and silk scarf. Maybe she was beginning to acclimatise to the island chill after all?

"If we can make a deal tomorrow, I'll be out of here on the first available ferry," Duncan continued. "Although I must admit, that would be slightly disappointing, in some respects." His green eyes held hers for a second, until Rachel looked away, uncomfortable.

"Don't hold your breath," she muttered.

Duncan nodded across the road, to where warm, golden light spilled out onto the pavement from the tiny square windows of the pub. Voices could be heard within, cheery and welcoming, and smoke puttered from the chimney into the twilit sky. Rachel knew there'd be a fire roaring in the wood burner, and her friends waiting for her in their usual spot.

"Shall we head in?" Duncan asked, thrusting his hands into his pockets. "I could do with the protection of a local; last time I walked in there alone, I thought it was all going to go a bit 'duelling banjos'."

Rachel frowned at him again, as he imitated holding a banjo and plucking the strings, his shoulders hunched over and one eye shut.

"Diddle-ing-ding-ding," he sang, and despite herself, Rachel couldn't help but smile.

"Fine," she sighed. "But once we're inside, you're on your own."

# CHAPTER 10

The warmth enveloped them as soon as Rachel opened the door, instantly spotting Una and Sorcha in their usual table by the corner, tucked in at the side of the wood burner. They looked up and smiled, waving her over, but their faces dropped when Duncan's tall figure stooped through the door behind her. Sorcha frowned, confused, while Una raised her eyebrows in an amused expression that Rachel didn't like one bit.

"Enjoy your night," she muttered to Duncan, not turning to look at him as she hurried over to her friends and gratefully accepted the large white wine spritzer Sorcha pressed into her hands.

"What are you doing with him?" she asked, incredulous. Duncan was hovering by the bar, looking uncomfortable, whilst some of the locals regarded him curiously.

"We ran into each other outside," she said, gulping down almost half of her drink in one go.

Una was still giving her that funny look, her lips pressed together in a knowing smirk. "The two of you looked very cosy together," she said, taking a casual sip from her own glass of merlot.

"Don't," Rachel said firmly. "He's a money grabbing, soulless, corporate goon."

"A good-looking one, though," Una persisted, smiling.

Rachel glanced back over to the bar. Duncan had got himself a drink now - a whisky, of course - and had taken a seat on a bar stool alongside Andrew. The two men were chatting amiably, Sorcha scowling at her husband's back.

"What's he playing at, talking to him as if they're old friends? Doesn't he know why he's here?"

"He's just being polite," Una said, sweeping her long dark hair over one shoulder. She wasn't wearing her dog collar tonight, dressed instead in high-waisted chinos and an oversized roll neck sweater. On Rachel it would have looked frumpy, but Una made anything look stylish. Even ministerial robes.

"Cut the guy some slack," she continued. "He's only doing his job; it doesn't make him a bad person."

"Easy for you to say," Sorcha said. "You've got to promote love and tolerance and forgiveness and all that shite; it's in the job description."

"Says the woman entrusted with the wellbeing and development of the future generation," Una shot back with a grin.

Shelagh, the landlady, was doing the rounds now, handing out answer sheets ready for the quiz to begin. She paused when she reached their table, lowering her voice conspiratorially.

"Sorry, girls," she said, screwing up her face as she followed their gaze to the bar.

Shelagh was a friendly woman in her early fifties who'd married an islander in her youth, and stayed on when, just two years later, he dumped her and ran off to the mainland with their next door neighbour. Rachel liked her; she didn't tolerate any nonsense, and could break up a bar fight between the burliest of her patrons, despite being so small that she made Rachel look positively statuesque by comparison.

"I dinna like them staying here, but I canna afford to have rooms lying empty, either," Shelagh finished.

"Don't worry about it," Rachel reassured her with a smile. "We've all got to earn a living."

"As does he," Una interjected. Rachel and Sorcha simultaneously scowled at her. "I won't mention it again," Una said, her hands raised innocently.

The usual teams had taken their places around the small pub - Rachel and her friends next to the fireplace, Andrew and a couple of the other odd-job men at the bar, and Tormod with some of his fellow fishermen in the opposite corner. A few other couples and individuals were scattered around, mostly just there to observe and eat peanuts. Cameron and Jenny weren't amongst them, Rachel noticed, although they usually were. And neither were Duncan's female associates, leaving him conspicuously alone. He was glancing around the room, his glass empty, before seeming to make up his mind and rising from his stool to head back upstairs.

Rachel breathed a sigh of relief, before, to everyone's surprise, Andrew stood up and called him back.

"We're a man down this week," he said. "You can make up the numbers."

Duncan glanced across the room, seeing Rachel watching them. He smiled, slowly. "I'd love to."

Sorcha was scowling at her husband once more. Andrew

caught her eye and gave an exaggerated shrug. "What?" he mouthed.

Frowning into her glass, Sorcha took a long gulp of gin. "Arse," she muttered.

"Things still no better with you two?" Rachel asked. She knew Sorcha and Andrew had been going through a bit of a bumpy patch.

Her friend shook her head sadly. "My mum takes the kids so we can have some time together, and we spend the entire night sitting at opposite ends of the bar." She ran her hands through her fair hair, sighing. "Just be glad you never had kids with your arsehole husband, Rachel. I'm stuck with Andrew now, forever. Whether I like it or not. Excuse me."

Sorcha pushed her stool back and stumbled into the toilets. Andrew didn't even notice, his head bowed as he remained deep in conversation with Duncan, revealing the bald spot at his crown which was growing increasingly difficult to hide.

Una looked across at Rachel, a sad and uncomfortable silence left in Sorcha's wake. "She didn't mean it," she said quietly.

Rachel nodded, swallowing down her own threatening tears. "I know," she said.

Grateful to hear Shelagh's voice booming across the room to kick off the quiz, Rachel picked up her pen and occupied herself with filling in their answer sheet.

They changed their name around every week, taking it in turns to come up with something; Una's choices were always clean and wholesome, whilst Sorcha's tended to be witty forms of word play or puns. Rachel, on the other hand, usually opted for something smutty or vulgar, much to Una's discomfort. This week, it was Rachel's turn to choose.

She looked up to see Sorcha emerging from the bathroom, with flushed cheeks and a somewhat sheepish expression.

"Sorry" she whispered, squeezing Rachel's leg under the table as she sidled back onto her stool. There was nothing else she needed to say. Rachel grabbed her hand and squeezed it in return.

Una glanced across the table at where Rachel had scribbled their team name at the top of the answer sheet, and scrunched up her pert little button nose.

"Is that it?" she asked. "Very tame, by your standards."

They rattled through the first round - TV trivia - with Rachel and Sorcha both managing to steadfastly ignore Duncan and Andrew on the opposite side of the room. It wasn't until Shelagh had gathered their answer sheets in and was scoring the first set of questions that, emboldened no doubt by the whisky in his belly, Duncan decided to approach.

"Ladies," he said warmly, flashing all three of them his trademark charming smile. "Can I get you all a drink? A peace offering, if you will."

"That'd be lovely," Una smiled back at him, displaying her own set of pristine white teeth. Rachel couldn't help but imagine what beautiful children the two of them could have - dark haired and olive skinned, with perfect smiles and fine-boned features. "A merlot, please."

"Una, am I right?" Duncan asked, lifting her glass from the table.

"You are indeed," Una replied, gesturing to her left where Sorcha was fixing him with an icy, blue-eyed stare. "This is Sorcha," she continued brightly, ignoring her friend's tight-lipped expression. "She'd like a G&T. And Rachel… well, you've already had the pleasure, of course."

"I have indeed." He smiled down at her, gesturing to her now empty wine glass. "I thought you'd be a whisky drinker?"

Rachel handed him the glass without looking up. "White wine spritzer. Large," she added.

Duncan sighed. "As you wish."

He fetched their drinks and brought them back to the table just as Shelagh was reading out the scores for round one. Both having been eyeballed by Una, who was as polite and friendly as ever, Rachel and Sorcha offered him an unenthusiastic thank you.

"And in the lead after round one," Shelagh finished, "we have The Big Fact Hunts!"

Hearing it read aloud, realisation suddenly dawned on Una and her jaw dropped, leaving her gasping at Rachel, open-mouthed and incredulous. The rest of the bar erupted into laughter, and eventually Una joined them.

"Well done," she conceded, when the laughter had subsided. "You got that one past me."

Rachel smiled, looking over at the bar to find Duncan watching her, a genuine, wide-toothed smile across his face and his eyes sparkling with laughter. He raised his glass to her, and with an uncharacteristic surge of confidence, Rachel raised hers back.

By the time the quiz had finished, Rachel was on her fourth spritzer and was exceptionally glad she hadn't brought the car. Una having made her excuses as soon as the last round was over, Rachel and Sorcha were left alone, finishing their drinks and comparing notes over this week's questions and scores. In the end, they'd narrowly conceded defeat to the imaginatively named 'Village Idiots'.

"Are the kids sleeping at your mum's tonight?" Rachel asked.

"Aye," Sorcha nodded. "She'll drop them at school in the morning, where they can complain about how I never make them pancakes on weekdays." She gave a rueful smile. "Andy and I are supposed to be using these date nights to 'reconnect'. Looks like he'd rather be heading home with your man Duncan than me." She glanced over to the bar, where both men were continuing to chat animatedly.

"You'll get back on track," Rachel said. "Why don't you skip the quiz next week? Stay home just the two of you and get an early night instead?"

Sorcha scoffed. "Fat chance of that happening. Andy would rather be on his computer than have sex. And I'd rather watch *Real Housewives* and eat biscuits, if I'm honest."

Rachel could empathise. Before she threw him out, it had been almost a year since she and Graham had had sex. She hadn't even missed it, at the time. She thought she'd just lost her libido; put it down to getting that little bit older, not to mention the fact that over the years, sex had become little more than a monthly chore based around whether or not she was ovulating. Now, however, Rachel was beginning to suspect that it wasn't that she didn't want to have sex; she just didn't want to have sex with *him*.

Before she had a chance to stop herself, her gaze flitted across the room and alighted on Duncan. The room had grown stuffy, and his zippy top was discarded on his bar stool, revealing the fitted tee-shirt beneath. Rachel had always had a bit of a thing for arms; his were lightly toned, the defined biceps clearly visible beneath the short sleeves, the forearms covered with a dusting of dark hair.

"Time to go," she said abruptly, tearing her eyes away. No good could come from being around him while she was slightly sozzled, on the rebound and - she finally admitted to herself - horny.

Rachel stumbled to her feet, picking up her jacket from where it had fallen to the floor whilst Sorcha finished the last of her gin. The pub was steadily emptying, and Andy approached with Duncan by his side, just as Rachel tripped over the strap of her handbag. She would have gone flying headfirst onto the flagstone floor, if Duncan hadn't stepped forward and caught her just in time.

"I think you need a taxi," he said with a smile, helping her up, his hands warm on her arm.

Andy emitted a brief, snorting laugh as he helped a very quiet Sorcha into her coat. "Nae taxis round here, mate. Yer no' in the city, now."

Duncan sighed. "I'll drive you then," he said, one hand still on Rachel's elbow.

"You've been drinking," she replied angrily, shaking him off and clumsily attempting to put on her coat. "I can walk; I'll be fine."

"You just fell over fresh air," Duncan argued. "If I let you walk up that cliff road in this state, we'll find you dashed on the rocks in the morning. That's the hood, by the way."

Rachel paused, looking down at where she'd been trying to force her arm into her jacket. Only he was right; her fist was currently trying to punch its way through the fabric of the hood.

She huffed, finally finding the right opening and pulling the jacket on. "You've still been drinking," she said. "You could end up driving us into the bloody sea in that stupid, mid-life-crisis-on-wheels car of yours."

Duncan smirked. "I had one dram, three hours ago," he said, quite reasonably. "I thought I'd best stick to the soft drinks after that. Some of us have an important business meeting tomorrow morning, after all."

Rachel felt her heart sink. "Ah, fuck," she muttered.

Duncan laughed, taking her scarf from where it dangled uselessly in her hands and wrapping it gently round her neck. "Fuck indeed," he said with a smile. "This way, m'lady."

# CHAPTER 11

Rachel awoke to the sun streaming in through her bedroom window. She rolled over, her head foggy and her mouth dry, pulling the duvet over her face to shield her eyes and wishing she'd remembered to shut the blinds before stumbling into bed the night before.

Cautiously, she peeled open one eye and squinted at the radio alarm clock next to her bed. Rachel breathed a sigh of relief - it was just after seven o'clock. Her alarm wouldn't go off for another twenty minutes. At least she hadn't slept in.

She rolled onto her back, dimly aware of the pounding in her skull but at least able to open her eyes fully now. She was naked, and for a split second a bolt of panic ran through her. But it was okay; she could remember Duncan helping her in the front door, but he definitely didn't come inside. He'd stayed on the step, a smile on his face as he gently reminded her to lock the door before she fell asleep. Rachel had laughed at him; no one around here worried about locking their doors.

And now she would have to face him, and try to look self-assured and professional, when he'd seen her bladdered and falling over not twelve hours before. At least the other two hadn't been there, although she was sure he'd waste no time in filling them in. He must be thinking this would be a piece of cake; easy to steal a business from some drunken floozy.

Cursing herself for not having thought to bring a glass of water upstairs, Rachel clambered out of bed and headed to the kitchen. Fluids, toast, a shower and some ibuprofen would deal with her most immediate problems; after that, she'd have to figure out how the hell she was going to get through this meeting without inadvertently selling off Edith's legacy before she'd even legally inherited it.

At a loss for any other form of back-up, and painfully aware that she was already outnumbered three to one, Cameron had agreed to sit in on the meeting with her. That was something at least; he was an islander born and bred, and had worked his way up through various roles at the distillery before eventually becoming the master blender. His knowledge of the business was thorough, and having him there would make Rachel feel more confident.

If she'd had more time she would have sent for Edith's lawyer, Ruaridh, or a representative from their accountancy firm on Skye as well. But regardless of what Duncan and his associates offered, she wasn't going to sell. She was just hearing them out so they could report back to their bosses that they'd done what they were sent to do, before hopefully pissing off back to the mainland and leaving them all alone.

The ibuprofen had taken the edge off her headache, and the shower and toast completed her transition back to an almost functioning human, so that by the time she was heading into the office just over an hour later Rachel actually felt relatively professional. After rummaging fruitlessly through her wardrobe once more, she'd settled on her usual work wear of branded polo shirt and jeans. Why should she put on airs and graces for their sake?

Rachel headed out the back door, pouring some more kibble into Doug's bowl as she passed. She hadn't seen him in a couple of days, which was unusual, but as the bowl kept getting emptied, she assumed he must be okay. The better weather probably meant he was happy to be outdoors, and wasn't as desperate for a warm knee to curl up on.

Cameron was already in the office when she arrived. He had his back to her as she entered, and jumped when Rachel closed the door, spilling the small half-measure of whisky he held in his hand.

"Jesus Christ, woman!" he declared, turning to see her, his hand shaking. "Ye scared me half to death!"

Rachel smiled. "Sorry. Are you in early for Iain again?"

Cameron hastily screwed the top back on the sample bottle on his desk, frowning. "I was, but Hamish offered him a lift instead. Thought I'd get a head start on this meeting, since I was in sharp."

"Do you think we should offer samples?" Rachel asked, nodding at the bottle in his hands as she flicked on her computer.

Cameron shrugged, placing the bottle back on the shelf and rubbing the palms of his hands against his trousers. "Probably not. Just an idea - thought it would be hospitable. But you're right, probably gives the wrong impression. Don't want things getting too friendly."

"I'm not going to accept, no matter what they offer," Rachel assured him, sitting down. "This is just to hear them out so that maybe they'll give up and go away."

Cameron frowned. "I wouldn't be so sure," he said. "Companies like this one don't give up without a fight; they've been chasing Edith for years. And we're no' exactly in great nick, on the financial side of things."

"I know." Rachel sighed, logging on to her computer and opening up the accounts and sales spreadsheets. "That's why we need to be prepared."

"Coffee?" Cameron asked.

"Yes please."

With the help of two pots of coffee and more of Jenny's homemade fruitcake, Cameron and Rachel eventually had a full picture of the distillery's current financial position printed out and assembled in front of them. Sales figures for the last six months, future projections, stock levels, budgets, plans and costings for Rachel's coffee shop project covered the table. They'd also dusted off their 'current' marketing strategy, which turned out to be three years old, and more than a little vague. Advertising had never been much of a priority. Their core consumers were extremely brand loyal, just small in number. The occasional feature in an industry magazine sometimes resulted in extra demand, but apart from that, drinkers of Inniscreag single malt were generally an unfluctuating market.

Cameron surveyed the table, before glancing up at the clock above the door. "Well, let's not give away the farm," he said, beginning to gather the papers together. "They'll be here soon. We know this business," he continued, giving Rachel's shoulder a reassuring squeeze as he dropped the papers into her desk drawer. "Just let them talk, and then we'll politely decline. Easy."

He smiled, and Rachel wished she shared his quiet confidence. Whilst they were managing - for now - she didn't feel anywhere near up to the task of getting their profits to where they really needed to be. Yes, she could install and run a coffee shop, but managing the whole site, including making decisions about product development, and marketing, and everything else? That was beginning to feel well beyond her capabilities.

They had ten minutes until Duncan and his team were due to arrive. Rachel quickly finished tidying around her desk - with no conference room of any kind, the meeting would have to take place here - before heading to the loo to freshen up.

Glancing in the mirror, she was relieved to see her reflection didn't look quite as rough as she'd expected. She swept some concealer over the dark circles under her eyes, added a fresh coat of mascara to her eyelashes, and puffed some blusher onto her cheeks. That would have to do, Rachel thought, tucking her hair behind her ears, tidying her fringe and hoping for the best.

She bumped into Hamish as she was coming out of the building's only toilet.

"I thought you went home?" she asked.

"Da sent me back," he replied. "This came over from the mainland yesterday. Postie left it with us; Da said I'd pass it along, but I forgot to bring it when I started my nightshift."

Hamish handed her a bundled-up pile of envelopes held together with elastic bands. Rachel recognised the spidery handwriting instantly; it was the last of Edith's personal effects from the nursing home. There must have been a few things hidden in drawers that she'd missed before she brought the body back to Inniscreag.

"Thanks." Rachel smiled sadly, taking the top envelope from the pile and strolling back to her desk. It was a padded jiffy bag, and there was a small, hard item within. She tipped it gently into the palm of her hand.

A gold locket fell out. It was oval, with initials engraved on the front in a curly script - 'M.M.G.' Rachel carefully unclicked the latch on one side, opening it to reveal an old, black and white photograph.

It was a baby; tiny and wrinkly and new. Absolutely perfect, in fact, except that the side of her little face was marked with a small, darkened imperfection. A port wine stain, perhaps? Rachel's mother had had one, although much larger - it had covered most of the right-hand side of her face.

She frowned, briefly wondering who on earth it could be. After all, Edith hadn't had any children of her own. Not even nieces or nephews, as far as Rachel was aware. Of all the trinkets and pieces of jewellery cluttering up her home, why would this be the one thing she took with her to the nursing home?

Placing the locket back in the bag, Rachel slipped it safely into her drawer before rifling through the rest of the pile. It all seemed to be basic correspondence; some bills, a few bank statements. Then, she stumbled across something familiar.

Pulling the letter out of the already opened envelope, Rachel quickly scanned her eyes over it. It was exactly what she expected it to be; a takeover proposal from Kindred Spirits, expressing their interest in the distillery and requesting a meeting. The signature at the bottom was equally familiar - Duncan Fraser.

The only difference between this letter and the one Ruaridh had shown her just after Edith's death, was the fact that this one had been scrawled upon, in Edith's own handwriting, with one word.

'*Never.*'

# CHAPTER 12

If Rachel had needed anything else to steel her resolve, that was it. By the time Duncan and his companions arrived, she felt the growing fire in her belly engulfing her earlier hopelessness. This was what Edith wanted; seeing it written in the old lady's own hand, resolute despite her failing strength, gave Rachel the conviction she was lacking. Come hell or high water, she would keep Inniscreag independent and make it work. Somehow.

She met Duncan at the door to her office, greeting him with little more than a nod and a cursory handshake as he introduced his companions.

"This is Fiona, from our finance department," he said, gesturing to the older looking of the two ladies. She had brassy, dyed blonde hair and a heavy face of makeup to go with her lime green silk blouse, pencil skirt and skyscraper heels. Rachel couldn't help but wonder how she'd negotiated the cobbles in the courtyard outside.

"And Louise, from marketing." The second woman was younger, with frizzy light brown hair and dressed in a slightly more understated pinstripe trouser suit paired with flat black ballet pumps.

Rachel offered them all coffee, which they declined, instead choosing to hover awkwardly in the small pocket of space between the door and Rachel's desk, obviously waiting to be led somewhere grander.

"So…?" Duncan began

"This is it," Rachel interjected. "This is the only office space we have, so take it or leave it."

Duncan frowned at her, clearly caught off guard by the hostility of her tone. So was Cameron; he laughed nervously before stepping into the fray.

"We've brought through some extra chairs," he said, herding them to the nearest side of the desk and urging them to sit, whilst he not-so-subtly guided Rachel to her own chair on the opposite side. Cameron perched nervously on his desk in between, like some kind of anxious mediator.

"We were expecting an interactive whiteboard?" Fiona said, peering down her nose and looking around the room with an expression that suggested she'd smelled something unpleasant. "I have a PowerPoint presentation to share."

Rachel gave her an insincere smile, not wanting to admit she had no idea what an interactive whiteboard was. "You'll just have to do your best to summarise."

Fiona saw her insincere smile and raised her a passive aggressive dig. "Well, I can assure you it won't take long. The financial evaluation of your company is decidedly... brief."

The other woman, Louise, was fidgeting nervously. She clearly lacked the easy confidence of Duncan, or the superiority complex of Fiona, and Rachel suspected that under other circumstances she might have actually quite liked her.

Rachel took a deep breath, thought of Edith's letter, and tried to remain calm. "You approached us," she said. "We haven't come looking for your help. Please, feel free to begin your pitch whenever you're ready."

Duncan spoke first, his tall frame cramped in the tiny room. Holding the meeting in here hadn't been a deliberate move - it genuinely was the only office space they possessed - but it seemed to have unintentionally worked in Rachel's favour. They were clearly out of their comfort zone, deprived of high-tech slideshows and infographics with which to dazzle them.

Despite his obvious discomfort, Duncan's voice conveyed a calm, insightful sense of authority. He gave an overview of the deal they were offering, and the many perks it would bring to the distillery. Rachel had to acknowledge that, like it or not, it did sound appealing.

Fiona was next, and her decimation of their financial position was every bit as brutal and as brief as she had promised. They were, to put it bluntly, fucked.

Finally Louise, the apparent marketing guru - whom Rachel assumed must be hiding her light under an enormous bushel - spoke quietly about their failure to diversify and broaden their appeal. The overall message was clear - they were skint, old fashioned, stuck in the past, and outdated. They didn't even have a social media presence, for crying out loud. Coming on board with Kindred Spirits Ltd, they promised, would change all that.

"So how much?" Rachel asked, when they had all eventually had their say.

"Well, to buy out the business in its entirety, all capital and intellectual assets…" Duncan began.

"Just give me a figure," Rachel interrupted coldly.

He sighed, fixing her with that almost confused expression once more, before scribbling a number on the notebook in front of him and turning it to face her.

Cameron peered across, letting out a low whistle and raising his eyebrows. Rachel didn't bat an eyelid.

"Double it," she said.

Duncan spluttered out something that wasn't even a word, whilst Fiona glared at her with barely contained venom. Louise's expression didn't change; she still just looked like she wanted to go home.

"I don't think you realise what an exceptionally generous offer that is," Duncan attempted.

"I don't care," Rachel said. "This distillery is not for sale. So, if you want it, you'll have to pay what we're asking. Double it."

Rachel wasn't entirely sure what she was doing. Negotiations at this level were not something she had ever participated in, so after seeing Edith's letter, she'd decided to have a go at playing hard ball. She was quite enjoying seeing Duncan squirm, and the look of abject rage on Fiona's face was proving to be equally satisfying.

The older woman spoke up now, rising furiously from her seat as she gesticulated with her pink fingernails. "Duncan, this is absurd! She cannot possibly believe we'd be authorised to double what is already an *exceptionally* generous offer. This girl hasn't got a bloody clue what she's talking about!"

Rachel felt her hackles rise at the condescending tone placed on the word "girl", but to her surprise, Duncan beat her to it. He frowned at his colleague, his voice low and measured.

"There's no need to be rude, Fiona. As the owner of the business, Ms McIntyre is entitled to ask for whatever she thinks it is worth."

Fiona stopped, clearly unaccustomed to being second guessed in front of an outsider. She scowled at Duncan now instead of Rachel, who sat back and allowed herself a small smile.

"I don't think there's anything further to say at this point," Rachel said. "If you can raise your offer, get back to me."

"What the bloody hell was that all about?" Cameron asked

when they had gone. "Whatever happened to 'listening quietly then politely declining'?"

"Change of tactic," Rachel declared, unfolding the letter from her drawer and showing it to him. "You said they'd been onto Edith before she died, and I think she's made her feelings pretty clear here. I didn't want them to think they could grind us down."

"But asking them to double their offer? Doesn't that just make it seem like you're willing to negotiate?" Cameron was clearly not on board with Rachel's approach. "What if they come back and agree to give you it?"

Rachel grimaced. It was a gamble, admittedly. "I don't think they will. You saw the look on that woman's face; it was a ludicrous demand. I've insulted them. With any luck, they'll be so disgusted they'll never want anything to do with us again."

Cameron frowned at her, still unconvinced. "If you say so," he said doubtfully.

Despite her outer confidence, Rachel had no idea if it had been the right move, but it certainly seemed to have pissed them off. Fiona could barely look her in the eye when she left, and even Duncan was slightly less effortlessly charming than usual.

Rachel glanced up at the clock. "I need to blow the cobwebs away," she said, feeling the ibuprofen wearing off and her white wine headache from the night before starting to return. "I'm going to take a stroll around the site, check in on everyone, then I'll pop home to grab some lunch. Can I bring you anything?"

"No thanks - Jenny's taken care of me," Cameron replied, pointing to the flask of soup and chunk of homemade bread sitting on his desk.

Rachel stepped out into the cool breeze, grateful to feel it on her skin. She was hot and sweaty after that meeting, and needed some fresh air and a moment to herself.

To her surprise, however, the courtyard was not empty. Duncan was still there, pacing back and forth with his back to her whilst he spoke on the phone. It clearly wasn't a business call; Rachel could hear the warmth and affection in his tone instantly.

"I miss you too, sweetheart," he was saying, one hand on his hip and a smile just visible as he turned halfway towards Rachel. He spotted her, smiling and giving a little nod of acknowledgement in her direction as he continued his conversation.

"I promise, I'll be home soon. Just wrapping up one last piece of business. Okay… yep, you too, baby. Love you, bye."

He hung up, turning his smile fully on Rachel as he slipped the phone in his pocket. Despite herself, she felt her spirits dip a little. He wasn't single after all, it would seem. Her years out of the dating field were telling; what Rachel had read as possible flirtation was obviously no more than simple friendliness.

"You were a complete bitch in there," Duncan said, walking towards her, and she flinched at the severity of his words. The amiable smile remained, however. "I mean that as a compliment, by the way; I didn't think you had it in you. But *double it?* You know there's absolutely no way that's ever going to happen?"

"I know," Rachel said, forcing herself to return his friendly smile. "Hopefully you'll get the message and leave us alone now."

They started walking together back in the direction of her house, outside of which Duncan had parked his car.

"I take it Mr McIntyre doesn't live on the island?" Duncan asked, hands in his pockets as he nodded towards the doorstep where he'd dropped her off the previous night.

"Mr McIntyre?" Rachel stopped and turned to face him, puzzled. Duncan pointed to her left hand, and Rachel followed his gaze to see the plain gold wedding band still encircling her third finger. She looked at it for a moment - she'd forgotten it was even there - before clenching her fist self-consciously and covering it with her other hand.

It had been her grandmother's. Graham had lacked the funds to buy her one of her own when they were married. When she left him, it had never occurred to her to take it off. Maybe it was time to at least switch it to the opposite hand, though?

"I'm not married," she said, looking up to see Duncan watching her curiously. "It's my grandmother's," she explained. "I started wearing it after she died…" she tailed off, and was surprised to find Duncan reaching out to touch her arm lightly.

"Sorry," he said. "I shouldn't have pried."

They stood together awkwardly once more, Rachel avoiding his gaze, until his hand slipped from her arm and found its way back into his pocket.

"Well, I guess this is it," he said, looking round at the sea which surrounded them. It was a soft, opaque blue today. "Farewell

Inniscreag."

"What will you do now?" Rachel asked.

He sighed deeply. "Head back to Edinburgh and the powers that be, let them know we were unsuccessful. Start looking for our next unsuspecting victim." He smiled. "I'm sorry we couldn't make this happen," he said, his eyes suddenly landing back on her. "I think it could have been… something." He was watching Rachel in a way that made her wonder if he was still talking about the distillery.

"Well, I guess we'll never know," she said, remembering the unknown woman waiting for him on the other end of the phone call, and chiding herself for being so stupid as to have ever thought he might actually be interested. He was a charming, good-looking flirt, with a knack for making all women think he fancied them; nothing more.

Duncan smiled sadly. "I guess not." He extended his hand and Rachel shook it, one last time. "Goodbye, Rach."

"Goodbye."

# CHAPTER 13

Nearly two months had passed since Edith's death, and Rachel almost felt that life on the island was returning to normal. Dealing with all of the issues the distillery had to address was an overwhelming task, so she decided to tackle them in bitesize chunks, beginning with the field with which she was most familiar - hospitality. They would get the coffee shop up and running, and hopefully that would bring in some extra revenue over the summer months.

Rachel's initial deadline of opening in time for the school Easter holidays had been and gone, all of her plans having been somewhat up-ended by Edith's sudden death. This week, however, the contractors would be arriving to start the initial preparations, with a six week projection for having the whole renovation completed. It was early May now, meaning they should still be up and running comfortably by the peak of the summer.

Tourists were already starting to become a more frequent sight on the island. Rachel could see a small group of them now, as she stepped out of the office door and into the early summer sun. They were standing with Jenny over by the working maltings, halfway through a tour. Cameron's wife helped out as an ad hoc guide during the summer season, along with lots of other occasional tasks around the site.

Rachel waved to them as she passed, on her way over to the disused floor maltings that was about to be converted. The contractors had arrived before her; she could see their van parked up outside, along with the old Volvo estate Andrew used for his plumbing jobs. Whilst the contractors from Skye would be overseeing things, Rachel had promised some of the locals work as labourers. Andrew would fit the little kitchen and required toilets when they got to that stage, but until then he was happy to muck in with anything else that needed done.

"Morning," he said, greeting Rachel with a smile. He knew the lead contractor, Bill, from previous jobs they'd undertaken together, and the two men were unloading tools from the van as Rachel approached.

Andrew had been very handsome in his youth, and he

maintained a craggy sort of manliness in his appearance even now, in his forties. However, what had once been a thick head of straw-coloured hair was starting to wear away rapidly, and the slide into middle age - aided by a fondness for real ale - had expanded his waistline from 'burly' to 'chubby'. Not that Rachel was in a position to judge; biscuits formed a staple part of her diet, and she didn't even have the excuse of being too busy raising three children to justify her own lack of exercise.

To Rachel, Andrew was still a very attractive man, but she knew his weight gain was an issue for Sorcha, who dedicated herself to maintaining her toned, firm figure at all costs. But Rachel also knew that while she did work at it, Sorcha's slimness was at least in part down to genetics.

Secretly, she wondered if part of the reason they were having issues was because her friend had lost sight of what a good thing she had. Despite their bickering, Andrew was a kind man and an attentive father, who worked hard to provide for his family. Rachel often thought that if Graham had been more like him, they'd have stood a better chance of making it work.

"Ready to get stuck in?" she asked.

Andrew nodded, while Bill started barking orders to the younger men currently drinking bottles of Irn Bru in the front seats of the van, his own teenage son amongst them.

The maltings was a large, rectangular building, similar to an old barn. Inside, a single open room was punctuated at regular intervals by tall, steel columns, set deep in the smooth concrete floor. A series of little square windows ran along the external walls, looking out to the ocean on one side and the courtyard on the other, and almost every surface was covered in a green, speckled mould. Stepping inside and breathing in the damp, musty scent, Rachel was reminded of just how much work this place would need to get it back in shape.

"Can I get you all some coffee?" she asked, once she and Bill had run over the initial phase of the plans one more time. "Tea?"

"I think Jenny's already taken care of that," Bill replied with a smile, as they emerged outside once more. A trestle table had been set up alongside their van, laden with flasks of hot water, tea bags, jars of instant coffee, milk and a variety of home baked treats. Rachel said a silent prayer of thanks for Jenny - she wasn't even an official employee, yet without her, she was sure, this whole place would have fallen apart years ago.

Turning to head back to her office, Andrew called out to her before she left.

"Ye'll no' see Sorcha the night, by the way."

Rachel turned back to him, frowning. It was Monday night - quiz night. "Is she OK?" she asked. "She's not ill or anything, is she?"

Andrew smiled, and gave her a secretive wink. "She's fine. But her mother's got the kids, like every Monday, and I've got a wee surprise up my sleeve."

Rachel smiled back. She hoped his surprise worked; Sorcha had been quiet recently. She needed cheering up.

"Have fun," she said. "Don't do anything I wouldn't do."

# CHAPTER 14

Sorcha and Andrew weren't the only regulars missing from the pub quiz that night. When Rachel arrived to find Una, waiting for her at their usual table, there were only another half a dozen people in the room, scattered around a handful of tables.

"Someone know something we don't?" Rachel asked, as Una rose to greet her with a hug and a kiss on the cheek. "It's like a ghost town in here."

Shelagh was en route with Rachel's customary white wine spritzer before she'd even had time to get her jacket off.

"No quiz tonight, ladies," she said with a sigh. "Barely enough folk in to justify staying open at all."

"I thought it'd be busier than this," Rachel admitted. "We had a group up at the still today for a tour. Are they not staying here?"

Shelagh shook her head. "Must be camping. Mind you, I'd have thought they might have come in for a steak pie or a pint at least, but no sign of them yet."

Rachel exchanged a sad smile with the landlady. Now that she was more au fait with the state of the distillery finances, she could only imagine how hard it must have been for Shelagh to stay afloat all these years with such a tiny pool of customers. Visitors wild camping, and stocking up on food at the larger shops on the mainland or Skye before making the journey over, was definitely having an impact on the tiny island economy.

"Never mind," Rachel said, raising her glass to clink it against the side of Una's in an attempt to be cheerful. "We'll always do our bit to support our local public house."

Shelagh smiled back at them both. "I knew I could rely on you. No Sorcha tonight?"

Rachel sipped her spritzer. "Date night," she said with a grin. Nothing around here stayed secret for long. "I believe Andrew will be seducing her as we speak."

"Rachel!" Una slapped her good-naturedly on the arm, while Shelagh giggled.

"Ah well, good luck to them," she said. "Any man that can keep it in his pants is worth holding on to, in my book."

Shelagh retreated back to the bar, just as the little bell above the door jingled to announce the arrival of Jenny and Cameron, along with their son, Iain. Rachel waved over to them.

"No quiz," Una said, turning to her and taking a sip from her merlot. "We'll actually have to have a conversation!"

"Heaven forbid!" Rachel replied.

Truth be told, she was actually quite looking forward to having a night just her and Una. Sorcha had been so down recently, and increasingly negative about everything. Hopefully getting laid would put a bit of a spring in her step, Rachel thought. It would certainly perk her up a bit, should the opportunity ever present itself. At this rate, however, she was beginning to think she would be doomed to a life of involuntary celibacy forever.

After they'd done the rounds of work and general island chitchat, discussion invariably swung back around to their personal lives.

"Do you ever hear anything from that guy - what was his name?" Una asked, with an affected air of casual enquiry. "The one with the dark hair and the fancy sports car."

Rachel shot her a look. "You know fine well, his name is Duncan," she said. "And no; he got the message, it would seem."

"What message? About the distillery, or…?

"The distillery," Rachel replied firmly. "And now he's back on the mainland, driving his fancy car and wearing his fancy suits, and no doubt shagging his fancy girlfriend."

"Which doesn't bother you in the slightest?"

"Why should it?" Rachel asked, her voice deliberately light. It was only then she realised how tightly she was gripping onto the stem of her wine glass.

"Right," Una gave her an unconvinced smile. "And Graham?"

Rachel sighed. She'd had word a couple of weeks ago from her solicitors back in Glasgow, explaining that he was still refusing to agree to her initial divorce petition, despite their circumstances being just about as straightforward as you could get. No kids, no major assets; just the flat Rachel had inherited from her Granny Peggy. And now the bastard was arguing that he was entitled to half of it, despite never having contributed to so much as a gas bill, never mind a mortgage payment.

"No change," she said. "Still an arsehole. Honestly, part of me just wants to give him whatever he's asking for, just to be rid of him."

It was true, especially now she was due to inherit the distillery. The financial aspect wasn't as much of a concern anymore. "But it's the principle. I supported him for fifteen years; he's taken me for enough of a ride."

Una nodded. "Go Old Testament on him. 'An eye for an eye' and all that."

Rachel wasn't sure if she was being sarcastic or not. "What about you?" she asked. "Any eligible bachelorettes on the scene?"

Una rolled her eyes at her. "Oh yeah, they're queueing up round the corner," she laughed. "Not a lot of Christian lesbians in the Western Isles."

"You could always try online?" Rachel said, half-joking, but the sudden flush of colour in Una's cheeks made her back up. She gave an excited gasp. "Ooh, you have!"

Una shushed her, panicking and looking self-consciously around the bar. "Draw a little more attention to us, why don't you?"

"Sorry, but I'm excited!" Rachel lowered her voice. "Have you met anyone?"

Una smiled coyly, twisting a long, dark tendril of hair around one finger. "I'm talking to someone who seems nice, but that's all it is," she emphasised. "Just talking."

"Can I see her?" Rachel asked, almost bouncing up and down in her seat with excitement.

Una rolled her eyes again, but pulled her phone out of her back pocket nonetheless. She quickly scrolled through her pictures, finally alighting on the one she was looking for and turning it to face Rachel.

It was an attractive young redhead, in her late twenties or early thirties, standing on a bridge over a river, the summer sun streaming on her copper hair. She was wearing a sundress and holding a takeaway coffee cup in her hand, freckled arms bare as she laughed into the camera. She was beautiful, and Rachel said as much.

Una blushed again, something Rachel had never seen her do before. She was obviously smitten already, try as she might to hide it.

"Her name's Lucy," she said. "She lives in Inverness. We've not been talking for long, but we're hoping to meet up next time I go home to visit Mum and Dad."

Rachel smiled again, reaching out to give her friend's hand a squeeze. "That's brilliant," she said. "I'm so happy for you."

"Don't get too carried away," Una warned, slipping her phone back into her pocket as she glanced nervously around the room. No one was paying them the least bit of attention, but she was clearly nervous.

"And please, keep it to yourself for now," she continued. "It took them long enough to accept a female minister, never mind a gay one. I might be pushing it to confront them with an actual, real-life girlfriend."

"Promise," Rachel said. "And you might be surprised; I'm sure everyone would just be happy for you."

They finished their drinks just before Shelagh called last orders, and as they stood to leave Rachel noticed a woman she didn't recognise sitting at the bar. She was dressed in a clingy leopard print top, white jeans and stiletto heels, sipping elegantly from a glass of prosecco. Shelagh only sold that stuff by the bottle, it not being in very great demand amongst the crofters and fishermen of Inniscreag.

The woman's long nails were painted a deep, scarlet red, and her highlighted blonde hair tumbled down her back in thick waves. Definitely a tourist, Rachel decided, although she didn't look like the average bird watcher or whisky aficionado. She glanced up at them as they passed on their way to the door, and flashed a dazzling set of veneers.

It was only as Rachel stepped out into the cool night air that she heard a familiar voice, causing her to turn back just as the door was swinging shut behind her. A tall, dark-haired figure had come through the internal door from the upstairs rooms and was pulling up a stool alongside the glamorous, unknown woman, while she reached out and handed him a second glass of prosecco.

Duncan Fraser had returned to Inniscreag.

# CHAPTER 15

Rachel didn't sleep much that night. She tossed and turned, desperately trying to get his face out of her mind, but it was useless. At just after two o'clock in the morning, prompted by the sound of Doug crying at the back door, she finally gave in, threw her dressing gown on and headed downstairs.

The reasons for Doug's late-night arrival at her door were twofold - first, it had started to rain; and second, he had actually managed to catch and kill a mouse, an achievement not unusual for most cats, but certainly noteworthy for Douglas.

He was sat on his haunches looking up at her, and if cats were capable of smiling then that's what Doug was doing now. His tail whipped back and forth across the floor as he mewed at her proudly, while the pathetic little body lay, bloodied and broken, in front of him. Rachel sighed, saddened more than she expected by the sight.

Letting Doug in from the rain, she grabbed the dustpan and brush from under the kitchen sink before gently scooping up the wee mouse and, at a loss for anything else to do with him, dropping him into the wheelie bin by the back door.

Something about that action; disposing of that tiny little soul as if it were nothing more than another piece of waste, brought the memory of Rachel's miscarriages flooding back. She'd never looked at what had been flushed away on those fateful nights - for it always seemed to happen at night, when she was alone and scared in the dark. Instead, she'd stayed firmly seated on the toilet, flushing two or three times, until she was sure it was gone, trying not to think about what she was doing. But the imagined sight still haunted her, along with the guilt; she'd flushed her babies away as if they had meant nothing to her. She never knew if they were boys or girls, never gave them a proper farewell. She didn't deserve to be a mum, she told herself. Not after doing something as awful as that.

And to make matters worse, no one else even knew they'd existed at all. Except for Graham, that is. But to him they had never been babies; not really. While Rachel felt that her heart had been ripped out, he saw only practicalities - nature had taken its course, getting rid of something that had never been viable in the first place.

It was a blessing, he'd said, and had only saved them greater heartache than if they'd lost them further down the line.

Rachel stood for a moment, staring up into the night sky. The drizzle landed wet on her cheeks as navy clouds scudded past, obscuring a twinkling carpet of innumerable stars. She breathed deeply, waiting for the urge to cry to subside. It always did, eventually. It didn't come as often these days, and when it did, she could usually control it.

Rachel breathed the night air in through her nose once more, feeling its biting coldness in her airways and lungs, pushing away the sadness. Not bothering to turn the key in the lock, she closed the door, before filling her espresso pot and digging a packet of chocolate digestives out of the cupboard. With sleep seemingly still a million miles away, the only way she was going to make it through the coming day was with the assistance of plenty of sugar and caffeine.

A steaming mug of hot, sweet coffee in one hand, and the biscuits in the other, Rachel crept through to the living room and curled up on the sofa, pulling a woollen throw and a still-damp Doug onto her knees as she did so. She switched the TV on and channel surfed through her limited options - reception wasn't great on Inniscreag - before finding a repeat of a cosy American sitcom she'd watched a thousand times before. She settled in numbly in front of it, letting the familiar words settle over her like a comforting blanket.

What was Duncan doing back here? she wondered. Clearly, the glamorous woman at the bar was the "sweetheart" she'd heard him on the phone to the day he left. She was every bit as beautiful as Rachel had imagined; well-groomed and preened, finely dressed, just like Duncan always was. While Rachel, on the other hand, lived in jeans and fleeces, and had only recently started slapping a box dye on her hair every now and then. Duncan's girlfriend had hair that looked remarkably timely and expensive to maintain, with caramel blonde highlights and, Rachel suspected, lots of extensions.

Maybe he'd brought her here on holiday? That would be something, at least. She might stand a chance of avoiding him if he was just another tourist. Few visitors stayed on the island for more than a handful of nights; they'd probably be gone by the weekend. After all, there wasn't that much to do here, if you weren't into birdwatching or other outdoor pursuits. Rachel knew for a fact that

Duncan definitely wasn't, and judging her purely on her appearance, it seemed unlikely that his girlfriend was, either.

Rachel caught herself suddenly, twisting her wedding ring where it still sat on her left-hand ring finger. She looked at it, the plain gold band dulled and scratched by the many rigours it had been put through over the years – first on her grandmother's hand, and then on Rachel's. Probably about seventy years of wear and tear, Rachel reckoned. She remembered Duncan's face when he asked her about it, the last time she had seen him. Would he even have noticed she was wearing a ring, if he hadn't been making a point of checking?

Telling herself it had nothing to do with Duncan's unexpected return, Rachel gave the ring an experimental tug. Unsurprisingly, it didn't budge. She twisted it a few more times, before accepting it wasn't going to move without some assistance. Lifting Doug gently from her lap, Rachel headed through to the kitchen. A good glug of Fairy Liquid dribbled around the base of her finger did the trick, and the ring soon slid loose with a satisfying 'pop'.

Placing it safely in a dish on the windowsill, Rachel flexed her fingers. The air against the newly exposed skin felt cool, and she gently rubbed the smooth, flat dent the ring had left behind. Hopefully it wouldn't take long for it to merge back in with the rest of her hand.

Even if he wasn't actually single, Rachel realised, her encounter with Duncan had at least proved one thing.

She was finally ready to move on.

# CHAPTER 16

The rain had cleared by the following morning, and when Rachel awoke just before nine o'clock, the early sun had already dried the concrete so there was no trace left of it at all. She opened her eyes, Doug still warm and purring against her neck, and sat up with a start when she saw the time; she was never in the office any later than half past eight. But then she remembered that she was the boss, after all, and even if she wasn't, she doubted Cameron would begrudge her a one-off lie in.

Rising from the sofa, she skipped her usual morning shower and ran upstairs to change her clothes as quickly as she could, before pulling her hair back up into a ponytail, leaving her overgrown fringe and some of the little tufts round the back loose. She never wore makeup anyway, so that at least wouldn't be an obvious omission. A banana in her hand, Rachel was out of the door and making her way across the courtyard within ten minutes of waking.

The workmen were already getting started over at the maltings, and Rachel made a mental note to pop in and check on them later. Jenny had replenished her trestle table of goodies, and when Rachel entered the office, she discovered a small supply had also been dropped off to them. A covered tray of caramel shortcake, tiffin, tablet and flapjacks - far too much for just her and Cameron - sat on Rachel's desk. That was the diet out the window for another day, then.

As it turned out, she was actually in before Cameron. By the time he arrived she was on her second coffee, and had already caved and was tucking into a slice of cinnamon apple flapjack. It contained fruit, she told herself, so surely it counted as acceptable breakfast fare?

"Tell your wife I hate her," Rachel said, her mouth full. "Her baking is impossible to resist."

Cameron laughed, helping himself to a slice as they settled into the comfortable rhythm of their working day.

Rachel spent most of the morning trying to source second hand furniture online, either on Skye or not too far into the mainland. She was hoping to find some bargains that could be upcycled cheaply, in hopes of giving the new coffee shop a fashionable, shabby-chic feel, without breaking the bank. She had just stumbled across a promising solid oak dining table in Broadford when there was an unexpected knock at the door.

Any of the operators or locals would just have walked straight in, so Rachel assumed it must be a visitor in search of a tour. Rising from her seat to direct them to the waiting room, Rachel was mid-yawn when she opened the door only to be confronted with the one person on the whole island she was trying to avoid.

Duncan was back in his three piece suit, dark hair combed to one side and his green eyes shining as he greeted her. Rachel could smell the sharp, fresh tang of his aftershave instantly; she could only imagine what she must smell like by comparison.

His expression was almost apologetic as he looked at her with a sad, lopsided grin. "Rachel," he said softly, before he was pushed to one side and the gorgeous, tanned, blonde woman he'd been with the night before bustled into the room ahead of him.

"You're Rachel?" she said, an angry glint in her blue eyes, and an accusatory finger pointing in Rachel's direction.

"Yes," Rachel replied, confused, as she glanced from one to the other. Duncan looked just as shocked as she was. Surely this woman didn't think anything had gone on between them?

Cameron had also risen from his seat and was watching them, a concerned frown on his face, as the unknown woman glared down at Rachel from her towering heels.

"You've taken something that belongs to me," she said. Involuntarily, Rachel took a step back, struggling to piece together what on earth was going on.

"Stephanie, we agreed you'd let me deal with this…" Duncan tried, attempting to put a hand on the woman's arm, but she shook it away.

"I haven't taken anything from you," Rachel protested. "I don't know what he's told you, but…"

"Oh, he's told me everything, you little liar." Stephanie had an accent Rachel couldn't quite place - American, possibly, but with an unusual twang - and was waggling an acrylic nail in her face. "I know all about you, and your sordid little scheme."

"What on earth is she on about?" Rachel cried, frowning at Duncan over this crazy woman's shoulder. "Can you rein your girlfriend in please?"

"Girlfriend?" The woman - Stephanie - stopped suddenly and laughed, as Duncan finally managed to squeeze his way into the room alongside her.

"He wishes," she was saying, tossing her blond hair over one shoulder as she coyly batted her eyelashes at Duncan. But he wasn't looking at her; his gaze was firmly fixed on Rachel.

"She's not my girlfriend," he said, breathless. "She's my client."

Half an hour later, with relative order resorted and a pot of tea shared out between the four of them, as well as Jenny's cakes, Stephanie was finally calm, and Duncan was explaining the chain of events that had led him back to Inniscreag.

"We conveyed your message to our superiors, after our last meeting, and explained that the distillery was most definitely not for sale. At least, not at a price we'd be willing to pay for it." He shot Rachel a surreptitious grin then, looking across at her with those green eyes that had been haunting her for weeks. She smiled back, trying to ignore the tell-tale tumbling sensation in her tummy.

"So, we'd moved on to other projects, when last week I was assigned our new client, Stephanie McLeod."

Cameron sat up straighter. "McLeod?" he repeated.

Duncan nodded, swallowing deeply and suddenly looking quite uncomfortable. "Miss McLeod claims to be…"

"The rightful owner of Inniscreag distillery," Stephanie interrupted, fixing Rachel with a satisfied grin. Rachel glanced back at Duncan, who shrugged helplessly and shifted in his seat. She had expected him to gloat, but on the contrary, he looked like he wanted the ground to swallow him up.

"How?" Rachel asked. "Edith didn't have any children."

"Miss McLeod is not a direct descendant of Edith's," Duncan explained, sifting through the sheaves of official looking documents he had lifted from his briefcase. "Her claim runs on her father's side; his grandfather was Edith's uncle, apparently."

"Hey; lose the 'apparently'," Stephanie barked, frowning. "I've got proof right there -" she jabbed one finger at the top piece of paper, yellowed with age. "A birth certificate naming my grandfather's father as Malcolm McLeod of Inniscreag."

Duncan slid it across the table to Rachel; not that she'd have been able to spot a fake, but it looked genuine enough.

"We've had it independently verified," Duncan confirmed.

"Why now?" Rachel asked, looking back across at Stephanie. "Why didn't you get in touch with Edith - your Great Aunt? - while she was still alive?"

"Miss McLeod has only just become aware of the relationship," Duncan interjected, leaving Stephanie sitting with her mouth hanging half-open. "She was doing some research into her family tree, and discovered that her Great-Grandmother, Kathleen, had been in service to a wealthy family from Scotland immediately prior to her emigration. It seems that although he was a confirmed bachelor, Malcolm McLeod was still something of a lady's man. When Kathleen left Inniscreag for Canada, as an eighteen year old, unmarried woman, she was in possession of enough money to fund her new life in the new world, and a baby."

"My grandfather," Stephanie added triumphantly.

Rachel paused for a moment, letting it all sink in, Cameron silent by her side.

"But Edith made a will," she said eventually. "She named me, specifically; surely her wishes can't just be overturned?"

Duncan coughed uncomfortably, fiddling with his pen and avoiding Rachel's gaze, while Stephanie's grin broadened. "Miss McLeod would like to make a claim of facility and circumvention," he said. Rachel raised her eyebrows at him questioningly, as he finally looked at her.

"She claims that due to Edith's frailty and advancing age," Duncan began, before being interrupted by a derisory snort from Cameron.

"Be thankful she's no' around to hear you describe her as 'frail'," he said.

"Due to Edith's age," Duncan continued, "Miss McLeod feels that she may have been vulnerable to undue influence, from…"

"Me?" Rachel said incredulously, slumping back in her seat.

"That's bloody ridiculous!" Cameron declared, jumping immediately to her defence.

"Be that as it may," Duncan said, whilst Stephanie folded her arms and watched the proceedings with barely contained glee. "She has the right to make her claim and have it heard in a court of law. We'll be submitting our case to the judge this week; I thought it would only be fair to forewarn you."

Rachel scowled at him, feeling delayed fury bubbling up beneath the shock. She wasn't buying his apologetic 'Mr Nice Guy' act anymore.

"Why you?" she asked. "You work for Kindred Spirits, don't you? Why are you representing her?"

Duncan swallowed deeply before he answered. "Because Miss McLeod has agreed that should her claim be successful, she will be selling the distillery to Kindred Spirits Ltd immediately."

# CHAPTER 17

Rachel managed to contain her rage just long enough for them to leave. As she shut the door behind them, a fixed grin on her face, she turned to Cameron and was pleased to see that he was obviously equally incensed. The cheeks above his moustache, already ruddy from a lifetime of exposure to the island winds, were positively blazing.

"This is fucking ridiculous!" he shouted, shocking Rachel with his choice of language. She'd never heard him swear.

"Sorry," he said, flustered, standing up and pacing restlessly around the small office. "It's just… to give it to someone who's never even set foot on the island, who Edith never knew existed… just for them to flog it to the highest bidder. It's not on."

He paused, both hands on his hips, nostrils flaring. "We won't let this happen," he said, resolute.

"I'm not sure there's much we can do to stop them," Rachel replied, reaching for her phone. "I should call Ruaridh; see what he says."

The discussion with Edith's lawyer was brief. He had received formal notification of their intention to challenge the will that morning, and confirmed that it was, despite Rachel's protestations, a legitimate argument to make.

"They'll have to prove it, though," he explained. "It's not enough just to say she was old, and therefore facile. It's up to them to prove that she was vulnerable, and that you knowingly abused that."

If anything, Rachel was even more enraged when the phone call ended. The suggestion that she would ever have tried to influence Edith, or that Edith would even have been susceptible to it if she had, was outrageous.

It did seem, however, that Duncan really had just been doing them a courtesy by dropping by to tell them in person. Although Rachel suspected he might regret having brought Stephanie along with him; that woman's temper seemed like it could be something of a liability.

She was surprised to find them both, nearly half an hour after they'd supposedly left, still in the carpark. Needing something to take her mind off the recent developments, Rachel had been on her way to check on the progress of the maltings, but paused outside the office door when she saw them. Stephanie was gesticulating wildly as Duncan attempted to speak to her.

"All I'm saying is, you can't go storming in like that, all guns blazing," he said. "She hasn't done anything wrong."

Stephanie glared at him, one hand on her hip, the other brandished in front of her, counting off Rachel's perceived transgressions on her manicured fingers. "Are you serious right now? She's taken my birth right, my inheritance…"

"Which you only found out about three weeks ago. And she hasn't taken anything. She was *given* it." Duncan had his back to Rachel, still carrying his briefcase, unaware of her watching their exchange. "If you want to be mad at anyone, be mad at Edith. In fact, no, she never even knew you existed. Be mad at your philandering great-grandfather; if he'd done the decent thing and married your great-grandmother you wouldn't be in this mess."

Stephanie paused, her arms folded across her chest and the toe of her high-heeled boot tapping against the cobbled floor. She'd spotted Rachel, and was glaring at her over Duncan's shoulder.

He turned, following her eye line, before lowering his voice and bustling Stephanie into her hire car. His own vehicle was parked further along; a tiny part of Rachel thrilled at the realisation they hadn't travelled together. Then she remembered he was a lying, conniving piece of shit. He and Stephanie were welcome to each other.

"I'll meet you back at the pub," he was saying, as Stephanie executed a rather lurching three-point turn and bumped her way out of the gates towards Craigport.

"Struggling with the manual gear stick, is she?" Rachel asked, walking slowly towards him.

"Please don't," Duncan replied, spinning to face her and running a weary hand through his hair. He looked shattered.

"Please?" he repeated. "I've been trying to rein her in ever since we got here last night; she's bloody exhausting. She'd have been knocking your door down at dawn if I'd let her have her way." He looked at her, his head cocked to one side, his expression suddenly soft. "I'm sorry, Rach. It wasn't meant to go down like this."

"Spare me the act," Rachel replied. "You're getting what you wanted, aren't you? By any means necessary. Just like you people always do." She paused, not wanting to ask what was on the tip of her tongue, but needing to know nonetheless. "Did you go looking for her?" she asked. "After I said I wouldn't sell?"

Duncan's jaw dropped, aghast. "Of course not. She approached us." He took half a step towards her and Rachel retreated, her arms folded defensively across her chest. Duncan flinched visibly, as if he was trying to tame a bad tempered, unpredictable lion who had just swiped a paw at him.

"Look, this should all have been handled very differently," he said, "and I'm sorry. It was a stupid idea to bring her here, but she insisted. I know how you feel about this place, and just because I'm representing her doesn't mean that *I* believe you did anything underhand to get it. But I can't change the fact that we are taking you to court."

"Just following orders, as usual," Rachel interjected.

"I just wanted to do you the courtesy of telling you to your face."

He looked at her earnestly, and for a moment Rachel felt herself softening. Maybe he really was telling the truth? But he was a lawyer, after all; he lied and manipulated people for a living.

"Well don't think we'll give up without a fight," she sniped back. "We've got a lawyer too, you know, and we won't make this easy for you."

Duncan sighed. "I didn't think for a second that you would." He paused for a moment, half a smile hovering on his lips as he looked at her. "I really am sorry about all this, Rachel. Although if I'm being honest, I can't say I'm entirely disappointed to be back."

Rachel glared back at him in response, her expression stern. "Don't do that."

"What?"

"Don't turn on that bloody fake, charming, flirty thing that you do. It won't work on me. Not this time."

Duncan recoiled, offended. "It's not fake…"

"Aye, very good. Go and tell it to your Canadian Barbie doll; she's much more your type, I'm sure." Her fury was giving vent to unrelated frustrations now, she knew, but Rachel couldn't help herself. Meanwhile Duncan just frowned at her, his dark brows knitted together in confusion.

"Rachel, I don't know what you're implying…"

"And whatever happened to your girlfriend back home?" she interrupted. "The one you were on the phone to last time you were here? Traded her in, have you, when you found some dolly bird with pneumatic tits who's about to make a small fortune selling off something that was never even hers in the first place?"

Duncan took a deep breath, and reached out a hand to her. "You're angry, I get it. But mine and Stephanie's relationship is strictly professional. And I don't know what you think you heard…"

Rachel interrupted with a derisory laugh. "Oh, aye, it certainly looked very professional, the two of you snuggled up sharing a bottle of prosecco at closing time last night. I thought there was some rule about lawyers not shagging their clients?"

Duncan paused, seemingly running out of patience. He pursed his lips together, inhaling deeply, while the hand that had been reaching out to her now pinched the bridge of his nose.

"We're in separate rooms," he said eventually, looking back up at her, his normally bright green eyes dull and empty. "Check with Shelagh, if you don't believe me. There's no conflict of interest for me here. Not with Stephanie, anyway."

He brushed past her, down the road towards his car, taking the keys from his pocket and beeping the locks open as he went. Rachel watched, finally lost for words, as he threw his briefcase into the back seat.

"We'll be here until this thing is settled," he said, without turning back. "I'll see you around, Rach."

# CHAPTER 18

Miraculously, Rachel made it through the rest of the week without crossing paths with Duncan at all, although that didn't mean he was ever far from her thoughts. The look in his eyes before he'd left tormented her. What if she really did have this all wrong? What if he *wasn't* the bad guy?

Then there were his parting words, still ringing in her ears. *"Not with Stephanie, anyway."* What did that mean? Rachel daren't allow herself to imagine. And besides, even if he had been implying what she might - in her dreamier moments - hope, there was nothing she could do about it anyway. He had a girlfriend, and they were on opposite sides of what she was sure would be an extremely acrimonious court case. No good could come of it.

So, instead of thinking about Duncan, Rachel attempted to keep herself distracted with busy days at work - the maltings renovation was progressing surprisingly well in a short space of time - and evenings focusing on projects at home which she had long been putting off. The nights were beginning to stretch now, and the weather continued to be unusually fine, so that she found herself feeling much more motivated than she had during the darkness of winter.

She started with the front garden, mowing and weeding, before washing the windows and sanding back and filling the cracks on the front door in preparation for a fresh coat of paint. Something bright, Rachel thought, instead of the dull, peeling brown that currently greeted her when she arrived home. Maybe red; or turquoise, to reflect the colour of the sea on a sunny day.

On Wednesday night, Sorcha rang and suggested meeting up for a coffee at her mum's tearoom the following afternoon, and Rachel found herself making excuses. It wasn't because she was worried about running into Duncan or Stephanie in the village, she told herself; she was just enjoying being productive. She suggested catching up on Sunday instead, and invited Sorcha and Una round to hers for lunch, after Una's Sunday service.

Sorcha sounded unconvinced. "Are you sure you're OK?" she asked. Rachel could picture her on the other end of the phone, twiddling her fair hair around her fingers, frowning, which seemed to be her default expression these days.

"I'm fine!" Rachel answered brightly. And she was. As long as she had minimum contact with him, she'd be fine. It was a crush. She'd get past it.

Hanging up, Rachel decided to call it a night. The front door was now packed with filler, and would need to dry before she could sand it one more time and apply the undercoat. After a quick shower, she came downstairs and sat on the back step, a cup of tea in her hand as she watched the sun - a deep, blood orange orb in the sky - sink steadily towards the horizon.

She'd placed an open tin of tuna on the step beside her, and it didn't take long for Doug to come slinking out of the encroaching darkness, led by his nose, mewing happily. He weaved in and out of Rachel's ankles as she tickled his back, before he buried his little ginger chin into the tin and started to noisily gobble up the contents.

"Enjoy," she said, letting his soft tail run through her fingers. "A little treat for you; you've been wandering a lot recently."

Doug didn't answer. Not surprising, really.

He crawled into her lap when he was finished, nudging her chin with his little fishy-smelling face before settling down into a fuzzy ball, purring contentedly.

Rachel cradled him against her, running one finger gently from the tiny pink nose, with a speck of brown right in the middle, and over the top of his head. She suddenly realised that he was the closest thing to a family she had left, and without warning, a crushing loneliness overwhelmed her.

"Love you, Doug," she whispered, her voice thick, but the only reply was the distant crashing of the waves.

She let him sleep at the foot of her bed that night, a furry little ball, warm against her feet. There was something comforting about the knowledge that there was another heartbeat in the house, and Rachel slept more soundly than she had in some time.

But the following evening, when she got home from work and had finished painting a thin layer of primer on the front door, Doug had not returned from his usual daily adventures. Rachel put out another tin of tuna, and waited patiently on the back step, but to no avail. It wasn't particularly unusual, she told herself. Cats were known for being masters of their own destiny, after all.

The tuna was gone the following morning, but that wasn't necessarily down to Doug; a passing fox or hedgehog could easily have stumbled across a fortuitous supper. Rachel filled the bowl up again, but with kibble this time - less appealing to the local wildlife, she figured - and hoped it might be enough to tempt Doug home.

Her general feeling of foreboding intensified when she returned from work that evening and went to inspect it, finding it still untouched. A heavy sense of dread settled in her belly, and nothing she could do would shift it.

By Saturday morning, with the bowl of kibble still conspicuously full, Rachel had made up her mind. Stupid or not, she couldn't shake the image of Doug, hurt and alone somewhere, or worse. After a sleepless night, she rose early, pulled on her jeans, fleece and walking boots, and set off in search of him.

The sky was still pink as she strode out across the moor, unsure of which direction to head. She knew he wasn't in the distillery grounds - she'd have stumbled across him by now if he were - and all there was to the West was the ocean. If he had somehow fallen off the cliffs, there was no way she'd ever find him.

That meant the only direction she could search was East; through the various crofter's fields and bare stretches of moorland, up the island's only peak - barely a hill, really - and down the other side towards Craigport. She'd go as far as the village off-piste, Rachel decided, and head home along the coastal road. That was about as thorough a search as she could conduct single-handed.

It was a much longer walk to Craigport taking this route, and Rachel trudged over the bare, rock-studded ground for almost an hour, following vaguely trodden footpaths, her head down to ensure she avoided the deepest divots and fissures. Inniscreag deserved its name; the thin, patchy grass rooted itself in a meagre layer of topsoil, with thick bands of granite running not far beneath it and protruding from the ground here and there in craggy lumps.

It was as she negotiated one of these lumps - a quite substantial boulder which required her to scramble down it on her bum - that Rachel spotted another walker coming over the ridge towards her. He was a long way off still, but even from here, she recognised that long-legged stride and shock of jet-black hair instantly.

Looking in vain around her, despite knowing there was

83

nowhere to hide and no way he hadn't already spotted her by now too, Rachel clambered ungainly to her feet and dusted herself down.

Duncan was smiling as he approached, his dark hair uncombed and tousled by the slightly damp, early morning wind. The sky had grown heavier as Rachel walked, promising rain to come.

As he drew closer, Rachel couldn't help but smile back. The designer jeans were gone, replaced with conspicuously new and shiny weatherproof trousers, a bright blue North Face jacket, and chunky, brown leather hillwalking boots.

"I took your advice," he called, by way of a greeting. He stopped a few steps away from her, and Rachel noticed that a couple of days' worth of stubble now coated his chin. To her dismay, this new, outdoorsy, rugged Duncan was even more attractive than the city boy she'd first met, all those weeks ago.

"I figured I'm going to be around for a while, so I'd best take the advice of the natives," he said with a relaxed grin.

"I'm not a native," Rachel replied, marvelling at his easy friendliness after their last encounter.

Duncan shrugged. "More native than I am. And you were right, as it turns out; much more fun to explore on foot." He looked around him, taking in the three hundred and sixty degree views. Even with the grey sky, it was always beautiful here.

"Where are you heading?" Rachel asked, as casually as she could.

"Anywhere and nowhere," he said. "Inniscreag isn't exactly huge. I figured I'd just see where the wind takes me." He was buffeted suddenly by an unexpected gust, knocking him off balance so that he stumbled forward. Rachel reached out instinctively, and he caught hold of her arm.

"Literally," she laughed. He smiled back, his hand warm in hers, before Rachel realised what she was doing and released it like a hot potato.

"What about yourself?" Duncan asked, nonplussed. "You're a bit off the beaten track just to be heading into the village, aren't you?"

Rachel hesitated for a moment. "My cat's missing," she admitted eventually. There you go, she thought, kicking herself; you've officially confirmed your status as a single, dumpy, almost middle aged, mad cat lady. Maybe she should get more cats? Rachel wondered fleetingly. Might as well accept the inevitable.

To her surprise, however, Duncan's face fell. "Oh no," he said, with what sounded like genuine concern. "Can I help?"

Rachel brushed the offer aside, not wanting to let on how worried she was. He was just a cat, after all. "No, there's no need for that. I'm sure he's fine."

But Duncan wouldn't take no for an answer. "I insist," he said, turning back the way he had come and urging Rachel to follow. "I had a cat when I was a kid," he said, as they continued up the gentle incline. "Loved that thing - Ollie, his name was. He got hit by a car when I was twelve and I was gutted. Cried for days."

Rachel walked a half step behind him, watching him carefully. She still couldn't figure him out; was this easy-going, chatty, friendly guy the real Duncan? Or was it all just an act?

"What's his name?" Duncan asked.

"Sorry?"

"The cat. What's his name? Or hers," he added.

"Doug," Rachel replied.

Duncan stopped abruptly, turning to look at her. One side of his mouth twitched upwards in a smile. "Doug?" he asked. "Doug the cat?"

Rachel nodded. "Short for Douglas."

Duncan laughed properly then. "Obviously," he said, nodding enthusiastically. "Excellent name."

They walked on in silence for a while longer, taking it in turns to call Doug's name, their voices echoing in vain across the empty hillside. It wasn't long until they rounded the flat peak of the moor and the rooftops of Craigport came into view below.

Suddenly, Rachel couldn't contain herself any longer.

"I'm sorry," she blurted out, as they started the final descent towards the village.

Duncan was walking on her right-hand side, both hands shoved in his pockets to keep them out of the chill breeze. He didn't look at her straight away; just continued walking for a moment as if she hadn't spoken at all. "About what?" he asked eventually.

Rachel sighed, jogging a little to keep up with his long strides. "About what I said, after you and Stephanie came to the still the other day. In the car park."

"Oh that?" He stopped walking at last, his voice still light, although he kept his eyes averted, turning and gazing across the moorland instead of looking at her. "You mean when you accused me of sleeping with a client, so that I could share the proceeds if she wins the case I'm representing her in?"

"Amongst other things."

"That's right," Duncan nodded, suddenly turning and fixing her with those green eyes, his eyebrows raised as the wind lifted the dark fringe of hair from his forehead. She couldn't decide if his expression was amused or annoyed.

"I chucked my girlfriend into the bargain, didn't I?" He shook his head, laughing and absent-mindedly scuffing the toe of his boots against a nearby rock. "You really do think I'm a class A prick."

Rachel felt herself flush with shame. "I don't," she whispered, looking down at her feet. "I'm sorry; I overreacted. I have a tendency to make rash judgements."

To her surprise, Duncan smiled, albeit half-heartedly. "I appreciate the apology." They held one another's gaze for a moment, and Rachel felt her heart skip a little beat in her chest.

Duncan broke the silence, his voice quiet. "I'm not the person you seem to think I am, Rachel. I don't know if you'll ever believe me; but maybe for now, we can call this a fresh start?" He extended his hand to her. "Deal?"

Rachel looked back at him, feeling the return of the butterflies in her belly. Before she could talk herself out of it, she reached out and grasped his hand firmly.

"Deal

# CHAPTER 19

By the time they had clambered back down to sea level and reached the curving bend of the coastal road, the clouds had gathered threateningly above. It wasn't even lunchtime, and yet all of a sudden, it was as if someone had turned out the lights.

"You can go back to the pub if you like," Rachel said, glancing along the road to the welcoming lights of the village. "It's going to throw down soon. Don't worry about Doug; he'll find his way home eventually."

Duncan seemed to hesitate for a moment, then shook his head. "No," he said firmly. "I said I'd help you, and I will. Let's get a wriggle on, though."

They turned, heading West once more, along the road where they'd first met. Conversation dwindled to nothing as the wind picked up, and both of them focused their energy on battling against the increasing gusts and periodically calling for Doug.

Not far from the distillery gates, Rachel's heart silently sinking, Duncan suddenly froze. It took her a moment to realise that he was no longer trudging alongside her, and she turned back in search of him.

He was standing by the verge, one hand holding his hood away from his face as he peered around. Suddenly, his eyes alighted on something and he called Rachel's name, excitedly waving her back.

She jogged the few steps back to where he was standing, looking up into a stunted, gnarled tree. New leaves were just starting to sprout from its branches, and Duncan was parting the ones closest to him as he looked up the trunk.

"Is this Doug?" he asked, beaming at her and pointing into the midst of the tangled branches.

At the very top of the tree, a damp, ginger ball of fuzz was clinging to the branches and crying like an abandoned baby. Rachel nodded, tears of joy springing unexpectedly to her eyes.

"How will we get him down?" she asked. Doug was well out of her grasp, and even beyond the reaches of Duncan's six foot plus frame.

He was already assessing the situation, one foot against the trunk as he gave it an experimental push; it was solid, despite its old and decrepit appearance.

"I'd climb it if I could," he said, "but the branches wouldn't take my weight. I could give you a leg up?" he suggested. "You're only small, but I think together we'd reach him."

Rachel shook her head. "You couldn't hold me," she said. "I'm too heavy."

Duncan laughed dismissively. "Don't be daft; you're tiny. Come on - up you get."

Bracing one leg at the side of the tree, Duncan crouched and interlocked his hands to provide her with a step. Then, as thunder rolled threateningly behind them, he gestured with a nod and Rachel was faced with very little choice. Trying not to imagine the embarrassment if he couldn't actually hold her, and ignoring the muck on her boots, she stepped into his grasp and he boosted her up the trunk of the tree.

Doug mewed more excitedly when he saw Rachel's head pop up amongst the young leaves, his claws fully extended as he grasped the branch and tried to wriggle closer.

"You bloody stupid animal," Rachel muttered under her breath, pulling twigs out of her hair as she attempted to reach him. "I go halfway across the island to find you, and you're stuck up a tree right outside my front door." Bit by bit, Doug scampered closer and eventually threw himself into her arms.

Rachel grabbed hold of him, his claws digging into her jacket, as she toppled backwards and overbalanced. Unable to right her, Duncan had no choice but to let go of her foot completely as she, and Doug, came tumbling down on top of him.

They landed in a crumpled heap in the muddy verge, Doug clambering excitedly over Rachel as she struggled to her feet, mortified.

"I'm so sorry" she said, helping Duncan up. At the bottom of the pile, he had come off the worst of the three of them; his brand new outdoor gear was covered in mud, as was his hair, and to finish the effect it was also splattered across his face. He was grimacing and rubbing one knee as he stood up.

"I'm sorry," Rachel repeated. "I told you I'd be too heavy. Are you OK?"

Duncan looked down at Doug, who was currently standing

on his hind legs and attempting to climb up Rachel's back, before breaking into a broad grin.

"We got him!" he cried, punching the air triumphantly.

He gathered Rachel into an impromptu hug, just as a crack of lightning lit up the sky around them. They jumped apart, and Rachel could feel the first drops of rain landing, fat and heavy, on her cheeks.

"Home?" Duncan asked, and she nodded enthusiastically in response.

They half-ran through the torrential downpour of rain, Doug tucked up inside Duncan's jacket as he grabbed Rachel's hand and led the way through the untimely darkness. By the time they were stumbling through the distillery gates and up to Rachel's front door, they were all soaked through.

Rachel pushed the door open, having left it unlocked as always, and Duncan fell through it behind her, unzipping his jacket and releasing Doug, who bolted straight for the warmth of the nearest radiator.

They stood for a moment, dripping on her carpet, and looking at each other uncertainly. Duncan's eyebrows were raised, that little half-grin on his face. Rachel suddenly felt awkward again.

"Do you want to come in?" she asked.

Duncan laughed, brushing the wet hair out of his face. "If that's OK? I don't much fancy the walk back to Craigport right now."

Thunder rumbled once more outside, while Rachel peeled off her coat, kicked off her boots and ran through to the bathroom to grab them each a towel. She came back into the hall to find Duncan, shoes and jacket off, in the middle of undoing his waterproof trousers. He caught her eye and grinned as she froze on the spot, the towel dangling from her outstretched hand.

"It's alright," he reassured her. "I've got shorts on underneath."

Rachel laughed nervously, watching Duncan take the towel and begin rubbing it briskly through his hair. The butterflies that had taken up permanent residence in her stomach fluttered back into life; his hair was damp and dishevelled, the sodden t-shirt clung to his obviously toned torso, and his green eyes crinkled delightfully at the corners when he looked up and smiled at her.

"Are you sure you don't mind me sitting out the storm here?" he asked.

"Of course not!" Rachel replied, masking her nerves with overstated cheeriness. "It's the least I can do to thank you for helping me find Doug."

She led him through to the living room and gestured to the sofa. "Have a seat; I'll get you a drink to heat up. Coffee?"

"Yes please. Just black, thanks." Duncan flopped onto the couch, stretching out his long legs and crossing them at the ankles, instantly at home. Rachel suspected he would be like that anywhere, but there was something nice about seeing him in her environment, relaxed and comfortable, as if he belonged there.

When she returned with their coffees, along with some hastily assembled ham sandwiches and a packet of Penguins, Duncan was no longer on the sofa. He was crouched on the rug in front of the open fireplace, peering curiously up the flue.

"Oh, I've never used that," Rachel said with a dismissive wave of her hand. "Not even sure it works. If you're cold I can turn the heating up?"

Duncan put his arm up the chimney. "There's a definite breeze," he said. "I think it'd draw. Do you have any wood?"

"There's an old store by the back door..." Rachel began, but Duncan was already springing to his feet.

"Wait there," he said with a smile, hurrying out into the hallway and throwing on his damp boots and jacket. "I'll be back in a minute."

And sure enough, not long after, an even soggier Duncan had returned with a rusty old bucket full of wood. He crouched back on the rug, smiling.

"Takes me back to my days in the Scouts," he said, piling wood into the grate and striking a match from a packet that Rachel handed to him.

"I thought you weren't into the 'great outdoors'?" she asked, remembering their very first conversation.

But Duncan didn't answer. He had created a careful little pyramid within the fireplace; the tiniest flakes of wood gathered at the bottom, with taller pieces propped up around the sides. He was concentrating on gently puffing air into the smouldering flames, until they built and engulfed the whole lot.

Rachel sat back and sipped her coffee contentedly, enjoying the opportunity to observe him without him knowing. His legs were long but muscular, covered in the same dark hair as his arms. She sighed; she could get used to this.

When Duncan was satisfied, he placed the largest chunk of wood on top and rose to his feet, looking very pleased with himself.

"I haven't been, not for years," he said at last, picking up the mug Rachel had placed on the coffee table for him. "Not since I turned seventeen and discovered fast cars and girls." He grinned at her, sitting down on the sofa, just a little closer than he really needed to.

"What about you?" he asked, taking a sip from his coffee.

"What about me?"

"What were you like as a kid? Did you go to Brownies, ballet dancing, clay pigeon shooting?" he asked, his tone teasing.

Rachel shrugged noncommittally, burying her face in her mug. She didn't talk to many people about her childhood; not even Graham.

"The usual," she said. "I was quiet, really. Didn't go out much."

Duncan nodded, taking another long sip from his coffee. The fire crackled comfortingly in the background, and Rachel curled her feet up under her. Part of her wished she could stretch them out into his lap.

Duncan didn't speak; just watched her, waiting for her to continue. At a loss for anything else to say, Rachel plumped for the truth. "It was just me and my mum, you see. And my granny. Mum was... ill, quite a lot, when I was little. So, I stayed with Granny Peggy whenever she couldn't look after me. Didn't have much chance for extra-curricular activities."

Duncan looked at her, long fingers holding the coffee cup gently in his lap. "That's a shame," he said sadly.

Rachel shrugged. "I didn't know any different. It was fine, really."

"Doesn't sound fine. Sounds lonely," Duncan said, and suddenly Rachel felt the lump she kept locked in her chest creeping up towards her throat. She swallowed it down, nodding silently.

"You were in the Scouts?" she asked when she could speak

91

again, in an attempt to lighten the tone.

"Got all my badges," Duncan replied with a grin.

"So how did you go from do-gooder boy scout, to soulless legal rep for a massive conglomerate like Kindred Spirits Ltd?"

Duncan smirked at her. "Ouch."

His story, as he told it, was an unremarkable one; he grew up in a fairly affluent Edinburgh suburb, the youngest child of a GP and a secondary school French teacher.

"I did pretty well in my exams," he said modestly.

"Despite all the fast cars and girls?"

He shot her a look, choosing to ignore the dig. "Then I started my law degree. I never really knew what I wanted to do, but Dad was insistent that I shouldn't 'waste my results on an arts degree' – his words, not mine. And actually, it turned out I was pretty good at it."

"So why didn't you just become a normal lawyer?" Rachel asked. "You could be putting murderers in jail, or prosecuting human rights violations. What made you go into the drinks industry?"

Duncan shrugged. "Mum and Dad were comfortable, don't get me wrong. But I wanted to be an advocate, and to do that you need to do an unpaid pupillage – basically you're everyone's dogsbody and get no money for the privilege."

He was twisting one finger around the handle of his mug. "If I'd asked, they'd have supported me through it, but I didn't want them to do that. I wanted a job, with a salary. So, I started looking for graduate schemes. But once I was in, I was 'encouraged' into the legal department, they funded my qualifications to become a proper solicitor, and I've kind of been stuck there ever since. Golden handcuffs, as it were."

Rachel shifted uncomfortably in her seat. She felt bad for insinuating that he could have done something more valuable with his life. Who was she to judge?

"What about you?" Duncan asked. "What brought you to this little lump of rock in the middle of nowhere?"

She sighed, not wanting to go into the full story so deciding to simplify things instead. "I was in hospitality, before I came here. Just needed a change, really, after years of doing the same thing. I ran a coffee shop, in a department store."

Rachel paused, feeling the urge to confide in him but not sure if it was wise. "At least I knew what I was doing there, though. Honestly, here… most days, I feel like I haven't got a bloody clue."

Duncan smiled at her again. "Can I give you a little friendly advice?" he asked. "As someone who's been a soulless member of the international drinks industry for over twenty years?"

"Go on," Rachel said, smiling back.

"Your product's too niche," he said. "Yes, you've got a handful of rich old men who'll only drink Inniscreag single malt, but not to put too fine a point on it, they'll all be dead before long. Who's your market then?"

Rachel chewed her lip. He had a point. Their current batch of regular customers wouldn't keep them going for long - they were already starting to feel the pinch.

"The island itself and the odd tourist who stumbles across this place can't keep you running forever," Duncan continued. "You need to diversify, and broaden your market appeal. You need to produce a blend, or a younger spirit. Something you could make cocktails with; something you could serve in a bar in Glasgow or Edinburgh, to people who don't wear flat caps and tweed."

Rachel nodded reluctantly. She knew he was right; these were the kind of issues she'd been mulling over ever since her first meeting with him. But she had no idea where to begin.

Duncan sat up, leaning towards her. "If I were you, I'd bring in a specialist marketing company. It'll cost, but they'll be worth it. Come up with a product no one would expect from you, that will appeal to a totally different market, and run a major campaign. It's a risk, but the only way you'll survive is if you change. Adapt. If not, you'll die out."

"Like the dinosaurs," Rachel said.

"Like the dinosaurs," Duncan echoed. He was looking at her earnestly.

"Why are you helping me?" Rachel asked. "I thought you'd want me to fail miserably, so that I give up and you lot can swoop in and buy us out?"

Duncan paused, a slow smile creeping across his face as he leaned even closer. "Don't tell anyone," he said, "but I actually kind of like it here. It would be sad if this place got swallowed up and became part of just another multi-national."

He'd put his empty coffee cup on the floor beside him, one

hand reaching out until the tips of his fingers very gently grazed Rachel's thigh. "And the last thing I'd want is to see you fail."

Rachel watched his fingers on her leg, feeling the hairs on the back of her neck stand on end and little shivers of anticipation course through her body.

"What are you doing?" she asked quietly, looking up at him.

He shifted closer, his eyes holding hers as his hand travelled up her leg and around her waist. "If you want me to stop," he said, his face now so close that she could feel his breath on her skin, "I'll stop."

Rachel closed her eyes, trying not to think of the mysterious voice at the other end of that overheard phone call. Was this all just a game to him? Was she just another conquest; a bit of fun on a business trip away from home? But then his lips grazed hers, and she lost all self-control.

He kissed her, gently at first, then harder. Rachel slid her arms around his neck and he pulled her into his lap.

As suddenly as they had come together, they simultaneously jumped apart again. The cup of tepid coffee balanced on Rachel's knee had been tossed into the air, sending brown liquid flying all over the two of them, as well as the sofa. They stood up, the mug clattering to the floor.

"Shit!" Rachel cried, giggling, before rushing to the kitchen in search of towels.

They both helped to mop up the mess, from the sofa and each other. But by the time they were done, the momentary madness that had enveloped them was gone, and they regarded each other nervously once more.

"That probably wasn't a very good idea," Duncan said, rubbing one hand back and forth over his hair until it stood out in dark tufts. Rachel resisted the urge to reach out and smooth it down.

"Probably not," she agreed. "Not with…"

"Everything," Duncan finished, watching her helplessly.

He turned and looked out of the window. The rain was easing, and a few scattered shards of sunlight could even be seen peeking between the clouds.

"I should probably go," he said, gesturing to the hallway.

"I guess so," Rachel agreed, trying to hide her disappointment. "Thanks again for your help with Doug."

"No problem," he said, but he was already hurrying back into his outdoor clothes, and had opened the door before Rachel could say anything further.

She stood awkwardly in the hallway while he made his way out, his jacket only half on, when suddenly he turned back. "Do you think we could just go back to our 'fresh start' from earlier?" Duncan asked. "Forget this ever happened?"

Rachel forced a smile onto her face. "Of course," she said quietly. "See you around, Duncan."

And with that she shut the door, gathered Doug into her arms, and headed upstairs to bed.

# CHAPTER 20

Rachel spent most of the afternoon ensconced under her duvet, silently berating herself for being so stupid. What was she playing at, letting him kiss her? Probably just another ploy, she thought; a way of getting under her skin and charming her, so she'd be easy prey come the court case. Given the way he'd rushed out of there before anything else could happen, it was obvious he didn't actually fancy her.

And even if he did, she told herself, there was still the question of the suspected girlfriend back on the mainland. There was something he wasn't telling her, that much Rachel was sure of, and she would never knowingly be the other woman. She didn't have any respect for someone who would treat her as one, either.

So as the afternoon slid into evening, Rachel eventually shook off her malaise, rose, put on her DIY clothes, and tackled the final coat of paint on her front door. The earlier storm had passed and the sky was now clear and bright. By the time she was done, the old stone house had a shiny, new, light blue door to go with its neat front garden, and was actually beginning to look quite cheerful.

The following morning, Rachel cleaned the interior of the house from top to toe, ready for her girls' afternoon with Sorcha and Una. She'd never been much of a cook, but a couple of pizzas from the freezer, along with salad, coleslaw and a few bottles of wine, would be more than enough to keep everyone happy.

Her friends arrived with even more wine in tow, of course, as well as crisps and a box of chocolates. They exchanged hugs by the door, before gathering around the coffee table in the living room.

The girls made themselves comfy on the sofas, getting started on the crisps whilst Rachel popped open a bottle of red for Una, and white for her and Sorcha, topping her own up with her usual lemonade.

"The house is looking great," Sorcha said admiringly. "Is this why you've been M.I.A. for the last week?"

"Thought it was about time I got properly settled in," Rachel said with a smile. "I'm planning to be sticking around for a while, after all."

"And cheers to that!" Una declared, all three of them clinking their glasses together lightly.

Rachel took a sip. She hadn't had a chance to tell them yet about Duncan's return to the island, or what it might mean for her own future there, but she knew it couldn't be long before it came up. News didn't stay quiet for long on Inniscreag.

"I did wonder if you might have had another motive for staying away from the village the last few days," Sorcha said, a gleam in her eyes. Una was smiling too.

Rachel sighed. "You've seen him, then?"

"And the bottle blonde on his arm," Sorcha replied, crossing her long legs and wrinkling her nose as she settled back on the sofa. "Is she his girlfriend? The one you heard him on the phone to?"

Rachel shook her head. "He says not."

Una sat up excitedly. "You've spoken to him?"

"We had a meeting at work," Rachel explained, taking a deep breath before continuing. "The blonde is his client, Stephanie," she said, trying to hide the disdain in her voice. "She claims she's Edith's niece."

Una and Sorcha just about spat out their wine. "What?" Sorcha declared, incredulous. "But Edith didn't have any family? She was the 'last of the McLeods', or so she always said."

"Well, apparently she was mistaken, "Rachel replied, briefly summarising Edith's uncle's affair with the servant girl, and the resulting baby she fled with to Canada.

Sorcha sighed, pressing her lips together in a resigned sort of grin. "I do remember my granny saying there were stories about him… Nobody on the island, mind, but women he visited, back on the mainland. But never a child."

"Well, Stephanie claims there was, and it was her great-grandfather."

"But Edith left the distillery to you," Una said, helping herself to another handful of crisps. "Surely this woman can't just come along and override her will?"

Their expressions were even more appalled when Rachel explained Stephanie's anger towards her, and the fact that she was claiming Rachel had somehow pressured Edith into bequeathing her the distillery.

"So obviously you're going to fight it?" Una asked.

"Of course I am! I never asked for this place, and to be

honest part of me doesn't even want the responsibility. But Edith wanted me to have it, and she was adamant about not selling it, so I don't see that I have any choice. I can't let this Stephanie person take it, and then give it to the very people Edith asked me to protect it from."

"So that's why she was with Duncan…" Sorcha said quietly, realisation dawning.

"Yep." Rachel sighed. "He's her lawyer. Kindred Spirits have a very strong vested interest in making sure she's successful."

"Is that even allowed?" Una asked, an unimpressed scowl on her face. "You'd think that would be a conflict of interest - having the company lawyer represent her?"

Rachel shrugged, reminded of their awkward parting in the distillery car park when she'd accused him of exactly the same thing, albeit for slightly different reasons. "I don't know. He says it's fine; I suppose it'll be up to Ruaridh to challenge it when the time comes. Anyway," she said, keen to change the subject. "What's going on with you guys? Any word from the pretty redhead?"

Una blushed and looked away, while Sorcha leaned forward with interest. "What's this?" she asked.

"I've sort of… been talking to someone," Una replied shyly.

Sorcha narrowly avoided falling out of her seat with shock, and Rachel left Una to fill her in on the lovely Lucy while she nipped out to put the pizzas in the oven.

When she returned, with a bottle of wine in each hand to top up the girls' glasses, conversation had turned to the possibility of Una actually meeting Lucy in the flesh. When Sorcha asked her about it, Una's already flushed cheeks turned an even deeper shade of crimson.

"We've actually got a date this week," she said sheepishly. "I was due to go through to Inverness to see my folks anyway, so I'm meeting her for coffee while I'm down. Don't get too excited," she said, in response to Rachel and Sorcha's barely contained giggles. "It's just coffee."

"We all know where coffee can lead," Rachel teased, before instantly wishing that she hadn't. The very mention of it had brought the memory of her own coffee-flavoured kiss with Duncan rushing back.

"Your turn," Una said, ignoring Rachel's implication and

turning her attention to Sorcha instead. "How are things with you and Andy? Any better?"

Sorcha sighed, draining her glass and topping it back up with the remainder of the bottle, before responding with a noncommittal shrug. "I guess. We had a proper date night last week, and to be fair he made a real effort." Sorcha went on to describe Andy's evening of romance, which involved a homemade steak dinner, a bottle of wine and an action movie.

"That sounds nice," Rachel said.

"It was," Sorcha replied, somewhat unconvincingly. "It's just… I mean, I appreciate the thought, I do. But it felt like a date night he'd planned for himself; do you know what I mean? It was all things *he* liked to do. I prefer seafood to steak, he'd got red wine instead of white, we streamed a movie *he* wanted to see…"

She sighed deeply. "I mean is it too much to ask that after nearly twenty years, he should be able to plan an evening full of the things that *I* love?"

Rachel and Una both fiddled with the stem of their wine glasses. As much as there were many things about Andy that Rachel admired - and sometimes felt her friend didn't fully appreciate - she could empathise with that feeling of not being noticed. Of someone assuming you always liked to do the same things they did, rather than taking the time to find out what *you* actually wanted. It had been like that with Graham for a long time before she finally decided to call it a day.

"Maybe I am just being ungrateful," Sorcha said, shifting on the sofa and placing her now empty wine glass on the coffee table. "I know he's a good guy; maybe this is just how things go when you've been together forever."

She looked enviously at Una. "But you've no idea what I wouldn't give to be back where you are," she said. "Back when it's exciting, and they make you feel fun, and interesting, and you can't think of a single bad thing about them."

Una smiled. "Don't get carried away," she said. "I haven't even met her in the flesh yet. She might be an absolute pain in the arse face to face. Or her pictures could all turn out to be ten years out of date. She could be a balding, middle-aged man for all I know."

Sorcha laughed. "You know I envy you too, Rachel. You were brave enough to walk away; you get a chance to start over.

Where would I go? Even if I did leave him, my whole life is on this island - my kids, my mum, my job… I could never really get a fresh start."

Rachel was grateful to be saved by the beeping of the oven timer. "The grass isn't always greener, you know," she said, rising from her seat and heading through to the kitchen.

As they shared pizza and chatted, the conversation thankfully moved on to more light-hearted topics. Rachel hoped Sorcha was just venting, and not thinking about actually leaving Andrew. They had three kids to consider. When she walked away from Graham, all she left behind was some shabby second hand furniture and a chronically broken-down car. Surely Sorcha would never leave her kids?

They opened the box of chocolates in lieu of dessert, and Rachel dug out a bottle of Baileys to go with them, not bothering to check the use by date. The much-maligned Andrew was collecting Sorcha and Una later, which meant they could make the most of the afternoon together. The only thing they had to worry about was being hungover at work the next day - or on the boat to the mainland, in Una's case.

As the sun started to dip lower in the evening sky, Rachel decided to light some scented candles. After rummaging in all the usual places, however, she couldn't find the matches anywhere.

"Here they are," Una said, spotting them where they'd fallen behind the wood basket next to the fire. "Oh, you finally managed to light it!" she said brightly. She was looking down into the fireplace, where the fresh ashes of the recent fire lay.

Rachel felt the colour rise in her cheeks. "Um, yeah," she said, attempting to sound casual. "I had a go at it during the storm yesterday, and eventually got the hang of it."

She lit the candles, not turning round until she was sure her complexion had returned to normal. But when she met her friends' eyes, she knew they hadn't been fooled.

"You've tried to get that fire going a million times." Sorcha's blue gaze was fixed on Rachel, unblinking. "What changed this time?"

Floundering for an answer, Rachel babbled incoherently before muttering, "Well, I didn't actually light it."

Sorcha narrowed her eyes. "So who did?"

"Duncan," Rachel admitted quietly.

"He was in your house!" Sorcha sat up abruptly, nearly sloshing Baileys over the edge of her glass. "What happened to him being a soulless, corporate goon?"

"A tall, dark and handsome, soulless corporate goon," Una chipped in with a smile.

Rachel sat down, taking a deep glug of Baileys before she continued. "I bumped into him while I was out for a walk," she said. "Doug didn't come home the other night, so I went looking for him, and he helped me find him. I couldn't very well leave him to walk home in the pissing rain after that."

"So you just invited him in and the two of you had a cosy wee chat over a roaring log fire?" Sorcha said.

"Something like that…"

"What else?" Una asked, narrowing her eyes at Rachel suspiciously.

She paused for a moment before answering. "There may have been a teeny, tiny kiss," she admitted eventually, bracing herself for the response.

Sorcha threw a cushion at her, while Una cheered gleefully.

"You *kissed* him?" Sorcha cried. Rachel wasn't sure if she sounded angry or jealous.

"It was nothing," she said. "Probably just him trying to get under my skin. He was out of here like a shot before anything else could happen, anyway."

Sorcha raised her blonde eyebrows at her, unconvinced.

"I still don't get why you're both so down on him." Una stood up, topping up her glass. "He's just a guy doing a job. Maybe he actually likes you, and just wanted to kiss you *because he likes you.* Did you ever think of that? Not everything he does has to have some kind of conniving, ulterior motive."

Sorcha snorted. "Spoken by someone who's never dated a man."

"Fair point."

"It doesn't matter whether he fancies me or not," Rachel said, mustering as much conviction as she could, and trying to forget the way her skin had tingled when he touched her. "He's got a girlfriend, and I don't fancy him anyway, so it's irrelevant. All I'm interested in is winning this court case and getting him off our island as quickly as humanly possible."

# CHAPTER 21

Another week passed, in which Rachel spent the vast majority of her spare time at home, as it became clear that there was little hope of her wish coming true anytime soon. Ruaridh had warned her that it would take a while for the case to get to court, and she had fleetingly hoped that would mean Stephanie, at least, might retreat back to the comforts of the mainland.

On the contrary, however, the glamorous Canadian seemed determined to connect with the island heritage of her great-grandfather. After just a few days, she moved out of her cramped room above the pub to take on an extended booking at one of the local AirBnBs instead. Duncan remained at the pub alone, a fact which gave Rachel a tiny thrill deep inside, no matter how hard she tried to pretend otherwise.

With little in the way of alternatives, Rachel tried her best to carry on with life as normal. Work continued to progress on the maltings renovations, with the interior now freshly painted and ready to be furnished. Rachel was often to be found sifting through second hand furniture listings online, as well as browsing the Facebook pages of various Hebridean artists and photographers. The long, bare walls of the maltings were crying out for something to brighten them up, but despite the plethora of talent she uncovered, nothing seemed quite right. The idea of having some artsy shots taken of the distillery itself was appealing, but Rachel couldn't justify the cost of commissioning anything original. Short of taking the photos herself on her mobile phone, she wasn't sure what exactly she could afford.

She was grateful when Saturday rolled around, and brought with it the opportunity for some light relief. Una was holding a fun day to raise money for the church, including a shinty match and early evening barbecue, as well as the usual raffles, tombolas, games, home baking and bottle stalls. Rachel offered to help out, donating a bottle of twenty-five year old Inniscreag single malt to the raffle and agreeing to supervise the hook-a-duck stall. Duncan and Stephanie were bound to be there, she was sure - there was little else around in the way of entertainment - but at least Rachel would have something purposeful to do to keep herself distracted, even if it was just monitoring plastic ducks in a blow-up paddling pool.

It was a beautiful day, and Rachel rose early enough to shower and blow dry her hair - as well as apply a little make up, just in case - before walking along to the village to meet Una and Sorcha at the church. Sorcha's mother, Ishbel, along with Jenny, had been busy baking for the tea stall, and Sorcha and the kids would be helping Andy out at Beat the Goalie. The whole island was sure to be in attendance, with the event culminating in the shinty match and barbecue at four o'clock.

Rachel arrived at the church just in time to muck in with assembling the various stalls. The fun day was taking place in a fallow crofter's field next to the manse on the outskirts of the village, and some of the local men had erected the tents the night before. Mercifully, the usually powerful island wind had slowed to a gentle breeze, and the neat rows of canvas structures were all pretty much just as they'd been left.

Between the tents, garlands of brightly coloured bunting had been hung, the little flags dappled with sunlight and fluttering lightly. Rachel felt silly to admit it, but as she crossed the grass and felt the quiet buzz of activity, she was excited; she'd never really been to anything like this before. It was all a bit twee, admittedly, but she'd only ever seen a sight like this on *Midsomer Murders*; never in real-life.

Una was in the midst of the general hubbub, giving directions to the helpers around her, as Rachel headed across the grass to say hi and see what she could do. She hadn't spoken to her friend properly since her trip to Inverness, and she was keen to hear how things had gone with Lucy. Other than a quick text affirming that they had indeed met - and she wasn't a middle-aged man - Una had refused to divulge anything further.

"Morning," Rachel called, her trainers sinking into the damp, thick grass as she approached. Una responded with a frazzled wave - clearly, things weren't going smoothly.

"Hi," she said, briefly pausing in the instructions she was giving to the group before her. Rachel waited until she was finished before speaking again, watching the helpers scuttle off to their various tasks.

"So," she asked. "How was it? Did you like her?"

Una grimaced, eyes wide as she took her by the arm and led her to the opposite side of the field. "Not so loud," she whispered, grinning, despite her scolding tone. "And yes, I did. But I'll fill you in properly later."

The day lived up to its early morning promise, the sky clear and cloudless. By the time the stalls were all set up and the first visitors started to arrive - a nice mix of locals and tourists, Rachel noticed - the early summer sun was warm on her skin. It wasn't long before she was wishing that she'd thought to put on sun cream. Despite her dark hair, her complexion was decidedly Scottish - white, with a hint of blue.

By midday, Rachel could feel the tell-tale tingle across the back of her neck and knew she'd need to find some shade.

"Hamish," she called, spotting his russet head above the crowd. He probably wasn't the best choice actually, given the circumstances, but it wouldn't be for long.

He turned and smiled when he saw her. "Whit can I dae for ye?"

"Do you mind manning the stall for a bit? I need to get some shade or I'll be a lobster in the morning."

He raised one orange eyebrow at her. "And ye thought it was a good idea tae ask the nearest passing ginger?"

Rachel shrugged, but Hamish laughed it off. "Aye, nae bother. Awa ye go tae the tea tent; my freckles have near enough joined up anyway, I'll be fine."

Relieved, Rachel squeezed his arm as he passed and whispered a quick thank you. There was something inherently likeable about Hamish; a softness to him that didn't quite match his gruff appearance.

As suggested, Rachel decided to take refuge in the tea tent. She hadn't had a drink all morning anyway, and was never one to turn down the possibility of cake. She joined the queue, waving to Jenny and Ishbel as they scurried about, delivering pancakes thick with butter and homemade shortbread to the many busy tables.

Helping herself to a piece of deid fly cake - a fruit slice, to give it its proper name, with shortcrust pastry on the bottom, a thick layer of raisins in the middle and sticky white icing on top - Rachel was waiting patiently for her cup of tea when a cool hand suddenly pressed against the back of her neck.

"Bloody hell, you're burnt to a crisp!" the male voice said. Rachel jumped about a foot in the air, narrowly avoiding dropping her cake. She turned abruptly, to see Duncan's green eyes and straight nose pointing back at her, his dark brows knitted together in a concerned frown. "You should put some after sun on that," he said, "or it'll peel and you'll itch like crazy."

Rachel shrugged his hand away, trying to ignore the sudden drumming of her heart in her chest.

"It'll be fine," she said. "But thank you for your concern."

Ishbel handed Rachel a cup of tea, accompanied by a curious smirk and raised eyebrows. Ignoring the obvious glances of the inquisitive islanders, Rachel turned her back on Duncan and headed over to the tables to find a seat. To her surprise, he followed, and sat down opposite.

He was dressed casually in jeans and a green half-zip jumper that only served to enhance the brightness of his eyes. The sleeves were rolled up in the early afternoon warmth, revealing dark hair on his forearms, and a pair of sunglasses was perched on his head, nestled in the thick dark tufts of his hair. He took a seat, smiling at her in that way that made Rachel's tummy flip. She was glad at least that she'd done her hair and makeup, and chosen one of the slightly less tatty tops from her wardrobe.

"How are you?" he asked quietly, leaning forward, his hands clasped on the table within touching distance of her own.

"Great," she replied, her voice forcibly bright as she kept her own hands tightly wrapped around her warm polystyrene cup.

Duncan shuffled nervously on his seat, ducking closer and looking up at her through thick, dark lashes. "I've dialled your number a thousand times this week, you know."

"Why's that?" Rachel asked. "Something to discuss about the case?"

Duncan frowned. "No… I just wanted to talk to you. I kind of panicked the other day, and I wanted to apologise…"

"Nothing to apologise for," Rachel said, downing a mouthful of tea and feeling it scald her throat. She stood up, abandoning her cake on the table. "You can let me know if there's any developments with the case. Other than that, I don't see that we have anything to talk about."

Without giving him the chance to reply, Rachel turned and walked back out into the sunshine.

She spent the rest of the afternoon trying to focus on her

stall, but sadly hook-a-duck didn't offer much in the way of mental stimulation. It certainly couldn't distract her from the pit that had settled in her stomach, especially when she was constantly reminded of Duncan's presence on the playing field. He didn't approach her again - she couldn't blame him, really, after the way she'd spoken to him - but he always seemed to be somewhere in her peripheral vision.

Rachel was relieved when the church bells finally rang out for four o'clock, marking the closure of the stalls and the start of the shinty match. She could already smell the coals for the barbecue warming up, and saw Cameron on the other side of the field, in his pinny with a set of tongs in one hand and a bottle of beer in the other.

Shinty was a game peculiar to the Highlands of Scotland. Whilst Inniscreag didn't have an official team, some of the locals played in a league for the Skye team, and Craigport had its own rather ramshackle pitch, which was sufficient for weeknight practice and informal games of six-a-side.

Enough participants had been gathered to make up two teams. The aim of the game was simple - get the ball across to the opposite side of the field and score a goal; the team who scores the most goals wins. In this case, however, the ball was small, hard and made of leather, and it was transported using a long, curved stick, called a caman. A good shinty player could make that ball travel over one hundred metres at very high speed, and that was precisely what made the game so dangerous. Despite this, the players rarely wore helmets, and the hardy residents of Inniscreag would never have been seen dead in one.

As she tidied away the paddling pool and plastic ducks, Rachel noticed Duncan standing across the field, chatting to Andy. Some of the other men were nearby, changing into team colours - one white, one red - and handing out camans. Duncan was nodding enthusiastically whilst Andy spoke, and Rachel stopped in her tracks when suddenly he stripped off his jumper, along with the t-shirt underneath, and reached out for a crisp, white team shirt.

"Alright, alright, put your eyes back in their sockets."

Sorcha was strolling towards her across the field, her arms crossed over her chest as she regarded Rachel, a smirk on her lips and one eyebrow raised. She had slipped into Una's house to change, and was dressed in a white strip identical to her husband's, and now,

Duncan's. Sorcha was one of the few women on the island who joined in with this ancient sport, and was a force to be reckoned with on the pitch, even amongst men who were twice her size.

"I'll admit, he is handsome," she said, pausing to watch Duncan pull the shirt on over his firm, hair-covered torso.

"He can't seriously be considering playing, can he?" Rachel asked, turning to her friend.

Sorcha shrugged. "Looks like it," she said. "Our team's a man short - Iain's had one too many and had to be taken home to his bed."

The two women walked over to join the crowd gathering around the perimeter of the pitch, watching the two teams finish their preparations. Andy was running through the basics of the game while Duncan listened attentively, trying out the weight of the caman in his hands. Seeing Sorcha and Rachel approach, the two men looked up and waved.

"Do you know what you're letting yourself in for?" Rachel asked, nodding at Duncan. He smiled, making her flinch – there was a solid row of black where his teeth should have been. A gum shield, she realised. At least he was taking some precautions.

"What's to know?" he asked. "It's just hockey, basically, right?"

Andy laughed. "Just you wait," he said.

Andy and Sorcha headed off to join the other team captain, their kids waving excitedly at them from the edge of the pitch, where they stood with Ishbel.

"He assured me it had been thoroughly disinfected," Duncan said, turning back to Rachel and indicating the borrowed gumshield.

Rachel laughed. "I wouldn't count on it." Looking around at the crowd, she suddenly realised there was a rather conspicuous missing person.

"Stephanie not here to cheer you on?" she asked.

It was Duncan's turn to flinch now, breathing in sharply between his teeth as he turned and flashed her a grin.

"I'm kind of in her bad books at the minute," he admitted.

"Why's that?"

Duncan rocked back and forth on his heels, swinging his caman experimentally at the long grass and not looking at her.

"You know that day your cat went missing?"

Rachel nodded.

"Well, we were supposed to have a 'business lunch' at the pub," he explained, putting the words in air quotes. Duncan paused and looked at her, leaning a little closer. "But I stood her up."

Rachel tried not to betray any reaction, holding his gaze. "I bet she didn't like that," she said simply.

"Not one bit," Duncan agreed. "But I got a better offer." He leaned even closer, his voice barely a whisper against her ear. "And I'd do it again."

With one last smile, he spun on his heels and made his way across the field, the sun highlighting the flecks of silver in his hair, Rachel grinning at his back.

# CHAPTER 22

Unsurprisingly, Duncan's team was resoundingly thrashed, and he found himself the proud new owner of more than a few lumps and bruises in the process.

"Not as much like hockey as I thought," he admitted to Rachel, while they hobbled back to the pub for drinks with the rest of the players. Laughing, she found herself offering him her shoulder to lean on. She'd enjoyed a few beers while watching the game, along with one of Cameron's excellent homemade pork and apple burgers, and was feeling a lot friendlier than she had done in the morning.

"Your back's red raw," Duncan said, putting his arm around her shoulder and tenderly brushing aside her hair. His fingers were cool where they touched the burnt skin lightly.

The two of them were at the back of the meandering group, following a winding trail of people down the hill towards the sea and along the front to Shelagh's waiting refreshments. Rachel watched the evening sun sparkle on the wide carpet of azure water before them, the coastline of Skye just visible in the distance.

"It's beautiful," Duncan said, before leaning down and whispering in her ear, "You really should have someone rub some cream on this, you know."

"Is that right?" Rachel smirked, impulsively linking her arm around his waist as they continued down the path towards the pub. It was nice; she fitted snugly under his shoulder. "If only I didn't live alone," she continued. "I'm not sure Doug would be up to the task - no thumbs, you see."

"A serious evolutionary flaw," Duncan smiled in agreement. "I, on the other hand, am fully equipped with two functioning thumbs." He held them up, head tilted to one side as he flashed her a suggestive smile.

"Functioning? Are you sure about that?" Rachel nodded at the left one, which had a large swelling at the base and was now pointing in a slightly unnatural direction.

"Well, maybe not that one," Duncan admitted. "You could ice it for me?"

Rachel rolled her eyes at him, disentangling herself just before they reached the pub, and the prying eyes of her fellow islanders.

By the time they'd entered, Duncan just had one hand resting on her forearm for support. Rachel knew, however, that they'd still drawn some curious glances from the assembled locals, not to mention a glare from Stephanie, who was sitting at the bar eating smoked salmon salad and drinking a glass of prosecco.

"Oops," Duncan whispered. His face was splattered with mud, the thick dark hair jutting up all over his head in various directions. There was a smear of blood by the corner of his mouth, and a fine bruise starting to spread across his right cheekbone. This Duncan bore little resemblance to the smooth, polished lawyer Stephanie was accustomed to. Rachel saw her do a double take as she belatedly realised who the bedraggled, battered man currently staggering through the doorway actually was.

"I'd better go and make amends," Duncan said, adding quietly, "I'll catch you again in a bit."

For a fleeting moment, Rachel thought he was about to kiss her - just an absentminded peck - but he stopped himself, squeezing her elbow instead before limping off across the room to speak to his client.

Rachel watched him go, trying not to react when Stephanie reached out a hand to gently touch the bruise on his cheekbone, her heavily made up face shrouded with worry. Feigned worry, Rachel wondered? Either way, she knew there weren't many men who'd turn down the chance of being nursed and fawned over by someone who looked like Stephanie.

"Ignore them," Una said firmly, taking Rachel by one hand and spinning her round, before placing a large white wine spritzer into the other. She spoke firmly, her brown eyes boring into Rachel's. "He likes you; any idiot can see that. Just relax and let it happen. And don't tell me you don't feel the same way," she said, when Rachel opened her mouth to protest. "Any idiot can see that, too."

Una smiled, her expression softening. "You're allowed a little bit of happiness, you know. You don't have to be alone."

Rachel returned the smile, taking a sip from her wine and feeling it settle comfortingly on top of the beers from earlier. "Neither do you," she replied.

Una smiled again, tucking her long hair behind one ear in an uncharacteristically girlish gesture. "I don't intend to be," she said, leading Rachel over to join Sorcha at their usual table.

"Do I take this to mean things went well in Inverness?" Rachel asked, as Una handed Sorcha her G&T.

Una nodded, eagerly - but quietly - filling them in on the details of her date. Lucy, it turned out, had been everything she'd hoped for and more; beautiful, funny, sweet and a regular church-goer.

"She's a nurse, and does loads of volunteer work as well," Una was gushing. "She showed me pictures from when she was in Malawi last year, helping to build a school. And she fosters pets for people who are in hospital and can't look after them. On her days off she even goes back into work to read stories to kids on the children's ward."

"Almost sounds too good to be true," Sorcha teased.

"That's what I thought," Una agreed. "But she seems genuine - just a nice, kind, caring, *normal* person."

"So what now?" asked Rachel.

Una affected a noncommittal shrug, despite her obvious excitement. "A few Facetime dates, I suppose. We said we'd maybe meet up on Skye sometime. I wouldn't want her coming to the island - meeting parishioners and everything - unless I knew it was actually going somewhere."

They were interrupted by the arrival of Andy, along with the rest of the shinty team, laden down with pints of ale and bags of crisps. Stealing a surreptitious glance, Rachel noticed Duncan at the rear, bringing Stephanie with him to introduce to the crowd.

It was, of course, horrendously awkward, but Stephanie plastered a megawatt smile on her face and brazened it out as Duncan made the introductions. The males in the group certainly seemed taken with her, swishing her honey-blonde hair and batting her eyelashes at them. Her presence on the island had clearly not gone unnoticed, but as yet, few of the locals were privy to exactly what it was she was doing here.

"So, do you work for Kindred Spirits too?" Ben - one of the operators at the still - asked. He had a ruddy complexion and unruly, curly brown hair, with matching chestnut eyes that were staring longingly at Stephanie like a Labrador stares at food.

Stephanie giggled, a girlish noise that didn't match her age. Late twenties or early thirties, Rachel thought? Definitely younger than she was, not to mention infinitely more toned and well groomed.

"Oh no," Stephanie said, brushing her hand casually against Ben's arm. "I'm a client. Duncan here is representing my claim to inherit the distillery."

The mood in the room shifted quickly, like an unseen wave suddenly capsizing a boat. The warmth that had been emanating towards Stephanie - mainly from the men, granted - suddenly vanished, to be replaced by an icy chill.

She giggled again, but this time her laughter betrayed a nervous edge. "What?" she asked, tucking a stray lock of honey gold hair behind one ear.

"You're here for the still?" Ben asked, frowning.

After a brief pause, Stephanie jutted out her chin and looked squarely at him, opting for defiance. "I am," she said. "I am Stephanie McLeod; my great-grandfather was Malcolm McLeod."

A chorus of murmurs wound its way around the room - everyone was, by now, blatantly listening in. Rachel heard the usual whispers about Edith having had no relatives, but no one openly challenged her.

Duncan coughed, coming to his client's rescue.

"Stephanie means no ill will to anyone here," he said, glancing unconsciously at Rachel. "She merely wants to connect with her heritage and explore any claim she may have to inherit a part of her great-grandfather's legacy."

"Aye, and sell it off to you bastards," a voice slurred from the back of the crowd. It was Cameron, who had clearly had one too many beers himself. He was standing unsteadily, pointing an accusatory finger at Duncan. Jenny hushed him loudly, pulling him back into his seat with a frown on her face.

"It's mine by right; I can do whatever I want with it," Stephanie declared over the growing hubbub. "Not like her." She pointed to Rachel now, who suddenly found the eyes of everyone in the village on her. "She's nothing but a common little thief!"

A number of voices jumped to Rachel's defence. Duncan shrugged at her apologetically, before stepping in front of Stephanie with his hands outstretched, shielding her from the growing animosity of the crowd. The sudden interruption of a loud, authoritative voice quietened them all.

"That's enough!" Shelagh's deep alto was a stark

juxtaposition to her tiny frame. She punctuated it with the sudden slamming shut of the flap at the end of the bar, which came cracking down with a thud and made everyone jump.

"We're here to raise money for a good cause," she said, lifting the tray of stovies she had been carrying through from the kitchen, "and anyone who wants to behave like hooligans will no longer be welcome in my pub. These people are our guests, and they'll be treated accordingly."

The assembled crowd shifted uncomfortably, everyone looking at their feet. Surprisingly, it was Hamish who spoke up first. "Shelagh's right. We may no' like it," he said, glancing in Rachel's direction, "but if what this Stephanie's saying is true then she deserves a chance to stake her claim. And Duncan's alright," Hamish added, with a grudging tip of his half-empty pint glass in the lawyer's direction. Clearly, Duncan's ability to take a bashing on the shinty field had raised his standing amongst the men of Inniscreag.

"Leave them be, and let's just enjoy Shelagh's fine cooking." Hamish finished.

"Hear, hear," someone echoed, as the usual friendly hubbub of the pub returned, and the patrons fell hungrily upon Shelagh's stovies; warm diced lamb mixed with mashed potato and neeps, topped with oatcakes.

Whether it was due to his speaking out in her defence, or just his overwhelming size and innate manliness, Stephanie gravitated towards Hamish. It wasn't long until she was comfortably ensconced in a corner with him, tucked up on a stool gazing at him adoringly and alternating between sipping prosecco and emitting high-pitched, girlish giggles. Hamish looked as nonplussed as ever, although Rachel couldn't help but notice a hint of additional redness in his cheeks.

"They look cosy," Duncan said, sidling up alongside her and spooning stovies into his mouth. "These are bloody delicious," he added, his mouth full.

Rachel nodded her agreement. "Shelagh's a great cook. I'm hoping she might help me out when we get the cafe up and running."

"Cafe?" Duncan asked, his head cocked to one side in a way that made him look quite adorable, bruised and bloodstained face notwithstanding.

Rachel felt her own face flush, realising she hadn't meant to let that slip. "You said we needed to diversify," she said with a shrug.

"This is my first step. Thought it might entice a broader range of visitors to the site."

Duncan nodded slowly, chewing on his stovies before scooping more up with an oatcake and taking another bite. He swallowed before answering.

"Not quite what I had in mind," he admitted, "but it's not a bad idea. Might bring in some revenue to keep you floating a little while longer. Long enough to get some new products on the shelf."

"Maybe," Rachel agreed. "Baby steps - this distilling thing is all new to me, remember? But coffee and cakes? I know what I'm doing with coffee and cakes."

Duncan pulled out a nearby bar stool for her, and the two of them found themselves sitting together as she explained her plan for the old maltings.

Rachel fleetingly wondered if this was such a good idea; after all, if he really was manipulating her just so his company could take over the distillery, then she was playing right into his hands. But he was easy to talk to, and he listened when she spoke. Really listened, and asked questions, and made helpful suggestions… It was too easy to let herself get carried away when she was with him.

"I just need to get it furnished now," she was saying, as Duncan ordered her another white wine spritzer and she found herself accepting it without argument. "Furniture and some decorations, then we should be ready to open in time for the summer holidays. What I'd really like to finish it off properly, is to get some photos taken of the distillery itself, maybe blow them up and hang them on big canvasses? But there's no way I could afford to commission a photographer to do them."

"What kind of thing were you thinking?"

Rachel shrugged. "Just some black and white shots of the buildings, or the copper stills, that kind of thing."

"I could do it if you like?" Duncan said, sipping from his fresh pint, his eyes slightly droopy. Rachel wasn't sure if that was a result of the multiple beers, or the very likely concussion he was nursing after his shinty debut.

"I'm a bit of an amateur photography geek," he continued. "I usually just go to car shows and the like, but I was thinking when I was out for that walk the other day - before I bumped into you - that it might be nice to take some landscape or wildlife shots while I'm here."

He paused, swallowing another glug of ale before continuing. "I'm going back to Edinburgh tomorrow, actually. Just for a couple of days; there's some family stuff I need to see to. But I was going to pick up my camera gear while I'm there."

Rachel felt her heart drop at the mention of 'family stuff'. That was the mysterious wife or girlfriend, no doubt.

"I couldn't ask you to do that," she said, shifting away from him slightly.

"It's no problem," Duncan said. "I won't be offended if you think they're shit," he added with a smile, sleepy green eyes twinkling. "But they might tide you over until you have the budget for something more… professional."

Rachel smiled uncertainly. "Lawyer, boy scout, shinty player, cat rescuer, photographer… What other talents are you hiding?"

"Wouldn't you like to know?" Duncan grinned, his hand finding her knee under the cover of the bar. He nodded over his shoulder. "You know, my room is just through that door," he said conversationally, looking around the room. "No one else is paying the least bit of attention. I bet you and I could nip through there without anyone noticing, and pick up where we left off the other day, before I ran out on you like an absolute fucking idiot."

His hand was travelling up her thigh, and Rachel felt a momentary weakening of her resolve. *She* wouldn't be cheating on anybody, after all. But the thought of him squeezing her in as a one-night stand right before he headed back to his home and partner was too much for her to bear.

"No, I'm sorry," she said, shaking her head and moving her leg out of his grasp. "We shouldn't."

Duncan's face fell. "You're right," he sighed. "I don't like it, but you're right. I'm going to jump in the shower and get an early night," he said, downing what was left of his beer. "I'm on the first boat in the morning and no doubt I'll have a fucker of a headache to contend with. Goodnight, Rach."

"Goodnight." She smiled sadly at his retreating back, as he pushed his way through the door and Rachel found herself alone once again.

# CHAPTER 23

In the end, it was nearly three weeks before Rachel saw Duncan again. The same, however, could not be said of Stephanie. Rather than keeping her head down and doing her best not to further antagonise the locals, it seemed their Canadian visitor was on a mission to irritate or offend as many people as possible.

First, there was the half an hour she spent quizzing Ishbel over the lack of gluten free options in the village shop. Then, just over a week into her stay on Inniscreag, came her utter disbelief when she discovered that there was nowhere on the island to have her gel nails infilled, closely followed by barely contained horror when she was informed that there wasn't even a resident hairdresser.

"But what about my roots?" Stephanie had exclaimed, eyes wide in shock, drawing the attention of most of the pub to her conversation with Shelagh.

The landlady shrugged, her own grey-streaked hair clearly of little concern. "Most folk go over to Skye for a trim when they need it, and if they want it dyed, they just do it themselves at home."

"Box dye?" Stephanie screeched, her hands clinging to her precious honey coloured locks.

The lack of personal grooming services and alternative dietary options was just the tip of the iceberg. There were few realities of life on Inniscreag that failed to draw a disparaging comment, from the painfully slow internet connection to the fact that Amazon Prime didn't guarantee next day delivery to the Highlands and Islands. Stephanie was, quite frankly, amazed that people had survived in this desolate part of the world for as long as they had.

As the days wore on, and it became increasingly clear that the novelty of life on Inniscreag was wearing off, Rachel began to tentatively hope that Stephanie might give up completely on her quest to take over the distillery and piss off back to Canada. Sadly, despite her many protestations and complaints, that didn't seem to be the case. And in a turn of events which no one could have foreseen - least of all Rachel - the one person who seemed to be making her stay on the island in any way bearable, was Hamish.

Much to the horror of the resident curtain twitchers - of which there were many on Inniscreag - the two of them had been seen together on multiple occasions, walking arm in arm along the seafront or sharing a drink at the pub. There were even whispers that Hamish had been caught leaving her AirBnB, under cover of darkness, very early one morning.

All of which left Rachel in a somewhat uncomfortable position. Obviously, Hamish's personal life was absolutely none of her business. But she couldn't help but worry - what if Stephanie got in his head and he ended up supporting her claim on the distillery?

And although she knew it was no different to her own dalliance with Duncan, there was a protective, sisterly instinct that worried Stephanie might only be out to use him to her own ends. Rachel knew Hamish to be strong willed, bordering on obstinate, but who was to say what he might succumb to when faced with the lure of Stephanie's physical charms?

In her usual passive manner, however, Rachel opted to deal with these concerns by doing absolutely nothing. Hamish was a big boy, and despite her misgivings she would just have to let him make his own mistakes. Besides, she had enough on her own plate to deal with, without worrying about Hamish too.

In the time since Duncan had returned to the mainland, on his mysterious 'family business', Rachel had been kept busy putting the finishing touches to the maltings. They were now just a matter of weeks away from opening, and all the structural work was complete - Andrew had installed the simple kitchen where they would produce food, as well as the staff and visitor toilets. Bill and his construction team had also sectioned off a small area at the opposite end to be used as a gift shop, although at the moment this would remain closed. Once the coffee shop was up and running, Rachel's next job was to explore options for putting distillery branding onto nosing glasses and decanters, and any other merchandise they could get a hold of easily and relatively cheaply.

Today, however, brought the final hurdle before the coffee shop could officially be opened. After spending the last two weekends, and most of her evenings, scavenging second hand furniture from around the island, hanging curtains and attempting to artfully place scatter cushions, rugs and vases around the room, today was the day of their inspection by the local authority food and hygiene department.

Rachel awoke with a pit of dread lying heavy in her stomach.

She'd never liked exams, least of all ones where she had to actually speak to someone face to face. The friendly lady she'd spoken to on the phone had assured her that this was 'merely a formality', but Rachel still dreaded the thought that she might get a telling off for having done something wrong.

They'd prepared as much as possible; Shelagh had coached them on everything from labelling to how to organise the fridges, and Jenny - who was now officially employed as the coffee shop head cook and supervisor - had taken her food hygiene certificate online and passed with flying colours. They weren't even handling high-risk produce, having restricted their menu to vegetable-based soups, home bakes and fresh bread, but still Rachel fretted. She needed this to go well, or all the money they'd spent on the refurbishment would have been for nothing.

After a quick shower, and a pep talk in the mirror which she would never admit to anyone, Rachel went for one last walk around the maltings to check everything was in order before meeting the food inspector off the morning ferry.

It was a beautiful day, the sun bright in the early summer sky, and Rachel tried to let its warmth ease away some of the tension in her body. Rounding the corner and seeing the finished building, she allowed herself a small smile; an outward sign of the little glimmer of pride swelling in her chest.

The long outline of the maltings stretched out before her, with a panoramic view of the wide, blue ocean behind it. The once tired and grubby white walls were now dazzlingly bright, and the little square window frames that dotted the length of the building had all been newly edged in black. Potted plants lined each of the sills, spilling cheery sprays of violas and pansies over their sides in a splash of bright yellows, blues, purples and pinks. Rachel still couldn't believe the change, compared to the tired, unloved old building that had stood there less than two months before.

She opened the door to find Jenny and the other two new employees, Martha and Irene, hard at work. The three of them smiled in greeting, from their various positions sweeping, mopping and wiping every surface they could reach.

The inside of the building had come together pretty well too, if she said so herself. Interior decorating wasn't a natural talent, but with a combination of tasteful but eclectic furniture, some nice rugs and cushions and mismatched vases filled with fresh flowers on each table, the room was charming, if not exactly plush. Only the long white, interior walls remained conspicuously bare.

After checking in with the ladies, and being reassured by Jenny that there was nothing to worry about, Rachel glanced at her watch and realised she could procrastinate no longer. The morning boat would be berthing any minute.

"It'll be grand," Jenny said, giving her arm a squeeze and smiling warmly. "Just you wait and see; all this fretting will have been for nothing."

As she usually did, Jenny proved, in the end, to be correct. The food inspector was a rotund and suitably jolly man named Peter, who was not in the least bit as officious or aloof as Rachel had been expecting. He oohed and aahed appreciatively over the various changes they had made to the maltings, was more than happy with the setup of their fridges, sinks and toilet facilities, and when Jenny offered him one of her empire biscuits and a coffee he gladly accepted, settling himself in one of the old church pews that Rachel had repurposed as benches around the larger tables.

"I'll have to file my official report once I'm back in Inverness," he said.

Rachel was sitting opposite, sipping her tea nervously, still waiting for him to suddenly find something amiss and bring all her plans crumbling down around her.

"But I think I can safely say you have nothing to worry about. How could I possibly stop you from selling wee beauties like these?" Peter held up the icing-covered biscuit in his hand, spilling yet more crumbs down the front of his shirt.

"Thank you," Rachel replied, pleased, but not quite able to relax just yet.

"When did you say you were planning to open?" Peter asked.

"Two weeks. I was hoping to have a bit of time to iron out any teething problems before the schools break off for summer."

"Good thinking." He smiled. "You should have my report in a few days at most."

Peter finished his coffee, heaped yet more praise upon the home baking, and Rachel had him back in Craigport - along with a few more samples of Jenny's cakes to take away with him - with plenty of time to spare before the afternoon ferry.

"I'm afraid there's not all that much to do around here," she said apologetically, the car engine idling as she worried about whether or not she would be expected to entertain him until he was able to make the crossing to Skye.

"Not to worry," he said, his eyes alighting upon the exterior of the pub across the road. "My colleague told me your local public house offers excellent meals; I should very much enjoy the opportunity to sample them."

"I'd recommend the langoustines," Rachel replied with a smile. "Landed fresh, right here on Inniscreag."

"Excellent."

He was clambering out of the car and crossing the road as Rachel slid the gear stick into reverse, glancing back just in time to see him holding the door open for someone who was making their way out of the pub. Her heart had recognised him before her brain had time to catch up, and was already pulsing excitedly the base of her throat. It was Duncan, casually dressed, his dark hair noticeably shorter, having obviously been cut during his trip to the mainland.

He had noticed her, too; could hardly miss her, really, in her distillery branded car and parked not ten feet away from him. Duncan glanced at where the door had just swung closed behind Peter, and back to Rachel again, one eyebrow raised as he crossed the road and headed purposefully in her direction. She rolled the window down to greet him.

"Is no man safe?" he asked, his tone teasing. "I've been gone just over a fortnight and you've already moved on."

Rachel rolled her eyes at him. "He's the food hygiene inspector. He's been out to sign off the cafe before opening."

"Oh, that's good," Duncan sighed. "You had me worried there for a second. Thought maybe you were trying to make me jealous." He smiled, and carried on speaking before Rachel had a chance to reply. "Mind if I jump in? I was heading your way anyway; save me a walk."

He was carrying a large rucksack, which he deposited in the boot without waiting for an answer, before climbing into the passenger side and buckling his seatbelt.

"And if I said no?" Rachel asked, bemused.

"But you didn't."

# CHAPTER 24

"I got back this morning."

They were driving along the coastal road to the distillery, the sea gradually dropping away below them as they climbed the gentle rise of the island's spine. Rachel's eyes were on the road, but she could feel Duncan watching her. "A few things at home held me up a little longer than I expected. I take it there's been no developments here?"

Rachel frowned. "Why would I be telling you if there were? We're not on the same side, remember?"

"I know, but no reason we can't be friendly about this," Duncan replied with a shrug. "It's nothing personal, remember?"

"Well, tell that to your client."

"What's that supposed to mean?"

"She's practically shacked up with one of my operators," Rachel announced. "This island's full of unmarried men and she picks one of the handful that work at the still to get her claws into? Seems pretty personal to me; probably just another tactic to try and undermine us from within..." She trailed off, realising what she'd just implied.

There was a moment of loaded silence, which Duncan broke. "What do you mean, 'another'?"

They were passing through the distillery gates now, and Rachel pulled in to park in her usual spot outside her house. She said nothing, her face flushed while she focused an unnecessary amount of concentration on making sure she didn't get too close to the little stone garden wall on the driver's side. Turning the key and removing it from the ignition, the interior of the car was abruptly plunged into silence.

"You don't think that's what I was doing, do you?" Duncan asked. "When we..."

She shook her head, wishing she hadn't said anything. "No... I don't know. It's just..."

"Rach," Duncan reached out one hand and placed it gently on her knee. "I kissed you because I wanted to kiss you; simple as that."

His hand remained there as Rachel looked at him, his green

eyes soft and sincere.

"I'd very much like to do it again some time, as a matter of fact." He was looking up at her through those dark lashes. Why did men always get the best eyelashes? Rachel wondered. She'd kill for eyelashes like those.

Rachel stared back at him, her head battling with her heart. And her libido, if she was honest. Her skin tingled beneath his hand; the same way it had every time he'd touched her.

"We shouldn't," she said eventually, pulling herself away and looking out of the window instead.

"Okay," Duncan sighed, leaning back in his chair. He was silent for a moment longer, before speaking. "If you ever change your mind, Rach, you know where I am."

"And your girlfriend?" she asked, turning back to him.

He paused, one hand on the door handle. "What girlfriend?"

Rachel looked back at him, taking in his confused frown. Was it genuine? she wondered. She tried to keep her voice steady.

"The one I heard you on the phone to; the one you presumably spent the last three weeks with, back in Edinburgh."

Duncan sighed again, raking one hand through his hair. "There's no girlfriend, Rach. And I wouldn't cheat on her if there was. But then you already think I go around seducing people just to win cases, so why on earth would you believe me?"

He stepped out of the car without saying anything else, grabbed his rucksack from the boot, and crossed the courtyard to the office without looking back.

The rucksack turned out to contain camera equipment. Duncan unpacked it in her office, the awkward tension between them still there, but both of them doing their best to ignore it.

"I promised you some pictures," he said, not meeting her eyes. "So, I'm here to take some pictures."

"Thank you," Rachel replied meekly, hiding behind her computer. "If you need any help finding your way around, just ask."

"I'll be fine," he assured her.

The thought briefly flitted through her mind that this would be the perfect cover for sneaking around and finding out all the business' secrets, if it had any, but Rachel quickly dismissed the possibility. Industrial espionage was pointless, at this stage; ownership of the still would all depend on whether or not some unknown judge thought Rachel had hoodwinked Edith into leaving it to her in the first place. Nothing he could discover on his walkaround today would give Duncan further ammunition one way or another.

It was late afternoon when he returned, windswept and pink-cheeked. The position of the still on this narrow, high, exposed outcrop of rock made the wind virtually unavoidable, even on the calmest of days.

"Did you get what you were hoping for?" Rachel asked.

"I think so," he nodded, seemingly back to his old self. "Do you want to have a look through them? I need to do a bit of processing and editing on my laptop before they'd be ready for printing, but it might give you an idea of any you particularly like."

"Just whatever ones you think are best," Rachel said, not wanting to be around him for any longer than was absolutely necessary. Her resolve was weakening by the minute. "I've written down the dimensions here."

While Duncan had been out photographing the site, Rachel had popped over to the maltings and measured the biggest spaces, to get an idea of what sizes and orientations of image might work. Duncan looked over the list and nodded.

"If it's easier I could just order them for you? There's a good site I normally use; not sure how much these bigger prints would be, or how quick they could ship to the islands, but I could check it out for you if you like?"

Rachel smiled. "Thank you," she said, and she meant it. Why on earth he was still being so nice to her, she had no idea.

"Canvas?" he asked.

"Sorry?"

"The pictures. Do you want them printed on canvas? That way you can just hang them straight on the wall; no need to worry about getting frames."

"That would be perfect," she replied. "Just let me know what it costs and I'll square you up straight away."

"Will do."

He started packing up his camera gear, delicately taking apart lenses and loading each part into its own cushioned, perfectly sized cubby hole.

"Would you like a lift back into the village?" Rachel asked

impulsively.

Duncan looked up at her, surprised, and shook his dark head. "No, it's okay. I might try and get some shots of the scenery on my way back. Thank you though."

"No problem," she muttered, turning her attention back to the empty screen on her computer.

He was halfway to the door when she finally spoke again.

"Thank you again," she said. Duncan turned back to look at her, his shoulders slumped under the weight of his bag. "I really do appreciate this," Rachel continued, rambling. "I know you don't have to do it, and it's very kind of you, and I really am sorry if I offended you, or implied anything…"

Duncan smiled. "It's okay. I meant what I said, Rach. If you change your mind, you know where to find me."

He smiled once more, before stepping through the doorway and closing it gently behind him.

# CHAPTER 25

Peter's report came through within the week, as promised, giving 'The Maltings' the official seal of approval to be able to begin trading. As soon as it arrived, Rachel threw herself into preparations for their grand opening, if you could call it that. It was really just a Friday afternoon get together, to which they had invited all the residents of the island to sample the food and see the interior of the renovated building.

They would open for business properly the following morning, when, Rachel hoped, they might tempt in their very first tourists. It was only a couple of weeks until the school holidays, and although Inniscreag wasn't really the destination of choice for very many families, the visitor numbers, she was assured, always surged in July and August.

Rachel was in The Maltings with Jenny just after lunch, setting out tables of baking and warming massive vats of soup, ready to be served in little cups accompanied by homemade oatcakes. A fire had been lit in the hearth, the weather outside being unusually dreich and overcast for the season. The sky was heavy with low clouds and persistent drizzle, but inside The Maltings - with bunting strung across the room and the gentle crackle of burning logs in the background - everything was feeling suitably cosy and cheerful. As they finished laying out the buffet, Rachel pulled Jenny into an impulsive hug.

"Thank you," she said. "I couldn't have done any of this without you."

"Och, wheesht, lass," Jenny replied, returning the hug but brushing aside the compliment. "It's us should be thanking you; you've breathed new life into this place."

They were interrupted by the sudden jangling of the little bell above the front door. Rachel glanced down at her watch, wondering who it could be; the party wasn't due to start for another three hours.

A long box entered the door first, with smaller boxes precariously balanced on top of it. The person carrying them was stumbling blindly into the room, attempting to hold the heavy door open with one knee whilst simultaneously battling the unpredictable gusts of wind and the fact that his arms were stretched to breaking point to manage the load. Rachel and Jenny both rushed to assist him, un-piling boxes from his grasp one at a time, gradually revealing Duncan behind them.

Rachel preoccupied herself with placing the damp boxes on nearby tables, whilst he and Jenny exchanged pleasantries.

"What dae we have, here?" Jenny asked, either oblivious or choosing to ignore the obvious tension in the room.

"Pictures," Duncan replied. "Arrived just in the nick of time." He smiled at her, and Rachel smiled back.

He was wearing jeans and a plain white tee-shirt, with a checked shirt open over the top. His dark hair was uncombed and there was a coating of stubble over his chin and jaw; he could almost have passed for an islander these days, Rachel thought. She hadn't seen him in a suit in weeks.

Jenny oohed excitedly. "Can we open them?" she asked.

Duncan nodded, and Jenny grabbed a serrated knife from the kitchen to begin carefully slicing open the parcel tape around the seams.

They opened the largest one first, Duncan standing back with his arms folded over his chest and one hand rubbing his chin, as he rocked nervously back and forth on his heels.

"Do you like it?" he asked. Jenny propped it up against the wall and Rachel stepped back to admire it.

"It's beautiful," she gasped, lost for words.

He must have taken it from the end of the jetty, she figured. There was a ramshackle path down the cliffs on the northern shoreline, leading to a seldom used wooden platform, which jutted out into the water on half rotten legs. It was the only conceivable way he could have achieved that angle, unless he'd learned to walk on water.

The shot was a long panoramic one, which somehow managed to stretch all the way from the westerly tip of the island to the distillery entrance. It was black and white, which made the long, low outline of the whitewashed storehouse stand out even more, with the word 'INNISCREAG' emblazoned upon it in tall, black letters. The sky tumbled away above in a moody swirl of greys, interrupted only by the two pagoda chimneys in the distance, whilst the bottom of the image showed the blurred outline of shiny pebbles, tossed by the waves crashing to shore.

"By God, lad, that's bonnie," Jenny exclaimed, her hands clasped over her mouth. "Aren't you clever!" she added, pulling him into a one-armed embrace and patting his back soundly.

"Really?" he asked again, but he wasn't looking at Jenny. Rachel nodded mutely, suddenly overcome with an emotion she couldn't quite put her finger on and unable to speak. Duncan smiled back at her, relieved.

"Have a look at the others," he said.

The rest were similar in style - black and white, like she'd requested, a mixture of sizes and orientations, some of the maltings and the copper stills, as well as close-ups of little quirky features, like the hand painted sign on their duty paid warehouse. There was even a shot of Doug; he was sat on his haunches on top of a branded barrel outside the cooperage warehouse, looking straight at the camera with his head cocked to one side.

"How did you manage to get that?" Rachel asked.

Duncan shrugged. "That was a lucky one," he admitted. "I was passing and he just happened to be sitting there. I thought he'd scarper as soon as I got the camera out, but he posed quite the thing."

Rachel smiled at the image. She'd quite like a copy of that one herself, she thought. "They're all brilliant," she said. "Thank you so much."

The three of them spent the rest of the afternoon hanging the canvases around the room, debating which ones should go where. They proved to be the perfect finishing touch. By the time they were done, with Duncan's pictures on the wall, the smell of Jenny's leek and potato soup wafting through the room and the comforting crackling of the open fire, The Maltings felt more complete, and more welcoming, than Rachel could ever possibly have imagined.

"Bloody hell, it's half three already!" Jenny exclaimed suddenly, looking at her watch. "I'd better head home and freshen up. You too," she instructed, pointing Rachel in the direction of the door. "This is your big night!"

Jenny undid her apron and rushed out, but Rachel found herself hesitating by the door. "Will you be coming tonight?" she asked, turning to face Duncan.

"Wouldn't miss it for the world," he smiled back.

As it turned out, no one on the island missed it. When Rachel arrived just before five o'clock, The Maltings was already buzzing with activity, people milling here and there helping themselves to bowls of soup. To get around the fact that they weren't licensed, most people had also brought a bottle or two of wine or whisky, and one table had already been turned into an impromptu bar.

Duncan arrived not long after Rachel, dressed in a smart shirt and chinos, smelling of aftershave and with his hair still damp from the shower. He hadn't shaved, though, which Rachel was secretly quite pleased about.

"Congratulations," he said to her, holding out the white wine he'd brought with him. "The place looks great."

"In no small part down to you," she replied with a smile, accepting the bottle.

Rachel was dressed in the smartest outfit she could pull together, her hair was shiny and smooth from the fresh blow dry she'd given it before leaving the house, and she'd even managed to apply a full face of makeup, albeit in a bit of a rush. For once, she actually felt quite confident.

Or she did, at least, until Stephanie arrived. The other woman waltzed in on Hamish's arm, blonde hair flowing at her back, in a floral print party dress and matching pink heels. The whole room fell into a hush at their arrival; they'd obviously decided to go public, and Rachel couldn't help but smart at the fact they'd chosen tonight to do it.

Hamish coughed uncomfortably as the room regarded them both, his simple fisherman's jumper in stark contrast to Stephanie's glamorous attire.

"So glad you could come," Rachel said, sidestepping Duncan and heading across the room to greet them. She couldn't bear to see Hamish standing there like that, as if he were an outsider amongst a community he'd been part of his entire life.

Stephanie turned to her, a surprised grin on her face. If she had expected Rachel to be angered at her unexpected presence, this friendly welcome had obviously thrown her.

Hamish flashed Rachel a relieved smile as she directed them both to the buffet table. "Help yourself to the drinks as well," she added, gesturing to the table now laden with bottles of donated booze.

When she turned back around, Duncan was smiling at her. "That was very big of you," he said.

"Don't get your hopes up. I did it for Hamish, not her."

"She's not all bad," Duncan said, following Rachel as she picked up a bin bag and started a quick sweep of the room. Duncan helped pick up discarded cups and paper plates as they went.

"Is that right?" she asked.

"We've spent a bit of time together. Not like that," he added, when Rachel shot him a look. "Honestly, I think she's just... confused. She never knew her own father, and I think now she's just looking for somewhere to belong."

"Yeah, well, I never knew my father, either," Rachel retorted. "I still didn't fly halfway round the world to try and take something that wasn't mine." She stopped, bin bag dangling in one hand, looking at him as something occurred to her for the first time.

"You know, I don't think I'd care as much if she was actually going to keep it in the family," she said. Duncan came to an abrupt stop, almost bumping into her. "I think Edith would be OK with that. It's the fact that she's going to sell it to your mob that she wouldn't be able to stomach. And I promised her I wouldn't let that happen."

It wasn't until she stopped talking that Rachel realised she'd been pointing her finger at him, practically jabbing him in the chest.

"OK," he said, palms facing her in surrender, his voice low. "But between you and me, Stephanie hasn't actually signed anything binding with us yet. I'm here speculatively; she's under no legal obligation to sell anything."

Rachel narrowed her eyes at him. They were still standing closer than was necessary, but neither one of them moved.

"Why are you telling me this?" she asked. "You shouldn't be telling me this."

"I shouldn't," he agreed. "I could get the sack for telling you this. In fact, I could probably be struck off for telling you this. But I just wonder if the two of you might not be able to find a mutually agreeable solution that *doesn't* involve Kindred Spirits."

Rachel didn't know what to say.

"If you trust me," Duncan continued, the pinkie finger of his right hand gently entwining itself around her own, "you should speak to her. There might be a way of avoiding a court case at all."

Rachel looked over his shoulder, seeing Una and Sorcha entering the room, and the spell was suddenly broken. She pulled her hand away from him.

"I'll think about it," she said, before painting a grin on her face and heading across the room to greet her friends.

# CHAPTER 26

As was always the way with social gatherings on Inniscreag, at one point or another someone pulled out a fiddle, and the night descended into a blur of drinking, singing and dancing. Rachel spent most of it with Sorcha and Una, chatting and drinking wine, until the ceilidh began. The tables had been pushed to one side, and the long room proved to be an ideal dance venue. She did the Gay Gordon's with Cameron and a Virginia Reel with Ben, and was just catching her breath when Hamish claimed her for Strip the Willow.

"Won't your girlfriend mind?" Rachel asked, glancing across the room. Stephanie actually looked like she was genuinely enjoying herself, chatting in a corner with Jenny and sipping from a glass of whisky, not paying the least bit of attention to what Hamish was up to. She wrinkled her nose a little each time she took a mouthful of the neat single malt, but she wasn't complaining, and actually seemed quite happy.

"She's nicer than people have given her credit for," Hamish said, as they took their places on opposite sides of the set. "She's just different from us; she isn't used to life here."

Rachel shrugged, Duncan's words echoing in her ears. "Or maybe she just has you blinded by her beauty."

"She is beautiful," Hamish replied, looking across the room at Stephanie, a besotted expression in his eyes that Rachel had never seen on the gruff, red-headed islander before.

The musicians started up then, and Rachel had to save her breath for the exertions of the dance. Strip the Willow was one of the most energetic ceilidh dances, and by the time she'd skipped and twirled the length of the room with every man in her set, she was sweating and out of breath.

Hamish caught her for a quick hug and a kiss on the cheek before they parted. "Give her a chance," he said, looking down at Rachel earnestly. "You're a great boss and I don't want that to change. You've been good for Inniscreag. But maybe she could be good for us too? She's got a hot temper, that's all; underneath it, she's really quite sweet."

Rachel sighed. Hamish was opinionated, and possibly in love, but she knew he wasn't stupid. Could Rachel, in her haste to defend

Edith's final wishes, have overlooked a potential compromise? She'd never wanted to own the distillery in the first place, after all; she just didn't want Kindred Spirits to have it.

"Let me talk to Ruaridh first," she replied quietly. "Then maybe we can think of a solution to all this that doesn't involve going to court."

Hamish smiled gratefully, before heading back across the room to Stephanie, who nestled in comfortably against his vast chest. Rachel felt a little pang of jealousy. Not because she wanted Hamish for herself; more that it had taken Stephanie a matter of weeks in a foreign country to seemingly fall into a very happy relationship. Rachel, meanwhile, was hopelessly lusting after someone she couldn't have, whilst still being technically married to an arsehole ex-husband who refused to divorce her. Why did some people have it so easy?

"You alright?" Una asked, meeting her at the drinks table. It was nearing midnight and the illicit drinks supply had been pretty much decimated. Rachel rummaged through it, eventually finding a half empty bottle of prosecco and pouring them each a splash into a paper cup.

"I'm fine," Rachel replied, not entirely convincingly. Andrew and Sorcha were across the room, caught in what seemed to be a rather heated conversation at one of the little tables. "What about them?" she asked.

Una shrugged. "They were fine, I think. But now they've had too much to drink and got themselves into a stupid argument."

"Easily done," Rachel replied, taking a sip from her prosecco.

The crowd had started to thin, various islanders drifting home to their beds as the night wore on, and Rachel briefly wondered how on earth she was going to get this place cleared up and fit for service by ten o'clock the following morning. Jenny and Cameron had already left, she noticed, along with Martha, who was on shift the next day. Irene was still up dancing, caught in a Dashing White Sergeant trio between Ben and Jamie.

"I saw you talking to Duncan earlier," Una mentioned casually.

"I saw you talking to him, too," Rachel replied. She'd spotted the two of them chatting intensely, matching dark heads bowed, whilst she had been dancing with Hamish. If Una had been anyone else, she definitely would have been jealous.

"Just talking you up," her friend replied with a smile. "What's holding you back? You don't trust him?"

"Is that what he told you?"

"Implied it. As much as admitted he's interested, but said you'd already made up your mind that he was a liar, and he doesn't know how to change it."

Rachel sighed. "I don't know who he is."

"Then maybe you should find out." Una finished the rest of her prosecco. "Anyway, it's past my bedtime," she continued, grabbing her coat from the nearby bench. "I'll talk to you soon." She gave Rachel a quick peck on the cheek, before slipping out into the night.

The combination of Una's words, a belly full of wine and nearly two years of celibacy soon had Rachel drifting towards where Duncan was sitting on the other side of the room. He was alone, watching a few couples perform an unusually slow ceilidh dance - the Canadian Barn Dance, fittingly - as the atmosphere naturally quietened and the revellers drew things to a close.

He smiled up at her as she approached, his expression tired but warm. "I think you can safely call tonight a success," he said, sliding along the bench to make room for her beside him.

"Getting this place cleaned up and ready for business tomorrow morning will be the next challenge," Rachel replied.

"You'll have plenty of help, I'm sure. I'll gladly pop back first thing if you need a hand?"

Rachel shook her head, suddenly nervous. "You don't need to do that."

"I don't mind," Duncan said. "I was going to head soon, anyway. Can't handle the pace these days," he added with a laugh. "I'm shattered."

"I meant you don't need to pop back," Rachel said quickly, before she lost her nerve. "Or you wouldn't need to pop back, if you wanted to just… stay here."

Duncan didn't speak for a moment, then a slow grin spread across his face. "Like a sleepover?"

"I guess," Rachel smiled back shyly.

"You're sure?" One of Duncan's hands gently cupped her knee.

She nodded, covering his hand with her own and forcing any

lingering doubts from her mind.

They waited until the last of the crowd had gradually drifted away, before walking slowly across the site and back to her house by the gates. Duncan had his arm around her shoulder, the island air cool on her face as he toyed with her hair.

Rachel slipped her arm around him in return, hooking her thumb into the waistband of his trousers. They didn't speak, just listened to the night sounds of the island around them - the distant crashing of the waves against the shore line below, the echoing call of a lone owl - and enjoyed the sense of anticipation.

Their pace slowed as they approached Rachel's front door, and Duncan turned her to look at him, taking both of her hands in his.

"You're really sure?" he asked. "I don't want you to rush into anything if you're not ready."

Rachel looked up into his beautiful green eyes. She wanted to trust him so badly. "There's definitely no girlfriend?" she asked.

"Not yet," Duncan teased. "But I'm open to offers."

Rachel smiled, feeling her tummy twist itself in knots. She knew she wanted this, but she was also bloody terrified. It had been a long time, and the suspense was killing her.

Thankfully, he bent his head to hers then, and kissed her gently, and all of her fears melted away.

They stumbled through the front door and up the stairs, alternately kissing and fumbling with each other's clothes, depositing them on the ground where they fell, giggling like teenagers. By the time they collapsed onto Rachel's bed she was unbuttoning Duncan's shirt, revealing the firm chest covered in dark hair, as he struggled with the clasps on her bra.

"Sorry," he laughed self-consciously. "It's been a while."

"Me too," Rachel smiled back, kissing him again and reaching behind her back to help him out.

It certainly had been a while, and although her memory of their last hurried union was admittedly sketchy at best, Rachel was pretty sure sex with Graham had never been anything like this.

Duncan was gentle but in control, and spoke to her throughout; sometimes hushed, urgent words of passion breathed in her ear, sometimes checking that she was comfortable or quietly seeking her consent. She might have thought the latter would ruin the moment, but if anything, it heightened it. Knowing what he was thinking and what he wanted, and that he wanted to know what *she* wanted, was empowering. With Graham, she'd had to try her best to interpret a series of grunts and silences, and then it was over.

Duncan, however, took his time. After he had undressed her, he lay her back on the bed, and Rachel expected him to follow. He didn't. Instead, he knelt back and looked at her, and for a moment Rachel enjoyed the sight of him; bare chested, in just his boxers, hair dishevelled as he gazed at her with obvious longing. Quickly, however, she became distracted by her own nakedness, and moved her arms to conceal the rounded curve of her belly.

"Don't," Duncan said, putting his hand out to stop her. "You're beautiful."

He lay beside her and kissed her again, his hands starting in her hair before wandering lower. They slipped between her legs, causing Rachel's breath to catch in her throat, and all the while his voice was in her ear. It didn't take long for her to stop worrying about what she looked like, and allow herself instead to sink beneath the sensation of his touch, her hands wrapped in the bed sheets as Duncan's mouth took over from his hands and brought her quickly to climax.

"I'm glad you don't have any neighbours," he said, moving back up the bed to kiss her. "You're noisy."

"Shut up," she gasped, batting his arm playfully.

"No, I like it," he said. "In fact, I could barely contain myself."

"Well, you don't have to now," Rachel replied, swapping places as he settled onto his back and she returned the favour.

"Not yet," he breathed, just as she thought he was about to come. "I want to see you." He shifted, sitting himself upright and pulling her into his lap, his eyes never leaving hers as he gently entered her. One hand remained behind her neck as he began to move inside her, the other cupping her bum while she straddled her legs around him, urging him deeper.

He came quickly, clasping her to his chest, the two of them slicked with sweat. When it was over, Rachel expected him to pull away, but he didn't; he held for a moment longer, kissing her deeply before they parted.

"That certainly wasn't how I expected tonight to end," he

said, dragging the duvet over them both and extending his arm, inviting her to cuddle in. Rachel did so gladly, snuggling in alongside him and running her hands gently over his firm, hairy stomach.

"Me neither," she breathed, before closing her eyes and drifting off to sleep.

# CHAPTER 27

She awoke in the same position she'd fallen asleep, her head tucked in beneath Duncan's shoulder, the hairs on his chest tickling her cheek. Rachel opened her eyes cautiously and glanced up at him; he was sound, his head tossed back against the pillow and one arm crossed behind his neck as he slept. All Rachel could see was the dark, pointed triangle of his stubble covered chin and the Adam's apple bobbing up and down his neck as he breathed.

It was early, the first shards of daylight just beginning to slip between the edges of her curtains. Rachel sat up to look at him, pulling the sheet over herself.

He was beautiful. Long dark lashes lay flat against his cheeks, his hair ruffled and his face relaxed in sleep. She wanted to reach out and touch him, to stroke the hair at his temples where the sprinkling of salt and pepper glinted against the surrounding darkness. But she didn't want to risk waking him, so instead, she sat in the early morning light, drinking in his presence.

He woke suddenly, sitting upright as his eyelids flew open, causing Rachel to fall backwards off the bed in fright.

"Jesus Christ, I'm sorry," he cried, rushing to help her up from where she'd landed on the floor, in a tangled mess of blankets and naked limbs, banging the back of her head in the process.

"Are you alright?" Duncan asked, helping her to her feet before switching the bedside lamp on. Rachel tried to ignore the throbbing pain in her head.

"I'm fine," she lied, unconvincingly.

"Liar." Duncan gently turned her head so he could inspect it; there was a lump forming already, he informed her.

"Well if our first night together wasn't memorable before, I've certainly made it memorable now," he said, kissing her tenderly on the bump. "Nothing says romance like concussion."

"It was already memorable," Rachel said quietly.

"I thought so, too." He pulled her in for another kiss, which quickly deepened. His hands soon began to wander, curving over her bum and pressing her closer, before he suddenly pulled away.

"About before," he said, a nervous grimace on his face. "I just realised; we didn't use a condom. Like a pair of bloody stupid, horny teenagers." Duncan laughed awkwardly.

Rachel smiled, rubbing her hands up and down his arms. "It's okay; I'm on the pill," she reassured him, which was true. She didn't bother to add, "but you needn't worry, because my uterus is a dry, barren, husk anyway."

Duncan sighed with relief, encircling her in his arms once again. "In that case, if your head isn't too sore, I could do with a shower…"

Afterwards, they lay wrapped in each other's arms, damp and tired. Duncan had opened the curtains so they could see the view out of the window, where the land at the end of Rachel's little garden dropped away dramatically to the ocean below. They watched the sky gradually lighten, from deep navy with a hint of green at the horizon, to a light blue streaked with pink and orange as the sun crept higher.

Rachel had her head on Duncan's chest, neither of them speaking, while he trailed his fingertips absentmindedly up and down her side. "This place is like nowhere I've ever been before," Duncan said eventually.

"My bedroom?" Rachel asked.

"No," he said, laughing. "This island. It's like… it's got a *soul*, or something. Like it's alive. Is that stupid?" He turned to look at her.

"No," Rachel replied, nestling closer. "I know what you mean. It casts a spell on you. Although some don't realise its charm straight away," she added, remembering his supposed aversion to the great outdoors when they had first met.

"Well I'm definitely under its spell now," Duncan said, pulling her closer and kissing the top of her head. "In fact, I'm starting to think civilisation might be overrated."

He paused for a moment, and Rachel could feel the muscles in his torso tense before he spoke again. "I'm afraid I do need to head back there for a few days, though."

"Oh." Rachel sat up, struggling to hide her disappointment. "For long?"

"It shouldn't be," he said, reaching out to take her hand. "I just have a few things to take care of. Work, and… personal."

She narrowed her eyes at him, that old sense of suspicion beginning to sneak its way up her spine. "Family?"

"Yes, but it's not what you think," he rushed on, attempting to pull her back into bed as Rachel abruptly stood up and began picking up her underwear from the floor.

"Rach, please, give me a chance to explain."

"It's fine," she said with an affected shrug. "It was one night, we both wanted it. You don't owe me anything."

"It wasn't just one night to me, Rach. I promise." He carried on, but Rachel refused to look at him. "There are just things back home that I have to take care of. Responsibilities I can't just forget about."

She finally turned, snapping. "Of course, because you're the big, important lawyer and family man, aren't you?" Why had she been stupid enough to believe him; to let him into her bed? Not just let - *invite*. How humiliating.

"Rach, don't be like this," Duncan clambered out of bed after her, pulling on his boxers as he went. "Let me explain."

"There's no need," Rachel repeated, grabbing a fresh work polo shirt and jeans from her wardrobe. "We're both grown-ups here. It was a drunken shag while you were working away, and now you can go home to your *family* and I'll go back to my sad little life with my cat."

She wrestled into her clothes, anger making her clumsy. Duncan reached out a hand to help her, but she brushed it away.

"Rachel please," he pleaded. "There's things I haven't told you about, but I haven't lied to you…"

"Oh great! You haven't lied, just been economical with the truth. What is it then – she's not your girlfriend, she's your wife, is that it? And you can get off with it on a technicality, because you didn't *actually* lie to me." She shook her head in disgust. "I should have known better than to trust a lawyer; you wouldn't know honesty if it hit you in the face."

There was a little flash of anger behind his green eyes. "Rach, if you'd just calm down and let me explain…"

"Just go, Duncan," she said, stopping at the top of the stairs and turning back to face him. "Go back to Edinburgh, and your fancy car, and your fancy job, and be with your family. We both know that whatever *this* has been, it was nothing more than an amusing little diversion before you have to go back to your real life. So go. Don't worry about locking the door when you leave."

# CHAPTER 28

The first day of trading in the cafe went better than Rachel could have hoped for. If it weren't for how she'd left things with Duncan, she would have been on a high.

After heading in early, drying her tears and setting to work clearing up from the party the night before, she'd been joined by Jenny and Martha around eight o'clock. Between them they had the place ship shape and ready for opening just a couple of hours later, with the first paying customers - a German couple on an island-hopping tour of the Hebrides - coming through the door not long after. From then, business was steady until they closed up at half past four.

"No' bad for the first day," Jenny said, when Rachel returned to check in on them, indicating the till heavy with cash.

"Not at all," Rachel replied with a forced smile. The professional success pleased her, but the mess she'd once again made of her personal life made it bittersweet.

She'd regretted her outburst before she'd even walked as far as The Maltings, after the first surge of hot, angry tears had subsided. She had no idea what he even meant by 'family', Rachel realised. Aside from work conversations and a few flirtatious chats, they knew very little about each other. Maybe he had a sick mother, or a disabled sibling that he cared for? 'Family' didn't necessarily mean 'wife'.

And even if it did, she thought, the overheard 'sweetheart' conversation still echoing in her ears, Rachel hadn't exactly been honest, either. She'd never told him about Graham, and although they were most definitely not together, neither was she technically single. Why couldn't she just have calmed down and heard him out? And now he was back off to the mainland, and all she had to contact him was a tatty business card buried somewhere amongst the mess on her desk, which - even if she found it - she wasn't sure she could actually bring herself to ring.

Rachel was still berating herself the following day, when she finally tackled a job she had long been putting off. It would be laborious and most probably upsetting, but given her current mood, now was possibly the best time to get it over with.

Ever since Edith had died, her house had lain dormant, just up the hill on the opposite side of the site from Rachel's. She knew there was no one else around to clear it out, and as the beneficiary of her will, assumed the responsibility must fall to her. Not that she'd throw anything away - as her only relative, Stephanie might want to see some of it, she supposed. She'd just sort through it and organise it a bit.

The night shift was clocking off just as Rachel was leaving, laden down with cleaning spray, kitchen roll and bin bags. Sorcha and Una had agreed to come and lend a hand later, but she was awake and restless and wanted to get a head start on things. Ben and Hamish were just leaving the still house, yawning and bleary eyed, and waved to her as she passed.

"Hamish!" Rachel called after them, jogging over. She might regret this, but if Edith really did have a living relative, she supposed it was only right.

"Something the matter?" Hamish asked, turning to her with a frown on his face.

"Are you going back to Stephanie's?" she asked, causing him to blush fiercely, his rosy cheeks clashing with the orange beard below.

"Aye," he nodded.

"I was thinking about what you were saying the other night, and you're right; I should give her a chance." Rachel hurried on before she could change her mind. "I'm going over to Edith's today to start clearing out her things. Tell her if she wants to find out more about her family, she'd be welcome to join me."

"Really?" Hamish asked, a surprised smile spreading across his face. "That's awfy good of ye, Rachel."

"It's the right thing to do," she replied with a nod, hoping to convince herself more than Hamish. "She's Edith's family."

"Aye," Hamish nodded back. "She is. I'll tell her."

By the time Sorcha and Una arrived a few hours later, Rachel was covered in a thick layer of dust and had already filled three bin bags with rubbish - mainly consisting of a stash of individual sugar packets and tomato sauce sachets she'd found at the back of a kitchen cupboard, along with three years' worth of local newspapers. Edith, it turned out, was something of a hoarder.

They found her in the ground floor bedroom, sitting on the purple swirly carpet with an old leather suitcase open in front of her. It was crammed full of snippets of Edith's life - photographs, newspaper cuttings, letters. Rachel knew she probably shouldn't be snooping; she should just have zipped the suitcase back up again and left it for Stephanie. They were her heirlooms, after all. But she'd been sucked in, peering at the yellowed, wrinkled images, wondering who these people were and what role they'd played in Edith's life.

"How are you getting on?" Sorcha asked, entering without knocking. Una had already changed out of the ministerial robes from her Sunday morning service, and they were both dressed casually in leggings and hoodies.

"I may have got distracted," Rachel admitted, clambering up from her position on the floor and feeling her bones creak.

They worked on companionably for another hour or so, Una folding clothes from the old wardrobe into an empty suitcase, while Sorcha stacked books and worn-out video tapes into boxes.

"Even the charity shops on Skye won't take VHS now," Sorcha observed, throwing another armful into the box nonetheless.

Rachel looked around the room. She couldn't believe that as full and vibrant a life as Edith's could be reduced to this; a suitcase of old photographs, some clothes, and a pile of random belongings that no one else would want.

"Maybe it wasn't such a good idea to do this today," she said, unplugging a lamp from the bedside table and then standing with it aimlessly in her arms, no idea what to do with it. "I'm in a crappy enough mood as it is, and this isn't exactly helping."

"What do you have to be upset about?" Sorcha retorted. "The opening night party went down a storm, the coffee shop's doing well…"

"It's not work stuff," Rachel admitted, putting the lamp back down on the table and flopping onto the bed. "It's… personal."

Her friends both stopped what they were doing and eyed her carefully.

"Ex-husband personal, or…" Una started.

Rachel shook her head. "Nope - no change with him. Still won't agree to the divorce."

"So it's Duncan then?" Sorcha asked, to which she nodded sadly.

"What happened?" Una came over to sit beside her. "You seemed to be getting on quite well on Friday night. I thought he was interested?"

"He was." Rachel sighed, wondering if that sentence would now forever live in the past tense.

Taking a deep breath, she told them everything; from her inviting him back to spend the night, to their argument, culminating in her storming off the morning after.

"But he told you outright he was single, right?" Una observed, perfectly reasonably.

"Sort of. He said he didn't have a girlfriend, at least. But when he said 'family', all I could think about was his face when he was talking to that woman on the phone, and how she must be his wife, and he'd tricked me into sleeping with him."

"At least you got a shag out of it," Sorcha said, a gleam in her eyes. Una shot her a look. "What?" she replied. "I'd give anything for a good fuck with a fit guy. How was he?"

"Sorcha!" Una was openly glaring at her now, her dark eyes wide.

Sorcha merely shrugged, and tossed a strand of fine, white-blond hair out of her eyes. "Prude," she muttered.

"It was nice," Rachel admitted. "But it won't be repeated. Even if it turns out he's not married, I've fucked it up now, haven't I? You don't go back to the crazy girl who stormed out on you after your first shag."

Una put an arm around her shoulder and gave it a gentle squeeze. "You never know," she said half-heartedly.

Rachel was saved from any further platitudes by a sudden, gentle tapping on the front door.

"Come in," she called, standing up from the bed and heading into the hallway to greet their visitor.

Rachel heard the audible gasps behind her as Sorcha and Una spotted Stephanie standing hesitantly in the doorway, one high-heeled foot over the threshold. She certainly hadn't come dressed for manual labour.

"Hi," she said, looking unusually nervous. The bolshy, loud-mouthed attitude she'd displayed on their previous meetings was nowhere to be seen.

"Hi," Rachel replied. "Come in."

"This is really kind of you," Stephanie said. "Thank you for letting me be a part of this."

Rachel shrugged. "We're just tidying up, really. But I thought you might like to see some of the old photos and things. Maybe there'd be someone you recognise?"

Stephanie shook her head, loose blonde curls shimmering around her face like strands of gold. "Oh, no. I never met my Dad. He died before I was born, so I never really found out anything about my family in Scotland."

They drifted naturally into the living room, Stephanie placing her handbag down on one of Edith's worn, green velvet sofas. The old woman's decorating style had been indulgent, to say the least, and the whole house was draped in jewelled colours and rich fabrics.

"Well, your great-grandfather, Malcolm, would have lived in this house," Rachel explained. "Before Edith inherited it. I guess it'll be yours, soon, if the court case goes your way."

She hadn't meant it to be a dig, but Stephanie's gaze instantly fell to the floor. "I am sorry, about all of that," she said quietly. "Hamish has told me what brilliant things you've been doing for the business, and how much everyone here loves you." Rachel blushed at the unexpected praise. "I really didn't come here to upset all of that. But when I found out about this place... I just wanted to know where I came from."

"And then sell it off to a massive corporation so they can suck the heart and soul out of it?" Sorcha interrupted, her hands braced on her hips. Clearly, she wasn't feeling nearly as forgiving as Rachel.

"That's not what I wanted," Stephanie admitted. "But when Kindred Spirits approached me, and offered legal representation... I could never have come all the way over here on my own, hired a lawyer... I wouldn't know where to begin."

"Hang on," It was Rachel's turn to interrupt now. "*They* approached *you?*"

Stephanie nodded. "I'd been doing my own research online, and I guess when you refused to sell, they must have started looking into other possible avenues."

Rachel breathed in deeply, trying to control the seething rage that had sprung to life deep in her belly. Wife or no wife, Duncan had been lying to her about something after all.

"I'm sorry," Stephanie rushed on, misinterpreting Rachel's look of fury as being directed at her. "I never really wanted to sell; I thought once the court case is settled, if I win, I could just... tell them I changed my mind."

"I doubt it would be quite as straightforward as that," Rachel said, suppressing her fury, for now at least. "But it's not you I'm angry with. They've been playing us all, right from the beginning."

Rachel was pacing, looking around the room at the three other women as her mind flew through the possibilities.

"So, what do we do?" Stephanie asked eventually.

"We find a way to play them back."

# CHAPTER 29

They spent the rest of the afternoon sorting through the ground floor of Edith's house, a new and tentative sense of camaraderie suddenly existing between the four women. For now, at least, they were on the same side. All they had to do was figure out how to get Kindred Spirits out of the picture, and then maybe she and Stephanie could come to some sort of compromise about the future of the distillery.

It was mid-afternoon, the four of them sitting around Edith's now slightly tidier living room, drinking tea from mismatched china cups. Black bags were stacked up around them, waiting to be taken to the dump on Skye or given away to charity. The family heirlooms and sentimental trinkets remained, for now, until such time as Edith's legal heir - whomever that should prove to be - decided what to do with them.

Rachel had dragged through the old suitcase stuffed with photos and keepsakes, and was rifling through it absentmindedly. She'd suddenly remembered about the locket stashed in her desk drawer - the one that had been returned from the care home after Edith died - and was wondering if there were any clues in here as to who that little baby might be. It must have been precious to her if, out of everything in this house, that was the one personal item Edith hadn't wanted to leave behind.

"Would your mum remember any of these people," she asked Sorcha, passing her a black and white photo of a group of distillery operators from years gone by. The men all had moustaches and wore dark trousers with braces, standing in a row outside the stillhouse, arms folded across their chests and grim smiles on their faces.

"Probably," Sorcha replied, glancing at the picture. "Do you want me to ask her? She's a decade or so younger than Edith, but she might recognise some faces."

"I wish she'd written on the back of them," Rachel said, remembering how her granny had done that with old family photos. Names and dates and locations were always scrawled on the back in her narrow, slanted handwriting.

"Rach, this one could almost be you!" Una exclaimed, picking up a photo of a young couple standing by the front at Craigport.

Rachel took it from her. She had to admit; the short frame, shiny dark hair and rounded nose were similar.

"I wonder who it is?" Stephanie asked, peeking over her shoulder.

"It's Edith," Rachel said. She could tell straight away; the sharp eyes hadn't changed. The young man next to her had his arm around her, and they were both smiling. She was probably only in her early twenties, although Rachel always thought people in old photographs looked middle aged.

"Are you sure?" Sorcha said, taking the photo from her. "Huh," she exclaimed, glancing from Rachel back to the photo. "Una's right; she does kind of look like you."

"How strange," Stephanie said.

"If anything, you'd expect her to look like you, wouldn't you?" Sorcha replied, an edge of animosity in her voice.

"I take after my Mom," Stephanie said simply, not taking the bait. "Tall, and blonde."

Rachel turned the photo over in her hand. This one had been written on, although not by Edith. The words were Gaelic, and in an unfamiliar hand.

*Tha gaol agam ort,*
*Fionnlagh x*

"One of Edith's many suitors, then," Sorcha said, glancing over Rachel's shoulder while the others looked at her blankly. "It's Gaelic - 'I love you'. Mystery solved."

"I guess," Rachel replied. But something about the photograph had unsettled her, and as the rest of the girls tidied up and loaded the bin bags into Sorcha's car, she hung back, rescuing the photo from the box and slipping it into her pocket.

She went outside to wave Una and Sorcha off, but Stephanie was lingering awkwardly by her hire car.

"Thank you for today," she said again. "It meant a lot, just to see inside her home, and those old pictures... I really do appreciate it."

"No problem," Rachel replied. They hadn't come to any decision about what to do next, but for now at least, they had called a truce.

"And I'm sorry," Stephanie added. "About the things I've said before. I don't think you're a liar, or a thief."

"Okay," Rachel nodded again, waving an awkward farewell and turning to make her way home. "I'll see you around."

"Please remember that," Stephanie called after her, causing her to turn back. "Whatever else happens, please; just remember that I'm sorry. I never came here to hurt you."

Without saying anything else, Stephanie suddenly ducked into the car and was off as quickly as she could, wheels spinning against the tarmac.

"She got the hang of that gear stick, then," Rachel muttered to herself, heading down the hill towards home.

Rachel was awoken the following morning by an unprecedented banging on her front door. With her bedroom facing the back of the house, she had to throw on her dressing gown and rush downstairs to the front door to see what all the ruckus was about.

She was greeted on her doorstep by a flashing camera and a woman she didn't recognise, firing questions at her like a machine gun.

"Rachel McIntyre? Are you the manager here? May we have a word please? Isobel Lawrence, Glasgow Mail, mind if we come in?"

The woman was already shouldering her way in the door, and Rachel had to brace her arms against the frame to block her way. The camera was still in her face, flashing away incessantly

"Pardon me?" she asked. "What are you doing here?"

The woman sighed, exasperated. She was dressed in smart trousers and a blazer, her reddish-brown hair pulled back into a severe ponytail.

"Isobel Lawrence," she repeated, slowing down slightly. "I'm here from the Glasgow Mail. We're doing a story on Stephanie McLeod and her claim against the distillery; I just need to get your side of the story."

"Journalists?" Rachel asked numbly.

"Yes. I just need a few comments from you. What's your take on Stephanie's claim that she's the true heir? And did you influence the will of the former owner, in order to be named beneficiary yourself?"

"No!" Rachel declared, suddenly realising the severity of the situation. "No comment," she repeated, slamming the door shut and

- for the first time since her arrival on Inniscreag - turning the key in the lock behind her.

Just over an hour later, when Rachel should have been leaving for work, the journalist and her photographer were still standing guard by her front gate. She paced nervously by the door, unsure of what to do. Presumably, this was what Stephanie had been apologising for last night. Whatever compromise they might have reached suddenly seemed to have been blown out of the water. What was she playing at, getting the press involved?

Eventually, Rachel took a deep breath and marched out of her front door, head held high, as confidently as she could. Isobel and the photographer instantly flocked after her, but Rachel batted off each question with a calm "no comment", until she reached the sanctuary of her office and hurried inside.

Cameron was already there. "Who the hell are they?" he asked. "I saw them standing outside your house when I arrived."

"Journalists," she replied, filling him in on Stephanie's surprise visitors as briefly as she could.

"No way," Cameron sighed, disbelieving. "She sent the press after you? Why would she do that?"

"I've no idea," Rachel shrugged. "I didn't speak to them, and I don't intend to. Although the photographer must have got some very flattering snaps of me, half asleep in my goonie this morning."

They were interrupted by Hamish, who came storming into the room, as close to angry as Rachel had ever seen him.

"Rachel, I'm so sorry," he said. "She's just told me this morning."

"What is she doing?" Rachel demanded. "I thought we were going to try and settle all this amicably?"

"So did I," Hamish assured her. "She says she spoke to them a couple of weeks ago, when she thought everyone hated her; called and gave them a telephone interview. They're here for some photographs and a comment from you, apparently. If you'll give them one."

"Well, I won't."

"Good." He was pacing, as much as his large frame would allow in the small room. "I'm not having this, Rachel. Do you want me to see them off?"

"God, no, don't do that," Rachel begged. The last thing she

needed was Hamish assaulting members of the free press. "I just won't speak to them, that's all."

"Stephanie says she regrets it…"

"I'm sure she does."

"But I've told her we're over."

"What?" Rachel looked at him, shocked. His anger she had expected, but not that he would break up with Stephanie over it. If anything, now that the shock had passed, Rachel wasn't even really that angry. It was a stupid thing for Stephanie to have done, but she could see it in her face last night; that apology was genuine. She knew she'd screwed up.

"I told you Rachel, I'm not having it. She canna lie to us, go after one of our own like this, and then expect everything just to go back to how it was. Trying to drag you through the dirt in the tabloids? It's despicable. We're over."

He was breathing deeply, one solid fist pointing at Rachel. "This distillery is *yours*, just like Edith wanted, and we'll make damn sure it stays that way."

# CHAPTER 30

The story ran, inevitably, just over a week later. The residents of Inniscreag weren't the Glasgow Mail's usual target audience, but thanks to social media and online news websites, they were soon aware of the article's existence. The distillery was named and photographed, and Rachel was also mentioned, although thankfully they hadn't published any of the doorstep pictures of her in her dressing gown.

If Stephanie had thought airing her plight in the national press was going to win her some sympathy, she was sorely mistaken. The grudging acceptance of the Canadian incomer that had emerged - aided by her fleeting romance with Hamish - faded just as quickly. Of everyone, Rachel was surprised to find that she seemed to be the only one that had any sympathy for her. She'd done a stupid thing, because she was angry and emotional; Rachel could certainly relate to that.

A steady stream of supporters had made themselves known to Rachel in the couple of days since the story broke, and whilst she appreciated knowing that the small community had her back, to Rachel, nothing much had really changed. She was more annoyed at Kindred Spirits, for their role in bringing Stephanie to Inniscreag in the first place. And she still intended to do everything she could to prevent the distillery from falling into their hands.

Her plans to go over to Skye and discuss with Ruaridh how to actually do that had to be put on hold, however, when Rachel woke up in the middle of Tuesday night with terrible stomach cramps and nausea. After spending the next three hours mostly in the foetal position on her bathroom floor, there was no way she could contemplate being on the morning ferry to Uig by ten o'clock.

Instead, she spent the first half of the day curled up on the sofa in front of the telly, periodically sipping water until her tummy settled enough to tempt her into risking a bit of dry toast.

It was as she was shuffling back from the kitchen to the sofa, wrapped in her dressing gown and snuggly socks and still shivering, despite the fine summer's day outside, that the front doorbell rang. Putting her half-nibbled piece of toast down on the arm of the sofa, Rachel padded back through to the hallway to see who it was.

She was expecting Cameron, or perhaps Jenny with a bowl of warm soup from the cafe, having emailed first thing to explain the reason for her sudden change of plans. Instead, she opened the door to find herself looking at the suit-clad chest of a tall, dark haired figure.

"Duncan?" she said, stepping back in shock. "What are you doing here?" Rachel pulled her dressing gown closer around herself, and made a futile attempt to tidy her bedraggled, sweaty hair.

"I'm back," he said simply. He was smooth-shaven again, his thick hair neatly combed and the sharp smell of his aftershave wafting in on the breeze.

"Now's not a good time," Rachel began.

"I can see that." He smiled, stepping in the door without waiting for an invitation. "What's wrong with you?"

"I'm sick," Rachel replied. "You don't really want to be here," she continued, following him into the living room, where he was propping his briefcase against the sofa and sitting down as if he lived there. "It's a stomach bug. Probably highly contagious."

"I'll take my chances." Duncan flashed her another easy smile, leaning back and crossing his long legs. "I'm here on business, anyway. I won't get too close."

"Good," Rachel shot back, deciding that if he wasn't going to take no for an answer, then she might as well make the most of having him here.

"I've got some business to discuss with you, too, as a matter of fact" she said, sitting herself on the sofa opposite, and surreptitiously wiping away the toast crumbs.

Duncan looked surprised, and frowned at her curiously. "What business?"

"You told me you didn't go after Stephanie."

"I didn't."

"That's not what she says."

Duncan sighed. "Rach, I really don't have as much clout at work as you think I do. If they pursued her, that's news to me. I don't make these decisions. I just go where they send me, and represent the cases they assign me."

"Just following orders."

"Yes. Although not for much longer." His eyes dropped, and it was Rachel's turn to be confused.

"What do you mean?"

"When I got back yesterday, Stephanie informed me that she wishes to withdraw her claim against the distillery. As soon as I let my bosses know, I'll be called back to Edinburgh, and out of your hair for good."

"Oh," Rachel said, slumping back in her seat.

"Yup."

They sat in silence for a moment, neither sure what to say next. She should have been pleased; this meant the distillery was hers, no more questions asked. Life could carry on as normal. So why did she feel so disappointed?

Before she could say anything else, Rachel was forced abruptly from her seat by a rising queasiness in her tummy.

"I'm sorry…" she started, running across the room to the downstairs toilet and slamming the door shut behind her.

The offending toast having been thoroughly ejected from her stomach, Rachel was resting her head against the toilet seat when she felt a warm hand on her shoulder.

"Here," Duncan said quietly, reaching round and handing her a towel. She heard his footsteps make their way back out of the kitchen, before returning with a glass of water. He knelt down beside her.

"Sorry," she mumbled, embarrassed.

"Don't be."

Duncan reached out and peeled a damp strand of hair from her cheek, tucking it gently behind her ear. His hand stayed there, cupped gently around the back of her head as he looked at her.

"If you hadn't just thrown up," he started, but Rachel shrugged his hand away.

"Don't," she whispered.

Duncan sighed, standing and offering a hand to help her to her feet. She took it, but even once she was upright, he didn't let go.

"Rach," he began, "I was going to come here today anyway, and not to talk about the case. I wanted to explain things to you. I know the way we left things a few weeks ago wasn't… great. I know you were angry. And I owe you an explanation."

"No, you don't," she interrupted with a sigh. "I jumped the gun, as usual. I should have trusted you."

"It would have been nice," Duncan said with a smile. "But

there are a few things I need to tell you. Can I make you a cup of tea or something, and we can talk?"

Rachel was just about to accept his offer, when they were interrupted by another unexpected knock at the door.

"It'll just be Jenny," she said, heading to intercept her before she let herself in. "She said she'd pop over with some soup for me; I'll be back in a minute."

Rachel walked to the front door, part of her mortified that he'd heard her throw up, and the other part excited that he'd come back to see her after all. Whatever he had to tell her, surely it couldn't be that bad? He'd come back; that was all that mattered.

Rachel had opened the front door fully, mouth open ready to greet Jenny and send her away again as quickly as possible, when she got her second shock of the morning.

"Alright, babe? Long time no see."

Rachel had to put out a hand to steady herself, her brain battling with what her eyes were telling it. Because he shouldn't be here, but he was. He shouldn't even know where she lived, but obviously he'd found out. And now he was standing on her doorstep, with a holdall at his feet and an innocuous smile on his face, those brown, slanted eyes she'd once loved so much running lazily over her from top to toe.

"Well then?" he asked with a grin. "Aren't you going to invite me in?"

"Do you take milk?" Duncan's voice carried through from the kitchen. When Rachel didn't answer, he came round to check on her.

"Rach? Everything OK?"

The two men's eyes alighted on each other, and suddenly Rachel could hear her heart pounding in her ears as panic engulfed her.

"Duncan Fraser," he was saying, slipping into his easy, habitual smile and extending his hand to the other man before Rachel could do anything to intervene. "And you are...?" he asked, glancing awkwardly between this stony faced, unknown man and Rachel.

"I'm her husband," Graham said, muttering through an insincere smile. "Who the fuck are you?"

"Husband?" Duncan turned to her, his expression almost amused, as if he thought this was all one big joke. But then he saw the alarm in Rachel's eyes, and his face fell.

"Right then," he said, walking briskly back into the living room and grabbing his jacket and briefcase, Rachel spluttering helplessly at his back.

"Duncan, please, let me explain…"

He paused briefly, looking back at her, before shaking his head and letting out a bitter little laugh. "And you had the cheek to accuse me of being a liar."

Without another word, he strode past Graham, out of the door and down the garden path, not looking back.

# CHAPTER 31

"What the actual *fuck* are you doing here?" Rachel said, struggling to control the rising fury that was pressing against her chest, like a volcano waiting to erupt. All the while Graham was watching her, an amused grin on his stupid bloody face, which Rachel suddenly had the overwhelming urge to smack.

"Is that any way to speak to your husband?" he asked, grabbing the bag at his feet and stepping inside. Not wanting to have an all-out barney on her front doorstep, Rachel had little choice but to follow him into the house.

"I said, what are you doing here?" she repeated. Graham was standing in the middle of her living room, looking around.

"Nice wee place you've got here," he said. "Big place, actually. What is it, three bed? Miles better than the miserable flat share I've been stuck in, that's for sure."

Rachel ignored the dig, not wanting to be drawn into one of his rows. This was what he did - ignored her perfectly reasonable complaints, then ground her down until she gave up trying to get through to him. But not this time.

"I asked you what you're doing here?" she said again, trying to keep her voice calm. But once again he ignored her, unzipping his holdall and taking a couple of minutes to rummage through it instead.

When he eventually stood up, he was holding a newspaper in his hand. Wordlessly, he dropped it down onto the coffee table, his brown eyes watching her carefully.

It was a copy of the Glasgow Mail, of course. "Page twenty-three," he said, but Rachel refused to pick it up.

"That's how you found me, then?"

Graham shrugged. "What's a man to do when his wife chucks him out, then moves halfway across the country without telling him? You didn't leave me much choice, did you?"

"You could have taken the hint," Rachel replied, pacing back and forth across the room, suddenly full of restless, pent up energy. "You could have agreed to the divorce and put me out of my misery, instead of digging your heels in just for the sake of it."

Graham made a show of looking wounded. Round two of his

usual strategy had clearly begun - making her feel sorry for him.

"I haven't agreed to the divorce because I still love you," he said. "I understand you were angry, and you wanted me to change... I get that Rachel. And I can change. But I was gone barely a week, came home to try and speak to you, and you'd changed the locks and buggered off to the arse-end of nowhere without telling me! I'm still your husband."

"You had over a decade to start acting like my husband, instead of a useless bloody lodger. And now you want half of a property you never even contributed to? Is that why you're here; to talk me into giving you what you want? 'Cos if it is you can piss off. I'd sooner go to court and take my chances letting a judge decide."

Graham took a moment to wander around the room, looking out of the window and across the courtyard to the still house. "You're going to own all this soon," he said, turning back to her with a leer. "What's a wee high rise in Glasgow worth in comparison?"

"It's the principle," Rachel replied. "And if you'd read the bloody article, you'd know I might not own all this, so I'll need the proceeds from my wee high rise in Glasgow, thank you very much."

To her dismay, Graham sat down on the sofa.

He was square and stocky, not that much taller than her, and the jet-black hair she'd once loved running her fingers through was now shorn short and faded to a dull grey. He still looked good though, she had to admit; square jawed and tattooed, with a thick beard. A million miles away from Duncan, and his wholesome, clean cut appearance.

"I spoke to my lawyer the other day," Graham was saying, his tone conversational, although she sensed the thinly veiled threat coming. "He mentioned that if you inherit this pace while we're still married, *technically*, it becomes a marital asset. So, you could argue, that I'd be entitled to fifty percent of all this, too."

Rachel felt her heart sink, the righteous fury she'd felt just a moment before instantly deflated. She hadn't spoken to her own solicitor back in Glasgow in months. She'd been so preoccupied with everything on Inniscreag; this possibility had never even occurred to her.

"You can't be serious?" she asked. "You'd actually come here and try to take this, too?"

"You're my wife," Graham said, rising from his seat and

walking over to her. Rachel had lost the strength to fight, and didn't stop him when he took both of her hands in his. He glanced down at them, seeing the ring finger conspicuously bare.

"You can try to hide it all you like, but we're still married, you and me. The way I see it, you have two choices; you can take me back, and we can make a go of this new life together. I won't even ask any questions about lover boy back there. Or, divorce me." Graham's voice lowered to a whisper. "But I won't make it quick, Rocky." Rachel flinched at the old nick-name. She'd always hated it, but had never told him.

He went on. "And I won't make it easy. If you inherit this place while you're waiting to get rid of me, I'll fight you for half of it, along with half of everything else you own."

He paused, still holding her by the arms, and placed a kiss on her hair. "You look like you need some rest," he said, rubbing her arms and making her skin crawl, although she didn't have the strength to shrug him off. "I'll let you think about it, and you can call me in a few days. Unlike you, *I* haven't changed my number. I'll be staying at the pub."

He let her go then, picking up his bag and heading out the door without another word, leaving Rachel to crumple in a heap on the floor and cry.

Nausea and vomiting notwithstanding, Rachel was showered and on the afternoon ferry to Skye without a second thought. Two large bowls of kibble had been left on the back step for Doug, and after a quick chat on the phone with the hotel where she had been supposed to be staying that night anyway, Rachel had rearranged her booking and was now going to stay for the rest of the week and into the weekend, too. Anything to get away from Graham and give her a chance to think. She couldn't bear the thought of him being on the island. It was her safe place; the place that had brought her peace and refuge. More than anything, Rachel needed space and time to think, so she could be prepared before she had to face him again.

In the meantime, no doubt, Graham would charm everyone around him, like he always did. Only Una and Sorcha were aware of Rachel's true marital status; she'd never seen any need to divulge it to anyone else. If she'd been more open about it, maybe things with Duncan wouldn't have been irretrievably fucked up at the same time.

"You sure you're OK?" Cameron had asked, when a suitably wobbly and pale-faced Rachel appeared in the office just after lunchtime. She nodded.

"It's just a stomach bug," she said, trying to keep her voice light. "I'll sleep it off tonight and see Ruaridh in the morning; try and sort out what to do about the whole Stephanie situation. Then I thought I'd have a couple of days holiday on Skye. I need a wee break. The last few weeks have been manic; getting the coffee shop up and running, and everything." She watched him carefully, hoping he believed her.

Cameron's face broke into a broad grin. "I don't blame you," he said. "You've worked hard this last wee while; Jenny and I can keep things ticking over while you're away. Dinna worry about a thing."

"You can still call me if anything comes up," Rachel assured him.

Cameron nodded. "It'll be fine, lass. You have a wee rest and some time to yourself; you've earned it."

Just a couple of hours later, Rachel found herself standing on the tiny ferry bobbing across the water towards Skye, the late afternoon sun setting the outline of the Cuillins alight in an orange glow.

She breathed in deeply, keeping her eyes on the horizon ahead. Thankfully, the worst of the nausea had passed, blasted away beneath a cold shower after Graham had left. But every time the boat rolled, even slightly, she felt a threatening bubble rise at the back of her throat. Rachel was grateful when she drove off the other side, and along the familiar road from Uig to Portree.

Knowing that she and Graham were no longer sharing the same patch of ground, Rachel felt instantly lighter. The evening was mild and bright, and she rolled down her window as she coasted through the beautiful scenery and into the island's main settlement.

This was the right thing to do, Rachel decided, pulling into a parking space alongside the brightly coloured houses that lined the front of Portree. A few days away from everything to clear her head - no Graham, no Duncan, no one else to influence her decisions. She would have time to think, and on Sunday night she would go back to Inniscreag, ready to finally deal with all the shit she'd been trying to run away from.

# CHAPTER 32

Rachel arrived for her meeting with Ruaridh the following morning, not entirely sure what she was hoping to get out of it. Officially, the case with Stephanie was still going ahead. But after hearing from Duncan that she now intended to back out, Rachel was beginning to wonder whether this whole meeting was a waste of time.

"Not at all," Ruaridh assured her, as they sat in his office and he handed her a cup of coffee. The room was above a bakery, in one of the little coloured houses along the front - pink, in this case. The warm, buttery smell of freshly baked shortbread wafted up the stairs as they spoke, making Rachel's tummy rumble.

"It's important we're prepared," Ruaridh went on, shuffling through a pile of papers on his desk as Rachel sipped the coffee. It was watery and tasteless, but she swallowed it eagerly nonetheless. The little hotel where she was staying didn't do breakfast, and after eating practically nothing the day before, now she was ravenous. Her stomach tied itself in knots as the coffee hit it, and Rachel squirmed in her seat to try and cover up the sound of it rumbling.

"Until the claim is officially withdrawn, we proceed as if there's a case to answer. Although I doubt there will be, in this instance," Ruaridh said.

"You do?" Rachel asked, sitting up eagerly in her seat. "Why's that?"

"There's three elements to being able to prove a claim of facility and circumvention," Ruaridh explained, scribbling on a notepad and pointing to it with a stubby finger to punctuate his argument. He had a slightly abrasive manner, but if anything, it gave Rachel a reassuring glimpse of what he might be like in court. She didn't think he'd take any prisoners, that's for sure.

"First, you need to prove that the individual concerned was facile in the first place; that they were vulnerable to undue influence. This could be due to age, illness, injury, mental decline... In Edith's case, I presume, they'll be hanging most of their hopes on her age. Second," he went on, jabbing his finger at the next item on his scribbled list, "you need to prove, with evidence, that the person benefiting from the will - that's you, in this case - knowingly deceived

160

the testator, took advantage of their vulnerability and placed pressure on them to leave the will in such a way that benefits them."

"I didn't," Rachel interrupted. "There's no way they could prove that."

"I know," Ruaridh said, with an impatient sigh. "But even if there was, the third point here is the killer." He moved onto the last item on his list, a little gleam in his eyes. "The person challenging the will - Stephanie - has to show they have been harmed or suffered loss as a direct result of the circumvention. She hasn't..."

"Because Edith never knew she existed in the first place," Rachel finished, her heart soaring as the penny dropped.

"Exactly." Ruaridh was smiling at her properly now. "Edith could never have left the still to her, even if she'd wanted to, because she never knew about her. It's irrelevant whether she left it to you, specifically, or anyone else; as long as she left it to *someone*, and didn't die intestate, Stephanie would never have inherited it anyway."

"So, you don't think it'll even get to court?"

"Doubt it," Ruaridh said, leaning back in his chair and folding his arms over his belly. "And this little stunt she pulled getting the press involved; that won't have enamoured her to any of the judges around here, I can tell you that much. I reckon they'll throw it out, soon as look at it."

Rachel allowed herself a little smile, before her heart fell again. If Ruaridh was right, and this thing could all be settled soon, then what were the chances of her inheriting before her divorce with Graham was finalised? His threat had sounded tenuous, even to her, but was there really a chance he could stake a claim against the distillery too?

"Do you practice family law?" she asked casually.

Ruaridh shrugged. "Now and then," he said. "Why?"

Rachel took a deep breath, and filled him in as briefly as she could on the situation with Graham - his refusal to consent to the divorce, their argument over the division of her flat, and his threat over claiming half of the distillery as her legal husband.

"How long have you been separated?"

"Just over nine months."

"Right - unless you can prove unreasonable behaviour, you'll have to wait at least another three months to begin full divorce proceedings on the grounds of separation. Over a year, if he still won't agree to it. Since there's a dispute over property you'll likely have to go to court either way, unless you can come to some agreement privately. Have you tried mediation?"

Rachel shook her head.

"It might be worth a shot - easier and cheaper for everyone if these things can be settled out of court. I can recommend some organisations if you like? But I wouldn't worry about the distillery - inherited assets stay with the person they were bequeathed to, and you were already separated when Edith left it to you. No judge would class it as a marital asset. I suspect he's just trying to scare you into agreeing to his other demands."

The lawyer paused for a moment. "As for your granny's flat - that might be different. Yes, it was inherited by you prior to the marriage, but it was also the marital home. A judge could feel he's entitled to part of it. I really do think the two of you coming to an agreement privately would be your best course of action, if that's possible."

Rachel nodded. The thought of having to be married to Graham for another year was soul destroying, but it helped to know the distillery was safe. She wondered if just giving him half the flat might be the easiest solution after all? Whether or not she thought it was fair, if it sped things up a little, it might be worth it.

"Keep me in the loop," Ruaridh said, standing up and drawing their meeting to a close. He shook her hand, and gave her an uncharacteristically warm smile. "I'm happy to help in any way I can. As a friend," he added. "No charge."

"Thank you," Rachel replied, unexpectedly touched by the gesture.

She headed down the stairs and back out into the summer sunshine, the gentle island breeze tangling her hair. It had grown longer than she'd had it in years; her usual bob, after months on Inniscreag with no hairdresser, was now past her shoulders.

Rachel toyed with the idea of finding somewhere for a trim, but decided on breakfast instead. Catching sight of her reflection in a shop window and seeing how it framed her face in a shiny brown curtain, she realised that she quite liked it. Long hair could be part of her reinvention.

Wandering along the front to a cafe, Rachel treated herself to a cooked breakfast, and wondered how she should spend the rest of her time off. Having a few days to herself was an unexpected treat, and although she would rather not have had Graham arrive unannounced on her doorstep like that, maybe it would turn out to be a good thing? She'd been burying her head in the sand, wishing she could just run away from their marriage and forget it had ever happened. Clearly, that was naïve. She had to face up to it, and get him out of her life once and for all.

After breakfast, Rachel decided to walk off her full belly. The island was busy, the school holidays having just begun, and Skye's convenient bridge to the mainland making it one of the Hebrides' most popular holiday spots. She strolled happily amongst holiday makers, popping in and out of little gift shops and enjoying the relaxing, summer atmosphere.

She was coming out of one of those little tourist shops - having treated herself to a new necklace, handmade on the island by a local silversmith – when Rachel saw him. He was strolling in the sunshine, relaxed and happy, his checked shirt open and flapping in the wind. A pair of sunglasses concealed the bright green eyes, and one arm was around the shoulders of the woman walking beside him - dark and curvaceous, with curly hair - whilst his other arm was being clung to by a little girl. She was staring up at him, glasses perched on the end of her nose as she chatted happily, the wind blowing her dark ringlets haphazardly around her face. Duncan laughed at something she'd said to him, before releasing the woman at his side and scooping the little girl up into his arms for an impromptu hug.

Rachel froze, part of her brain willing her back inside the sanctuary of the shop, the other rooted to the spot as she stared at them, this oh-so-happy family that were rapidly advancing on her. She finally made up her mind to move, spinning on her heels to head back inside the shop she'd just exited, but it was too late. He'd seen her, and had frozen mid-sentence, staring back at her as the little girl by his side followed his gaze. The woman was looking at Rachel too, and back to Duncan, curiously.

Feeling the colour rise in her cheeks, along with a disorientating wave of shame at being confronted unexpectedly with his wife and child, Rachel abandoned her plan to hide in the shop, turned her back on them and marched down the street in the opposite direction instead.

She was prepared for him to ignore her; to walk past her, avoiding her eye and acting as if they had never met. She could have handled that, as much as it would have hurt. What she wasn't prepared for, however, was for him to chase her down the street calling her name.

"Rachel! Rach, wait up," Duncan cried, jogging towards her. She walked faster, not turning back, until he caught up to her and grabbed her by the elbow, spinning her round to face him.

"Rachel, it's me," he said, out of breath.

"What are you playing at?" she muttered, wrenching her arm out of his grasp. She glanced over his shoulder and saw the woman and girl following at a leisurely pace, a curious frown on his wife's pretty face. Blondes really weren't his type after all, Rachel thought.

"I just wanted to talk," he said. "I know I walked out on you the other day, and I shouldn't have. I should have given you a chance to explain, like I wished you'd given me…"

"You mean explain about your wife and child?" she fired back, as the pair got closer.

"And your husband?" he retorted. "I think it's clear we've both not been entirely honest with each other."

"And you want to have this conversation now, in public, in the middle of the street, and get your missus in on the chat as well?" Rachel whispered furiously, the woman and the little girl finally catching up with them.

"Hi," Duncan's wife said brightly, smiling a white toothed smile and tucking her dark wavy hair behind one ear. She looked a little older than Rachel had thought at first glance, but was impeccably dressed, in a black cotton dress and summer wedges, a lightweight cardigan draped elegantly over her olive-skinned shoulders. She was tall - nearly as tall as Duncan, with the heels - and Rachel felt small and scruffy next to her.

"I'm Morag," the woman said, filling the void left by Rachel's stunned silence, still flashing that relaxed, easy smile. Quite a familiar smile, Rachel suddenly thought, glancing back at Duncan.

"My sister," he said, watching her.

It was only then that Rachel realised she'd been holding her breath. Inhaling deeply, she glanced back and forth between the siblings. It was obvious, now that he said it; the green eyes were identical.

"And this is Violet," Duncan continued, gesturing to the little girl who smiled up at Rachel, displaying buck teeth and dimpled cheeks. Duncan took a deep breath.

"My daughter."

# CHAPTER 33

"You have a habit of popping up when I least expect you," Rachel said, cupping the warm mug of coffee in her hands.

"So do you," Duncan replied.

They were sitting in the window of a little cafe along the front, Rachel's frazzled nerves gradually recovering themselves. At Morag's insistence - having obviously sensed the weird tension between them - Duncan and Rachel had been dispatched to 'catch up' somewhere more private, whilst she took Violet to play down on the beach. Rachel could really have done with something stronger than coffee, but alcohol probably wasn't a wise addition to their situation right now.

"You have a daughter," Rachel observed.

"I do," Duncan nodded. "She'll be nine in December."

"She's beautiful."

"She is," Duncan smiled back at her. "And you have a husband."

"Technically..."

"He is not so beautiful." There was a twinkle in his green eyes. Despite the circumstances, Rachel couldn't help but laugh.

"I guess not," she admitted. "I'm sorry; I should have told you about him sooner."

"You should have. And I should have told you about Vi, too. We could have avoided rather a lot of unnecessary misunderstandings, if we'd been a bit more honest."

Rachel toyed with the spoon in her coffee, scooping the thick, frothed milk off the top and dropping it back in again. "So that really wasn't a girlfriend, or a wife, I heard you on the phone to that day?"

He shook his head, smiling at her. "Nope. That was Vi."

"Sorry, again," Rachel replied, exhaling deeply. "Another stupid, rash judgement."

Duncan reached across the table and took her hand in his.

"You're not the only one who makes them," he said. "I'm sorry for storming out when your husband - ex-husband? - showed up like that. I should have given you a chance to explain. I was going to come back, but I'd already arranged for Morag to bring Violet here to meet me, now that the school term is over, and I didn't want to let her down..."

"It's OK," Rachel said, squeezing his hand. Suddenly everything made sense, from that first overheard phone call, where he'd spoken with such warmth and affection to the person on the other end of the line, to the mysterious trips home and family commitments. Rachel was amazed she hadn't clicked sooner, but then she'd been blinded by stupid, petty jealousy. "Do you have shared custody?"

Duncan shook his head. "Her mum left just before her second birthday. Having a kid wasn't what she'd hoped it would be, apparently." His voice was matter of fact; not bitter or accusatory, as Rachel might have expected.

"She gets the odd postcard or telephone call, but apart from that it's been just me and Vi for nearly seven years now."

"Wow," Rachel breathed. She couldn't fathom what would make a woman, who'd been lucky enough to have a child in the first place, decide to leave it. "So, while you've been up here...?"

"She's been staying with Morag, in Edinburgh. Morag's kids are all grown up now - one's at uni, the other's travelling - so she looks after Vi when I'm not able to. It's school holidays now, and Morag's a teacher, so she said she'd bring Violet up to Skye for a few weeks. Make it easier for me to see her more."

While he'd been talking, their fingers had intertwined, and his thumb was now rubbing the back of Rachel's hand. She couldn't believe she hadn't trusted him, and that she'd come so close to fucking this up.

Duncan was looking down at her fingers, where they rested in his own. The dent had smoothed out, but the little line where her ring had been was still paler than the skin around it. His mouth curved upwards in a small smile.

"I take it you and your husband..."

"Separated," Rachel confirmed. "Over nine months ago. I left him just before I moved to Inniscreag. He wasn't supposed to know where I was, but then Stephanie did that story with those journalists from Glasgow..."

His eyes widened as realisation dawned. "Ah, shit... this is all because of Stephanie?"

Rachel nodded. Duncan was leaning across the table, and his

voice lowered to a gentle whisper. "Why didn't you tell him where you'd gone?" he asked. "Was it because he… hurt you?"

"Oh, God, no," Rachel said. "Nothing like that - he's not dangerous. He's just a twat, and I didn't want him chasing after me, trying to change my mind. He's been refusing to agree to the divorce, and now that he thinks I'm about to inherit a distillery…"

"He wants you back."

"Not me," Rachel said. "Not really. He just wants someone to look after him. And I'm not going to be that person," she added. "Not anymore."

"Good," Duncan replied with a grin.

He sat up suddenly, letting go of her hands and waving out of the window. Violet was there, curls bobbing around her face as she jumped up and down and waved excitedly at her father. Morag stood beside her, an apologetic smile on her face.

"Can I take you out for dinner tonight?" Duncan asked, digging out his wallet and leaving a ten-pound note on the table. "Morag won't mind watching Violet, and I'd like us to clear the air, properly."

Rachel smiled up at him. "I'd like that, too," she said.

Duncan reached out impulsively and touched her cheek, before remembering his daughter was watching him through the window and retracting his hand quickly. He gestured outside with a nod of his head. "I'll meet you by the harbour, seven o'clock?"

"OK," Rachel nodded. "I'll see you tonight."

"Can't wait."

# CHAPTER 34

After that, Rachel found the rest of her day was rather quickly eaten up by a flurry of trips around the local shops, followed by a long, hot soak in the bath back at her hotel room. She'd been to the chemists to buy razors, shaving cream and hair dye, as well as a tub of body cream, foundation and some new perfume.

There weren't any mainstream clothes stores on the island, but she struck it lucky in one of the little charity shops and managed to find a mid-length, floral print dress in her size, with flattering flutter sleeves and a plunging, button neckline. Rachel looked at the label; it was French Connection, and only five pounds. Deciding it was meant to be, she grabbed it without trying it on, hoping it would look okay with the lace up canvas flats she'd packed, and her denim jacket. Pretty enough to look like she'd made an effort, without being overly dressy.

By the time she emerged from her room at just before seven o'clock, Rachel had been shaved and buffed and moisturised from top to toe. The natural chestnut brown of her hair had been suitably 'refreshed', and with a full face of makeup and her new second-hand dress on - which fit like a glove - Rachel was actually feeling pretty confident.

He was waiting for her, as promised, by the harbour; leaning casually against the old stone wall, long legs stretched out in front of him and hands in the pockets of his jeans. Rachel was pleased to see he hadn't shaved; she liked him with his five o'clock shadow.

Duncan turned to her as she approached, arms wide and a smile on his face, drawing her into a hug and placing a kiss on her cheek. "You look beautiful," he said, and the expression in his eyes when he looked at her actually made Rachel believe him.

He took her hand as they strolled together along the front, making small talk.

"Where are we going?" Rachel asked eventually, suddenly getting the feeling that their aimless stroll, lovely as it was, wasn't leading them anywhere in particular.

"Nowhere too fancy, I'm afraid," Duncan admitted. "But I thought we should make the most of the beautiful evening."

They'd wandered along the front, past the picture-postcard

painted houses by the harbour, and were now standing in front of a row of ordinary looking buildings which housed various shops and cafes, including the one they'd sat in earlier. It was closed now, but next door there was a fish and chip shop. The smell of batter and frying potatoes wafted temptingly out into the evening air. Duncan stopped outside it and looked at her sheepishly.

"A chippie?" she asked.

"Is that alright?"

"Of course!" Rachel didn't need to pretend; she'd take a good seaside chippie over a fancy restaurant any day.

They went in and Duncan ordered them both a fish supper, which was made fresh to order. He sat on the windowsill as they waited, pulling Rachel down into his lap.

That feeling he gave her of being a teenager once again washed over her. She was giddy, her arm around his shoulder, fiddling with the little tuft of hair at the nape of his neck, while one of his hands rubbed absentmindedly up and down her bare shin.

They didn't speak; she just rested her head on top of his and enjoyed the sensation of being with him. Rachel couldn't remember feeling this relaxed around anyone else before. Her usual nerves had been replaced with a sense of security and contentment.

When the fish suppers were ready, they carried them down to the beach, Duncan popping into a corner shop on the way and returning with two cans of cider.

"Classy," Rachel commented with a smile.

"Only the best for you," he said, drawing her in with his free arm and kissing her properly for the first time all day.

The beach at the front in Portree did not have the white sands of nearby Harris, or the shiny, cascading pebbles that characterised the shores of Inniscreag. The beach here was made up of mostly loose, greyish shingle marked with trails of seaweed, showing the tidelines of the advancing waves. Not the most romantic beach anyone could have envisaged, but Rachel didn't care.

Duncan took off his jacket, laying it on the ground for her to sit on, before plonking himself down beside her and unwrapping their newspaper parcels of steaming hot battered fish and chunky, golden chips.

"Something light and refreshing for the lady?" he asked, presenting her with the can of cider balanced on his forearm, as if he were the sommelier at a fancy restaurant.

Rachel giggled. "Thank you, sir."

He opened it, cracking the seal with a fizz, before raising his own can. "Cheers," he said. "Here's to us, finally having a proper date."

"Is this what you call a proper date?" Rachel teased.

Duncan lay back on one elbow, propping himself up on the pebbles and breaking off a bit of fish before he spoke. "If I'm with you, and we're alone, under a beautiful sky, with food and drink... then it's a date."

"I'll drink to that," Rachel answered.

They ate in silence for a while, listening to the gentle lapping of the waves at the shore, and the cry of seagulls far above. One or two crept close, pecking at the ground and watching them with interest, but other than that they were alone. It was a beautiful night, and behind them Rachel could hear couples and families out walking along the front, but no one else ventured onto the beach.

When they had finished, Duncan cleared away their wrappers and drew Rachel into his arms. He kissed her again, one hand soft against her cheek. "Get comfy," he said, encouraging her to lie with her head in his lap as he toyed with the long strands of her hair.

"I'll fall asleep if you keep that up," she said, lulled by the nearby ocean and the gentle sensation of his hand stroking her head.

"Well we can't have that," he replied, withdrawing his hand from her hair and letting it run down her side instead, squeezing her hip gently. "What I had in mind for later very much involved you being awake."

Rachel wriggled beneath his touch, feeling a pleasant tingle of anticipation.

They stayed tangled up on the beach, alternating between kissing and talking, as the sun began its slow and gentle descent towards the horizon. Rachel found out he was allergic to strawberries, and she told him about the time, back in her waitressing days, when she'd accidentally poured an entire pizza into a customer's handbag. It was all quite superficial still, but it was nice. Eventually, however, conversation shifted to deeper topics.

"Don't you hate her?" Rachel asked, when Duncan casually mentioned his ex-wife, and she was once again blown away by the calmness in his voice. "For leaving you. And Violet?"

Duncan shrugged. "I think I did, for a while. But then I realised, what's the point in using up all my energy hating someone who'll never change? It won't achieve anything, other than making me feel like shit. And besides, I'm the lucky one. I get to spend every minute I have with Vi - still not as much time as I'd like, granted, with work and everything. But her mum's the one who's really missing out. If anything, I feel sorry for her."

Rachel sighed, amazed at his magnanimous attitude. "You're a better person than me," she said.

"I don't think so," he replied, his hand snaking around her waist as he pulled her closer. "What about your ex?" he asked, punctuating his question with a little kiss on her hair. "What's the story there?"

"We were too young," Rachel replied, honestly. "And I wasn't in a good place. My Mum hadn't long died, followed by my Granny, then Graham showed up…" she sighed, wondering how to explain it. "I guess I needed something to hold on to, and just grabbed the first person that came along."

"You were together a long time though? There must have been something keeping you with him."

Rachel looked up at him, wondering if a little bit of him was jealous, and how honest she should be. This was technically a first date, but she felt like she knew him, and trusted him, already.

"I wanted a baby," she said. "A proper family, like the one I'd never had. I wanted to be a mum…" she stopped, her voice suddenly thickening and that little lump of grief she kept locked deep inside threatening to break forth.

"It's okay," Duncan murmured, his lips brushing her hair and the fingertips of one hand gently caressing her shoulder.

Rachel sniffed, embarrassed. She couldn't believe she was greeting like a baby, on their first proper date. This really would scare him off.

"I kept thinking that if we could just have a baby then we'd make it work. But every time it would happen, I'd lose them…" she stopped again, choking down a sob.

"Shhhh," Duncan whispered, enveloping her in his arms, strong and steady against the waves of her sadness. "I'm here. You don't have to hold it in."

Those were the words she'd waited years to hear someone

say, and the minute he'd spoken them Rachel couldn't contain it any longer; she sobbed against his chest while he held her, unwavering, murmuring in her hair and stroking her back until she was spent.

When the crying had slowed to a sniffle, Rachel pulled away from him, rubbing the damp patches she'd left on his shirt.

"Sorry," she sniffed.

"Don't worry about it," he replied, smiling at her kindly. "I'm sorry you went through all that."

Rachel shrugged, opening her mouth to dismiss it, the way she always did. There were lots of people who'd been through worse than she had; they weren't really 'babies' in the first place. Those were the mantras she'd chanted, over and over again, as the years went by, trying to talk herself out of the darkness.

Duncan spoke before she could.

"Don't brush it aside," he said, turning her to look at him. "They were your babies, just like Violet is mine. You're allowed to grieve for them."

Rachel nodded mutely, burying her face in his neck and clinging to him, not trusting herself to speak.

"Thank you," she whispered eventually. Duncan was silent, just squeezing her closer in response.

# CHAPTER 35

They lay together on the shingle until the sky deepened to turquoise, and the breeze around them grew chill. They must have drawn some looks from the passers-by on the street above, but Rachel didn't care. With her head on Duncan's chest, and his hands in her hair, she could have lain there forever.

Eventually, though, he stretched out his long limbs, and rolled her half on top of him for a kiss.

"Your hands are like ice," he said, flinching when she slipped them beneath his shirt and onto the contours of his torso. "I think we should get somewhere warmer."

"I agree," Rachel replied.

The town had emptied as the hour grew late. Duncan and Rachel strolled along the deserted street towards her hotel, stopping periodically to kiss, their bodies pressed together.

"Don't you need to get back for Violet?" Rachel breathed half-heartedly against his mouth. They had stopped outside the door of her hotel, Duncan pushing her hungrily up against the wall. He paused.

"Do you not want to…?" He let go of her suddenly, his eyes clouded with worry. "I'm sorry if I've moved too fast," he said, taking a step back. "I just assumed…"

"No, no, it's not that," Rachel said, taking his hands and pulling him back to her. "I do want to. I just… thought I should ask. I wouldn't like to think she was worried, wondering where you were."

Duncan smiled, stroking one hand over her hair and smiling. "You're very sweet," he said, "but Violet will have gone to bed hours ago. As long as I'm home by breakfast, she won't know a thing."

He lowered his mouth to her neck, nibbling gently down towards her shoulder. Rachel shivered, the gentle scratching of his stubble against the soft skin intoxicating.

"We'd better get inside then," she whispered, opening the door and pulling him up the stairs behind her.

They fell on each other the minute they were in her room, Duncan pulling her jacket off while Rachel kicked off her shoes. He lifted her into his arms, cupping her bum, Rachel wrapping her legs around his waist before they collapsed together onto the bed. Rachel was pulling his shirt open, when suddenly a button popped off and bounced across the wooden floor.

"Sorry!" she giggled, shifting her attention to the belt of his jeans instead, unfastening it and pulling them down. Meanwhile Duncan had undone the top couple of buttons of her dress, revealing her bra. He cupped her breasts together and squeezed gently.

"God, I want you," he whispered urgently, his teeth scraping her flesh.

"Take me then," she replied, pulling him to her. Rachel wrapped her legs around him, and Duncan pushed her dress up around her waist. This time, he wasn't gentle, and Rachel cried out.

"Shit, are you okay?" he asked, stopping and looking down at her with concern.

"Yes," she breathed, smiling up at him and wrapping her arms around his back, urging him closer. "Don't stop."

Rachel lost herself in the sensation of him inside her, and the pressure of his body on top of her as he moved deeper. It was fast and urgent, and before long he came, burying his head in her neck and biting gently into the soft skin as his breath came in short, ragged gasps.

She held him on top of her for a moment, running her fingers down the smooth, shallow dip of his spine, to the little hollow just above his bum. Duncan smiled, gently resting his forehead against hers and stroking her cheek with one hand, his green eyes looking intently into her own. For a moment, it felt like he was going to say something, but he stopped himself, rolling off of her instead.

"It's times like these I wish I smoked," he grinned, settling back on the pillows. His dark hair was dishevelled, the shirt half undone to reveal the top of his lightly defined chest. Rachel sat up to look at him for a moment.

"What?" he asked, eyes dancing in amusement.

"You're gorgeous," she admitted.

"You're not so bad yourself," he replied with a playful smile.

"No, I mean it," Rachel persisted. "You're like, objectively, movie star, kind of handsome. I'm... presentable, at best. What are you doing, slumming it with me?" She tried to keep her voice light and jokey, but knew she'd failed from the way his expression immediately changed.

Duncan tilted his head to one side, frowning at her. "You're serious?" he said quietly. Rachel nodded.

"Come here." He spread one arm wide and urged her to cuddle in beside him. "Do you know what I thought, the first time I saw you?"

"Doesn't she look practical?"

"Shut up," he scolded lightly, squeezing her closer. "I thought, who's this gorgeous, curvy wee brunette, with the big brown eyes, pouty little lips, and great tits?"

Rachel laughed. "Even with the anorak?" she asked.

"*Especially* with the anorak," he teased. "As a matter of fact, I don't suppose you brought it with you...?"

He started to get out of bed, heading for the wardrobe, but Rachel pulled him back. "Shut up yourself," she whispered, kissing him. They sank into the embrace for a minute, the kiss deepening as Rachel felt another surge of desire begin to grow.

"It occurs to me," Duncan said, pulling away slightly and looking at her, "that whilst I am fully satisfied and, let's be honest, probably out of commission for a little while; I wonder if you might have any needs that haven't quite been seen to yet?" His hands ran over her breasts as he spoke, slowly pulling at the nipples beneath the lacy fabric of her bra. Rachel sighed and closed her eyes.

"There's one way to find out," she breathed.

He was as attentive and thorough as he'd been the first time they slept together, taking his time to peel her clothes off gently one layer at a time, until Rachel thought the anticipation might kill her.

He kissed her tenderly on the lips, before moving to her ear and down her neck, planting little kisses and nibbles over her collarbone and down towards her breasts. When he reached these, he cupped them together, taking the time to roll each nipple between his teeth, applying just enough pressure to make Rachel squirm beneath him.

His lips travelled over her belly, and this time she let him, without trying to cover it up, until he parted her legs. He was gentle at first, responding to her moans and movements, guiding him gently to the right spot to begin increasing the pressure. Rachel felt the intensity build inside her, her hands in his hair, until she came in undulating waves, her back arched and her body trembling beneath him.

"Better?" Duncan asked, looking very pleased with himself.

He crept back up the bed to find Rachel, sweaty and breathless, her hair strewn across her face in damp strands.

"You sure you're done?" he teased, trailing one hand gently between her legs and making her jump.

"Definitely," she replied, squirming away from his touch and giggling.

"Good," he replied, kissing her. "Can't leave a job half done."

Rachel smiled, sinking back onto the pillow alongside him, a deep sense of fulfilment settling over her that she hadn't felt in quite some time; possibly ever. It could just have been the post-coital glow - hormones, oxytocin and all that - but deep down, she suspected it might be something more.

They must have dozed off then, because when Rachel awoke the room was bathed in a strange glow. This far North, in the height of summer, it wasn't unusual for the sky to remain bright late into the night. But when Rachel glanced at her watch, she knew they should have been in the middle of the brief, fleeting hours of darkness. It wasn't the streetlights below, either, or a passing car; this light was green, and moved in organic, rippling waves. She climbed out of bed, pulling a sheet around her, and crept to the window.

Drawing aside the curtain, Rachel was met with quite possibly the most beautiful sight she had ever seen. It was like the sky was alive; ribbons of light were travelling across it, pulsing and moving in shades of deep green and blue, shot through with streaks of pink.

"What are you looking at?" Duncan asked from behind her, rising from the bed and rubbing his eyes sleepily.

"Put your boxers on," Rachel urged in a hushed whisper, turning to find him standing, in all his glory, stark naked in front of the open window. "It's the Northern Lights."

Duncan tiptoed up behind her and wrapped his arms around her waist, his modesty now suitably protected.

"Wow," he breathed against her hair, kissing it gently before resting his chin on top of her head as they took in the sight.

"This place really is magic," Duncan said eventually.

Rachel smiled. "Not such a city boy anymore, then? Have we converted you?"

She felt him nodding his head above her, both of them still enthralled by the swaying lights outside their window.

"I think you might have. The last few times I've been home,

it just hasn't felt right anymore. The noise and the smells and the people… They never bothered me before, but now… I can't explain it. I'm restless there. Whereas here, I feel at peace. As if I've found something that I never knew was missing in the first place."

He wrapped his arms tighter around Rachel. She wanted to say something; she wanted to tell him that she knew exactly how he was feeling. She wanted to tell him that it wasn't just the spell of the islands that had made her feel that way; it was him. But she was scared, and so instead she leaned gently into the comfort of his strong chest, and the feel of his arms around her, and silently watched the dancing sky above them.

# CHAPTER 36

Duncan crept back to his AirBnB just after three o'clock, waking Rachel with a gentle kiss.

"I didn't want to leave without saying goodbye," he said, stroking her hair. "Don't get up; I've left my number on the side."

He gestured over to where a little notepad sat next to the phone on the bedside table. "Call me later? I wondered if you might want to join us for lunch?"

"Are you sure?" Rachel asked, sitting up with a frown. "What about Violet?"

"She'll love you," he said simply, kissing her once more on the head, before quietly sneaking out of the room and down the stairs to the street below.

When Rachel woke later, she might have believed that last part had been a dream, if it weren't for the fact that when she went to check, his number was indeed there, scribbled on the pad alongside his name. His full name, at that; as if she might have had some other Duncan creeping out of her bed in the wee small hours of the morning and leaving his phone number on the bedside table.

Rachel smiled. They'd had no need of phones on Inniscreag, the tiny community meaning they always managed to bump into each other without really trying. Something about tapping his number into her phone and pressing save suddenly made the whole thing feel real.

She dialled it around eleven o'clock, when she'd had a shower, dressed and eaten a breakfast of smoked salmon and scrambled eggs in the same cafe as the day before. Ordinarily, she'd never have called a guy so soon after their first date, but it was him who had mentioned having lunch.

Rachel was surprised at the warmth in his voice when he realised it was her; she'd half expected him to freak out and back pedal, withdrawing the invitation or making up some kind of excuse not to see her.

"How are you?" Duncan asked

"I'm good." Her voice caught in her throat. Rachel was suddenly reminded of the time when she was thirteen, before the world of mobile phones and social media, when she'd finally plucked up the courage to phone David Paterson from her French class and

179

ask him out. He'd said no, unsurprisingly. Everyone had fancied David Paterson.

"Free for lunch?"

"If you're sure, I mean, I don't want to intrude…"

"Don't be daft. Morag's desperate to meet you properly, and Violet's a chatterbox. She'll just be happy to have someone new to talk to."

He invited her to drive out to their AirBnB, which was in the south of the island, near a little hamlet named Torrin. Morag was insisting on cooking, apparently, and there was a stretch of coastline a short walk away that Violet enjoyed playing on. Rachel agreed, and after a quick pop into the corner shop to pick up a bottle of wine - she didn't want to turn up empty handed, after all - she was in the car, windows down, and the refreshing island breeze in her hair.

Following the directions Duncan had given her over the phone, Rachel had been expecting to find a little cottage on the outskirts of a village, overlooking the water. Whilst she was correct on the last two counts, the AirBnB Duncan and his family were renting was anything but little, and certainly not a cottage.

It was a double height, modern structure, with a dramatic view over Loch Slapin towards the Isle of Eigg. Rachel pulled in at the back, to find a large but relatively ordinary looking box, rendered in white plaster with crisp, anthracite window frames and a bright green door. On the other side, however, where the house faced onto the water, it boasted a full height, apex window, affording the inhabitants jaw-dropping views that ran the full height and width of the building.

Duncan greeted her at the green back door, which led through a utility room about the same size as Rachel's living room, and into a stunning, glossy, white kitchen. The ceiling here was lower, studded with spotlights, and rose to the full height of the house where the kitchen extended into the open plan living and dining room. A huge, free standing wood burner was lit at one side of the large room, while the rest was stylishly furnished with low-backed sofas and a minimalist white dining table surrounded by eight chairs, each a different colour.

"This place is amazing," Rachel breathed, Duncan's hand light on her hip as he led her into the room. He'd planted a chaste kiss on her cheek by the front door, and remained close by her side, the gentle touch just enough to reassure her.

Morag was stirring something at the hob, an apron covering her summer dress and her bronzed limbs exposed. She too greeted Rachel with a kiss, graciously accepting the bottle of wine and saying how pleased she was that Rachel could join them.

Up close, and in a calmer frame of mind to notice it, the similarity to Duncan was striking; they each had the same straight, pointed nose, bright green eyes framed by long lashes, and dark hair. Morag's curled effortlessly around her shoulders in a way that reminded Rachel of a beautiful, exotic gypsy.

"Can I get you a drink?" Morag was asking, the smell of what Rachel suspected was freshly baked bread filling the room.

"White wine, please."

"And lemonade," Duncan added, opening the door to the huge, American style fridge freezer. Rachel cringed. Morag was so elegant and mature; she was probably one of those people who thought adding lemonade to wine was tantamount to heresy.

"Don't blame you," Morag said with a smile, taking the proffered bottle of lemonade from her brother. "I'm not a wine drinker, myself. I prefer vodka."

Rachel smiled, feeling more at ease. Morag mixed herself a vodka and orange juice, and poured a glass of red for Duncan.

"Cheers," she said, the three of them raising their glasses.

"Where's Violet?" Rachel asked, taking a sip and feeling the warmth of the wine settle comfortingly in her belly, belatedly realising that she'd brought the car. It was fine, she told herself; it was still early, and she'd only have one. By the time they'd had lunch, she'd be fine to drive home later.

"In her room," Morag replied, returning to the stove. "She's a bookworm; back home, we have to bribe her to get her out in the fresh air. But she loves the beach here – such a big change from life in Edinburgh. We'll take a walk down after lunch."

"It smells delicious," Rachel said.

Duncan was sitting at one of the stools by the kitchen island, and gestured for Rachel to do the same.

"Is there anything I can do to help?" she asked, perching on the stool next to his and feeling the reassuring warmth of his palm against her thigh.

"No, thank you - I'm better left alone when I'm cooking,"

Morag said with a laugh. "Too much of a control freak. You two go and sit on the sofa, enjoy the view. I'll call you when it's ready."

Duncan and Rachel did as they were told, taking a seat before the wall to ceiling glass windows that gave them a panoramic view of the loch. The water was calm today, reflecting the clear cobalt blue of the sky above.

Duncan slipped an arm around her shoulder, brushing her hair gently to one side. "You look lovely, as always."

Rachel opened her mouth to dismiss the compliment - she was just in skinny jeans, trainers and a blouse, after all - but stopped herself.

"Thank you," she said instead. "Your sister's beautiful. Good looks obviously run in the family."

Duncan smiled, one hand rubbing her shoulder.

They were interrupted by the sudden clattering of footsteps on the wooden floor in the hallway, as Violet came bounding down from upstairs. "Is she here, Daddy?"

Duncan smiled. "In here, sweetheart."

Rachel was suddenly overcome with nerves, but she needn't have worried - Violet proved to be a happy, friendly, chatty little girl, who wasn't the least bit perturbed by this strange woman gate crashing her holiday. In fact, she seemed rather excited by the new arrival.

"Vi, this is Rachel. She's a friend of Daddy's."

"Hello," Violet said, smiling at Rachel brightly as she gripped onto the arm of the sofa, swinging back and forth. She was wearing the glasses from the day before, her wild hair frizzing around her face in a halo of dark curls, a handful of freckles dappling the bridge of her nose.

Rachel smiled back. "I love your tee-shirt," she said. The little girl was dressed in pink jeans and what looked to be a hand-crocheted cardigan with rainbows on it. But underneath, her white tee-shirt was emblazoned with a slogan; *Though she be but little, she is fierce.* "Shakespeare, right?"

Violet's grin broadened at the comment, and Rachel silently congratulated herself.

"*A Midsummer Night's Dream,*" Violet said. "Do you know it?"

"Not as well as I should," Rachel admitted.

"I'll go get it," Violet said, turning and scampering excitedly back up the stairs. When Rachel looked back over at him, Duncan was smiling.

"Well played," he said, reclining in his seat and crossing one long leg over the other. "Recognising a Shakespeare quote earns you major brownie points with my daughter."

"How old is she again?" Rachel asked.

"Almost nine. She's... advanced, in certain areas. Not so much in others. In the absence of a mother figure, Morag has taken it upon herself to ensure my daughter has a suitably thorough literary - and feminist - education."

"I'm a lecturer," Morag explained, bringing them over a tray of olives, cheese and posh little crackers. "University of Edinburgh - Literature, Feminism and Gender Studies."

"Wow," Rachel said, feeling suddenly inadequate once again. She'd barely scraped four passes in her Highers.

Morag shrugged. "I mainly do it for the holidays," she said with a smile. "I was able to spend every summer with my own kids, when they were little. Now I get to spend them with Vi."

"How many kids do you have?" Rachel asked.

"Twin boys, all grown up now. One's on a gap year in Cambodia; the other's at uni in Glasgow and just moved in with his girlfriend. The way things are going, I could be a granny, before long," she added, with a wide-eyed grimace.

Rachel struggled to picture this glamourous, exotic woman as a grandmother. "You must have had them very young," she said.

"Twenty-five," Morag said with a shrug. "Not much older than they are now. Can't imagine either of them raising one baby on their own, let alone two."

"Oh. Is their dad not...?"

"Not on the scene," Morag confirmed, taking another sip of her Screwdriver before popping a large, green olive in her mouth. "Legged it, as soon as he saw the positive pregnancy test. My little brother and I seem to share a knack for picking arseholes with whom to procreate."

She grinned at Duncan, but Rachel felt the edge of warning behind her words; Morag may have been gracious, and friendly, but it was clear she was also fiercely protective.

Violet reappeared then, a huge tome grasped in her skinny, bird-like arms, and Rachel spent the next half an hour curled up beside her on the sofa, as she read aloud and told Rachel all about her favourite plays.

"Have you ever seen any, in the theatre?" Rachel asked.

Violet shook her head. "Daddy says he'll take me, one day. But he's always busy at work."

"Well your Daddy has a very important job," Rachel replied.

"Nothing's more important than you, though, sweetheart." Duncan dropped a kiss on his daughter's curly head, passing the sofa on his way to fill up Rachel's drink. "We'll go when this case is finished, I promise."

"He always says that," Violet whispered, when her father had returned to the kitchen. She smiled at Rachel; a perceptive little grin that didn't quite match her age.

"But it's okay. He has to work to pay for my school, and our house, and all my clubs and things, so I understand."

Rachel felt her heart sink for her a little, but Violet was very matter of fact about it. She thought back to Duncan's comment about Rachel's own childhood, and it being lonely, and wondered if that was a worry he was trying to combat for his daughter.

Morag called them to the table just then, which was now laden with food. She was carrying a steaming casserole dish filled with some kind of spicy stew, and on the table there sat a huge bowl of fragrant rice and a homemade, elaborately plaited loaf.

"Wow," Rachel breathed, for what felt like the millionth time. "This looks incredible." Duncan came up beside her, slipping his arm around her waist briefly, while Violet was at the bathroom washing her hands. "Is this a normal Friday afternoon lunch for you lot?"

He kissed her shoulder gently. "Morag may have gone to a wee bit more effort than usual," he whispered, "but don't let on. I think she wants to impress you."

"She's succeeded," Rachel replied. "But I'd be impressed with any meal that didn't come out of the freezer, so the bar wasn't set very high to begin with. She could have saved herself some effort."

Duncan gave her one last squeeze, as Violet wandered back into the room and they all took their seats. "She knows I like you; you're worth it."

"Bon Appetit!" Morag declared, gesturing for them all to dig in.

"I don't know where to start," Rachel admitted. "It all looks so good."

"Have some goulash." Morag rose from her seat to spoon some of the smoky, spicy stew onto Rachel's plate without waiting for an answer. "It's Anyu's secret recipe," she added, smiling across the table at Duncan.

"Anyu?" Rachel asked, scooping some into her mouth; it was delicious.

"Mum," Duncan explained. "Our mum was from Hungary."

Rachel spent the rest of the meal hearing about their family history. Both of Duncan's parents had now passed away, but his Hungarian mother had been an impressive linguist. She'd been a translator across Europe, before meeting her husband and retraining as a secondary school teacher, so she could have more time with her children. Their father had been a GP at the local medical surgery. The Fraser siblings' childhood sounded like everything Rachel had dreamed of; stable, and loving, and uneventful.

It was after they'd finished the main course - when Rachel's offer to do the dishes had been rebuffed and Morag was bringing them each a large portion of raspberry roulade topped with whipped cream - that it suddenly hit her. Violet was regaling them all with an in-depth assessment of the book she'd just finished, offering a detailed critique of the author's perceived failings. Her aunt and her father were asking questions and, occasionally, gently teasing her. Rachel was content just sitting quietly and sipping her wine, listening to their easy, relaxed conversation.

That was when she realised - this is what it feels like. The warmth, the comfort, the connection. Even though she was just on the outside looking in, she could sense it. This was what it was like, to be part of a family.

# CHAPTER 37

As promised, they walked down to the beach after lunch, Violet skipping ahead through the trees and bushes to lead the way. Morag followed after, a shawl wrapped around her bare shoulders, while Rachel and Duncan lingered at the rear. With Violet far ahead, Duncan took the opportunity to catch Rachel's fingers as they walked alongside one another, and grasped them lightly in his own.

"She likes you," he said, nodding ahead to where his daughter's dark curls were bouncing periodically into view, beyond the gentle upwards rise of the path. He was smiling, his free hand in his pocket, the breeze catching in his hair.

"Do you think?" Rachel asked, hesitant. She didn't want to come storming in and turn some poor wee girl's life upside down when she wasn't even sure what this whole thing with Duncan was, or where it might be heading.

"Definitely," Duncan nodded. "Not everyone gets treated to the entire works of Shakespeare on their first meeting, you know."

Rachel paused. A question had been gradually creeping to the forefront of her mind over the course of the afternoon.

"Have there been a lot?" she asked, keeping her voice light but unable to look him in the eye. She gazed down to the shoreline instead, where Violet had raced ahead and was now skipping delightedly along the sand.

"A lot of what?"

"Women. That Violet's had to meet."

To her surprise, Duncan smiled; a small, sad little grin that was directed mainly towards his feet. They were drawing closer to the others now, and he gently let go of her hand.

"No," he said, shaking his head. "I don't introduce just anyone to my daughter, you know. And I wouldn't have introduced you so soon, if we hadn't run into you the way we did." He paused, taking a deep breath. "And if I didn't like you quite so much."

"Oh." Rachel stopped walking and looked at him.

"I'm not trying to put any pressure on you," Duncan said, watching her carefully. "I just wanted to spend some time with you, away from Stephanie, and the distillery, and the prying eyes of Inniscreag. I saw an opportunity to do that, and I took it. I'm sorry if

I've made you feel uncomfortable."

"You haven't. It's been wonderful, really." She laughed nervously. "Honestly, this has been the nicest day I've had in a very long time."

Unexpectedly, Rachel felt tears sting the back of her eyes, and she wasn't exactly sure why.

"Then enjoy it," Duncan said with a smile, reaching out to squeeze her arm gently. "I am."

Rachel smiled, nodding. "Okay."

They spent the rest of the afternoon exploring the beach, Violet running from end to end, the wind in her wild curls. She was fascinated by the distinctive, swirling patterns of the razor clam casts in the sand, and gathered as many different shells as she could fit in her pockets.

"I'm going to make something with them," she explained to Rachel, her hands overflowing with empty limpets, cockles and periwinkles.

"Let me help," Rachel suggested, opening up the pockets of her denim jacket and encouraging Violet to deposit some inside.

They headed home when the wind picked up and the sky started to darken, not long after four o'clock. The first fat drops of rain splashed to the ground just as they were rushing in the back door.

"Perfect timing for an afternoon dram!" Morag announced, taking a brand new bottle of Inniscreag from one of the cupboards. "Duncan tells me this distillery of yours produces a very fine whisky," she said with a smile, nodding in Rachel's direction.

"Which I can take absolutely no credit for," she replied.

"But you're going to own it soon, right?" Morag asked, uncorking the bottle. "Now that this Canadian woman's changed her mind?"

Rachel shot Duncan a look. "Whatever happened to lawyer-client confidentiality?"

He shrugged. "It kind of goes out the window when your client calls in the press without talking to you, then storms around the island telling all and sundry she's made a huge mistake and begging their forgiveness."

"Fair enough," Rachel replied, "but I'll have to pass. I should be getting back now; I've intruded enough on your family holiday.

Thank you so much for having me."

Morag gave her brother a knowing smile, before splashing a generous measure into a cut crystal glass and retreating to the living room, where Violet was sat cross-legged on the rug, browsing films on Netflix.

Once they were alone, Duncan sidled closer to Rachel, his voice lowered. "I thought you might want to stay the night?"

Rachel shook her head. "No, I couldn't," she said. "It wouldn't be fair on Violet."

"Let me worry about my daughter," Duncan said, one hand caressing her waist. "There's a spare room; I'm not suggesting anything improper."

He smiled at her, his dark hair flopping over his forehead. Rachel had to resist the urge to reach up and brush it out of his eyes.

"As a matter of fact, the spare room just so happens to be at the exact opposite end of the house to Violet's..."

"Is that right?" Rachel smirked, feeling her resolve weakening. "But I haven't brought any pyjamas?" she teased.

"Maybe you don't need them..."

"Dad! We're watching *Shrek*. Hurry up, it's starting!" Violet's voice burst through from the living room.

"On my way," he called back, smiling at Rachel one last time, before pouring her a fresh glass of wine and heading through to the living room.

The rest of the afternoon was spent engaged in the kind of stereotypically happy, family activities Rachel had only ever seen in films, or other people's smug Facebook posts. They watched movies under blankets on the sofa, shared bowls of popcorn, toasted marshmallows on the wood burner, played board games and had a pizza picnic on the carpet for dinner.

Rachel was surprised at how relaxed and at home she felt with them; more so than she'd ever felt with anyone else. So, when Duncan carried a sleeping Violet up to her bedroom, while Morag and Rachel tidied the dirty plates and glasses into the dishwasher, she couldn't understand the sense of heavy sadness that suddenly settled in her chest. She'd had the loveliest day, she told herself; so why did she feel so down?

Duncan brought her one of his tee-shirts and a pair of joggers to sleep in, while Morag made herself a cup of tea and wished them goodnight before heading upstairs to her room.

As soon as his sister was gone, Duncan took Rachel in his arms and kissed her. "I've been dying to do that all day," he whispered, his breath warm on her cheek.

Rachel shrugged him off, turning to stack the dirty oven trays in the sink to soak.

"Everything okay?" Duncan asked.

"Mmm hmm," she nodded, not looking at him. The lump in her throat was back, and she didn't know how to explain it.

Duncan came up behind her, rubbing her arms gently and kissing her neck. "What's up, Rach?" he whispered.

She blinked, feeling a couple of rogue tears roll down her cheek. "It's nothing," she said, brushing them aside. "I'm sorry; I'm just being silly. I've had a lovely day."

"Then why the tears?" Duncan asked, turning her to face him. He reached out and followed the trail of one with his thumb, dragging it gently down her cheek before coming to rest on her chin.

"I don't know," Rachel admitted, looking up at him. "I really have had the best time. I guess…" she hesitated, not wanting him to think she was stupid, or to scare him off. "I think I'm just sad that it's over," she admitted, smiling self-consciously.

"That's not stupid." Duncan squeezed his arms tighter round her waist, drawing her close. Rachel snaked her arms around his neck in response. "We can have lots more days like this, if you want them," he said, kissing her gently on the lips.

Rachel frowned at him. "Do you mean that?"

"You still don't trust me?" he asked, dark eyebrows raised and his green eyes fixed on hers. "You think this is all a ruse? Violet and Morag are actually actors I've hired in an elaborate hoax to make you fall in love with me, so I can steal the distillery out from under your nose?"

Rachel laughed, trying not to fixate on his casual use of the 'L' word.

"I trust you," she said.

"Good." Duncan planted a little peck on the tip of her nose. "Now let's go to bed."

As soon as they'd closed the door behind them, Duncan kissed her, and began to undress her, slowly, in the dark. Rachel felt a sudden wave of nerves sweep over her. Somehow, this felt different from the other times they'd slept together; as if something had shifted between them, and they could never go back.

Duncan was unusually quiet, too, as he undid Rachel's bra and trailed his hands gently over her breasts, coming to rest on her hips, his fingertips just grazing her skin. He was still for a moment, his eyes downcast, and Rachel felt her skin prickle in anticipation. His face was millimetres from hers, his breathing suddenly heavy. He swallowed nervously before he spoke.

"Rach?" he whispered.

"Yes?"

"I love you."

Her answer came quickly, and, much to her surprise, without a single moment of hesitation or doubt.

"I love you, too."

# CHAPTER 38

Rachel awoke the next morning still wrapped in Duncan's arms, his head buried in her shoulder and one long leg slung over her, entwined with her own. He stirred slightly as she moved, rolling over with a low grumble to glance at the clock on the bedside table.

"Shit," he breathed, rubbing his eyes.

Rachel enjoyed the sight of his long body stretching out beside her. The duvet had ridden down his chest to reveal the outline of ribs rippling beneath the hair covered skin, the firm muscles of his stomach tensing as he yawned.

"So much for being back in my room before Violet woke up."

Rachel draped herself over him, placing a little kiss on his belly and looking at the clock. It was already after nine.

"Oops," she whispered, rolling out of bed and pulling on the joggers and tee-shirt he had lent her. "Maybe you could sneak out and pretend you'd just been for a run or something?"

Duncan smiled at her, reclining back on the crumpled pillows and sighing deeply. "It's okay," he said. "I need to talk to her anyway. About us. Now's as good a time as any."

"Us?" Rachel asked, pausing in the middle of doing up her bra. He nodded in reply, the sleepy green eyes crinkling round the edges.

Climbing back on to the bed, Rachel crawled over to him, running her hands over the grey sparkles at his temples and down to the dark stubble of his jawline. "So... is this officially a thing, now?"

Duncan's smile widened, his arms around her waist pulling her closer. "Yes," he said, "or it is as far as I'm concerned. I told you; I love you."

Rachel grinned. She didn't think she'd ever get tired of hearing him say that.

"I love you too," she replied, kissing him and trying not to think about everything that stood in their way. For now, she just wanted to be with him. They would sort everything else out in time.

Duncan got dressed and headed down the stairs before her, Rachel listening to the distant murmur of voices as he entered the living room. She hovered uncertainly by the bedroom door, until

191

their footsteps came creaking back up the steps, father and daughter disappearing into Violet's bedroom for a chat. Only then did Rachel creep out and sneak down the stairs, feeling more than a little embarrassed.

"Morning!" Morag greeted her brightly as she wandered into the kitchen, dark curls piled high on her head and dressed in a floaty, floral dressing gown. Rachel should have guessed she'd be the kind of woman who wore elegant nightwear, rather than the naff jammies and old hoodies that were Rachel's usual night time attire.

"Morning," she smiled back, accepting one of the large mugs of coffee which Morag was currently pouring from a freshly brewed cafetiere.

"Milk and sugar?"

"Both, please," Rachel replied.

The two women sipped their coffee in companionable silence for a moment, leaning against the kitchen counter and basking in the sun that was streaming in from the panoramic windows opposite.

"It's beautiful here," Morag observed.

"It certainly is," Rachel agreed. "How long are you staying for?"

"We've got this place booked for another week," Morag said. "Although Duncan suggested we might come over and spend a couple of nights on Inniscreag. He's quite taken with that place, you know." She flashed Rachel a mischievous grin from over her coffee cup. "He's quite taken with you, too, for that matter."

Rachel blushed. There was obviously no use denying that something was going on between them. "The feeling's mutual," she said eventually.

"Good," Morag declared, turning and placing her now empty coffee cup in the dishwasher, seemingly satisfied. Rachel was relieved; if that was the extent of the big sisterly interrogation, then hopefully she'd passed.

"I was going to do bacon rolls for breakfast, if you're hungry?" Morag asked.

"I should probably get back to my hotel." Rachel swallowed the last of her own coffee and slipped the mug in alongside Morag's. "I need to get some clean clothes; ones that actually fit," she explained, gesturing down to her feet. Duncan's ridiculously long joggers were scrunched up around her ankles.

But Morag was insistent. "Stay for breakfast, at least. Violet was asking for you this morning; she'd be disappointed if you left without saying goodbye." She paused for a second. "She likes you too, by the way."

Rachel smiled. "The feeling's mutual there, as well."

"Even better."

Rachel was buttering rolls, while Morag fried the bacon, when Duncan and Violet re-emerged from the bedroom. The little girl ran into the living room, shouting good morning to Rachel and grabbing the book she'd left abandoned on the sofa. She picked it up and carrying on reading, as if nothing out of the ordinary had occurred at all.

Duncan wandered into the kitchen, kissing Rachel's head as he passed.

"She's okay?" Rachel asked.

Duncan poured himself a coffee before answering. "She'd already figured it out, apparently. She said - and I quote - 'your face goes all mushy when you look at her'."

Morag laughed. "Out of the mouths of babes," she said, squeezing her brother's arm affectionately.

They sat around the dining table they'd eaten at the night before, the same warm, effortless atmosphere surrounding them as they chatted and shared out the food and drink. The bacon rolls were augmented with a selection of cereals and juices, along with some croissants which Morag had warmed in the oven. The food here was even better than being at a hotel, Rachel decided.

When they'd finished eating, and a contented silence had descended on the table, Rachel judged it as the right time to take her leave.

"I really need to get back to my hotel," she insisted, "take a shower and get dressed. I haven't got any clean clothes here."

Violet protested first. "I wanted to go back to the beach, to find more shells," she said.

Rachel looked across at Duncan, who was sitting opposite her. He raised his eyebrows at her and grinned. "You'd be welcome to come back here after?" he suggested. "You could even bring your stuff back with you, and spend the rest of the weekend?"

"Oh, yes please!" Violet cried excitedly. "Can she stay?" she asked, turning to her aunt.

"It's fine by me," Morag confirmed.

"Are you sure?" Rachel looked around from one Fraser to the next; their matching dark heads and green eyes were all nodding back at her.

It was unanimously agreed that Rachel should go back to her hotel, pack up her things, and return to spend the rest of the weekend at the holiday home. She would have to go back to Inniscreag the following day - as would Duncan - but a quick phone call arranged for another room to be booked above the pub, so that Morag and Violet could come, too. Rachel batted aside Shelagh's enquiry as to who exactly her new guests were going to be - no point giving the already extremely efficient island rumour mill a head start.

As promised, Rachel made it to Portree and back just in time for lunch - a picnic of sandwiches, fruit and crisps, which they carried down and ate by the shore of the loch, despite all three of the adults protesting that they were still too full from breakfast.

Duncan had brought his camera with him, so while Rachel and Morag lay back on the blankets, nibbling crisps and talking, he followed Violet around the beach, snapping off photos while she ran and explored, and generally did her best to ignore him.

After they'd eaten, Morag took Violet further down the shore in search of more seashells - she'd brought a bucket with her today, and fully intended to fill it - while Duncan roamed further afield with his camera, experimenting with different lenses. Rachel had last seen him lying on his belly in the long grass above the bank of shingle at the top of the beach, facing out towards the water and focusing on something she couldn't see.

Deciding to make the most of the peace and solitude, Rachel stretched out on her tummy to read her book. The sun was warm where it hit her back, but the perpetual island breeze was soon giving her goose bumps. She pulled the checked rug over her shoulders to keep off the chill.

Losing herself in her book, it was a while later when Rachel was startled by the sudden, rapid clicking of a camera shutter. She sat up, seeing Duncan crouched in the sand a short distance away, camera pointing in her direction.

"Stop it," she said, sitting up self-consciously. Duncan rose to his feet, smiling and striding towards her.

"I couldn't help myself," he said, folding up his long legs and collapsing onto the sand alongside her. "You looked so beautiful lying there, with the wind in your hair, and absolutely no idea I was watching you."

Rachel bit back her innate urge to dismiss the compliment, looking at him instead. His green eyes were squinting at her in the sunlight, the wind ruffling his hair. "Do you really mean that?" she asked.

Duncan laughed. "Of course I do," he said. "You're gorgeous." Reaching out one hand, he tucked a strand of hair behind her ear. "And don't you forget it," he added, wrapping an arm around her and pulling her in for a kiss.

They walked back up to the house later, Violet laden down with as many seashells as she could carry, and spent another cosy afternoon watching films. On her trip back into Portree Rachel had popped into a shop to buy more microwave popcorn, as well as Haribo, much to Violet's delight.

"Is she allowed them?" she asked Duncan, seeing Violet's eyes light up in a way that suddenly made her think these might be considered contraband goods.

"Occasionally," he said with a begrudging smirk. Violet had already grabbed them, before her father had the chance to change his mind, and was scampering back over to the sofa.

"Bribery and corruption," Duncan whispered, wrapping one arm around Rachel's shoulders and kissing her on the head. "The way to every child's heart."

Violet disappeared to her room before dinner, which Morag insisted she didn't need any help with, so Rachel and Duncan found themselves alone on the sofa, drinking wine in front of a kids' film that neither of them were watching.

"This is nice," Duncan said, trailing his fingers up and down Rachel's arm. She had her head on his chest, and could feel his heartbeat reassuringly strong and steady against her cheek.

"It is," Rachel agreed.

"So, back to Inniscreag tomorrow. Are you okay with this all being public? You and me - official?"

Rachel smiled, and ran one hand over his taut stomach. "Yes," she said. "My ex might not be too pleased, mind you, but hopefully he'll get the message and piss off soon."

"Will you need to see him again?" Duncan asked. "I can be

195

with you, if it helps?"

"Oh God, no." Rachel sat up. "Honestly I can handle him. He's just throwing his weight around." She sighed. "He's trying to manipulate me into giving him something in the divorce settlement. When he realises I'm not going to cave, he'll give up."

"What is it he wants?"

Rachel filled him in on everything, from her grandmother's flat in Glasgow, to Graham's thinly veiled threat about trying to claim half of the distillery as well, should her inheritance come through before the divorce was finalised.

"But I spoke to a lawyer the other day; that's why I was here, on Skye, in the first place. I know he's talking shite - about the still, at least. I might just give in on the flat though," she conceded. "It'd be worth the sacrifice, just to get the whole nightmare over with."

Duncan nodded. "You know you've got me, too, right? For anything. I'd even do a special mate's rates for legal advice, just for you," he added with a smirk.

Smiling back at him, Rachel couldn't believe how much her luck, and her mood, had changed in just a few short days. "Thank you."

Violet came running back down the stairs then, the sudden loud clattering on the steps disproportionate to her tiny frame. Shooting straight over to the sofa, her hands were clasped behind her back and a huge grin plastered across her face.

"I've made you something," she said, the green eyes, identical to her father's, fixed on Rachel.

Rachel sat up, surprised. "For me?"

Violet nodded eagerly back at her, pulling her hands out from behind her back and presenting the contents to Rachel proudly.

She was holding a huge clamshell, almost as big as both of her little hands held together, deep white ridges fanning out from the centre to the perfectly smooth, unchipped edges.

"It's beautiful!" Rachel declared.

"Turn it over."

Rachel did as she was asked, pressing her fingers to her lips when she saw what was underneath.

The smooth, pearlescent pink underside of the shell had been decorated, using what looked to be coloured Sharpies and glitter. The words 'Torrin Beach' had been inscribed in purple, while underneath

Violet had written today's date. Around the edges, she'd added all of their initials - R, D, V and M - each one floating in a little red love heart.

"Oh, Violet, thank you so much," Rachel said, her voice thick. She found herself blinking wildly to hold back the tears that were threatening to spill over her eyelids.

"You're welcome," Violet said, impulsively throwing her skinny little arms around Rachel's neck. Rachel squeezed her back fiercely in return.

"I'll keep it forever," she said. And she meant it.

# CHAPTER 39

They travelled back together on the afternoon ferry the following day, the three cars - Rachel's, Duncan's and Morag's - taking up the majority of space on the little roll on roll off boat. Having crossed the bridge with her aunt on their outbound journey to Skye, Violet was more than a little excited at being out on the open sea, even if it was just the short crossing from Uig to Craigport.

She bounded out of the car as soon as they were allowed, eagerly peering over the barrier, the wind whipping her long brown ringlets wildly around her face.

"This is brilliant!" she cried, her excitement reaching fever pitch when the boat was suddenly accompanied by a pod of dolphins, their blue-grey bodies breaching and rolling in the surf.

"Daddy, look!"

Duncan was bent over the railings alongside her, the two of them thoroughly soaked with sea spray, but neither of them cared.

"I've never seen her like this before," Morag said to Rachel. They were standing near the back of the boat, watching father and daughter marvel at the creatures. A flock of gannets had now joined the melee. Violet was enthralled by their dramatic swoops and dives, watching wide-eyed as their large white bodies and black-tipped wings criss-crossed the sky.

"She doesn't get out in the countryside that much at home," Morag was explaining, pulling her shawl closer around herself to shut out the biting breeze. "They live in a flat, you see, same as me. No garden, although we're just across the road from the Meadows. Should make an effort to get her out more, I suppose, but she's always been so content just being inside, with her books."

Morag was chewing her bottom lip, and Rachel didn't know what to say to reassure her. "She's a happy wee girl - anyone can see that. You've both done a great job raising her."

Morag dismissed the compliment with a shrug. "I just help out now and then. I love her as if she were my own, mind you, but she's Duncan's pride and joy. If anyone's to take credit for the person she's turning into, it's him."

Rachel smiled across, watching him crouching down beside Violet as the two of them gazed out over the water, pointing here and there at the passing seabirds. Why couldn't she have met him years ago? It was clear to anyone that he was a brilliant dad.

After everything she'd been through, Rachel thought she had resigned herself to the fact that she would never have kids of her own. Now though, for the first time in years, she began to wonder. Would it be possible that with a different partner, she'd be able to have a successful pregnancy? Rachel daren't let herself hope. And besides, it was early days with Duncan; far too early to be thinking about having a baby with him.

"Duncan mentioned that you're separated," Morag said. "No kids yourself?"

She asked the question casually, as so many people had before. Women who no doubt were lucky enough to never have struggled, and never considered that things might not be as easy for everyone else. Rachel knew the question wasn't intended to wound, but it did, every single time.

"No kids," she answered, as breezily as she could. She wasn't going to say anything else - she never did, after all. Just batted it aside as carelessly as she could, not wanting to make other people feel awkward. Or worse - pity her.

But suddenly Duncan's words were in her ears, and as she watched him with Violet, she decided not to lie anymore. He was right; those babies were hers, and she had loved them.

"I lost four," she said, breathing deeply to calm the rising wave of emotion. She blinked, swallowing it back down. "Stopped trying after that. It was too difficult, and going through it all made me wake up and realise that my husband was actually a bit of a dick."

For a moment, Rachel worried that she'd gone too far. Morag was silent, the two women staring out to sea, side by side. Then, her hand found Rachel's, and squeezed it gently.

"I'm sorry," she said.

Rachel waited for the platitudes to follow; the things people said to fill the empty space that existed after a revelation like that. But Morag said nothing more. She just held her hand, and watched as the distant outline of Craigport bobbed gently into view.

They disembarked, Rachel saying farewell to the three of them outside the pub, before Shelagh's curious eyes could spot her. She'd already agreed with Duncan that it was best for him to spend the night just with Violet and Morag - it was their holiday after all, and she'd already taken up lots of their time.

"They'd be happy to have you join us," he said.

"I know. But I have things to sort before work tomorrow, anyway. And it's important Violet knows that she's still your first priority; I don't want to make her feel pushed aside."

Duncan smiled, taking her hands in his. "You're a very, very close second."

"And that's where I belong," Rachel replied, standing up on her tiptoes to kiss him.

He picked up their cases and turned to join Morag and Violet in the bar, before pausing and spinning back suddenly. Dropping the cases, Duncan rushed to her and gathered her into his arms, kissing her in a way that made her hope no one she knew was passing.

"Thank you," he said. "For being so understanding. I never thought I'd meet anyone who accepted Violet the way you have."

Rachel smiled. "I love you," she said. "And I love her, too. She's great."

Duncan smiled at her again. "Still on for dinner tomorrow?"

Rachel nodded. Technically, he was meant to be on annual leave for the next week, but he'd need to speak to Stephanie as soon as possible. The two of them were in a bit of a bubble for now, but sooner or later they'd need to work out what was happening with the case, and whatever impact that might have on them. Rachel's relief at knowing they might not have to go to court after all, had been replaced with the sinking knowledge that if the case was truly over, then Duncan had no further need to remain on Inniscreag.

"Duncan?"

"What?" He frowned, reading the look of worry in her eyes. Something had suddenly, and somewhat belatedly, dawned on her.

"Graham's staying at the pub too. If you see him, just..."

"Don't worry," he said, giving her hand one last squeeze. "I'll stay well out of his way. But I can be with you, if you want me to, when you do have to see him."

"It's fine," Rachel replied, forcing a smile. "I can handle Graham."

Despite her words of reassurance to Duncan, Rachel locked her doors when she got home that night, and there were no late-night cuddles on the back step with Doug. Instead, she waited until she heard his frenzied scratching at the door, before letting him in and hurriedly locking it once more behind him.

Thankfully, Graham didn't appear on her doorstep that evening. Rachel let Doug into her bed for company, where he curled comfortingly against her feet, and managed a few broken hours of sleep. But her nerves were on edge; she woke every time the old house creaked, as it did often. It was as if its weary bones settled down in the darkness, after a long day in the wind and sun.

There was no sign of him in the morning, either, when Rachel crept from her door and scurried over to the office. She had purposely waited until shift changeover, so that Ben and Hamish were crossing the tarmac to their car just as Iain and Jamie were arriving. She felt less vulnerable, knowing there were other people around.

Cameron arrived not long after she did, and as she'd expected, news of Graham's identity hadn't stayed quiet for long.

"So, ye've a husband, then?" he said conversationally, getting settled at his desk and sifting through his to do list for the day, not looking directly at her.

Rachel sighed. "We're separated."

Cameron smiled at her, an almost fatherly expression. "It's fine, lass. Ye must have had a reason not to tell us, and a reason not to tell him where ye'd gone. He's asking anybody that'll listen where ye are, and trying to track ye down." He hurried on, seeing Rachel's wide-eyed expression. "But dinna fash; none of us will tell him. As far as he's concerned, ye've left Inniscreag on business and we're no' sure when ye'll be back. We look after our own," he added, his hazel eyes warm.

"Thank you," Rachel breathed.

Burying her head in work, for the time being at least, Rachel had a quick look over the sales figures from the coffee shop. They'd only been open just over a fortnight, but the numbers were consistent - with the schools being on holiday and tourist season in full swing, they were busy pretty much every day, and making a decent profit.

Rachel smiled to herself, wondering if it would be premature to start thinking about ordering in some merchandise and getting the gift shop up and running, too. It seemed silly to miss out on all these extra visitors they were attracting, who might very well decide they'd like a wee souvenir to take away with them.

She suggested as much to Cameron, while they were sharing their mid-morning coffee, accompanied by some home-made tablet which Jenny had dropped off. The distinctive Scottish fudge was sweet and crumbly, and melted on her tongue.

"I'd been thinking the same myself, funnily enough," Cameron replied, brushing some crumbs from his tawny moustache. "All these people hanging around after their tours are finished, when they used to just get back in the car and leave; seems daft no' to take advantage."

Rachel nodded, mulling it over. It'd mean more investment, but if they didn't do it now, they'd have to wait until next season to make it worthwhile. And the coffee shop was paying for itself rather more quickly than she'd expected.

"There's folk askin' about the pictures, as well," Cameron said.

"What do you mean?"

"The ones yon lad took, Duncan? The one tryin' to buy us out, who for some reason now seems to be helpin' us out instead?" Cameron's eyes twinkled at her, although he didn't delve any further.

"They're asking about them?" Rachel repeated, not taking the bait. "As in, they want to buy them?"

Cameron nodded. "Aye. Jenny says folk keep askin' if we do them on postcards or wee prints or anythin'."

If Rachel had needed a final push to make up her mind, that was it. Printing out postcards couldn't be that expensive, and along with a few engraved decanters and nosing glasses, they could soon stock a wee gift shop, even if it was a bit rough and ready for the time being.

"I'll speak to Duncan tonight," she said, without thinking. "See if we can have his permission to use the images on merchandising."

"Oh, tonight, is it?" Cameron asked, one corner of his mouth curving up in a little smile. "Having business meetings in the evenings these days, are ye?"

Rachel smirked back at him. "Shut up," she said, as he broke into a wide grin and laughed.

# CHAPTER 40

Rachel was panicking. Not being a natural born cook, she'd made some gentle enquiries at work as to something simple, but special, which she could prepare for Duncan that evening. They were all very diplomatic, not one of them enquiring as to who her mystery guest was, although she was pretty sure the cat was out of the bag on that one.

It was Jenny who came up with a solution. The two of them were enjoying a bowl of soup in the coffee shop during their lunch break, and quietly soaking up the atmosphere. Rachel was pleased to see it was pleasantly busy, most tables occupied with a mixture of families and couples, and a warm, gentle hubbub of chat enveloped them.

"Why don't you ask for some seafood from Tormod's boat?" Jenny asked. "Hamish could bring it in tonight, at the start of his shift."

Rachel looked at her with a dubious frown. "Are you sure?" she asked. "I don't want to give him food poisoning?"

"Och, ye'll be fine," Jenny said, grabbing a napkin and scribbling down instructions. "It's easy peasy – just steam whatever he's landed today in a nice white wine and garlic broth, and add a wee splash o' cream at the end. Mussels would be best, but this will work for just about anything - it's impressive, but easy. I'll bake ye a fresh loaf of bread to have with it and drop it in before I finish up for the day. Ye can pinch some salad veg from the kitchen fridge." Jenny's eyes were twinkling mischievously. "The way to a man's heart is through his stomach," she teased.

Jenny was on the phone to Hamish without waiting for an answer, relaying the message through his mother, who assured her that Tormod would save the best from his catch, and Hamish would drop it in that evening. Rachel, however, remained unconvinced - she loved seafood, but cooking it without killing anyone seemed a bit beyond her capabilities.

She had showered and dried her hair, full face of makeup applied, and was wearing the dress she'd bought on Skye when Hamish knocked at the door. He smiled at her, holding up a plastic bag in each hand triumphantly.

"My, don't you look bonny?" he said.

"Don't sound so surprised," Rachel replied, accepting the bag in his right hand, which was obviously heavy with mussels. Jenny had already dropped off the crusty bread, and Rachel managed to chop an onion and dig out the cupboard store supplies for the sauce - butter, wine and garlic - so all she'd have to do before Duncan arrived was clean the mussels. She'd cook it all fresh when he got here, and hopefully not make a complete arse of herself in the process.

"What's that?" she asked, gesturing to the bag in Hamish's other hand as he followed her through to the kitchen at the back of the house.

"Da' thought ye might like something a wee bit special, as an added extra," he said, a smile on his ruddy face. He'd trimmed his beard recently, and the little orange hairs were cropped in close against the skin.

Plopping the bag down on the kitchen counter, Rachel jumped when she noticed it moving.

"What the hell is that?" she cried.

"Lobster," Hamish said, nonplussed.

*"Alive?"*

"Aye," he replied, looking at her as if she were mad. "Freshest lobster you could get, landed today, and big buggers, too," he said, reaching to remove one from the bag.

"No, don't, put it back," Rachel said, withdrawing across the room, but it was too late. He was holding it out to her, the expression on his face suggesting that he had absolutely no idea why she might find this disturbing.

The lobster was dark blue, and its beady eyes - or what she assumed were eyes - were out on stalks, veering wildly from side to side, while the little front legs waved around madly, seeking some purchase to allow it to scurry away. The large front pincers were, mercifully, held together with elastic bands.

"Ye've got tae cook them live," Hamish was explaining. "The mussels are alive, too, ye ken…"

"But they're not trying to crawl across my kitchen counter," Rachel almost screeched in response. "And I don't think I'll be able to sauté that bloody great thing in garlic butter - it'll have my fingers off!"

Hamish sighed, returning the poor little lobster to its plastic bag. He adopted a very patient tone of voice, the kind you might use when explaining to an obstinate two year old why it wasn't a good idea to stick their fingers in an electrical socket.

"They're nae bother tae cook," he said. "Ye just put them in the freezer for ten minutes, so they're nice and sleepy, then head first into a pot of boiling water. They dinna feel a thing."

Rachel didn't think she'd very much like to be put in the freezer then plunged into a pot of boiling water, but she bit her tongue.

It was completely hypocritical, she knew - she'd eaten plenty of lobsters and langoustines since she'd been on the island, and she supposed it was no different to what she was going to do to the mussels. But Rachel wasn't sure she could bring herself to kill something that looked quite so sentient.

There was another knock on the door just then, and Hamish shot her a knowing smile. "There's yer date then," he said. "Dae ye want me to sneak oot the back?"

"No, it's fine," she sighed, knowing that Duncan's arrival at her doorstep was hardly likely to go unnoticed. His bright red sports car parked outside was not exactly inconspicuous.

But when she and Hamish reached the front door, it was not Duncan's tall, lithe figure that greeted them. This visitor was square, and stocky, with a shaved head and thick dark beard.

"Alright, Rocky?" Graham said when she opened the door. Rachel felt her heart start to beat faster, and she was grateful for Hamish's looming bulk behind her, although Graham barely flinched.

"Another one?" he said, his eyes scanning Hamish from head to toe. "Working your way around the island, are you?"

She breathed deeply, taking a minute to compose herself. "This is Hamish," she said. "He works here. Hamish, this is my *ex*-husband."

Hamish nodded, frowning slightly at the smaller man. He could obviously tell from Rachel's tone that this was not who she had been preparing the seafood dinner for.

"D'ye need me tae hang around, boss?" Hamish asked. He had never called her 'boss' before, but it gave her the little injection of confidence she needed right now, and she was grateful for it.

"It's fine," Rachel said. "He won't be staying long."

Hamish squeezed through the door, giving Graham one last

glare as he passed. "I'll just be at the still if you need me," he said pointedly, glancing back at Rachel as he left. She noticed that he took his time crossing the cobbled courtyard, and paused at the door to the stillhouse, watching them from a distance.

"Can I come in then?" Graham asked. "You did your disappearing act again before we had a chance to sort things out."

"There's nothing to sort," Rachel said, standing her ground and blocking the doorway, as best as she could. She noticed Graham taking in her appearance, his gaze lingering on the low-cut neckline of the dress.

"You're all dressed up," he observed.

"I've got a visitor on his way."

"Loverboy?"

"None of your business."

Graham sighed, changing tack. "So, have you thought about my... proposition?"

"You mean, when you threatened to try and steal my inheritance unless I got back together with you?"

"Rocky..."

"Don't call me that," she snapped. "I hate it. I've always hated it."

For a second, he looked genuinely hurt, but Rachel tried not to let it weaken her.

"I've seen a lawyer," she continued, "who assures me there's no way you'd have any legal claim to the distillery. As for the flat... we can discuss it, if you'll agree to proper mediation. Go back to Glasgow, and stop showing up on my doorstep unannounced."

Graham said nothing for a moment, and Rachel could almost see him trying to think of some reason to argue back in the face of her perfectly reasonable suggestion.

As he finally opened his mouth to speak, the still evening air was suddenly fractured by the low, throaty grumble of an Italian sports car engine. Hamish was still watching them from the stillhouse door, and he stayed there as Duncan's car pulled up outside and came to a standstill.

Rachel's breath caught in her throat as he got out, despite the circumstances. He was wearing tan trousers, with a crisp white shirt and navy blue blazer, his dark hair gleaming in the sunlight and a bunch of flowers in his hand. The easy smile that was on his face, however, dropped when he saw Graham standing on her doorstep.

Calm and measured as always, Duncan approached them slowly, his voice light. "Everything okay, Rach?"

"Fine," she smiled back, echoing his breezy tone. "Graham was just leaving."

Her ex looked from side to side, and back over to where Hamish was still watching them, clearly weighing up his options.

"I should name him in the divorce, for adultery," he growled, glaring at Duncan as he approached.

"You're separated," Duncan retorted, continuing nonchalantly down the garden path.

"What do you know?"

"I'm a lawyer." There was a relaxed smile on his face as he casually regarded Rachel's ex. He was still a whole head taller than him, despite Graham being elevated a few inches on Rachel's front step. "This is sort of in my whole wheelhouse."

Graham drew himself up to his full five foot six inches, puffing his chest out. "I'll come back when you're not quite so busy," he said through gritted teeth.

"Please don't," Rachel said. "I've nothing else to say to you. Anything you have to say to me, can go through your lawyer."

Sharply exhaling through his nostrils like an exasperated bull, Graham finally gave up and retreated back down the steps, narrowly avoiding shoulder barging Duncan on his way past. Duncan didn't flinch. He merely stepped aside lightly, and let Graham storm back down the path and out of the distillery gates.

Rachel glanced over Duncan's shoulder to see Hamish give her a little nod, before stepping through the open door of the stillhouse. She waved, thankful for his presence, and turned back to Duncan.

"You've still got time to back out of this?" she said, eyeing him carefully.

"Not a chance." Duncan swept her into his arms and over the threshold, pulling the front door shut behind them.

# CHAPTER 41

Rachel turned the key in the lock once they were safely indoors, causing Duncan to look at her curiously.

"I thought no one locked their doors around here?"

Rachel shrugged. "Better safe than sorry," she said.

"Are you scared of him?" Duncan asked, reaching out for her, his hands warm on her arms. She was holding the flowers he had given her, and wishing that all of this could have been much, much simpler.

She shook her head half-heartedly. "No, he just... He can't take no for an answer, that's all."

Duncan kept his eyes on her, trying to decide if she was telling him the truth. "You can tell me if you are, you know. I could have a non-harassment order drawn up for you? Make sure he leaves you alone."

"No, there's no need for that. He's all hot air, honestly."

Duncan clearly was not convinced, but he didn't push it for now.

"Okay," he said, pulling her into a hug and stroking her hair. He breathed in deeply. "I don't know about you, but I'm starving. What's for dinner?"

"That remains to be seen." Taking his hand, Rachel led him through to the kitchen and revealed the spoils from Tormod's fishing boat. He grimaced when he saw the live lobsters.

"Oh... So, do we need to...?"

"Yup," she said, hands on her hips as she watched them, making feeble attempts to crawl along her kitchen counter. "I'm not sure I can do it, to be honest. Total hypocrite, I know - I'd happily eat them..."

"I'm not sure I'm up for it either," Duncan admitted. "Do you think they know?" He crouched down, peering at the nearest one, and jumping away when one of its little claws waved pathetically towards him.

"I did have an idea." Rachel said. "But you might think it's stupid..."

Half an hour later, the two of them had scrambled down the

chain link steps that led down the cliffside and found themselves standing on the grey, tumbling shingle next to the distillery's disused jetty. Duncan was undoing his laces, carefully setting his brown leather shoes to one side, stuffing his socks inside them and rolling up the legs of his chinos. Rachel kicked off her own flat pumps and smiled up at him.

"Ready?" she asked.

He nodded, taking her hand in one of his, and carrying the plastic bag in the other.

They waded together into the cold sea, jumping as the first wave washed over their feet and up their calves. Slipping and sliding and giggling, they made their way as deep as they dared. Rachel had to gather her dress up in her free hand, and the rolled-up ends of Duncan's trousers were already damp.

"Do we just... chuck them in?" he asked.

"I don't know," Rachel giggled. "I've never liberated seafood before."

"Maybe we should give them names?" Duncan suggested. "Something to remember them by."

He slung the bag over one arm, reaching in and carefully lifting out the first lobster. Rachel took it from him delicately, keeping the still bound claws pointed away from herself. Duncan did the same with the other one.

"What do you think?" he asked. "Boys or girls?"

"I'm going boy for this one," Rachel replied. "Sebastian - like in *The Little Mermaid*." She'd loved that movie when she was little.

Duncan nodded. "Excellent choice - Violet would approve."

"What about yours?"

Duncan considered it for a moment. "Pinchy," he said eventually.

Rachel laughed. "Very imaginative," she said.

"From the woman who decided to name her cat 'Doug'," Duncan quipped back.

Rachel took a deep breath. "Okay then - ready for the big moment?"

They both crouched down in the surf. Rachel, at a distinct disadvantage from a leg-length perspective, struggled to keep her bum out of the water.

As carefully as she could, she used her free hand to peel off the elastic bands, before dropping Sebastian into the clear turquoise water, whilst Duncan did the same to Pinchy. The two creatures froze for a moment, as if they thought it might be a trick, before quickly scurrying off into the deeper water.

Duncan and Rachel stood up, arms around each other, watching them disappear into the surf.

"Bye Sebastian; bye Pinchy," she said, waving. Duncan squeezed her closer.

"I feel kind of bad about not setting the mussels free, too," he confessed. "But I'm bloody starving."

At Duncan's suggestion - given Rachel's lack of dining table - they ate on the grass in her back garden, looking out over the cliff tops to the sea far below. He had ended up taking charge of the mussel cooking as well, which Rachel was secretly grateful for. No point giving him the false impression that she was some kind of Michelin star chef, when in reality she struggled to coordinate timings on oven food.

"I wonder where Pinchy and Sebastian are now," she mused, peeling another mussel out of its shell and popping the chewy little orange blob in her mouth. The sauce Jenny had suggested was delicious, and accompanied with thickly buttered homemade bread and chilled white wine, Rachel couldn't think of a more perfect meal.

"Probably already eaten by something else," Duncan said. Rachel slapped his arm playfully. "What's a lobster's natural predator, anyway?"

"Damned if I know," she replied. "Science was never really my subject."

Duncan sipped his wine. "What were you into, in school?" he asked.

Rachel shrugged. "Nothing, really. I had too much on my plate at home, with mum and everything."

"Because she was sick?"

"Sort of. She was... troubled, more than anything else. She'd had a rough start - raised in a care home, no family or anything. I don't think she had any idea how to even be a mum, really. Don't get me wrong, it wasn't all bad - she was loving and fun a lot of the time. But then she'd hit a dark spell, and I'd try to cover for her, so school didn't find out. And then when it got really bad and I couldn't hide it

210

anymore, we'd go to Granny Peggy's." She sighed. "School just never seemed that important, in the grand scheme of things."

Duncan didn't say anything for a moment, taking the time to absorb what she'd said. She liked that about him; he really thought about things, rather than rushing to reply or fill the void. He just let it be.

"What happened to her?" he asked eventually.

"She died," Rachel said simply. "I was away at uni. We hadn't spoken for a while, and I guess things just got really bad. She finally decided enough was enough." Rachel paused, and when Duncan remained silent, she found herself prattling on, the words spilling out of her mouth before she'd really had time to consider them.

"I think if it had all happened thirty years later... well, people are more understanding about these things nowadays, aren't they? Mental health isn't as taboo as it used to be. I can't help but wonder sometimes, that maybe if she'd got the help she needed – counselling, or meds, or whatever – maybe she'd still be here?"

Duncan nodded thoughtfully, and Rachel took a moment to compose herself. She had never actually been able to bring herself to say the words out loud, but she could tell from his expression that he understood.

"I didn't even have any money for a proper funeral," she continued, suddenly finding herself admitting to something she had never told anyone else before. "I just let the council take care of it."

It was like a great, pressing weight was suddenly lifted from her chest, and Rachel realised for the first time how much guilt she had been carrying around all these years. But now she'd said it, out loud, and the world hadn't ended. She'd been a terrible daughter, and the universe had made it clear she wasn't fit to be a mother, either. But Duncan was still there, looking at her with those green eyes she loved so much, without an ounce of judgement in his expression.

Unexpectedly, tears sprung to her eyes. She nodded frantically, blinking them away. "Well, there you go," she said, standing up and busying herself with clearing away the plates. "You know all the very worst things about me now - abandoned her mother, can't have kids. Time to run for the hills!" she joked.

"Don't," Duncan said, rising and taking the plates from her grasp. He placed them on the grass, and took her hands in his instead. "Those aren't bad things *about* you. They're bad things that *happened* to you. There's a world of difference."

Rachel sniffed, as he drew her once more into the safety of his arms. "And I'm not going anywhere," he whispered quietly.

They made their way back inside, leaving the dirty dishes by the kitchen sink and heading straight upstairs, instead. Relishing the privacy of being in Rachel's own home, and the luxury of having all the time they needed, they made love slowly this time. Duncan was sleeping over, although he'd promised he'd be back in time to have breakfast with Violet at the hotel. They had the whole night together, and both of them intended to make the most of it.

Afterwards, lying in a sleepy knot, her head on Duncan's chest, Rachel realised that she'd completely forgotten to tell him about the popularity of his photographs.

"Seriously?" he asked, sitting up with a disbelieving frown on his face. "People actually want to buy them?"

Rachel smiled; she hadn't expected him to be so chuffed about it. "I was wondering - and you don't have to say yes, so please don't feel obliged - but would you give us permission to use them on some merchandise? Just postcards, that kind of thing. I was hoping to get the gift shop open sooner rather than later. We'd pay you commission, or whatever. I'm not sure how it all works. But we'd do it above board; I'm not asking for a freebie."

The words had tumbled out of her mouth in a hurried frenzy, so anxious was she in case he thought she was trying to take advantage of him just because they were sleeping together.

"I never thought I'd actually *sell* a photograph," he said, still looking rather pleased with himself. "Of course you can use them. I'll have my lawyer call your lawyer and work something out," he added with a wink.

Rachel settled down against his chest, comfortable and content. She was just starting to feel her eyelids droop when Duncan broke the silence. "I saw Stephanie today."

"You did?" She looked up. Rachel had actually been a little worried about Stephanie. She'd royally screwed herself over with all that carry on with the newspaper, and fucked up her relationship with Hamish into the bargain. Although she hadn't liked the girl much to begin with, she couldn't help but feel sorry for her - it was clear she'd been quite smitten with the gruff, but soft-centred, stillman.

"How was she?"

"She's standing by what she said - she doesn't want to pursue her claim. Honestly, I think she's just heartbroken that things didn't work out with Hamish. She looked devastated; kept saying how she wished she'd never even come here in the first place."

"And what does that mean for us?" Rachel asked, although she already knew. It had been inevitable, sooner or later.

"Well it's good news for you, first of all," Duncan replied, trying to cheer her up. "This place will be yours now, as soon as Ruaridh gets the probate concluded."

"But what about you?" Rachel persisted.

Duncan sighed. "I'll have to tell my boss that she's changed her mind. I can put it off 'til the end of this week, when my annual leave is up, but after that…"

"You'll have to go back to Edinburgh."

He nodded sadly. "We'll make it work though, Rach," he said earnestly, squeezing his arm more firmly around her shoulders. "What's a few hundred miles? I love you; I want to give this a proper chance."

Rachel forced herself to smile. "Me too," she said. And it was true; now that she had him, she wanted this to work out more than anything.

But as she settled down to try and go back to sleep, with Duncan spooned in behind her and his arm tucked reassuringly around her waist, Rachel couldn't fight the sinking feeling that somehow, things between them were destined not to last.

# CHAPTER 42

Between Hamish's watchful eye, and her evening's spent with Duncan and his family, Rachel managed to avoid Graham for the rest of the week. He obviously hadn't given up completely, though, and had declined to return to Glasgow as she'd suggested. Instead, he remained on the island, popping up in the distance here and there, but never venturing any closer.

"I really wish you'd let me do something about him," Duncan said. It was Friday evening, and Morag and Violet only had two nights left on the island. They'd just had dinner together at the pub, and now Violet and her auntie were scrabbling among the rockpools on the shoreline, while Duncan and Rachel watched on from the street above. Graham had appeared around the corner ahead, making a great show of huffing and crossing to the other side of the road when he saw them.

"He's keeping his distance," Rachel said. "He'll give up eventually and go home."

"He's keeping his distance now," Duncan said. "It's what he might try when I'm not around that worries me."

Rachel raised her eyebrows at him. "I'm a big girl," she said, "and I managed him for fifteen years. I can look after myself, thank you very much."

"I know you can," Duncan relented, draping one arm around her shoulder. "I just want to support you. Whatever you need, just say the word."

Rachel smiled. "Thank you. But trust me, just the fact that I'm not getting worked up by him being here will be pissing him off no end. He'll get fed up sooner or later."

In truth, on the nights that Duncan hadn't been staying over, Rachel still double and triple checked her doors, and didn't sleep as well. Whilst the rational part of her brain knew Graham was perfectly harmless, there was still something unnerving about knowing he could appear on her doorstep whenever he fancied.

"Did you order any of that merchandise you were talking about?" Duncan asked.

"I did." She nodded, perking up. "Andrew's going to kit out the gift shop for me next week - just a lick of paint, and a few shelves. I might have gone a bit overboard, to be honest. Hopefully it doesn't all turn out to be a huge waste of money."

"I'm sure it won't," Duncan said, giving her a reassuring squeeze. "Everything else you've done here has worked out - I have no doubt you'll make a success of this, too."

Violet came scampering up from the shore then, her bucket full and sloshing water over the edges. Morag sauntered behind, smiling.

"Daddy, look!" The little girl was shouting excitedly. "I've found a starfish!"

She reached them, panting and out of breath, holding out her bucket proudly. Sure enough, a tiny, five-legged, orange starfish was clinging to the side.

"Wow," Duncan breathed, crouching down to take a closer look.

A deep voice suddenly spoke from behind them, making them all jump.

"That's a fine wee creature ye've found. Common starfish - quite a young one too, from the looks of it."

Duncan and Rachel turned to find Hamish, beaming at them from ear to ear. Even more surprisingly, an unusually bashful looking Stephanie was clinging to his arm. Rachel tried to hide her visible shock, as she introduced the clearly reconciled couple to Duncan's sister and daughter.

"You look like Hagrid," Violet observed, causing Hamish to chuckle. He crouched down closer to her. "Well, I'm definitely no wizard," he whispered, "but I might just have a teeny, tiny wee bit o' giant in me."

Violet giggled.

"You two have worked things out, then?" Rachel observed. "I'm glad."

Stephanie smiled. "Not that I deserve it, after what I did," she said. "But Hamish has agreed to give me a second chance."

She pursed her lips together in a little pout. "I really am so, so sorry, Rachel. He told me about your ex showing up like that. I honestly never meant…"

"It's okay," Rachel said. "He'd have found me sooner or later anyway. Can't run away from the past forever."

"I know what you mean," Stephanie agreed, gazing up at

Hamish adoringly. They looked like a couple from a Disney movie – Hamish's giant hands could have encircled her whole waist, Rachel was sure.

"That's why I told Duncan - I don't want to pursue anything with the distillery any more. I'm sick of obsessing over my past; all I want now is to think about the future."

"Stephanie's moving to Inniscreag," Hamish blurted out suddenly, as if he couldn't contain himself any longer. Pure joy was written across his face. "We need to sort out her visas and things, but we're going to give it a go. Properly."

"Oh, I'm so pleased for you both," Rachel said, and she meant it. She wrapped her arms around Hamish's bull-like neck, and pecked Stephanie on the cheek. "You know when the time comes, there's vacant cottages at the distillery. They need a bit of work, but you'd be welcome to one."

"That's very kind of you." Stephanie smiled back at her. "We're just taking it one day at a time for now."

They exchanged goodbyes, Rachel turning to watch them stroll back along the road, towards Hamish's parents' house.

"I guess you definitely won't be going to court," Duncan commented.

"I guess you can definitely tell your bosses you'll be coming back to Edinburgh."

Duncan grimaced. "Let's not think about that now," he said, squeezing her gently round the waist.

Violet had wandered back down to the beach, her aunt trailing behind her, and Duncan's eyes followed them for a moment. "I promised I'd read Violet a bedtime story - can I come to yours once she's asleep? We can talk properly then."

Rachel nodded, watching Violet turn and wave to them, the wind catching her jacket and flapping it around her. She blew her a kiss in return, leaving Duncan to wander down to the shoreline and join them, whilst she made her way along the coastal road and back to the distillery.

By the time she'd walked home, Rachel just managed a quick shower and a run over the living room carpet with the hoover, before there was a knock at her door.

"That was quick," she said, turning the key and pulling the door open. "All that sea air must have tired her out."

But it wasn't Duncan standing on her doorstep; it was Graham.

Gone was the bravado and peacocking of their previous meetings. He seemed deflated; his shoulders slumped, as he looked at her with a doleful expression. In spite of her better judgement, Rachel actually felt sorry for him. There was even a bunch of flowers clutched in his hands.

"Hear me out," he said, before she had time to shut the door in his face. "Please, Rocky... I mean, Rachel. I only want to talk."

Rachel sighed. "What do you want to talk about?"

"The divorce," he said. "I can see you've moved on, and you're obviously happy now... maybe it is time we just draw a line under this whole thing."

She looked at him, her guard still up. "Duncan's on his way round," she said. "You've got ten minutes."

"Thank you."

They went into the living room, Rachel pacing back and forth by the door while Graham perched on the edge of the sofa.

"Peace offering?" he said, holding out the flowers.

Not wanting to be churlish, Rachel took them. "Thank you," she said. "So, you're finally ready to proceed?"

Graham nodded, slowly. "If we can come to an agreement. I know you don't think I deserve it, and I understand why you feel that way, but I have nothing, Rachel..."

"You maybe should have got a job fifteen years ago then, shouldn't you? Rather than expecting me to keep a roof over your head forever."

"Don't be like that. It was my home, too; I deserve something, surely? How would you feel if it was the other way around?"

"But it wasn't, was it? It was this way round - you moved into *my* home, *I* paid all the bills, did the housework, washed your clothes..."

Graham sighed dramatically, throwing himself back in his seat. "Aye, okay, fine - you did everything and I was a lazy, useless waster, is that what you want me to say?" Rachel could see him making an effort to remain calm. "But I have *nothing*, Rachel, and you have all this now, not to mention your fucking fancy man."

"Leave him out of this," she snapped back. "This is between

you and me."

Graham rose to his feet, causing Rachel to step back involuntarily. "I'm trying to be reasonable here, Rachel," he continued, although his tone had shifted - almost imperceptibly, but Rachel sensed it nonetheless. "You've moved on with your life - are you so selfish that you can't give me a chance to move on with mine?"

"Me? You're calling *me* selfish?" Rachel scoffed incredulously. "Are you fucking serious?"

"Well you are being fucking selfish!" Graham shouted. "Perfect fucking Rachel, can't even throw me some fucking scraps so I don't end up living on the street."

He was closer to her now, one hand pointing in her face. "Am I so beneath you, that I don't even deserve half of a fucking miserable wee ex-council flat?"

Rachel took a deep breath, trying to calm things down. "If you want to discuss this, then you need to agree to mediation. Go home, and we can let professionals sort it all out. You've known for ages that I want a divorce, and you've refused to even negotiate..."

"Because I don't want to fucking negotiate - I want my wife back!"

His fist slammed into the wall on the last word, making Rachel jump. She turned to see a dent in the plasterwork, Graham breathing heavily and looking at his hand as if it didn't belong to him.

"Fuck, I'm sorry..." he said. "I didn't mean to..."

"I think it's time for you to leave," Rachel said, breathless, her heart thudding in her chest. "If you want to discuss how we split the flat, you need to do it through our lawyers."

"Rach?" the voice came through the front door, which Rachel had purposely left unlocked. In the heat of their argument, neither of them had heard Duncan's car approach.

"In here," she called, trying to still the wobble in her voice.

Graham stepped back, rubbing the palms of his hands nervously against his jumper, and shaking.

"What's going on?" Duncan asked, peering round the door. His eyes danced back and forth, from where Rachel stood in the corner, to a red-faced Graham in the middle of the room, before alighting on the conspicuous dent in the wall.

"Get out." His voice was low but lined with fury, as he

218

marched across the room towards Graham.

"Duncan, don't," Rachel said, intercepting him and grabbing him by the elbow. "He was just leaving."

Duncan stopped when she touched him, but Rachel could sense the tension emanating from him.

Graham puffed his chest out again. He was silent, staring at Duncan for a minute, before pushing past him towards the door.

Duncan followed after him. "Don't come back here. If you have something to say to her, say it through your lawyer." He had reached the front door, Graham halfway down the garden path ahead of him. "If I see you here again, you'll have a non-harassment order landing on your doorstep before you know it."

"Is that a threat?" Graham growled, spinning on his heels and advancing back towards the house. "She's my wife, and this is none of your fucking business."

"She's not your wife anymore," Duncan muttered. "The sooner you get used to that fact, the better."

Graham squared up to him, his chin jutting out as he looked up defiantly at the taller man. "I ought to teach you a lesson, lover boy," he said, one stubby finger jabbing as close to Duncan's chest as he dared.

"Nothing would make me happier," Duncan replied. "Give me a reason and I'll have you arrested and charged so fast your head will spin."

"Stop it!" Rachel stormed out into the garden, pushing herself between them. "Cut it out, the pair of you. You - leave," she said, pointing furiously at Graham. "You," she spun on Duncan now, "get inside."

The two men eyeballed each other a moment longer, before Duncan turned and stalked back to the house.

Rachel lingered for a second. "I'll think about the flat," she said quietly. "But we do this through the proper channels now, you understand?"

Graham pointed his finger at her. "Fine," he said. "But this isn't a negotiation. You give me *my* flat back, and I'll agree to your fucking divorce. Then you and lover boy can sail off into the sunset."

# CHAPTER 43

"You told me he'd never hurt you."

Duncan was pacing back and forth in her living room, his hands clenching and unclenching by his side. Rachel went over to him, wrapping her arms around his waist and resting her head against his chest. His heart fluttered rapidly against her cheek.

"He hasn't," she said. "Yes, he slams doors, and shouts, and has - once or twice - punched a wall. But he never laid a finger on me."

"That doesn't make it okay."

"People fight," Rachel said with a shrug, pulling away from him. "I've done things I'm not proud of too, when I'm angry. I know it doesn't make it okay, but we're all just human at the end of the day, aren't we? We make mistakes."

Duncan was watching her curiously. "You should hate him."

"I do, sometimes. But most of the time, now, I'm just… indifferent."

They sat on the sofa together, Duncan keeping his arm around her, one finger drawing little circles around her shoulder. "Why was he here in the first place?" he asked.

"He says he wants to come to an agreement. About the divorce."

"Really? That's something, at least."

Rachel sighed. She knew she was being stubborn, and that on paper yes, maybe he was entitled to half of the flat they'd shared. But it just stuck in her throat to think of giving it to him, after all the years he'd let her shoulder the responsibility for, well, everything.

She explained it to Duncan. "Maybe I should just give him what he wants? At least that way I'd be rid of him."

Duncan continued stroking her arm. "Not wanting to sound like your lawyer, instead of your boyfriend," he said, "but given how long the two of you were together, I think a judge would probably award him something, at least."

Rachel sighed. She was so tired of stressing about all of this; deep down, she just wanted it to be over.

"Do you know, I don't think I even care anymore. As long as I still have this place." She looked around her house, and suddenly realised that it felt more like home than her granny's flat ever had.

"About that," Duncan said, shifting uncomfortably in his seat. "I phoned my boss today."

Rachel sat up suddenly, all thoughts of Graham pushed from her mind.

"I couldn't put it off any longer, I'm afraid. I had to tell him what Stephanie's decided. He wants me back in Edinburgh first thing on Monday morning. Kindred Spirits are officially - and permanently - withdrawing their interest in Inniscreag Distillery."

Duncan stayed over that night, although for the first time, they didn't have sex. Rachel fell asleep with her head in the crook of his elbow, both of them avoiding talking about the fact that in forty-eight hours he'd be gone, with no idea when they would see each other again.

Rachel knew she was being melodramatic - Edinburgh was hardly the ends of the earth, and they could easily drive to see one another. But something about it felt final, as if the magic that had come over them on Inniscreag might not last out in the real world.

The following morning, they walked the coastal road to Craigport to meet Violet and Morag. They were rendezvousing with Sorcha and her family at eleven o'clock by the harbour; Andy had offered to take them all out sightseeing on his tour boat, a prospect which - after her ferry trip a couple of days before - had greatly excited Violet.

Shelagh was just tidying up from the breakfast service when they arrived, stopping for a chat at the bar.

"Your ex has made himself scarce," the landlady said, direct as ever.

"What do you mean?" Rachel asked.

"Checked out this morning. Said he's off on the morning ferry, back to civilisation. Well, his actual words were, 'I'm getting off this Godforsaken lump of rock', but I'm paraphrasing."

Rachel glanced at her watch, instantly feeling a weight lifting from her shoulders; it was after ten, which meant the morning ferry had already left. He was gone. Maybe last night had been the catalyst he'd needed, to realise it was actually over?

His parting words still rang in her ear, though. Deep down, Rachel knew that if she wanted rid of Graham for good, she'd have to give him what he wanted.

With an excited yelp, Violet came bounding through the door from the bedrooms, and straight into her father's arms. Morag was close behind.

"Morning," she said, greeting Rachel and Duncan with a peck on the cheek each.

The four of them walked across the road to the harbour, where Andrew and Sorcha were due to meet them with the kids, but there was no sign of them. They eventually arrived - ten minutes late - the adults both looking harassed and the kids unusually quiet.

"Everything okay?" Rachel whispered, giving her friend a quick hug.

"I'll explain later." Sorcha's usually clear blue eyes were puffy and rimmed with red.

They were all grateful for the distraction of the boat trip, letting the kids carry the conversational burden as they chattered excitedly over one another. Maisie couldn't believe that Violet went to school in a class of thirty other girls.

"That's bigger than our whole school," she gasped, blue eyes wide.

The two girls were like negative versions of one another – Violet, dark and curly haired next to Maisie's smooth, flyaway mane of blonde – but they were hitting it off. Violet was younger by a year or so, but her maturity, and the fact that Maisie was used to having just her little brothers to play with, evened things out.

"Look dad, more dolphins!" Violet screeched, leaning over the side so far that Duncan grabbed onto her life jacket.

"We get whales too, sometimes," Maisie was saying. "Humpbacks and orcas. They hunt the seals that live on the colonies off of Skye."

Maisie took great pride in showing off her island, providing narration while Andrew steered them in and out of the little coves and caves that peppered Inniscreag's coastline. Sorcha, however, remained quiet, sitting on one of the benches and staring out to sea.

Rachel sidled over to her, while the men and children were looking over the opposite side of the boat; Fergus thought he'd seen an otter scampering around the shoreline, and they were all now hunting earnestly for it.

"What's up?" Rachel asked. But Sorcha just shook her head.

"Not now," she said.

"Okay. Do you want to come over for a drink tomorrow night? Duncan's going back to Edinburgh; we could cheer each other up? Maybe get Una over too?"

Sorcha smiled, but it didn't reach her eyes. "That'd be nice. It'll just be us though; did you not know Una's off to Skye for a couple of days?"

Rachel felt a pang of guilt; she'd been so wrapped up in her own dramas, she hadn't spoken to her friends in days. Una still didn't know that she and Duncan we're now 'official', and Sorcha had only found out because Rachel had arranged this little trip, mainly for Violet's benefit.

"She's meeting up with Lucy," Sorcha continued. "Sounds like they're really hitting it off."

"Just you and me then," Rachel persisted. "You look like you could use a girls' night."

"Okay." Sorcha nodded reluctantly. "I'll double check with Andy later; make sure he doesn't mind putting the kids to bed."

By the time they'd returned to shore, Violet and Maisie were confirmed friends.

"Can Violet come for dinner?" Maisie asked, as they were clambering to shore back at the harbour.

"Can I Dad? Please?" Violet echoed.

"Not tonight I'm afraid, darling. It's our last night; we're having dinner with Rachel."

Rachel tried not to notice how her little face dipped. She was no longer the most interesting person Violet had met on this trip, then.

They said goodbye, the girls exchanging contact details and promising to email.

"I'll send you pictures when the whales come," Maisie promised. "And you can send me some of Edinburgh castle, yeah?"

Violet nodded earnestly, and the two even hugged.

Walking back to the pub, Duncan slipped his hand into Rachel's.

"I've never seen Violet like that before," he said. "She's great with grownups, but kids... She's never really found other kids that she gets on with. I don't know why, but she and Maisie just clicked."

Rachel smiled. "Maybe they can see each other again, if you

guys ever come back?"

"Of course we'll be coming back," Duncan replied. He stopped, letting the gap widen between them and Violet and Morag.

"We're going to make this work," he said. "I love you; we can do long distance for a while. And further down the line, if everything works out like I hope it will... we'll figure out what comes next."

Rachel nodded, letting him pull her against his chest for a hug, and wishing that she shared even just an ounce of his certainty.

# CHAPTER 44

They left on the morning boat, allowing time for Duncan and Morag to negotiate the long drive home, whilst still getting Violet back at a reasonable time to go to bed.

Rachel stood at the terminal to see them off, willing herself not to cry.

"I've really enjoyed meeting you," she said to Violet, bending down to give the girl a proper hug. "I'll see you again soon, okay?"

"We can Facetime," Violet said brightly. She was clutching her notebook in her hands, complete with Maisie's email address and phone number - as well as Rachel's - and a dolphin teddy she'd uncovered in amongst Ishbel's eclectic selection of tourist gifts.

Rachel and Morag exchanged kisses, while Duncan helped Violet into his sister's car. Duncan's own sporty vehicle lacked a back seat, so Violet had no choice but to travel home with her auntie.

"I do have a sensible 'dad car' at home," he said lightly, lingering at Rachel's side as long as he could. "This is my 'wanky lawyer having a mid-life crisis car' that I save for work."

Rachel laughed. "Phone me when you get home?"

"Promise."

He folded her into his arms, resting his chin on top of her head before depositing a little kiss on her hair. "I love you, Rach. I'll be back to see you as soon as I can."

"I love you, too," she replied. "I might have to come down to Glasgow in a couple of weeks actually - I need to see my divorce lawyer about a few things." She tried to keep her voice light. "We could maybe meet up?"

"Sounds perfect." He looked at her earnestly, both of her hands in his. "We can make this work."

Rachel nodded, not trusting herself to speak. Just then, the car behind them pipped its horn impatiently; the queue of traffic had slowly started to creep towards the ramp and up onto the boat.

"Better go," Duncan said, giving her one last, firm kiss. "I'll speak to you soon."

Rachel stepped back and watched them as the cars were directed into their places on the deck of the ferry. She remained there, the wind buffeting her hair, until the boat set off and the occupants were allowed to leave their cars.

Even at a distance, she could recognise the Frasers clear as day - three dark heads, the little one in the middle, Violet's curls wafting wildly in the breeze as she waved her skinny arms as high as they would go. Rachel waved back, blinking away the tears, until they became nothing more than little black dots balanced on top of the bright red hull of the boat.

She sniffed, gathering her coat around herself - the unpredictable island weather had turned once again, so that it was chilly, even in mid-July. Una would be delivering her sermon right about now, Rachel realised, before leaving on the afternoon boat.

Firing off a quick text message, Rachel apologised for not managing to see her in the week since she'd returned from Skye. So much had changed in such a short space of time, she reflected, and Rachel had decided that it was time to take matters into her own hands. No more running away, or burying her head in the sand. She knew what she wanted now, and she was going to do whatever it took to hold onto it.

Opening the door later that evening, Rachel expected to find a smiling Sorcha, bottle of wine in hand, ready for what she was hoping would be a fun, light-hearted girls evening to take her mind off Duncan's departure, and cheer Sorcha up after whatever had upset her yesterday. But instead, Sorcha's face was drawn, her hair pulled back, and a heavily laden rucksack lay on the ground at her feet.

Rachel frowned at her, taking a moment to catch up with what was happening.

"Have you left him?" Rachel couldn't believe that she'd actually gone through with it; she thought it was all talk.

Sorcha shook her head, sniffing, tears rimming her blue eyes. "No," she said. "He's thrown me out."

Opting for tea instead of wine, Rachel bundled Sorcha into the living room, took her bag from her and got her settled on the sofa. She'd started crying again, and Rachel didn't know what to say, so she settled for boiling the kettle and piling chocolate biscuits onto a plate while she gathered her thoughts.

Andrew had broken up with Sorcha? She would never have seen that one coming, and from the looks of it, neither did Sorcha.

As a soon to be divorcee herself, Rachel should have had a font of advice for her friend. On the contrary, however, she felt woefully ill-prepared for this, and found herself wishing Una wasn't currently half way across the water to Skye.

"What happened?" she asked as she re-entered the living room, handing Sorcha a mug of tea and a brand new roll of toilet paper. She never thought to buy proper tissues.

"He checked my emails," she said. Her hands were trembling, so Rachel removed the mug of tea and placed it on the coffee table instead.

Sorcha went on, her eyes glazed. "He's never checked my emails before; why did he do it now? I was going to end it anyway, but now he won't believe me..."

"Sorcha, what are you talking about?"

The two bright blue pools that had been waving frantically back and forth suddenly zoomed in on Rachel. They were wide, and scared, and the mouth beneath them suddenly crumpled into an anguished sob.

"I've been having an affair," Sorcha admitted, bending her head over onto her skinny knees and sobbing.

Rachel sat back in her seat, preoccupied - for the moment at least - with the logistics of it.

"Who with?" she asked, all too aware that the eligible bachelors on Inniscreag were thin on the ground, and certainly none of them Sorcha's type.

She sniffed again, tearing off a great chunk of loo roll and blowing her nose in it. "I haven't actually met him," she said. "He lives in America. We just talked, online - he commented on an Instagram post I'd put up, then we started emailing, and it all just spiralled."

"So nothing's actually happened, in the flesh?"

Sorcha's face was already reddened as a result of her crying, but the colour in her cheeks deepened now. "There were some messages, where we, you know... talked about it. And I sent him some pictures. God, I'm such an *idiot!*"

She flung her head into her hands again, a fresh wave of sobs overwhelming her.

Rachel sat back. If she'd been at a loss for what to say before, it was even worse now. "You didn't tell Andy yourself?" she asked.

227

Sorcha shook her head. "You know what things have been like between us recently. This guy started messaging me, and he was gorgeous, and he complimented me… I just got sucked in. It's been years since Andy's talked to me like that. I'm not making excuses," she rushed on, "but that's just how it was. I'd decided to end it, then yesterday, Andy logged onto my emails - said he was checking an Amazon order I'd placed for him, but he must have been suspicious. And he saw all our messages."

"*All* of them? Including the…"

"Yep." Sorcha breathed in deeply, taking a sip from her tea. "I honestly was going to put a stop to it, but he won't believe me. We couldn't discuss it yesterday, with the kids around, and going out on the boat with you guys, but this morning he took them to my mother's, then kicked me out. Said he wouldn't spend another minute under the same roof as a cheat."

Her lip wobbled again, but she held it in. "I've fucked everything up, Rachel. And when the kids find out, they're going to hate me…"

Rachel crossed the room to sit on the sofa beside her, taking her hand. She could empathise, to a degree. Although Rachel had never cheated on Graham - unless you counted Duncan - she couldn't say with one hundred percent certainty that she wouldn't have been tempted, if someone had come along and said all those things she'd spent years wanting to hear.

"Don't think about that right now," she said, patting the back of Sorcha's hand. "You can stay here as long as you need. You're still their mum, no matter what - you just made a mistake, that's all."

Sorcha scoffed. "You know what this place is like, though," she said. "Nothing stays secret for long. Eventually everyone will know, and I'll forever be remembered as the adulteress school teacher."

Rachel squeezed her hand again. Nothing she could say right now was going to make Sorcha feel better. So, she said the only thing she could think of.

"Wine?"

# CHAPTER 45

Rachel tucked Sorcha in on her sofa, not long after ten o'clock. She'd fallen asleep halfway through her third glass of wine, so Rachel helped her get her head down on a cushion, lifted her long, skinny legs up onto the seat, and covered her over with a blanket. As an afterthought, she also placed the remote control, a glass of water and a packet of paracetamol on the coffee table, in case she woke up before Rachel, and presumably with a headache.

Their evening had been briefly interrupted by Duncan, when he'd phoned just before nine to let Rachel know they were home.

"Just got Vi to sleep," he said, stifling a yawn. "I don't think I'll be far behind her myself, to be honest."

In a hushed voice, Rachel filled him in on the circumstances surrounding the arrival of her unexpected house guest.

"Andy will come around," he assured her. "He adores her. I'll give him a ring in the morning though, check in on him."

"Thank you. I'd best get back to her - call you tomorrow?"

"Can't wait. Sweet dreams."

Rachel hung up with a smile; it was nice just to hear his voice. Maybe he was right - long distance might not be so bad, for a while at least. She'd always heard people say 'absence makes the heart grow fonder'. Now, she'd find out if they were right.

Sorcha had perked up slightly, after her second glass of wine.

"Check you two out," she said, only a slight edge of bitterness in her voice. "Young love - only been apart a matter of hours, and you're already whispering sweet nothings down the phone to each other."

Rachel shrugged. "Just checking in before he went to sleep."

"Your ex pissed off eventually then?" Sorcha sighed. "How come you've got two men fighting over you, and I can barely get one to pay attention to me?"

Rachel was going to point out that she *did* have two men interested in her - that was what had caused this whole mess, after all - but Sorcha continued mindlessly, drink obviously loosening her tongue.

"I mean I work out, I eat right; I've had three kids and I've still got a washboard stomach. Not like some women, who just let themselves go. I mean look at you - you've never even had one, and you've got more of a belly than me. But yet gorgeous Duncan can't get enough of you, and my tubby, balding husband doesn't fancy me in the slightest. That doesn't seem fair, does it?"

Rachel watched her for a moment, saying nothing, waiting for her friend's drink-addled mind to catch up with what her mouth had been saying. After a few seconds, regret dawned in Sorcha's blue eyes.

"Ah, shit, Rachel, I didn't mean that the way it came out…"

"What - that you're tall, and slim, and fertile, and therefore deserve a happy ending? But chubby little barren Rachel doesn't - or certainly not with someone who looks like Duncan. Is that about right?"

She kept her voice calm, but inside Rachel felt a little bubble of rage swelling. She loved Sorcha, but this selfish, superficial side of her was beginning to grate.

"I'm sorry, Rachel, please…"

"Did you ever think that your attitude might be the problem, rather than your looks? That maybe if you appreciated what you've got a little more, and put some effort into fixing your marriage, instead of falling for someone buttering you up online, then maybe - just maybe - you wouldn't be in this mess?"

Sorcha's blue eyes swelled once more. "You're right," she whispered, looking down at her feet. A big, fat tear hung precariously on the end of her long nose, before dropping on to the carpet. "I've been a bitch to everyone recently. I just feel so miserable, all the time…"

Softening, Rachel came and sat beside her once more. "We understand, Sorcha, we really do. And we're your friends, and we want to help you. But maybe if you started looking for the positives in your life, rather than the negatives, you'd find a lot to be grateful for?"

Sorcha nodded, as Rachel continued. "I'm not saying you have to stay with Andy - if you're miserable, and he doesn't treat you the way you want to be treated, then leave. Una and I, your mum - we'll all support you no matter what. And the kids will adapt. But if you still love him, and you're realising that you've made a mistake… Then you need to stop blaming him and start thinking about what you can do to put it right."

"Do you think I can?" Sorcha asked quietly. "He hates me now, and he's got every right to."

"He's angry," Rachel said. "And hurt. And I doubt he'll be able to trust you for a really, really long time. But marriages have survived worse; you just both have to want to make it work. Give him some time, and maybe he'll come to realise what he's missing, too."

Sorcha looked at her again, embarrassed. "I am sorry about what I said, Rachel. You're beautiful, inside and out. And you and Duncan are made for each other."

She had grown quiet after that, so that Rachel almost didn't notice when, half an hour later, she was nodding into her empty wine glass. Flicking out the light, and leaving Sorcha snoring quietly in the darkness, she climbed up the stairs to her bedroom, wishing more than ever that Duncan's warm, safe body was there waiting for her.

The next morning, leaving a very embarrassed and apologetic Sorcha at her house, Rachel headed across to the office early. Having ordered the new merchandise on Friday, she now needed to make sure that the gift shop would be ready when it arrived. And that would require a conversation with Andy, which, given last night's unexpected turn of events, might be a tad awkward. On top of that, she needed to phone her lawyer, and she wanted to speak to Cameron. If the lawyer confirmed that her plan was workable, then she was going to need another short leave of absence.

He arrived just after nine, when Rachel was hanging up the phone. The solicitor had given her suggestion the go-ahead, although it would require agreement at the other end before they could proceed with anything. Still, she wanted to get down to Glasgow as soon as possible, to make sure everything was in order.

"Morning," Cameron said. "Sorry I'm a wee bit late this morning. How's this week looking?" he asked, flicking through the open diary on Rachel's desk.

"A few changes, actually," Rachel replied. "I'm going to go and see Andy in a bit - see when he can fit in the work on the shop, between his boat tours and stuff. Then I'm going to be away for the rest of the week, if that's okay?"

Cameron's eyes sparkled. "Canna bear being away from yer man, can ye? Leavin' us already?"

"No," Rachel blushed. "I need to go back down to Glasgow. I've got a few personal things to see to."

Cameron nodded, but didn't pry any further. "Aye, nae bother."

"And just in case you see her around - Sorcha will be staying at my place while I'm away."

Cameron squinted at her curiously. "Everything a'right?"

"Just a tiff," Rachel said lightly. "She'll be back home soon, I'm sure. They just need a wee break from each other."

Cameron gave her a wry smile. "We've a' been there," he said. "I'll keep a wee eye on her - from a distance, mind."

After firing off a few emails, and checking in on Martha and Irene up at the coffee shop, Rachel popped home to quickly pack a case. She was only planning to be away for a few days, hopefully. When she explained her plan to Sorcha, however, her friend looked at her uncertainly.

"You're sure?" she asked. "I thought..."

"I've made up my mind," Rachel said. "It's time to move on, properly."

They hugged goodbye on the doorstep, Rachel reassuring Sorcha once again that she could stay for as long as she needed.

"I am going to have to pop in to see Andy before I leave, though," she said hesitantly, rushing on when she saw her friend's expression. "It's about work - I'm hoping he'll be able to start on the gift shop refurb this week. I won't mention you, unless you want me to. Does he know where you are?"

Sorcha nodded sadly. She'd showered and freshened up, but the same air of guilt and shame still hung over her. "Just tell him I love him. And I'm ready when he wants to talk."

Giving her friend one last squeeze, Rachel threw her suitcase in the back seat of the car, double checked that she had the keys she was going to need, and started down the road to Craigport.

When he answered the door, Andrew's expression bore a striking resemblance to his wife's. His face was drawn and crumpled, the brown eyes lined in red, and his thinning, straw coloured hair tousled. He looked as though he'd slept in his clothes, and eyed Rachel warily when he saw her.

"Did she send you?" he asked.

"No," Rachel shook her head. "I'm here about work. Can I

come in?"

"Aye." With a tired sigh, Andy stepped aside and led her through to the living room, which was scattered with toys and books. "Excuse the mess," he said. "I couldn't be arsed tidying up."

"Don't worry about it," she assured him, moving aside a forgotten football so that she could sit down. "Are the kids still at Ishbel's?"

Andy nodded. "She said she'll keep them for a couple of days. As far as they're concerned, they're just having an extended sleepover at Granny's."

"I'm not here because of Sorcha," Rachel repeated. "But she did ask me to tell you she loved you, and she was ready to talk whenever you are."

Andy grimaced. Rachel could see the pain, and the anger, lined in his face, and in the tension of his tightly clenched fists as he sat beside her. "She'll be waiting a while," he muttered.

Shifting awkwardly in her seat, Rachel attempted to move the conversation along to her original purpose. "You know how I spoke to you about the gift shop, a while back?"

Andy nodded.

"Well, I know you've got a lot on your plate just now, but I wondered if you might be able to get started on it this week? It's just, I've ordered in some merchandise and wanted to get up and running as soon as I can…"

He sighed heavily. "Aye, that should be fine," he said. "But make sure Sorcha knows I'm no' coming up there to speak to her - no' yet, anyway. I'll let her know when I'm ready."

"Okay," Rachel nodded. "Thank you."

They agreed a price, before Rachel phoned Cameron to let him know, and ask him to bung a hefty tip on top, too. After another phone call to check in on Sorcha, and relay Andy's message, Rachel was ready.

She sat in the little queue of cars, waiting to roll onto the ferry and cross the short stretch of water between Inniscreag and Skye. Then, she would follow almost exactly the same route Duncan had travelled the day before, through the Highlands and down to the Central Belt, before heading West into Glasgow. Her stomach churned with anticipation. Rachel was sure this was the right choice, but once it had been made, there would be no turning back.

# CHAPTER 46

It was late when Rachel finally arrived in Glasgow, coasting along the motorway that circled the city. The carpet of lights and the endless trail of traffic was dazzling, even at this late hour. After almost a year of driving on country roads, it took Rachel a moment to get re-accustomed to the cars whooshing past on either side, double and triple checking her mirrors before she dared execute a lane change.

She pulled up outside the familiar high-rise block of flats, feeling a strange mix of emotions wash over her. Rachel had never really liked it here - it was bland and depressing, the internal communal walls covered in graffiti and imbued with the smell of years of second hand cigarette smoke. Many nights, as a child, she had dreamed about running away from this place, and finding love and adventure on some foreign shore. She guessed she had now, in a way, although Inniscreag wasn't quite as far away as she had imagined.

But this was also the place where some of her happiest childhood memories had taken place - reading stories on Granny Peggy's knee, scattering breadcrumbs for the pigeons at her window ledge, and helping her carry the mop and bucket when it was her turn to clean the stairwell. Rachel had felt safe here, when life with her mother could be so unpredictable.

Even coming home with Graham after their wedding - a rushed ceremony at the registry office, followed by drinks with his bandmates at a pub on the Trongate - had been a happy time. It was bittersweet now, tinged with sadness at the eventual disintegration of their relationship; but she had loved him once, and for a while they'd been happy here.

Locking the doors manually as she exited the car, Rachel skirted the groups of teenagers crowded around the entrance way with her head down. She passed the concierge in his glass booth, who barely glanced up - he wouldn't have recognised her if he had, she realised. The housing association must have taken on some new employees during the time she had been away.

Rachel took the lift up to her old flat, on the seventh floor. Most of these properties were still rented, but her Granny Peggy had bought hers years ago, when Rachel was only little, thanks to Maggie Thatcher's right to buy scheme. It was worth buttons now, and as she rode up the lift and saw the peeling paint and vandalised hallways, Rachel realised how stubborn she'd been being. If it weren't for Edith's will then things might have been different, but as it stood, she was going to inherit a business - including a mortgage free home for life - in a beautiful location. Graham really did have nothing. And although she knew it wasn't her fault, she realised that she didn't want to feel responsible for him spending the rest of his days destitute, either.

Letting herself in, Rachel took a quick walk around the little two bed flat, with its net curtains and dingy wallpaper, before unravelling the sleeping bag she'd brought with her and settling down on the bare mattress. The sooner she got to sleep, the sooner she could get back home. And home, she now realised, was Inniscreag.

She woke early, and wasted no time in getting to work. A sandwich she'd picked up at a late-night garage on her way down provided breakfast, washed down with a bottle of room-temperature water. Rachel then lugged up the few empty suitcases she'd brought with her and started raking through the belongings she'd left behind. Things she wanted to keep went in the cases; everything else went in black bags, ready to be dropped off at the recycling centre later.

Rachel noticed, with a pang, how many of Graham's things were still here. Clothes, books, CDs; she'd shut him out and fled without a second thought, not considering what he might have needed. Things really must have been miserable for him.

It was early afternoon when the buzzer went, Rachel having lost track of the time. Her old wardrobe had been emptied, along with the contents of nearly all the kitchen cupboards. She wasn't planning on doing anything with the tired old furniture - he was welcome to it, if he wanted it.

"Hello?" she said, speaking into the little unit by the front door, and noticing how caked in dust it was.

"It's me. Please, don't hang up."

Rachel hadn't expected to hear his voice ever again. She didn't know what had possessed him to come here, or how he'd even figured out where she was.

"My lawyer called me this morning. Please, Rachel, I didn't

know you'd be here – I just came by for a look. But when I saw the lights on, I thought we could talk."

Sighing, and hoping she didn't regret this, Rachel pressed the buzzer to let him in.

He regarded her awkwardly as he got out of the lift, before walking slowly into the home they'd once shared together as husband and wife.

"Where does the time go, eh?" Graham said, looking around the little yellow painted hallway. Rachel remembered picking out the colour, thinking it would brighten up the windowless room in the centre of their home. Now it just felt drab.

She nodded, not sure what he wanted her to say.

He scuffed the carpet nervously with the toe of his tatty trainers. "I'm sorry about what happened the other day, at your house. I lost my temper. And I'm sorry it's ended this way, Rachel."

"Me too," she admitted, before adding in a rush, "and I'm sorry for running off the way that I did. That wasn't fair on you; I should have spoken to you first."

To her surprise, Graham smiled. "I understand why you did it, though. I wasn't much of a husband to you, was I?"

Rachel didn't say anything, the two of them wandering through to the living room and taking a seat on the old, sagging sofas.

"I have actually got a job now," Graham said. "I should have told you when I came to Inniscreag. Nothing exciting - just stacking shelves in Asda. But it pays the bills."

"So your lawyer has spoken to you?" Rachel asked, not wanting to be drawn into small-talk.

Graham nodded. "It's very generous of you. Thank you."

"And you understand the conditions?"

"Yes - my lawyer's drawing up the paperwork as we speak. I'm going to their office later to sign everything."

Rachel sighed, relieved. Part of her had expected him to rail against the proposal, to look for another excuse to fight or punish her. But if this proved anything, it was that he didn't want her back; not really. He just wanted the flat, and the mortgage-free security it offered him.

Returning here had only confirmed what Rachel had come to realise over the last few weeks; she didn't want anything from this part of her life anymore. She wanted a fresh start, with Duncan, and missing out on a few grand from the sale of this dingy little flat was, she now realised, a price worth paying to get it.

In exchange for Rachel transferring full ownership of the flat to him, Graham was agreeing to proceed with the divorce, uncontested, and officially sign away any claim - however tenuous - he might have against the distillery. She would have Inniscreag, and Duncan; she didn't need anything else.

"Do you want to grab anything while you're here, or just wait til everything's finalised?" Rachel asked. "I'll probably stay over tomorrow night again, but that should be me cleared out then."

Graham shook his head, rising from the seat. "It's fine - I've got what I need at my flat share, for now. You could leave me a key, though if you like? Save you making another journey back down?"

"No," Rachel said firmly. "I'll leave them at my solicitor's office. Once you've signed your half of the deal, then you can get them."

"Fair enough," he agreed with a shrug.

They walked back through to the front door, Graham hovering awkwardly at the threshold. He turned back to look at her, and Rachel was amazed to see tears welling in his eyes; Graham never cried.

"Rachel - I'm sorry. We did love each other once, didn't we? It wasn't all horrible? We were happy for a while, right?"

She smiled sadly, taking his hand and squeezing it gently. "We were, and I did. Very much. I'm not sure when I stopped."

"Was it because we could never…"

"No," she said fiercely. "Not that. Even if we had, it wouldn't have made us happy. Not in the long run, at least."

He nodded, sniffing and rubbing the moisture from his eyes. "I know I never really spoke to you about it - it wasn't because I didn't care." He laughed bitterly. "I just never knew how to. You were so sad, and I couldn't make it better. But they were my babies too."

Rachel swallowed deeply. "I know," she whispered.

He pulled her into a hug then, and for a moment Rachel remembered what it was like when they'd first met - a brief flashback to that first spark of connection. She hugged him back, knowing for certain now, that this would be the last time they ever saw each other.

"Goodbye, Graham," she said, letting him go.

"Goodbye, Rachel."

# CHAPTER 47

When he called that evening, Duncan was more than a little surprised to hear that Rachel was in Glasgow.

"I thought you said you weren't going down for a couple of weeks?" he asked.

"Change of plans," she said casually. She hadn't divulged the extent of her plan to him, as she knew he'd probably try to talk her out of giving the flat away completely. And maybe it was stupid, but with nothing now standing in the way of her inheritance at Inniscreag, bickering with Graham over a dilapidated flat just seemed unnecessary. One more night and she could say goodbye to this place, and this chapter of her life, forever.

"Did you see your lawyer? Has Graham agreed to the terms of the divorce?"

"Yes," she replied, relieved that she didn't have to lie. "I'll fill you in properly when I see you. Would you be free for lunch tomorrow? I thought we could meet up somewhere halfway - maybe Pitlochry? I need to go to the tip in the morning, but I'm hoping to finish packing up tonight and be on the road first thing."

"Sounds lovely," Duncan said. She could hear the smile in his voice, and pictured his crinkling emerald eyes.

They arranged to meet at Pitlochry Festival Theatre - it was located in a handy little location on the outskirts of the village, where it was quick and easy to pull on and off the A9.

"I love you," Duncan said, before they hung up.

"Love you, too."

Deciding to make the most of being in the land of international cuisine and home delivery, Rachel opened up her phone and went onto Just Eat, picking a local Indian restaurant she used to love. With a chicken chasni, mushroom fried rice and naan bread on the way, Rachel set about her final task.

The spare room had once been her Granny's, and still housed some of the things which Rachel hadn't been able to bring herself to get rid of after she died. There were a few trinkets and some jewellery, which Rachel popped into her case to take back to Inniscreag, and in the wardrobe she found shoeboxes full of old photographs. Unsure whether she should take them all, Rachel decided to sift through what she could just now, take home any that were of people she recognised, and accept that she would probably just have to chuck the rest. It seemed heartless, but she couldn't be doing with boxes full of photos of people she didn't know and had never met cluttering up her home.

The first few pictures she came across were of her mum and dad; Mum was short and dark, like Rachel, while her dad – of whom she had only the vaguest memories - was tall and blonde, with a thick eighties' moustache. They looked happy, and not for the first time, Rachel wondered what had made him leave so suddenly, when she was just two years old. There were even some photos of the three of them together, which Rachel moved into the 'keep' pile but didn't look at too closely. She had a feeling they would make her cry if she did.

As well as the photographs, there was an assortment of old family documents. Rachel found her results letter from the Scottish Qualifications Authority, showing her grades from her Higher exams twenty years previously, and was strangely touched that her granny had kept it all this time. There was also a zipped-up leather folder that held what had obviously been her grandmother's most important items of paperwork - insurance documents, bank statements and such. All decades out of date now, of course.

Rachel sifted through them one at a time, just in case there was anything worth keeping - like a hidden, secret bank account with thousands of pounds in it, perhaps? She laughed. That was the sort of thing that would happen in a film right about now - the protagonist would find some life changing item, hidden in amongst all the junk.

She was cross-legged on the floor, tearing off chunks of naan bread and dipping them in the deep red sauce of the curry, when it happened. At first, the piece of paper looked no different than all the others - tatty, and yellowed with age. But it was obviously official, like something from the government rather than a bank or insurance agency, so Rachel unfolded it to have a closer look.

It was a birth certificate, for a baby born on 13th June 1962; her mother's birthday. There were no details for the parents, but the child's full name made Rachel do a double take - *Mhairi McLeod Grant.* Mum had always been known as Mary, as far as Rachel was aware, and she didn't know she'd even had a middle name. McLeod was hardly an uncommon name in Scotland, Rachel told herself, but still, something about the revelation unnerved her.

Scanning quickly down the brief few lines of text, Rachel uncovered her next surprise - the place of birth was listed as Harris. How strange, she thought; she'd felt so at home ever since she arrived in the Western Isles, all the time never knowing that her mother had been born there.

A sudden sense of purpose and excitement overwhelming her, Rachel began digging frantically through the box that had contained the birth certificate. It didn't take long to uncover a notebook, every page scribbled over in her mother's own frantic, messy handwriting.

Rachel flicked through it - mostly, the contents made no sense. Just random words and names scribbled here and there, alongside the occasional date. From the looks of it, her mother had been trying to piece together some of the fragments of her past, but didn't seem to have had much luck.

Suddenly, one scrawled message jumped out at her: 'FATHER - FIONNLAGH GRANT'. The words were carved in thick black letters, multiple pen lines showing that they had obviously been traced over repeatedly.

Rachel felt her heart quicken in her chest - if this meant what she thought it did, could that mean that this Fionnlagh Grant was her own grandfather? And, presumably, he was from Harris, just a few miles across the water from Inniscreag? Rachel knew it was unlikely he'd still be alive, but there could be relatives left behind, other children even? She could have aunties and uncles, or cousins, she never knew anything about.

Rachel sat back, her mind racing and her takeaway forgotten. If her mother had been looking into this before she died, surely now it was Rachel's job to finish what she had started?

Deciding to take everything back with her to Inniscreag, just in case any of the old photographs she didn't recognise turned out to be useful, Rachel boxed everything back up and piled it by the front door to be put in the boot of her car in the morning. If there was a chance she had any long-lost family out there, she wanted to find them.

# CHAPTER 48

Rachel was still full of pent up energy by the time she met Duncan for an early lunch the following day. They pulled into the car park, from opposite directions, at almost the exact same moment.

"Very punctual," Duncan said, greeting her with a smile and open arms. He was carrying a gift bag in one hand.

"For me?" Rachel asked, standing up on tiptoes to kiss him. She couldn't believe it had only been two days - she'd missed him like crazy.

He dangled the gift bag just out of her reach. "Inside," he teased.

They found a comfy sofa by the huge glass windows, offering expansive views over the green banks of the River Tummel and a picturesque suspension bridge to the town beyond. Duncan left Rachel to get comfy while he went up to the little service hatch, returning with two bowls of soup, tuna sandwiches and a pot of tea. With it being a Wednesday, the place was deserted, even during the school holidays.

"How civilised." Rachel said, as Duncan poured them both a cup of tea. "It's like we've fast forwarded thirty years already."

Duncan smiled, handing her the teacup balanced on a twee little saucer. "I'll still think you're gorgeous," he said with a wink. "Even when you're old and grey."

"You should know, I'm pretty grey already," Rachel replied, sipping her tea. "It's only thanks to Madame Clairol that I've not got a full-on badger streak down the middle."

Duncan laughed, before nodding to the bag, which he had left sitting conspicuously on the table top. "You can open it now, if you like."

Rachel had always loved presents, and opened it like a little child, tearing apart the paper impatiently.

It was a double picture frame in solid wood; the kind with a hinge in the middle, so you can open it out to see the pictures on either side. On the left was one of the three of them - Duncan, Violet and Rachel - taken on Andy's boat. It was a selfie; three ruddy, windswept faces grinning broadly into the camera, Violet's wild curls being tossed in the wind and obscuring most of Duncan and Rachel.

The one on the right took Rachel a moment to recognise. It was black and white, and showed a woman lying on her stomach on a sandy beach, tartan blanket over her shoulders and the wind in her hair. Her ankles were crossed in the air behind her and her nose was stuck in a book, completely oblivious to the presence of the photographer. She was beautiful, Rachel thought, before it suddenly dawned on her who it was.

"It's me," she gasped.

"That's how I see you," Duncan said softly, one hand reaching out for hers. "That's how I've always seen you."

Rachel smiled, leaning over to kiss him. "Thank you," she said.

"Just a little something so you don't forget us, while we're stuck down here."

"How could I?" Rachel asked. "How is Violet anyway?"

"Gutted to be back in the concrete jungle," Duncan replied, turning his attention to his soup. "She loved it up on the islands; it was like she was a different child. Now she's back in her room, pining after the wildlife. And the people."

"Is she with Morag today?"

Duncan sighed heavily. "Yeah; same as most days. I hate not being able to be with her more, but my schedule at work... I should really look at cutting back. Morag's more her parent than me, these days."

"I'm sure that's not true," Rachel said. "She didn't think so anyway; she told me the reason Violet's such a great kid is all down to you."

"Well, that's kind of her, but she's understating her role slightly. If it weren't for her, I don't know how I would have managed these past few years. There's no way I'd be in this job right now, that's for sure. Or if I was, Violet would be spending half her life with a nanny or childminder."

"There's worse ways for kids to grow up," Rachel said, thinking back to her own childhood, and her mum's. She suddenly realised that by comparison, she herself had been positively blessed. Her childhood had hardly been idyllic, but she was loved, by her mum and her granny. She doubted now if her own mother had ever known what it felt like to be loved - abandoned by her birth parents, and raised in a children's home. Was it any wonder she'd struggled so much to find peace?

Rachel told Duncan about the birth certificate she'd found, showing that her mum had been born in Harris. She'd been thinking about it all morning, and the more she did, the more it just made sense.

"We used to go on holiday to Harris," she was saying, after Duncan had gone back up to the counter and returned with two slices of homemade Victoria sponge.

"That must be why - I guess she was trying to find out about her birth family."

"And she never told you about it?"

Rachel shook her head. "We were never that close," she said. "I wish I'd known that she was trying to find them. I could have helped her."

"Do you want to pick up where she left off?"

"I feel like I should," Rachel admitted. "It might make me feel a little less guilty about not being there when she died. Like I could make it up to her, somehow, by finishing what she'd started." She hesitated for a moment, before continuing. "I'd also like to give her a proper memorial."

This was something else that had been tormenting her. As a penniless student she'd been quite happy to stick her head in the sand and let the authorities deal with her mother's burial. But now, she felt awful about it.

She'd been Googling on her phone last night - court assisted burials, they were called - and she'd learned that her mother was probably in an unmarked grave somewhere in the city. The guilt was overwhelming. She hoped that having a proper headstone erected - now that she was in a position where she could afford one - might assuage that guilt slightly.

"I think you should do whatever's going to make you feel at peace with the whole situation," Duncan said. "But you've got a lot on your plate right now - Edith's will, the divorce. Don't put yourself under too much pressure."

"About that," Rachel began, realising that she should really tell him about how things had unfolded with Graham. She'd worried that maybe he'd be cross, or disappointed, thinking that she'd just given up without a fight. To her surprise, however, he smiled.

"That's exceptionally generous of you," he said. "It's more

than he deserves."

Rachel sighed, relieved. "I felt bad for him, and I don't need it anymore. My life has moved on." Duncan ran one hand up her thigh, smiling at her in that way she loved so much.

"I just want the divorce to be over, and I don't want anything else to feel guilty about. He's got a job, and a roof over his head; if he fucks his life up now, it's on him."

# CHAPTER 49

They said goodbye in the car park, Duncan pulling her close as he kissed her, his hands firm on her waist.

"I wish we had a little more time… and a little more privacy," he breathed.

"Soon," Rachel promised. "You'll let me know when you have a weekend that suits? I don't want to intrude on your free time with Violet…"

"She'd love to see you too," Duncan assured her. "But I might take a couple of days off mid-week and come up to yours - my flat isn't very big, you see, and you do have a tendency to make quite a bit of noise..."

"Shut up," she scolded, kissing him again before getting into her car. He stood and waved her off as she pulled out of the car park and back on to the A9.

Rachel cruised up the main artery into the Highlands, the late afternoon sun warm through her window and the radio blasting out suitably cheerful summer tunes. The landscape gradually grew more rugged the further North she climbed, the wild forests of Perthshire merging into the barren, rugged mountaintops surrounding the Drumochter pass. The temperature plummeted here too, before she pulled off and headed West along the shore of Loch Laggan and towards the coast.

An almost palpable feeling of serenity washed over Rachel the further she ventured into this wild countryside. It brought her a sense of peace she had never experienced back in Glasgow. Maybe, she wondered, it was because this was truly her home. Her mother had been born on these desolate islands - maybe something deep in the fabric of Rachel's being had been calling her back here all along?

As Rachel had expected, Sorcha was still at her place when she finally arrived home. She'd text her before she left Glasgow to say she'd be back that evening. What she wasn't expecting, however, was for Una to be there too, bottles of wine open and a big pot of homemade Bolognese sauce bubbling on the stove.

"This is a nice surprise," Rachel said, the smell of garlic, basil and frying mince greeting her as she came through the door, dragging her bags behind her.

Una quickly relieved her of the heaviest, dumping it on the floor in the hallway and replacing it with a glass of wine instead. "Welcome home," she said.

Rachel was pleased to see Sorcha looking a bit more like her old self. There was colour in her cheeks, and she greeted Rachel with a smile.

"Thank you," she whispered in her ear. "I think I needed that little talking to the other day."

Rachel smiled back. "What are friends for?" she said.

The three of them settled down on the sofa to catch up, clutching steaming bowls of spaghetti topped with the rich, fragrant tomato sauce and a plate of garlic bread to share on the coffee table. Rachel started by filling them in on events in Glasgow, first with Graham, and then the revelations about her mother.

"She's from Harris?" Sorcha said, delighted. "She's an islander! I always knew you were one of us, deep down."

"I've brought back her birth certificate, and some old photos. I thought I might try to track them down, and finish what she started."

"Do you know the names of her parents?" Una asked.

Rachel shook her head. "No - there were no names on the birth certificate."

"I thought they had to include that?" Sorcha interjected. "Andy and I put our names on all three of ours."

"It'll be a short entry," Una explained. "You have to pay for a full extract. They'll be in the system, somewhere - just not on the paper copy your mum had."

Rachel thought about it. It made sense, really, that whoever abandoned her mum would have been in difficult circumstances. Who was she, she wondered? A teenage girl, or a housewife having an affair? Having never given much thought to her own heritage before, suddenly Rachel was desperate to find out.

"There was a name, actually," she said, remembering the notebook her mother had scrawled in. "Just not on the birth certificate."

She got out of her seat and went to rummage in her bags, finding it and bringing it through. "Here it is" she said, flicking it open to the marked page and showing the girls.

"Fionnlagh Grant?" Una read, stumbling over the Gaelic

name.

"*Fionnlagh*," Sorcha corrected, the sounds rolling easily off her native tongue. Rachel tried it out; 'Fyoo-lah' was the closest she could come.

"Pretty common name on the islands unfortunately," Sorcha continued. "That picture we found in Edith's things; do you remember? With her boyfriend or whoever he was? His name was Fionnlagh."

Rachel paused. "Just a sec," she said, running up to her bedroom to where she had placed the picture, along with the locket, in the top drawer of her bedside table for safe keeping. She came back into the room, showing them to Una and Sorcha. Sure enough, the first name of Edith's long-lost lover was the same as the man Rachel now believed to have been her grandfather.

"What's this?" Una asked, picking up the little gold locket and turning it over in her long, elegant fingers.

"It was in amongst Edith's things at the care home," Rachel explained. "It was the only really personal item she'd taken with her."

"M.M.G," Una whispered, running her fingertips over the twirling, inscribed initials on the front, before popping it open. "It's a baby," she said, all three women gathering round to look at the picture within. "When was Edith born again?"

"Nineteen-forties," Rachel replied. "Middle of World War Two."

"It can't be her though, can it? She'd be E.M, not M.M.G."

Sorcha drifted back across the room, and started flicking through one of the shoeboxes Rachel had retrieved from her Granny's. She picked something up, frowning at it for a moment before she spoke. "What did you say your mum's name was, Rachel?"

"Mary Grant, as far as I was aware. I only found out when I saw that birth certificate that her birth name was actually Mhairi, and her middle name was McLeod."

Sorcha was looking at her, an inscrutable expression on her face. "So obviously, Mhairi is Gaelic for Mary, right?"

Rachel nodded.

"And up here, it's quite common for people to use the mother's maiden name as a middle name. I think we can probably assume that whoever your mother's mother was, she was most likely a McLeod."

"Okay?" Rachel wasn't entirely sure what Sorcha was getting at.

"So, Edith was a McLeod, wasn't she? The M.M.G inscribed on her locket *could* stand for Mhairi McLeod Grant. Only, I've found another baby photo in here, and I think you should see it..."

Sorcha held it out to them, and Rachel was suddenly hit with a wave of shock that forced her to sit back down on the sofa.

The child was slightly older, sitting upright now, wearing a frilly dress with a Peter Pan collar, unruly tufts of black hair sprouting from her head. But the birthmark on her cheek was unmistakable; it was just like the one on the baby in Edith's locket.

Rachel took the picture from Sorcha and turned it over in her hands. Written on the back, in her mother's handwriting, were the words, *'Me, Dec. 1962'*.

Rachel glanced back at the locket, which Una was holding out to her, her eyebrows raised in disbelief. She'd always thought that one baby looked much like the next, but even without the birthmark, it was obvious. The little upturned nose and high, rounded cheeks were identical.

"No way," she breathed, overcome with the urge to laugh. "It's impossible!"

"Bit of a coincidence, that's for sure," Sorcha said. "But they're definitely the same kid. A picture of your mum, hidden away in Edith's locket all these years? How do you explain that?"

Rachel sat with her mouth open, unable to think straight, let alone speak.

"It does seem unlikely," Una said, taking the photo herself and holding it next to the locket for a closer inspection. "But what are the chances that you'd randomly end up applying for a job at a distillery in the middle of nowhere, that just so happens to be owned by your long-lost Grandmother?"

"I didn't apply for it though," Rachel said, suddenly finding her voice.

"What do you mean?"

Rachel took a deep breath, thinking back to how everything had unfolded. It had seemed like fate, at the time - this job, miles away from Glasgow and with a house included, landed in her lap exactly when she needed. Now, it seemed suspicious.

"I joined LinkedIn when I chucked Graham out," she

explained. "Decided it was time for a whole fresh start. Within a week I had an email from the distillery, asking if I'd be interested in interviewing for a position? I figured it was just one of those blanket enquiries people send on LinkedIn - you know what it's like. But maybe...?"

"Maybe Edith had already found you."

# CHAPTER 50

Rachel tossed and turned in her bed that night, unable to sleep. It all seemed like far too much of a coincidence, but yet she couldn't think of any other explanation. Was it really possible that Edith had given birth to a secret daughter, fathered by the mysterious Fionnlagh Grant, and that daughter had grown up to be Rachel's mum?

Doing the maths, Rachel figured Edith would have been around nineteen or twenty when her mother was born. Old enough to be married, in those days; but also young enough that the scandal of a bastard baby would have tarred her for life. What choice would she have had, Rachel wondered? Get married, or have the baby in secret and send it away? She doubted there would have been a third option.

Sorcha was spending the night curled up on her sofa again, still quiet, but certainly in better spirits than when she'd last seen her. Andy had come round, apparently, while he was up working on the gift shop, and they'd talked. He wasn't ready for her to come home yet, but he had suggested that they go to see a counsellor on Skye, and Sorcha had agreed.

"I think we can fix this," she said earnestly, her blue eyes shining when Rachel asked her about it. "I've fucked up - majorly fucked up - but I'll make it up to him. I don't want to lose him, or our family."

"How are the kids?" Una asked.

"Still staying at Mum's. At least it's the school holidays - they're happy just getting to eat various forms of homemade cake at every meal. How about you?" Sorcha asked, turning to Una with a knowing grin. "You and Lucy have a nice time on Skye?"

"Yes," Una blushed. "It was really good."

"And did you... seal the deal?"

Una's eyes widened, but she didn't deny it. "We're official now," was all she would say, sipping her red wine coyly. "Girlfriend and girlfriend, as it were."

Sorcha laughed. "Check us out," she said. "Not so long ago, I was the smug married and you two were the singletons. Now me and Andy are on the rocks and you're both loved up."

She scoffed, but there wasn't the same edge of bitterness or jealousy in her voice as Rachel had sensed before. "Maybe if I can convince Andy to take me back, soon we'll all be happily settled down," she said.

As it turned out, Sorcha was back in the family home before the end of the week. Agreeing to the counselling had obviously been the first step in persuading Andy that she meant it when she said she wanted to make things work. Now, she just had to earn back his trust.

Rachel spent the rest of the week quietly mulling over the possible revelations about her family tree, eventually alighting upon a plan. She shared her idea with Duncan one night, during their daily phone call.

"Do you think they'll know one way or another?" he asked. "It's a pretty big secret to be carrying around all these years?"

"I think they're the most likely to," Rachel replied. "Their families have been here for generations, and before I came along, they were Edith's closest confidantes. If she'd told anybody about it, it would be them."

The more she thought about it, the more certain Rachel became that they would have the answers. So, not wanting to have this particular conversation at work, she waited until Saturday morning to take her car into Craigport and go and knock on their door.

"Wish me luck," she whispered to Doug, tickling him under his chin before she left.

It was Jenny who opened the door, her mouth forming a surprised little 'O' when she saw who it was. Rachel had never visited them at home before; not since her very first night on the island, when they'd invited her round for tea.

"Come in," Jenny said, ushering her into the cosy living room. It smelled of home baking - Rachel suspected it always did - and before she had a chance to say no, Jenny had boiled the kettle and brought her through a steaming hot mug of tea and a homemade scone.

"To what do we owe this pleasure?" she asked. "Cameron's just popped along to Ishbel's for a few supplies, but he'll no' be long. Everything okay?"

Rachel chewed her scone slowly, swallowing before she

spoke. She'd been thinking about this all last night, and all this morning, and had thought she knew what she was going to say. But now that she was here, she found the words died on her tongue.

"You know how everybody thought Malcolm - Edith's uncle - hadn't had any kids? And then Stephanie showed up?" she began nervously.

"Aye." Jenny nodded slowly, frowning.

"Well, this will sound stupid, but… Is there any chance Edith might have had a child?"

A strange choking sound came from Jenny's throat, and she stood and paced round the room, almost laughing.

"Och, no, lass, dinna be daft! It's one thing for a man to plant his seed in some poor girl and send her away, but Edith couldna very well have hidden a pregnancy! Someone would have seen her. Nothing stays secret around here, you know that."

But there was something in her eyes that caught Rachel's attention. Was it fear? Nerves? This certainly wasn't the calm, relaxed Jenny she was used to. She'd never seen her even close to being flustered.

"I know it sounds ridiculous," Rachel continued, reaching into her handbag and pulling out the brown envelope she'd filled with all of her 'evidence'. "But I found these, in amongst her things."

She handed Jenny the locket. "I think this was Edith's baby. And I think this was the father." She slid the photo across the table, of a young Edith and Fionnlagh, arm in arm by the harbour wall. Looking at it now, she was filled with sadness to think about the happy ending they had missed out on.

"And this," Rachel added, unveiling the final piece - the baby picture from her granny's flat. "This is my mother," she said, pointing to it.

Jenny barely glanced at them. "What does that prove - the baby in that locket could be anyone. Just because they've both got a birthmark… it's a coincidence, nothing more. And Fionnlagh was just a boy Edith courted for a while."

"You knew about him?" Rachel asked, sitting upright in her seat.

Jenny sighed. "He was my uncle." she said eventually, shoulders slumping. "My maiden name is Grant, ye see."

At that moment, the front door swung open and Cameron's

cheery voice carried through from the hallway to the lounge. Rachel could hear him, kicking off his shoes and hanging his jacket on the pegs by the door.

"Ishbel didna have any yeast," he called through, "but she said there's some coming in her next delivery. I got everything else. Oh," he said, spotting Rachel as he wandered into the living room. "Hello, Rachel. What can we do for you?"

Jenny spoke first, before Rachel could say anything.

"She knows."

Cameron joined them on the sofa, the three of them looking over the items laid out on the coffee table - the birth certificate, Fionnlagh's name, the picture of him and Edith together, the picture of her mother as a baby, and Edith's locket.

"You do look like her," Jenny said, picking up the picture of her uncle and Edith and looking at it fondly. "I thought it the first time I saw you - small, pale and dark, like she was.

"You knew that Edith was my grandmother" she asked. "You knew all along?"

Cameron sighed, running his fingers over his moustache. "Aye, we kent. No one else did, mind you. She swore us to secrecy. Jenny was Fionnlagh's niece, and when Edith took on the still, she made a point o' takin' care o' his family."

"That's why she always had work for me," Jenny chipped in. "And when I married Cameron, she took him on, too."

"And Iain," Rachel added.

"Aye," Cameron nodded. "The Grants, ye see… Edith's uncle - Malcolm - didna think a Grant was worthy to marry his kin."

"That's rich, coming from him," Rachel interjected. "He was the one having it away with the servant girl."

"The rules have always been different for women, though, haven't they?" Jenny observed. "Men can have as many mistresses as they like, but women were expected to be chaste and virtuous, and marry someone of good standing. Malcolm would have disowned Edith if she'd married Fionnlagh. We were just fisherfolk, ye see," she added.

"What happened to him?"

"He died." Jenny said. "I dinna mind him, ye ken. It all happened before I was born. He was washed overboard in a squall.

He was only twenty-four."

"And he left Edith behind, pregnant?"

"Aye - pregnant, and unwed. Not even betrothed. Her uncle couldna bear the shame, she said, but neither would he see her cast out without a husband to support her. So, she was sent away to Harris, to some distant relative there. Stayed out of sight, had the baby, then came home as if nothing had happened."

"And never married?"

Jenny shook her head. "She loved Fionnlagh til the last."

Rachel felt unexpectedly emotional. Edith had always been so brash, so fiercely independent; realising that she'd been mourning her lost love for sixty years was heart-breaking. That she'd been forced to give away their child on top of it all was even worse. Rachel didn't really have what you could call a faith, but part of her hoped that the three of them were together now, and at peace.

"How did she track me down?" Rachel asked. "That's what happened, wasn't it? It wasn't chance - or my excellent references - that brought me to Inniscreag?"

Cameron and Jenny exchanged glances, seemingly considering how they ought to proceed.

"She deserves to see it for herself," Jenny said firmly.

"See what?"

Cameron nodded his head, acceding to his wife's request. "There's a letter."

# CHAPTER 51

"She sent it to us in the post, before she died," Cameron was explaining, returning from the bedroom where the letter had obviously been hidden. "She said she trusted us to know when it was the right time to give ye it."

Rachel took the envelope from his hands. Her name was written on the front, and the seal was still closed; Edith must have sent it inside a larger envelope addressed to Jenny and Cameron.

"We'll give ye some privacy," Jenny said, ushering her husband from the room and closing the door behind him.

Taking a deep breath, Rachel carefully peeled open the envelope and pulled out the letter within.

*Dearest Rachel,*

*I don't know how to begin this letter; only that I owe you some sort of explanation for the series of events that led to your mother's birth, and brought you to Inniscreag. Forgive me if I wander, or retell events that you'd rather not hear. It is the privilege of old age to be able to record my tale, and I will do my best to tell it to you honestly. I can only apologise if time, or shame, prevents me from sharing everything you would like to know.*

*You will have figured out by now that I am, in fact, your grandmother. You're a sharp cookie, Rachel - I may flatter myself by believing you inherited that from me, despite my lack of presence in your formative years. I wish that had been different, and I hope that once you have heard the full story you may be able to forgive me.*

*I gave birth to your mother on a stormy Wednesday afternoon in June 1962, in the bedroom of a blackhouse on the Isle of Harris, looking out over the sea. A fire burned in the hearth and I screamed louder than any of the gulls outside, I can tell you that much. She was born at exactly four o'clock, and weighed exactly nine pounds - a squealing, pink, chubby bundle. Perfect, except for the red mark on her right cheek, which the women caring for me swore was a punishment; my child was cursed to bear the mark of her mother's sin. But I loved her. What happened next may cause you to doubt that, but I promise you I did. I loved her more deeply and more instantly than I have ever loved anyone, before or since.*

*I had been courting her father for two years before her arrival, unbeknownst to my uncle and guardian. He did not believe a future as a* fisherman's wife was fitting for a McLeod woman, and would not grant us permission to marry. I would have defied him anyway, Rachel, if I could have. But the night before we had planned to run away together - to the mainland and the first chapel we could find - my Fionnlagh was lost at sea. And so, I found myself alone, bereaved, and sent away from my home so I could bear the child without shaming my family.

If I screamed when I birthed her, it was nothing compared to the way I screamed when they tried to take your mother from me - I fought and I shouted and I clung to her for days. But one night, while I slept, the women caring for me took your mother from my breast and sent her away. They promised me she was alive, but would tell me nothing more.

It must seem silly to you now, Rachel - you are a modern woman, and you may wonder why I did not move heaven and earth to get my child back. I assure you that I could feel no deeper shame over my actions - or the lack of them - than I do already. But I was young, and alone, and knew nothing of the world beyond my own little island. I did the only thing I thought I could do; I went home, and locked my sadness away inside my heart, never to speak of it again. All I had left of her was a picture in a locket, which I swore I would keep with me forever.

In time, my uncle died, and I inherited the distillery. I never desired another husband, or a child; if I could not have my Fionnlagh, or my Mhairi, then I would live and die alone.

But then one day - I was watching some daytime talk show at the time, I believe - I decided to try and track her down. I was old by then, and Mhairi would be a woman grown, and I knew she may well hate me, and rightly so. But I wanted to find her, and at least see if she had had a good life.

Never having been short of money, I hired a private investigator. I was elated when he traced her so quickly; but then he told me that she had taken her own life. I blame myself for this completely, Rachel, and I am sorry; any troubles your mother had could, perhaps, have been avoided if she had been raised with a family who loved her.

My heartache turned to bittersweet joy, however when I learned she had borne a child of her own - you. You were an adult by now, Rachel, and I had no wish to disrupt your life. You were married and, I believed, happy. But I checked in on you now and then, in case I could offer any assistance - secretly, you understand. I imagined myself as your 'Fairy Grandmother', if you will. So, when I saw you were looking for a new job, and had separated from your husband, I took my opportunity. I offered you the job here, on Inniscreag, and to my endless joy, you accepted.

*I cannot tell you how happy it made me to see my own flesh and blood back on our island. You didn't know it, but I did - another McLeod lived, and would inherit the still when I was gone. I could die in peace now, knowing that you were here.*

*I want you to know, that even if you had declined my job offer, the still would always have been yours when the time came. But instead of it coming from a mysterious, long lost relative you had never heard of, I was blessed with six months of getting to know you, and seeing for myself the wonderful person you are. I know our family's heritage is in safe hands with you.*

*And so, darling Rachel, I will end this here. I am sorry that cowardice prevented me from telling you this to your face. I hope I have answered some of your questions, and if I may wish for anything, it is that you forgive me for my mistakes.*

*All my love,*
*Grandma Edith*

# CHAPTER 52

It still hadn't sunk in that evening, when Rachel had read the letter over and over, crying fresh tears each time. She relayed it all to Duncan over the phone.

"Edith had planned it all along?" he asked. She could picture him, rubbing his hands back and forth through his hair. "She knew you were her granddaughter?"

"And she'd have left me the still, one way or another. She offered me the job because she wanted to get to know me; to spend time with me."

"Wow," Duncan said. "So that means you and Stephanie…"

"Some sort of cousin, I guess? I haven't spoken to her yet, but I suppose I should, really."

"Well, I did not see this coming," Duncan said. "You're a McLeod."

"I am," Rachel said proudly. "I know now why Edith trusted me to see your lot off," she teased.

Duncan laughed. "Well, my boss still isn't very happy about how that all worked out, you know. But I wouldn't change it for the world."

They hung up, after making plans for him to come and visit the weekend after next. In the meantime, Rachel thought, as she rolled over to go to sleep, she had some good news to share.

She was at Hamish's door early the following day. To save money, Stephanie had given up the AirBnB and was now living with Hamish and his parents, in a little, low-roofed fisherman's cottage along the front in Craigport. When she opened the door, she was barefaced and wearing what looked to be one of Hamish's oversized shirts and a pair of leggings.

"Oh," she said, covering herself self-consciously with her arms, "I'm sorry; I wasn't expecting anyone. Rhona's still in bed, and Hamish is at the still… What are you doing here?" she asked urgently, her face suddenly dropping in panic. "Is he okay?"

"He's fine," Rachel assured her. "It's you I wanted to talk to. Can I come in?"

Reluctantly, Stephanie stepped aside and let her through the door. Not really knowing how to broach the subject, Rachel had blurted it out before they'd even sat down.

For a moment, Stephanie just stared, her mouth wide, a vaguely confused frown creasing her manicured, golden brows. "We're... cousins?" she asked.

"Yup," Rachel nodded. They couldn't be more different, physically - one tall, tanned and blond, the other small, pale and dark. And yet they shared some of the same genetic makeup, and bloodlines that tied them to this place over generations. "Your great-grandfather was my great-great-uncle... I think."

"Jeez," Stephanie breathed. "Ain't that a turn up for the books."

They regarded each other awkwardly for a moment, neither one knowing what to say. Rachel cleared her throat.

"It got me thinking, though. I know you're planning on staying here, and I guess if that's the case, then you're going to need a job. And I thought, if we really are family, then maybe you'd like to join the family business?"

Stephanie's nervousness vanished instantly.

"Yes!" she screeched, suddenly throwing herself at Rachel from across the sofa and enveloping her in a crushing hug. It was like being cuddled by a giraffe - long, bony arms and legs jabbed into her. "Thank you so much," Stephanie said. When she pulled away, Rachel was surprised to see tears in her eyes.

"We're family," Rachel said simply. "I thought this could be a fresh start, for all of us. The next phase of life for Inniscreag Distillery."

Stephanie squeezed her hand firmly. "Hamish won't believe this," she said.

"About Hamish," Rachel interrupted. "I was planning on moving into Edith's old house - traditionally, it's meant to be for the owner, so I'm told. But I wondered if you two wanted a place of your own, you might like to take on my house?"

Stephanie's answer was drowned out in another excited squeal, as Rachel was bowled backwards across the sofa once more.

# CHAPTER 53

*Three Months Later*

Rachel pulled her car into a space alongside the harbour wall, the village around her already buzzing with activity. It was only just gone four o'clock in the afternoon, but already the sky was dark blue and peppered with stars. In late November on the Western Isles, daylight didn't hang around for long.

The stalls had been set up, lining the main street along the front, and as Rachel got out of the car, she could smell Shelagh's cooking wafting down the road towards her. She would be serving burgers, hot dogs and stovies to the revellers, while Rachel and the distillery staff were going to be handing out free drams.

She waved to Hamish and Stephanie, who were getting out of their car on the opposite side of the road. Rachel's proposition had, so far, worked out perfectly - Stephanie turned out to have a background in marketing, not to mention more of a taste for whisky than Rachel had ever had, and so she naturally took charge of developing new products and promotion. They already had a cream liqueur tried and tested, which would be on the shelves just in time for Christmas, and a young blend for cocktail mixing was in development. Stephanie had even set them up with a few social media accounts; they were positively modern, these days.

Rachel, in turn, continued to oversee the manufacturing process and maintain the site, as well as running the coffee shop and gift shop. Their first season of trading had gone remarkably well, and now that they were closed for winter, she had enough money in the bank to invest in a luxury facelift before they reopened again in the summer.

They walked over to their tent together, where Ben, Cameron and Jenny were already setting up. It was a cold but clear night - perfect for the start of the island's Christmas festivities.

By the time they were ready, the crowds had thickened and there were already a few locals seeking a nip to warm them up. Rachel chatted with the familiar faces, every one of which she'd come to know and love. Had it really been just over a year since she'd arrived on Inniscreag? Her life was unrecognisable now, Rachel realised, and there was very little she would change about it.

Graham had stuck to his end of the bargain, signing away any possible claim against the distillery and setting up residence in Granny Peggy's flat once more. She hadn't heard from him directly since they said goodbye that day when she was in Glasgow, and was confident now that it would remain that way.

Just then, she saw Sorcha and Andrew coming out of their house a little further down the street, their three children bundled up in coats, hats and scarves, skipping ahead of them. Husband and wife were holding hands as they wandered down the road together, and Rachel smiled. Everything was far from fixed, she knew, but it seemed they were on the right track.

They came over and took a dram each, exchanging hugs and kisses. Rachel poured out some warm orange cordial for the kids and handed it to them.

"Have you heard from Violet lately?" she asked Maisie. The two girls had remained firm friends, exchanging emails and letters on an almost weekly basis.

Maisie nodded. "She's on holiday with her Dad just now."

"I know! Looks like they're having an amazing time."

Rachel smiled sadly. The way things were going with Duncan - that was the only slight blot on the landscape right now.

It had been over a month since she'd last seen him, and Rachel was finding it harder and harder to silence the little voice in her head, insisting that he was slipping away. *You're losing him,* it whispered, and she was starting to think the voice was right. Yes, they still talked on the phone most days, and text regularly, but he'd been so busy with work, and Violet, and Rachel was stuck on Inniscreag… She couldn't help but think that, no matter how much they might love each other, maybe their 'happily ever after' wasn't to be?

There was a steady stream of custom at their little stall to keep her distracted, at least, as the residents of Inniscreag milled up and down the front, eating and drinking happily. A fiddle and accordion had started playing by the Cenotaph, next to where a little podium had been set up, and where the as-yet unlit Christmas tree stood.

Rachel glanced at her watch; soon, Una would stand at the podium, give a short speech, and announce which one of the residents would be invited to turn on the lights. It was a little tradition on Inniscreag - the islanders would vote for the person they thought had made the greatest contribution to the community that year, and that person would have the honour of turning on the Christmas lights. They weren't likely to ever tempt a celebrity to their little unknown lump of rock, so they picked their own instead.

Just before six o'clock, the musicians fell silent and Rachel looked up to see Una at the podium. The assembled islanders gradually hushed, as everyone drifted towards the minister.

Rachel looked around the crowd, finally seeing her; her red hair glowed amber in the streetlights. Lucy had only been on the island for a couple of weeks, but she seemed to have been accepted by the parishioners. She was smiling up at Una, wrapped in a bright green scarf, her freckled cheeks ruddy from the cold.

"Good evening!" Una began, ignoring the microphone, her voice echoing around the village effortlessly. "Welcome to the annual switching on of Inniscreag's Christmas lights."

A little cheer and round of clapping reverberated through the crowd.

"I won't keep you long - I know you'd all much rather be enjoying a few drams from our local still, or some of Shelagh's fine cooking, than listening to me." Una paused, allowing the little ripple of laughter to die out before she continued.

"It is my very great honour to announce the name of this year's 'Community Hero'. This person has brought one of our oldest industries back to life, bringing increased tourism, and revenue, into the local economy. I think everyone here always knew she was 'one of us', but this was recently confirmed when we found out she is in fact the long-lost granddaughter of one of our most esteemed residents, who we sadly lost earlier this year. I'm sure none of you will be surprised when I tell you, that this year's Community Hero is... Rachel McIntyre!"

A loud cheer whooped round the crowd, while Rachel felt all the colour drain from her face.

"Go on," Hamish said, grinning at her and urging her forward with one great big freckly arm.

Reluctantly, Rachel weaved her way through the crowd, being patted on the back by those she passed, and made her way up the steps to the podium.

"Do I need to say anything?" she whispered to Una urgently.

"Just 'thank you', and then do the countdown."

There was a big red button next to the microphone, which Una hadn't needed, but Rachel now lifted tentatively to her face.

"Thank you very much," she said. "I am very proud to be a resident of Inniscreag, and I consider every single one of you to be my family." She looked down at the smiling faces around her, feeling unexpectedly emotional.

Before her voice could break again, she went straight to the countdown. "Ten, nine, eight, seven…" At 'one', she pressed the red button and the village around them sprung into light. The twelve foot tall Christmas tree to her left sparkled all the way to the star at the top, whilst the little buildings that lined the front were strung with heavy garlands of fairy lights. It was simple, but beautiful.

Rachel stepped down from the podium and made her way back to the stall, her face red with embarrassment. She was touched, but she hated being the centre of attention.

Just as she reached the stall, where her friends were waiting for her, Rachel found herself spinning round on her heels. Maisie was looking over her shoulder, an enormous smile breaking across her face as she screamed, "Violet!"

Rachel turned, her heart in her throat, to see the two little girls collide into each other in a tangle of arms and giggles. Violet was taller than she remembered - in just six weeks, somehow, she'd shot up. She ran up to Rachel next, without hesitation, throwing her skinny arms around her and squeezing with all her might.

"I've missed you."

"I've missed you too," Rachel whispered back.

She stood up, releasing Violet as she and Maisie scampered off together, and looking in the direction she'd come. Sure enough, there he was; walking casually towards her, hands in his pockets, wrapped up in a heavy tweed coat and scarf.

He sighed as he looked at her, a little smile on his face. "Hi."

"What are you doing here?" was all Rachel could manage.

"She's missed being on Inniscreag," Duncan replied, nodding over to where Maisie and Violet were standing with the others, chattering excitedly. "Prefers it to Edinburgh, actually."

"Is that right?" Rachel asked, as he took another couple of steps closer to her.

"So do I, as it happens."

"I thought the two of you were on holiday?"

He was within touching distance of her now, although he kept his hands in his pockets.

"We are," he smiled. "A holiday with no return date."

Rachel frowned at him. "What do you mean?"

"I quit my job. Sold the flat. Bought a campervan." He laughed at her incredulous expression, and Rachel made a conscious effort to close her mouth.

"We've been on the road for a month now; touring around, taking photographs. Violet's got me doing something called a 'blog'? I really haven't got a clue what it's all about - she writes most of it, I just take the photos. We've chatted lots - about life, the universe and everything - and we decided we both really wanted to come back here. For good."

They stood in silence for a moment, before Duncan finally took one step towards her, closing the gap and lightly taking hold of her hand.

"I realise I should probably have discussed this with you first," he said quietly.

Rachel smiled up at him. "I don't mind."

He kissed her then, gently, one hand soft against her cheek.

"I love you, Rach," he said when they pulled apart. "And I'm all in. I want you, and I want this life, here, on Inniscreag. If that's alright with you," he added with a grin.

"I suppose."

"Good," Duncan said, running one hand over her hair. "In that case, I don't suppose you know of anywhere with a spare room? Turns out sleeping in a camper van in November is fucking Baltic."

"I might have a vacancy," she laughed, burrowing closer to his reassuring warmth. Her Duncan, here on her island, forever.

Duncan enveloped her in his arms and kissed her once more, and for the first time in her life, Rachel finally knew what it felt like to be home.

# EPILOGUE

The wind blew in wild from the sea, despite the fact that it was almost June. A mass of seabirds swooped and screeched delightedly across the sky, their wings outstretched as they tipped and swayed on the breeze. Rachel smiled to see them; she loved the sound of their calls, and knew Edith, and her Mum, would have loved them, too.

Duncan took her hand as they reached the top of the hill, looking back down the road they had come towards the wide, curved bay of Craigport below. They could see all the way to Skye, the red hull of the morning ferry bobbing in the choppy waters as it made its way across.

"Ready?" he asked.

Rachel nodded, squeezing his hand back in return.

Violet was ahead of them, already making her way through the gates to the cemetery, carrying a bundle of wild flowers she'd been picking for the occasion. Rachel and Duncan carried their own bouquets - ordered from the florist on Skye - along with four, long stemmed, white roses.

She led them to Edith's plot from memory, the rectangle of turf she'd seen rolled over on the day of her funeral now merged indistinguishably with the rest of the grass, and covered in a thick spongy layer of moss and daisies. This was the first time she'd been up here since then, she realised, as they came to a standstill.

Beneath the carving on Edith's headstone, showing her name and the dates of her birth and death, a fresh message had been added.

*Mother of Mhairi McLeod Grant*
*13th June 1962 - 25th February 2002*

Rachel smiled sadly. It had only seemed right, she thought, to mark the fact that she had been a mother. It was right too, to give her own mother a proper memorial. And so, to the right of Edith's headstone, there now stood a smaller marker, carved in black granite.

*Mhairi McLeod Grant*
*13th June 1962 - 25th February 2002*
*Beloved daughter of Edith and Fionnlagh, and mother of Rachel*

Duncan's hand found its way onto her shoulder and squeezed reassuringly. "Do you want me to give you a moment?"

Rachel shook her head. "It's fine," she said, wiping a rogue tear from her cheek and bending down to lay her flowers in front of her mother's grave. Duncan placed his bunch next to Edith's, leaving Rachel holding the four individual roses.

In front of the two headstones, four little slate love hearts had been laid into the earth. Each one was inscribed with only a date - dates that Rachel would never forget, for lives that had never set foot on earth, but mattered nonetheless.

Blinking back tears, she laid a rose on top of each one. When she stood up, Duncan wrapped his arms around her from behind.

"Take as long as you need," he said.

"It's okay," she replied, sniffing. "I'm ready."

He placed a kiss on her shoulder, one hand running down from her waist to cup the gentle swell of her belly protectively. She wasn't really showing yet, but it wouldn't be long until she was.

"Let's go home," he said.

Rachel turned, one hand in Duncan's and the other in Violet's, as they walked together back down the hill towards the sea, birds circling and crying in the great blue infinity above.

# ABOUT THE AUTHOR

Elsie McArthur was born and brought up in Glasgow, a city she still holds dear to her heart. She now lives in Speyside, in the Scottish Highlands, along with her husband, their two children, a couple of badly behaved dogs and an exceptionally lazy cat.

Elsie has worked as a primary school teacher for over a decade, and after years of jotting down stories, she began writing more seriously during her first period of maternity leave.

*Love, on the Rocks* is her second novel.

Reviews – which are always greatly appreciated – can be left on Amazon or Goodreads.

Elsie may be contacted via Facebook, Instagram and Twitter.

Printed in Great Britain
by Amazon